GEORGE TURNER, who died in 1996, was a significant and award-winning Australian novelist before turning to SF in the 1970s and becoming one of the great living SF writers. His major books include *Beloved Son, Drowning Towers, Brain Child,* and *Genetic Soldier.* He was widely reviewed and was a winner of the Arthur C. Clarke Award for best novel.

This novel chronicles the future destruction and eventual rebirth of human civilization. It is linked to the future world of *Genetic Soldier* and *Drowning Towers,* as well as others of his works.

Down There in Darkness

"Turner creates a land reminiscent of Huxley's *Brave New World.* His narrative innovatively blends conceptual art, aboriginal philosophy, and genetic engineering, and his characters display a memorable vibrancy."

—*Publishers Weekly*

"Turner's lucid prose and bold imagination combine in a tale that contains elements of SF noir, police procedural, and metaphysical fiction. Published posthumously (Turner died in 1996), this compelling and disturbing exploration of the darkness of the human soul belongs in most SF collections."

—*Library Journal*

"The late Turner's last novel, full of allusions to his earlier work and with an ironic hope arising from his trademark dour future, fittingly ends his long career."

—*Booklist*

"In his final novel, George Turner joins Robert Heinlein and Isaac Asimov in forging his novels into a vast tapestry of future history. *Down There in Darkness* forms a startling bridge between the earlier gritty *The Destiny Makers* and *Brain Child* and his finest novel, *Genetic Soldier.* As always, Turner dramatizes evil lurking in human hearts, and the decency with which it can be surmounted. His driven characters plunge into the mysteries of the collective, timeless consciousness of the aboriginal Dreaming—and what they find there will alter the future of the whole world."

—Damien Broderick

Drowning Towers
WINNER OF THE ARTHUR C. CLARKE AWARD FOR BEST SF NOVEL

"An extraordinary feat . . . unequaled in contemporary cautionary fiction . . . No disaster novel yet written can hold a candle to this, in grace of writing, depth of characterization, breadth of vision, and sheer drama and suspense."

—Paul Preuss

"The best didactic novel I've read sin

"His most powerful novel . . . Georg

D0814032

DOWN

THERE

IN

DARKNESS

GEORGE TURNER

TOR®

A TOM DOHERTY ASSOCIATES BOOK
NEW YORK

DOWN THERE IN DARKNESS

Copyright © 1999 by The Literary Estate of George Turner

Chapter 2 of this novel appeared previously as a short story, "Worlds," in *Eidolon*, summer 1991. The present version has been slightly edited and a new character added.

This book is printed on acid-free paper.

Edited by David G. Hartwell

A Tor Book
Published by Tom Doherty Associates, LLC
175 Fifth Avenue
New York, NY 10010

www.tor.com

Tor® is a registered trademark of Tom Doherty Associates, LLC.

Book design by Lisa Pifher

Library of Congress Cataloging-in-Publication Data

Turner, George.
   Down there in darkness / George Turner.
     p.   cm.
   "A Tom Doherty Associates book."
   ISBN 0-312-86829-4 (hc)
   ISBN 0-312-87258-5 (pbk)
   I. Title.
 PR9619.3.T868D69 1999
 823—dc21   99-20078

First Hardcover Edition: May 1999
First Trade Paperback Edition: April 2000

Printed in the United States of America

0 9 8 7 6 5 4 3 2 1

This one is for
Leanne Frahm,
onetime pupil
and
excellent writer

ABORIGINAL TERMS

KOORI: This term for an aboriginal Australian applies, strictly, only to the tribes of southeastern Australia but is gaining acceptance as a generic term for all Australian aboriginal tribes.

KORADJI: Most easily translated as "medicine man" or "witch doctor."

KURDAITCHA: The descriptions given by Connor and later by Bill Gordon are accurate according to my references (mainly *Aboriginal Words of Australia*, A. W. Reed, 1965), but the ascription to some of them practicing "inner contemplation" is purely fictional.

However, the prevalence of out-of-body and other mystical experience in Australian native folklore suggests that some such awareness was common currency and almost certainly followed up by individuals.

DOWN

THERE

IN

DARKNESS

1.

HARRY OSTROV

1

My name is Ostrov, Harry Ostrov. My actual given names were Ian Juan Ivan John, a lighthearted and light-headed joke wished on me by my parents when I was born in the final year of the Dancing Thirties, before the realities of overpopulation, ineradicable pollution, rampant nationalism, and plain entrepreneurial greed—the four horsemen of the greenhouse apocalypse—closed around the planet.

I fought my parents to a standstill on the matter of the names, which had become a crown of thorns on my teenage head (what cruel little animals one's schoolyard peers could be, tongues alive with mockery of the odd man out), and arrived at an understanding that I was, thenceforth and forever, Harry Ostrov. I might be all those other aliases on official documents but I was Harry in the home and, after a few definitive fights—I was a big lump of a kid—in the schoolyard.

Looking back, it seems like the only victory I ever won. All the other encounters, however successful, have left me with a sense of outward victory and inner doubt, as though I had traded some secret part of me (my soul, if the word means anything) for a few words of routine adulation. Failure hurts, but success, if you have any brains at all, reveals the inner weaknesses you somehow survived.

You stand up straight for the public accolade but you know

the part sheer luck played, how you blundered from point to point until you practically tripped over the answers, how the opposition's mistakes were the real sum of your supposed brilliance, and how often you were simply, starkly afraid.

I had, at the age of thirty-two, the ghastly experience of being brought face-to-face with the suppressed, hidden expressions of my true beliefs and desires, the stuff that lies unrecognized in the sump of the mind, and that was a terrible confrontation. I know more about the human veneer of civilization than most because I have been down in the engine room of the mind to observe the thing in action, and I know I am no hero. We are reactive mechanisms driven by deep-buried forces.

My claim to a place in history is not that I achieved great things but that I happened to be present at a few seminal passages and know something of the truth of the people who fashioned, for good or damnation, the world we live in today.

All these things happened long ago. There's a temptation to write "on another planet." That's the measure of historical change in a single lifetime.

I had my one hundred thirty-third birthday last week, making me one of the few old enough to remember 2070 in Australia, when the long greenhouse was at its height and January was the hottest month of the year.

Adding insult to animal sweat, the south polar ozone holes had defied the predictions of science and common sense by refusing to close wholly over; they thickened and thinned like pranksters who had us all by the short hairs. For the temperate regions, meaning most of the world, this hardly mattered, but for the state of Victoria and my hometown of Melbourne, both uncomfortably close to Antarctica and within the radius of UV onslaught, it meant January ill-temper, dripping armpits, and the regular anticancer shots that turned the skin a dirty brown and was ineffective in at least 5 percent of cases.

So we all wore long-sleeved shirts in high summer, protective glasses and wide-brimmed hats to shade the vulnerable forehead, ears, and nose. We police wore "digger" hats of a lightweight cotton closely woven against UV penetration, so that we sweated like draft horses from the hairline down, and after an hour or so probably stank like them.

This account begins in 2070, a hundred years ago, in January, with the outdoor temperature in the mid-forties and Detective Sergeant Ostrov relegated to a desk job, in a condition somewhere between official tolerance and limbo.

Premier Beltane had died six months earlier, by his own hand, while I was on duty at The Manor as bodyguard to his father. Beltane was not strictly my business, but the commissioner considered it a stain on the force's image that I had been unable to prevent the suicide. He would have dumped me as a sacrificial gesture if Psych Section had not stepped in to defend me. They knew of my horrible encounter with my subconscious because, in a state bordering on schizophrenic confusion, I had begged their help and they had been able to convince him that sacking me might backfire as a publicized injustice. (Besides, they wanted me for study, didn't they?)

I was grateful because, with half the workforce permanently unemployed, he was a lucky man who found two jobs in his lifetime.

My area superintendent, Connor, had me on a desk job because he didn't know what else to do with me. He would not trust my mental stability until Psych Section gave me a clean bill—which they would not do while they could dream up more tests and interrogations—so I wasted my days consolidating the reports of others, constructing endless schedules, and answering the questions that lazy coppers could have researched for themselves.

Then Connor sent for me and, though I could not know it, my entanglement with history began.

There were no omens or portents of destiny, only his face in my desk screen saying, "My office right away, Harry," and snapping off the call on the final syllable as though terseness represented efficiency. Connor had a repertoire of roles and attitudes, and as usual I found myself answering an automatic, "Yes, sir," to an unhearing screen. I disliked him. We saw each other's existences as crosses to be borne.

In his office he had another demonstration of reform school efficiency ready for me. He handed me a sheaf of papers, said, "Read, consider, and report to me for orders in one hour," and began the scanning of some other printout as though I had vanished with his last word.

Still, I said, "Yes, sir," because there would have been disciplinary slaughter if I hadn't. The small dog must never aspire to the bad manners of the big dog. Besides, Psych Section would never have forgiven me if I had so far lost control as to override their careful training in repression of the assaulted ego.

Until the shocking night in The Manor, when Gus Kostakis and I had been subjected to a drug-induced mental probing that no one should have to remember, I had had the average copper's impatience with Psych Section as a group of cloud-niners, more immersed in theory than aware of the grim facts of human behavior, but when confusion came pretty close to breakdown on my part they raced to the rescue with a down-to-earth practicality that tossed preconceptions out the window. They understood the implications of what had happened to me and cushioned my initial despair of coping with the paradoxes and blind alleys of unbalanced thinking. Better, they devised mental exercises founded in what they termed "logical dislocation," allowing the brain to freewheel with a problem or a decision until the subconscious disgorged an appropriate conclusion. "Appropriate" as distinct from "correct." They recognized moral and ethical "correctness" as variables dependent on personal perception, changing with the winds of popular convention and philosophic fashion. What they shaped for me was a coherent personality, not my previous holier-than-thou, morally perfect one.

Nevertheless, I had a complaint: they refused to treat Gus, because he was not a member of the force. It is hard to realize in our more or less brave new world that human beings were little more than statistics in that day. Nobody cared a damn what happened to civilian Gus; he had no entitlement to police care and no money for impossibly expensive private specialists. In the end I taught him, night after night, what Psych Section taught me by day, and together we struggled back to a bearable level of humanity. You must believe me when I say that no two people ever knew each other, to the depths, better than Gus and I when it was over.

So I was able to put Connor's playacting behind me and give my attention to the sheaf of papers. They could represent a promise of better times to come. Connor had said. ". . . and report to me for orders," so it might be that my putting out to grass was over; the papers might signal some sort of trial run.

They had come from the Dead File, I had no doubt, from the repository of old documents that had not been fed into the Data Bank but preserved, only because if ever they were revived for attention and action their context might demand forensic testing of print and paper. In the age of microrecording, printed originals were curios with rarity value.

The slight stiffness of the sheets and the browning edges were witness to a long, undisturbed shelf life. The first page was headed: Unsworn Statement by Steven Parry Warlock, 8th October, 2036. It was older than I. I began reading with no expectation of more than routine interest and soon was wondering why this document without any apparent criminal relevance had found its way into a police file at all. Then it became intriguing in its own right—and finally engrossing.

It was the narrative of a bizarre tragedy that had played itself out three years before I was born.

2

UNSWORN STATEMENT BY STEVEN PARRY WARLOCK
8TH OCTOBER, 2036

ATTESTED BY: SERGEANT P. K. NEWELL
CONST. L. C. HARTLEY (VOXCODE)

You might think that with Brian Warlock for a father I would have at least the seeds of artistic appreciation in me, but the fact is that I belong with the peasantry who "know what they like" and treat the aesthetic others with puzzlement and a secret suspicion that artists are all slightly out of balance or that the whole gallery game is suckerbait.

I remember that I was fifteen (which places the year as 2025) when I remarked that I liked the Seurat painting of some bathers that happened to be on loan to the Victoria State Gallery.

I should have known better than to open my mouth because Dad at once asked, "What do you like about it?" He really wanted to know. He always wanted to know.

And of course I muttered, "I just like it."

"But why? What is the special thing in it that speaks to you?"

I didn't know about any "speaking to me," but I made a valiant teenage effort. "It's bright and happy; it's about things I like doing." Then the urge to mutiny overtook me. "I just like it. I don't have to know why."

He said, with some disappointment I think, "I suppose not," and would have turned the conversation, but I was roused by too many inconclusive encounters to carry the fight to the enemy for once. I asked, "Do you always know why you make things look half finished or twisted or colored all wrong?"

Maybe nobody had put it so directly to him before, because he looked down at his hands as if the answer might be something he could reach out and grab hold of, then said, "Sometimes. Not always. A thing is right or it is wrong."

I think that was as close as ever I came to pinning down the relationship between my plain and gentle father and the painter with secret fire in his mind. There was no lack of feeling between us; the father–son bond was powerful, but in each of us there was an area of the soul quite impenetrable to the other.

He for his part pretended to follow and applaud my fascination with machinery and later was noisily proud of my success as an engineering troubleshooter, but he had no real interest in the details of my work. He was much taken by the patterns created by moving machinery but not at all by the mechanical details of how the patterns were derived. In much the same way I was pleased when he had a successful show or a good critical response, but I attended the shows only as a gesture of family solidarity. His paintings were and for the most part remain meaningless to me. I don't say they aren't often pleasing to the quick glance or that there isn't sometimes an emotional fillip that recedes and disintegrates when I look more closely, but by and large they remain meaningless.

That offends my sense of order and purpose. I see colors (and some are purely colorful abstractions) or I see shapes (often agglomerations of form without overt relevance) but I see no meaning.

To which he says, "What you see is the meaning." Just once he said, "Ultimate meaning is inexpressible," and looked as if he might cry if I pushed him further. So he really didn't know what his work meant, either.

The critics categorized him as "involuntarist," as though giving style a name was explanation enough. He muttered furiously that one wrong name would do as well as another when it added 50 percent to the sale value of the canvases.

The nearest we came to mutual comprehension was when he remarked that I researched what I saw and thought, while he was satisfied to contemplate phenomena of the mind and not confuse them with realities.

Make what you will of that.

(What indeed! This was an extraordinarily long and discursive statement by common police standards and I wondered at the patience of Sergeant Newell with Warlock's maunderings about his dad. They had some interest for me because my own parents were children of those same Dancing Thirties, that last party before realities closed around the planet. Brian Warlock, I recalled vaguely, was a painter whose work had passed out of fashion after he had come to some sort of peculiar end whose manner eluded memory. In a world oversupplied with oddities only the truly fabulous stay in mind. I was about to be reminded.)

My work in the Bio-Engineering Research Complex is design and maintenance of low-pressure evacuation and heat pump installations, which means that every laboratory staffer knows me, so nobody became uptight and regulation-bound when I asked permission to give my minor-celebrity father a tour of those areas that were not closed to the public for reasons of sterilization or secrecy. He had asked for it in what was a wholly dutiful expression of interest in his son's daily drudgery among the philistines— and he fell in love with the place.

Rapt in his personal conception of the world, he had no idea of machinery beyond wheels and pistons, gears and fans, centrifuges and the stink of hot oil. Of the world of microtechnology, since it didn't enter his everyday observation, he had little idea. Trailing me through the complex, with at first a few questions to show he was awake and looking, his guard was pierced by the microreduction systems of the nanotechnic replication machinery, which to his wondering eye appeared to operate with blades and punches of light, making ballets of snap and whirl and spark in pinhead spaces. His startled eyes as he looked up from the viewer and pushed the protective lenses up onto his forehead set me guessing that a new style of painterly obfuscation struggled for birth. Microvoluntarism, perhaps?

Then, in the Liquid Physics section, he gaped like a child in Wonderland at the superficial but never still evolution of symmetries and adjustments, and (though he had little math beyond simple addition and subtraction) in the chaos patterns of random interference on the computer screens. Chaos seemed a new world. I suppose that in a culture of intense specialization in smaller and smaller fractions it is normal for one man to be ignorant of what is the whole life of others. He demanded exposition and explanation. So to the demonstration of visual math: the Mandelbrots he rejected as kid stuff, no more than a viewpoint watching itself watch itself shrink down to a vanishment (I didn't argue), but the Julia patterns held him spellbound. "Mysteries that express without revealing," he said—and as usual became distressed when pressed to elaborate. To him the remark was transparently plain.

Next day the visit produced expectable ribaldry among the staff and I came close to getting myself laid off over one loud-mouth who suggested that Dad's attitude "reduced art to the status of an idiot child fascinated by a wagging finger." Privately I thought he had a point, but he wasn't to be permitted to repeat it; Dad and I were strongly and mutually supportive on the one or two ideas we had in common and formed a stubbornly aggressive front on all the rest.

I soon found out that Dad was visiting some sections without telling me, and that the lab staff let him roam for the sake of the incomprehensible comments they noted down and argued over. The visits produced new paintings that Dad claimed were "reactions to new vision." I found them indistinguishable from his previous work, but the critics perceived new directions and labeled them "apprehensions of the impulse of research"—and so they became "apprehensionist."

It might have been comical if the money hadn't kept on rolling in, paid by undoubtedly intelligent people who saw meaning that escaped me. Whether their perceptions were genuine or fantastic, there certainly were depths that even the most profound failed to penetrate.

We know that now.

Those visits, with their half-comprehended ejaculations about art and attitude, finally brought Dad into the Isolation Project, one of the more esoteric (some said "scatty") investigations proceeding in the Psych labs. It turned out that they had been debating his paintings and gnomic utterances and that some of the theoreticians claimed to understand "in a relating sort of way" how the works grew from observation. I never could do that though my fiancée, Helen, had an eerie gift for relating the finished canvases to the mini-machines that had been the source of "apprehension," and this seemed almost proof that his art made valid statements and was not simply associative doodling in oils.

It amounted to this: my father, who could create difficulties over the insertion of a shoelace into the correct eyelet, was capable of mental associations beyond his own or anyone else's ability to elucidate.

So the Psych crew suggested Dad as a subject for isolation. When they told him what was entailed, which would have scared the stunned wits out of me, he merely asked what they hoped to discover. That they could not tell him; it was an expedition into the unknown, in search of those things a mind might perceive when utterly alone with itself.

Dad asked, "With all sensation removed, what is there to perceive?"

Someone said, "A better word might be 'apprehend.' "

I think that word did it. Genuine or merely sly, it sucked Dad in whole. From that moment he was an eager guinea pig while I wondered if a more meaningless abstraction than "mental apprehension" was possible.

"Apprehend what?" I asked him.

He told me, "You're too much a realist; in this context the word means 'discover.' "

•   •   •

The Isolation Tank experiment as a technique had exhausted its possibilities and fallen into disuse during the last century. Subjects floating in water at body temperature in the solitude of lightless, soundproofed tanks had experienced euphoria, hallucination, or passages of terror; some had exhibited physical symptoms involving muscular contraction and vomiting; others had merely slept, unable to stay awake in a desensitized universe. In the long run the tests had told more about the physical and mental makeups of the subjects than about any reproducible effects of sensory deprivation. Interest in them lapsed.

Now, with the introduction of EIH—electronically induced hypnosis—as a tool of investigation, new possibilities had become apparent and the complex had resurrected the technique. The Psychs saw Dad as a find.

He spent hours with them as they probed his mental processes in question-and-answer sessions with heavy emphasis on the creative faculty, looking for a lead into what took place in his mind between perception of an object and the finished painting, which rarely displayed visual relationship with the thing ostensibly represented.

He became unbearable at home, discovering in himself a unique mentality with a totally individual perception, until my exasperated mum told him, "You're like one of those cultists who speak in tongues and don't know themselves what they are saying. It will turn out to be something quite simple. A misplaced gene, most likely."

You can see that Mum was not strong on either psychiatry or genetics, but she was more worried by Dad's engagement in this experiment than she let him know. She let me know, however, and insisted that I probe the matter to the depths.

As if I could!

At least I tried. I began with Helen, who is a nursing paramedic on the General Aid Staff of the complex and consequently familiar with most of what goes on in the research sectors. I told her that

Mum was concerned about the projected tests and most perturbed about the "unknown," which to her was a word hung about with doubts and fears. I admitted for myself only an ignorant man's curiosity, but Helen's answer to my complaint—that the manipulations of the Psychs were often jabberwocky to a practical engineer—told me more about her morality than about the project: "Well, they won't let him come to harm. They wouldn't dare; he's a public man, not to be risked. I'm glad he has volunteered and saved some frightened criminal from being drafted."

Most of us feel a little queasy about the Experimental Science Provision—that is, when we think about it at all—though the use of criminals as research subjects is hedged about with protective rulings and in fact few of them ever come to harm. The use of them pinpointed a change in humanity's thinking as fear of the greenhouse subsided, to give way to the much greater fear of the unmanageable population problem. The one-time "sanctity" of human life became a guilty joke, underscored by the daily starvation deaths of hundreds in the more destitute countries. Life was not sacred. With backs to the wall we recognized that it never had been, outside of the pulpit. It had become an epidemic infecting its own flesh. We had learned to see death as it is, rid of its ritual and outward trappings, and to acknowledge that it made little difference to history who died and when.

Admitting all this to myself, I still had to correct her. "The crims aren't drafted; they volunteer and are rewarded with remission."

"Much you know! You haven't seen how Appraisal Group selecters maneuver to get the ones they want nudged and argued into the lineup."

Nor had she, but as a nurse she heard doctors' discussions and confidences. I hadn't expected her to be so vehement but I still had to argue: "That's as may be, but I still can't see too many Category F crims having the type of mind that led to Dad being asked to take it on."

It was the wrong tack, of course.

"You can't? Well, the criminal mind might surprise you if you ever got around to probing one."

"Not my can of worms, darling."

"And therefore not worth thinking about!"

How did we get from there to here? These spats start so easily. This one lasted half a day, with sulks, but eventually she told me what she knew.

The limiting factor in Isolation Tank work in the last century had been the impossibility of damping out the interference of the body itself; the mind of the subject had never been totally free of the active flesh. Suspension at precise body heat had removed the awareness of weight and orientation, but the heart had still pounded its engine beat, the lungs swelled and relaxed, breath made its tiny bat squeaks in the nose and throat, and even the muscles made faint, nearly unmeasurable protests against protracted immobility. All these sounds and pressures, subliminal in daily life, intruded when the exterior world was shut out by the tank; the body thrust forward its moment to moment changes as the only sensations defining itself, and the brain was not free of them. Chained to life, however minimally, it could not gaze into its pristine self.

EIH involved direct interference in the brain to match, amplify, or neutralize the tiny currents activating its processes; in this case it would be used to negate the body's input of sound and tactile experience.

I asked, without any joy, "That's what they'll do to him?"

"That's it, Steve, darling. Your old man will be left alone in his mind to see what he can make of himself, and report back."

I spent a day thinking it over. Then, the next morning, I managed a little time with Dr. Paulinus of the Consciousness Research Unit. He bought me coffee and a bun in the canteen and listened patiently to my doubts and fears, which sounded only ill-informed as I failed to express them in a psychiatric jargon I did not know. Psychs and engineers live in different worlds.

His round plate of a Dutch-Indonesian face beamed at me as

he said, "You seem undecided between Frankenstein's monster and a brainwashed idiot. Why either?"

"Because he's my father and I'm bothered by what I don't understand."

"That's what you should have said in the first place. Your father can't explain because he has been told nothing much; we don't want him going into isolation with a head full of preconceived ideas. We propose to do only what we have done with a dozen other voluntary subjects, none of whom have suffered harm. Has my behavior changed, for instance?"

That took me by surprise. "You've had it done to yourself?"

"Naturally. How else learn what you are doing? Does that make you feel better?"

It surely did. "But why Dad?"

"Because his mind displays apparent, ah, eccentricities."

A lifetime's familiarity had taught me more about that than Paulinus would ever know. "It's ordinary in most things; only his art is unintelligible. Otherwise, he likes games, reads thrillers, has a conventionally dirty mind, and behaves much as other men do."

"Only his art! There some irrationality is present, or seems to be. What do you think art is?"

I had to reach into my grab bag of half-baked ideas.

"Creativity?"

"Everybody is to a degree creative. Even an idiot."

"Communication?"

"Better. From whom to whom?"

"From the artist to the public, I suppose."

"And with whom does your father communicate?"

"Hard to say. People rationalize and he just stares at them. They ask what a picture means and he says, 'What's there, of course.' When some stupid critic tries to chart creative connections he gets short-tempered because he doesn't know them himself. Or says he doesn't."

"Be careful with critics; most are far from stupid. And your father does not know the connections. Listen carefully." He looked down on my intelligence (that's how it felt) from the certified height of all his professional years. "Some artists work from the outside inward; they have a theory of artistic expression and present visions in accord with their theories. They know exactly what they are doing and why. Others work from inside themselves to the canvas, transmuting a factual scene into an intellectual comment or philosophic exposition. Most are reasonably aware of the process of elaboration and can discuss it with some degree of self-reference; your father cannot because he is unaware of the mental leap between the stimulus and the canvas."

"You mean he doesn't know what he is doing?"

"I mean that he doesn't know why he does it in that particular fashion. His work is spontaneity with a vengeance. We have tried to tap in with deep hypnosis and achieved nothing; the answers lie deeper than hypnosis can reach."

"So it's his own mind that must tell what it is doing?"

Paulinus winced. "Crudely, yes."

"What happened with the other people you tried?"

"More or less what we expected. Specialized minds are oriented to their specializations; they report back in the terms of their orientation. Their processes are governed by purely intellectual factors, so we have learned from them a great deal about how education, dextral abilities, and emotional bias affect the world-view, but nothing of the impulses at deeper levels. From your father we hope to gain clues to the working of the seemingly irrational."

I thought of the Theorems of Order arising from the Laws of Chaos and muttered something about them.

"Why not?" he asked. "They seem as fundamental as quantum uncertainty; they may be much the same thing."

While I was relieved that the process was tested and safe, I still asked, out of curiosity, "Did you run the first trials on crim volunteers?"

"With procedures and parameters untested? Good God, no! We wanted relatively normal minds to establish the initial procedures."

"So criminal minds are abnormal?"

"Not usually; reactions to early experience do much of the shaping and can give the same result as tests on the dedicated professional, a skewed reading where something more generalized is required."

"But Dad—"

"Not at all generalized, of course, but we have the basic procedural data now and are feeling our way into personality variations." I started to thank him for giving me his time but he shushed me and said, "There will in fact be a criminal mind tested in tandem with your father. He's a volunteer"—I suppressed a desire to ask, A real one?—"chosen for much the same reason as Mr. Warlock. He is a child molester."

For the life of me I couldn't see the connection and must have showed it, for he gave me a smug professional grin as he explained, "His peculiarity is that he dislikes children intensely yet uses them for sexual frisson but never harms them physically. He shows no understanding of his actions and becomes hysterical with frustration when any attempt is made to rationalize them. Like your father he does not know why he does what he does. There may be neuron process similarities or there may not. We shall see."

The parallel between my dad and an unpleasant pervert seemed tenuous, but I was more puzzled by the idea of a mind regarding itself critically; it smelled of lifting oneself by the bootlaces. "But if all sensory input is removed, what has the mind to work on?"

"What it always has—knowledge, memory, experience, and the neuron paths linking them as processes of thought. The novelty here is that they operate without built-in distraction. We hope to tap into areas unmapped, below the level of recoverable thought—the preconscious. Even in the closed-circuit minds of our professional testees there have been hints of deeper processes."

Later, at home, I retailed all this to Mum, explaining as best I could. My best didn't penetrate far, because she sniffed and asked,

"Do they imagine art is some manner of perversion?" and hurried off to the bedroom.

To cry, I imagined. She had cried a lot, privately, since Dad had made his decision, but had never attempted to alter his mind. She rarely discussed his work and I have felt that she regarded genius or talent or whatever the description might be as part of the cross wives bear.

(No sign yet of a crime, though there must be something nasty in the woodwork for us to take an interest at this late date. It was surprising that Sergeant Newell had not tried to jolly young Warlock along and squeeze all this wandering kerfuffle into a few workmanlike essentials. It could be, though, that the background was necessary to understanding what was to come and that Newell had been instructed to let the man ramble. That may happen when the case team is fishing for a lead.

As it happened, this was the point where I stopped wondering because Steven Warlock, with a smart gear change, moved into the action.)

The test was conducted in one of the smaller assembly rooms, probably because a fair amount of floor space was covered by the experimental setup; it was easier than rearranging a cluttered laboratory.

Chairs were arranged around but back from the two bare operating tables and occupied mainly by Psych Section personnel.

To the end of each table was attached a board arranged with gauges that appeared to lead, by color-coded cables, to a cluster of terminals on a fairly bulky helmet, apparently intended for the head of the isolation subject.

About a meter from each board of gauges was a chair for the EIH man and beside it a metal box which only feature was what looked like small fingertip controls on its upper surface.

Close-by each table, chairs were occupied by a physician, a

nurse, and two male orderlies apparently chosen for weight and muscle. This crew was plainly ready for the unexpected, and I felt that some possibilities had not been passed on to me.

The two table assemblies were totally separated. The two examinations seemed unconnected with each other and this lent eeriness to what we were to learn only many months later.

Helen, sitting by Paulinus, waved briefly and then ignored me.

The two subjects came in naked from an inner room, where they had undressed, one of the orderlies told me, against the unlikely case of some bone-wrenching spasm requiring immediate action. I had been told nothing of possible spasms.

The two stood awkwardly by their tables, embarrassed and nervous and looking away from their audience. There could scarcely have been two more dissimilar subjects. Dad was fifty-three, at sixty-five kilos a little overweight for his slight frame, breathing self-consciously in his chest to hold in the small pot he pretended was not there. Reddish hair around a balding skull, plus his narrow mouth and chin, gave him the look of an aging, mortified fawn.

Frankie, the pederast (he really had been christened Frankie, not Francis) was an absolute contrast, younger and taller and heavier, well made, dark, and something like handsome—but not quite handsome because of some hard-to-pick flaw in his features. When he let his gaze sweep just once around the faces in the room I found the flaw. An enraptured girl might have seen an attractive, impish mockery but I glimpsed a deeper trait, an amused wickedness overlying some other different feeling. Even in the glimpse I formulated it in my mind as an unfulfilled regret, an expectation of sadness.

Two EIH men came in behind them, one pudgy and short and jolly, the other long and narrow, absorbed and strangely unnoticeable until he spoke.

Paulinus opened the proceedings with unfussy brevity. "You all know the nature of this operation and the characteristics of the subjects. There should be little to see other than two men apparently asleep on their respective tables. We hope there will be something interesting to hear from them later." He turned to the EIH men. "Dr. Graves"—he indicated the pudgy one—"will monitor Brian Warlock in his quest for the transmuting of the creative impulse." Dad grinned uncertainly. "Dr. Bentinck will monitor Frankie Devalera, who will be seeking the origin of physical activities springing from no definable impulse." Devalera unsuccessfully tried to look as though he didn't care what anybody thought of him. "Are you gentlemen ready?"

Bentinck said in an unexpectedly rich bass voice, "We can begin now." Then each doctor took up one of the helmets and asked his charge to lie on his table. The two naked men looked at each other for the first time since they had entered the room, exchanged bleak smiles, and climbed onto the tables.

The helmets were fitted. I had expected cables connecting subject and hypnotist, but there were none. What I had taken for simple terminals were in fact compact transmitters and receivers; there was no man-to-man wiring to figure in dangerous accidents.

Dad raised his head and said, "Come here, Stevie."

When I hesitated he held out his hand, wanting me to hold it. I did not recall that he had ever before made such a gesture of trust and need. I glanced at Graves, who smiled and nodded. I took his hand, felt it shake slightly, and bent to his ear to say, "You can still pull out of this."

He pressed my fingers. "Can't. The boys at the pub would never let me forget it."

So I stood holding his hand, feeling like a hovering nanny and ineffably stupid, waiting for the drama to begin. Then Graves said, "You can rest his hand on the table. He can no longer feel you."

Without fuss the process had begun. I went back to my chair as Graves said, "The subjects are isolated from sensory input. You can converse in ordinary tones."

Somebody asked a question and Graves answered in what sounded like a prepared monologue, "Through the encephalostats we read the operating voltages of the sensory centers of the brain and cancel them with precisely matched impulses. This is done by small computer units, eliminating human error. It is a purely electronic process, not hypnotic or in any sense telepathic. With the eleven senses canceled, we concentrate on monitoring the total mental and physical state of the subjects." He added with the off-hand arrogance of the expert, "Best not to address us again; our attention must now be wholly on the instruments."

I pondered those six additional senses. If "sense" meant "detection system," you would have to include all the mechanisms triggered by temperature maintenance, adrenaline release, hunger stimulus, tiredness warning . . .

Paulinus was plugging explanatory holes, forestalling misunderstanding. ". . . and they are emphatically not in communication with the subjects. They maintain surveillance only. They have no means of intruding on the subjects' observation or thinking . . ."

I wondered if glandular balance would count as a "sense" and decided against it.

". . . cannot reach the isolated minds by hypnotic command. If interruption to the isolation should be necessary, they will simply cut off the canceling frequencies and shake the subjects awake. This has never been necessary in previous trials."

Someone pointed out that previous trials had not used subjects with abnormal intellectual functions.

"Why abnormal? They are merely unfamiliar. In Devalera's case we may have only an unusually powerful repression at work."

I said, with sudden distrust of the whole thing, "Maybe self-knowledge will be more destructive than the self-imposed ignorance hiding it."

Paulinus's impatient stare made me feel like the kid who always asks the silly questions in class. "Devalera is aware of the possibility; we do not use subjects without prior counseling. If he suffers as a result of the freeing of blocked knowledge he will be given full remedial treatment."

I formed my own conclusion as to how much "volunteering" Devalera had done. Feeling I had him cornered, I asked, "What counseling did Dad get?"

Paulinus's frown meant shut up and stay shut, but he shifted to bland surprise. "He hasn't told you? Then I must respect his privacy." Down, Towser, down! My guess at the true answer was "none," because in Dad's case they didn't know what they were dealing with.

I had my eyes on Dad, of course, so I saw the quick twitch and the shrinking movement, as if on the flat table he tried to draw away from something unpleasant. It lasted a bare second but from the corner of my eye I noted that Graves stiffened and leaned forward to his telltales. Then Dad relaxed and lay still as before.

At the same moment Devalera made an indescribable sound, inarticulate, strangled, coarse, brutal, as though something sub-human bellowed in a private hell. His hands and feet thumped the table like a tethered animal trying to run.

Then his whole body rolled from side to side and the orderlies sprang to restrain him. Too late. Bentinck uttered a hoarse, de-spairing cry as Devalera's body, responding to commands from its own mental depths, convulsed away from their reaching hands, over the edge of the table and down to the floor.

In a relaxed fall he might have suffered no more than bruising, but every muscle was taut and his limbs projected rigidly from his toppling trunk. The sounds of breaking arm and shoulder were muted pistol shots.

Bentinck reached down and pulled the helmet free but De-valera continued to writhe and roll like the victim of a nightmare unable to wake. Bentinck put two fingers in his mouth, bent to the man's ear, and blew a street kid's whistle that would have wakened a cataleptic. At any rate it brought one sense into full function and I assume the others followed it. Devalera was in shocking distress and it needed three of them to hold him while Helen injected a pacifier.

Bentinck called to Paulinus, "Get him to surgery!"

"Full sedation?"

"No! I'll keep him under light hypnosis until we get some idea what happened."

Paulinus nodded. "What about Warlock? There was some re-action there."

Jolly, pudgy Graves said in his jolly, pudgy way, "He's hard to rouse." He was shaking Dad without effect. He prized open an eyelid and shone a torch beam into Dad's eye, then signaled Bentinck, who repeated his whistling performance. Dad did not stir.

He has not stirred since.

He lies in bed, at home now, with a feeding tube in his arm, at rest in the total seclusion of his mind.

Daily the isometric exercise machine works on him to maintain some physical condition against his eventual waking. But he does not wake.

Graves has stopped trying. He no longer comes near us.

(Contemporary art said little to me; my interest stopped at portraits of personable women, striking animal studies, or landscapes with some atmosphere about them. Brian Warlock was only a name with a tinge of forgotten mystery clinging to it. Mother was the aesthete of our family, visiting galleries and sketching a little when she could afford the equipment. It was she who had mentioned the Warlock name recently, rousing a tingle of familiarity—something to do with the man's extant paintings and the National Heritage Commission, a news item that had not registered among the daily trivia. What then rose to mind was the odd fact—one of the thousand or so odd facts in a day's scanning—that he was still alive. If his condition could be termed "alive."

It had been mentioned because the disposal of his paintings was in question.

None of this provided any clue to where my detective duty entered.)

Mum's heart broke—slowly—before she accepted that there would be no return from whatever far place had claimed him.

They had never been a publicly demonstrative couple, but her inability to cope with the happening or with the everyday world, her lostness, made our home a place to avoid. Friends did not know how to console grief that kept a private face and retreated from their goodwill while she communed within herself.

Silently she blamed all of us: Paulinus, Graves, myself, even Helen. She said nothing, but her eyes laid blame as an enduring weight.

A miserable year dragged by before she returned to something like a normal existence, but she never referred to the sleeper in the back room (though I knew she kept a lonely vigil there for hours each day) but spoke of him—rarely—in the past tense, as a memory. She cleaned him and changed the feeding tubes daily but never mentioned the mocking chore.

Marriage with Helen sagged into indefinite postponement. I could not in decency leave home while Dad lived—in his fashion— nor could I bring a wife into a mausoleum. Helen said nothing; we settled for a weary, receding future.

A few days before last Christmas I received a vidcall at the complex. The screen cleared on the unmemorable face of someone I should recall but did not. Only the profoundly bass voice, loaded with all the character the face lacked, stirred recollection of Bentinck.

He said, as though no lead up was necessary, "I have arranged with the complex for you to be free tomorrow. Frankie Devalera is now a reconstituted member of society and is willing to speak of his experience in the Isolation Project."

Ready to go public, probably for money, with the cheap hype of science-for-the-citizen.

"Should I care?"

Bentinck said, "He has much of interest to tell of your father."

"Clinical detail? I can live without it."

"Much of personal and emotional interest. I feel, and so does he, that you and your mother should hear what he has to tell before it becomes public property in the scientific journals."

The warning shook me. "I don't understand this."

The vague face took on a faint frowning. "There was communication . . . That is an inaccurate statement but there is no simple way of presenting it. There was a form of communication between Frankie and your father during the process. What he says will concern you deeply. And Mrs. Warlock more so. Much more so.''

This began to be a summons from a man who meant to have his way. I said, "That my be, but my mother is still in distress and I don't want to add to it.''

"Devalera may give her great comfort.''

"You should explain that.''

A little shrug accused me of being unnecessarily difficult. "I have learned, cautiously, from your neighbors and relatives, of Mrs. Warlock's emotional condition and, if I read her correctly, Devalera's news will be very welcome. She will be most proud.''

He promised without revealing; I supposed there was a matter of professional confidentiality, leaving only Devalera the right to speak freely. "Where will this meeting take place?''

"In Devalera's home.'' He gave me a time and an address on the seamier side of the city.

I said, "I will be there but I can't promise to bring Mother.''

"I urge that you do. I speak as a psychiatrist and as a man who has himself endured separation.''

The words carried a sort of mournful conviction. Only after he had beeped off did I think of the irrationality of communication between separated egos in isolation.

I broached the invitation, hesitantly, to Mother that night. She heard me out, plucking at her dress as sick people will pluck at their sheets. In the end she said, "I do not need to be made proud of Brian; that I have always been.''

I told her, "I'll go. One of us should know what's going on.''

"Suit yourself, Steven.'' I was not much in favor.

In the morning, however, she was dressed and ready to leave with me. She said rigidly, "I expect nothing of a meeting with a perverted criminal and a negligent scientist, but if there is to be publicity I shall at least make legally certain that no vicious gossip will be put about.''

It was not the moment to argue that scientific journals were not media for vicious gossip.

DOWN THERE IN DARKNESS

"So," she continued, "I have arranged for the younger Mr. Gregg to be present."

Our family lawyer, the "younger" Mr. Gregg, was pushing seventy.

With such interest shown, it seemed to me reasonable that I had wired myself unobtrusively to take a record of the meeting. What you will hear is verbatim.

The Devaleras were poor, not poverty-stricken but poor in the fashion of families with only one working member and he not a well-paid one. Their single-fronted house in a Richmond back street was a relic of the previous century, needing a coat of paint and some shoring up of the rear foundations, but the small garden was a miniature blaze.

Mother stopped on the violet-bordered path to examine every plant. "A fine gardener; a sign of humanity," she said, as if that lifted the child molester an inch or two out of the gutter. "Well, that is something."

From the front door Devalera said, "My father is the gardener; I am a laborer in Sewer Maintenance. I am Frankie Devalera and I think I'm all too human."

It was an assertion of personal dignity, not a declaration of war, but Mother surveyed him without speaking, lips pursed, eyes wary and unforgiving. She nodded with minimum courtesy and entered the house as he stepped aside.

As I passed him he said, "I remember you; you held his hand. He was frightened. At first he was frightened."

That was high-order recollection; his eyes had swept the audience just once. He himself was not easily forgettable; the sourly amused cast remained, under a new composure but not gone away. Perhaps he had discovered what aroused his amused contempt. Himself?

The rooms in these old houses are small and the sitting room was crowded with all of us. There were "the younger" Mr. Gregg, with Mother next to him, and a grimly aging man of fifty or so whose hard, prim features were his son's without the hint of mockery. There was a quiet, thin man in whom I did not at once recognize—Bentinck. I am sure his self-effacement was deliberate, a ploy of the trade that made him startlingly effective when he thrust himself into notice. When patients forgot his presence he no doubt collected intimacies that otherwise might have been glossed or withheld.

At that point I scarcely noticed a boy seated behind the elder Devalera. With all my interest centered on Frankie, I dismissed him as a younger brother.

Mother at once laid down the terms of her presence. Looking at no one in particular, she said, "I will not listen to defamation or derogation of my husband or permit him to be exposed to malice. I am not interested in research, only in personal values."

Gregg presumed on old acquaintance to say snappishly, "Do sit down, Millie. I am assured you will hear nothing against Brian and much that is favorable."

Frankie said, "Only what is favorable."

His voice was working-class though well enough schooled to make him an unlikely sewer rat, but in the greenhouse century and with his repellent criminal record he was lucky, in an automated world, to have a job at all. Somebody (Bentinck?) had pulled strings at rehabilitation. Manner and manners defined his economic stratum exactly when he asked, "Is the kettle on, Dad? It'll be easier over a cuppa." Then he became self-consciously formal. "I'm sure you would like some tea, Mrs. Warlock?"

It was a pretty obvious please-try-to-like-me but Mother only bowed her head slightly. She would take his tea as part of the visiting ritual, the formal dance allowing people to disagree without savaging each others throats.

The father went out to the kitchen with the faintly lumbering tread of the scrapheap unemployed, old before time for sheer lack of activity to preserve youth. He came back with a huge family teapot to set on a trolley laid with china. It didn't all match, but among the laboring classes its mere sufficiency was enough.

It seemed there was no Mrs. Devalera; it was the young boy

who helped the older man, silently bringing milk, sugar, and biscuits, then retiring to his chair at the rear. He seemed about twelve years old and skinny.

Frankie got up to do the honors, talking all the time, not addressing anyone but launching into a speech any man would have found difficult, as if by concentrating on cups and saucers he might forget he was under judgment.

"My name's Frankie, not Francis. It's important. It was a sort of wordplay on my mum's part because I was a twin—Frankie and Johnnie, you see? Only not like the song, we were both boys. We weren't just twins but joined at the hip, too. We were Siamese twins and that meant we had to be delivered by caesarean section and one way and another Mum had a hard time with us. She never really forgave us for it. That right for you, Mrs. Warlock? Pass her the milk and sugar, Dad."

Mother said in the strangled voice that afflicts her when she senses unpleasantness coming, "No milk, thank you."

Frankie plowed on, handing around tea with not quite steady hands and the desperation of a host out of his depth. "The join was just a flap of flesh so the doctors got on to it right away and cut us apart and put skin grafts in and there's not much scar left. You didn't see any scar that day, did you?" Pushing a teacup at me.

"No, none."

"There's hardly any to see, nothing to remind me there was another one, Johnnie. But there was a kind of memory started later on. Then there was the day in the complex, but I'm not sure if even that is a real memory."

Bentinck spoke suddenly in a staccato bass: "Stop fiddling, Frankie. Get to the point."

It was the tone of an exasperated chaperone and it seemed to work. "I couldn't remember him because we were only a few weeks old when I rolled over his face in my sleep and smothered him."

Mother clattered her cup and saucer and the younger Mr. Gregg frowned as if this sort of thing was outside his area of practice and should be discouraged, but I began to see Frankie as a human being with depths and compulsions outside my experience.

"Mum and Dad put it about as something they called cot death and I think the doctor must have helped them get away with it." The father's face changed not a fraction at this. He was stone. "I was going to school before I ever knew I once had a twin. I learned the hard way; the other kids found out about it and gave me schoolyard hell the way kids can. They even had a game of rolling on each others' faces and singing 'Frankie and Johnnie.' I used to get hysterical because I didn't understand and I still don't know how they found out!"

The father spoke without warning in a gritty, passionless voice. "Confidences! Your mother told her best friend, who told everybody—in confidence!"

"You don't know that, Dad. You shouldn't blame everything on her."

"She blamed you, didn't she? For her poor health and what she regarded as her ill fortune and for everything that happened for ten years! Then she deserted me for a younger man and blamed you for that, too."

His teeth snapped audibly as he closed his mouth on the words. He had had his say and that was that. He must have been a hard man to live with.

The interruption upset Mother. "What has all this to do with my husband?"

Bentinck answered, "There is a connection, leading to the Isolation Project. Also, Frankie is still my patient and this rehearsal helps him."

"Are you taking advantage of my presence to further his treatment!"

To her anger Bentinck said simply, "Yes," and for once she could find no immediate objection. She was, despite herself, involved.

When we were quiet, Frankie said, "You can see that I grew up with a sort of false memory of a twin called Johnnie. I made it

DOWN THERE IN DARKNESS

true by looking at myself in the bedroom mirror and pretending there were two of us exactly the same. We talked. I mean, he talked, too, because I could see his lips make the words as I heard them. And there was the tiny bit of scar on my left hip proving he was real. He was real to me though I couldn't touch him. I tried but there was only flat glass. I told my mum but she only screamed at me and called it nonsense, and I wasn't old enough to know that rage and pain go together to make hate and despair. One day she beat me. Hard. With the buckle end of a belt. Screaming that Johnnie was dead and I killed him. I never saw her again after that because when I got back from the hospital she was gone. I got belted for that, too. Don't blame Dad; he was half out of his mind between a wife gone off and a son who talked to the mirror."

He glanced briefly and smiled like a shy kid. The father's expression did not change; solid brick all through.

"But the persecution stopped because somebody got to the neighborhood parents and they spoke to their kids and suddenly there was no more Frankie and Johnnie talk." He looked again at his father, hoping, I think, that the old man would confirm the decent thing attributed to him, but he might as well have begged the Sphinx. "No use asking him. He won't admit he was trying to make up for everything going wrong."

I saw the young boy, from his seat behind the father, give a peculiarly adult approving nod, like a schoolmaster pleased with a promising pupil. It seemed the family formed a single psychiatric stew. And, indeed, Frankie's tale more and more left reality adrift in fantasy land.

"When there was nobody mentioning Johnnie, he went away—I mean I learned other things to do, games and friendships and all that. Girls, too, later on. But he didn't go right away; he was there in the back of my mind, out of sight. He showed up again when I was older, though I didn't know it was him. It was just that I loved little boys, the younger the better. I wanted to feel them and play the games with them that I had played with Johnnie in the mirror."

His eyes came up sharply, facing us all down. "Personal games. You understand me? Intimate!"

He wasn't excusing anything and yes, we understood him.

Mum shifted uneasily but said nothing. She had never seen sexual deviations as psychological imbalances rather than visitations of the Devil.

"That's what got me into trouble. Dr. Bentinck says I was looking for Johnnie where he was lost in the bottom of my mind. However it was, people started looking sideways at me. And some kids got frightened when I touched them. Then a couple of fathers made trouble and I had to leave home, run away. I started to hate kids, remembering how they gave me a bad time and were doing it again now. Love and hate together; it's a mad feeling. I couldn't keep my hands off them and I didn't know why. It was like being pushed against your will, like a voice saying, 'There, that one!' and 'It could be the next one!' and me not knowing what I looked for and hating each one that wasn't it. Then the police, of course, and the trial with nearly a hundred charges against me—and that was only the ones they found out about—and me with nothing to say because I didn't know why I did it. And jail. And then Dr. Bentinck."

I tried to imagine myself relating such a history, and found some respect for so much honesty. I stole a glance at Mother. She was grim (nobody loves a child molester) but puzzled, too, unable to come to grips with an obsession she saw only in terms of primary evil and so not subject to reason.

Bentinck spoke, with his usual effect of materializing suddenly. "I had been studying Frankie in prison, and the Isolation Project made a possible means of checking my tentative diagnosis by having the patient actually recall the forgotten processes I had rationalized into hypothetical existence. It turned out to be much more."

Frankie took up his tale. "You can't know what it is like—dark and silent and like floating and alone in a way you could never imagine." He appealed to Bentinck. "The doctor can explain better."

The beginning was familiar stuff until he got to ". . . the old isolation tanks were more like solitary confinement, with all the mental trauma that involves. Electrohypnotic isolation leaves the mind utterly unaffected by the physical universe. Sense of imprisonment is lost because there is no awareness of an 'outside.' But we do not cut the mind free to leave it open to nightmares; the subject is given his project theme before isolation begins. He takes with him the matters he is to pursue. What we call 'bad trips' are possible—repressed information can have its unpleasant aspects— but the encephalostat monitoring of reflexes allows us to intervene and restore the patient to normal surroundings with the flick of a switch."

Did it so? I said, "I was there. The flick of the switch was pretty slow. I saw him convulsing before he rolled off the table."

"Worse, the convulsions continued after I had canceled his isolation."

"So he must have had a hell of a bad trip."

"He will tell you."

Frankie said, "We had our preparation, Brian and me. A sort of hypnotic loosening up."

"Presensitizing," Bentinck interposed, as though that should be obvious to the lay mind.

"So when they put the helmets on us and canceled out the brain waves, our senses went blank like putting out lights one after another. I was alone. I never knew what the word meant before. It's as if nothing exists, not even yourself, but it isn't frightening; you just listen to your own thinking because there isn't anything else. I was caught up on the questions I had to find answers for; the preparation had fixed them in the front of my mind. I had been told Brian was trying to find out where he got his art from and of course I had to find out why I had to explore kids' bodies.

"So there I was, thinking about some kid who turned out to be me in a mirror, about six years old because that was when I first heard about him, with both of us reaching out to touch. Except it wasn't a mirror; it was real because we could grab hold of each other. That other me—because both of us was really me, not me and Johnnie—pulled me toward him, making me go some-where I didn't want to. Somewhere down and terrible, somewhere I knew about and was afraid of. I started to panic.

"That was when I felt Brian in there with me. Nobody had thought of this happening. He was in trouble, too, but his trouble was different. He was pulled somewhere, too, but he knew where and he felt guilty about it. And he knew my mind, too. Don't get this wrong; we didn't talk to each other or anything like that. It was as if we were in a place where people know each other com-pletely without having to speak or wait to find out. We could even share experiences a bit; I saw what he saw and he saw what I could see, like as if we had come together in the same place though we were going different ways."

He looked directly at Mother. "It was you he was guilty about. Some others, too, but you most of all. I saw you there."

I thought she would weep but he held up his hand with a quite strange authority, his knowledge superseding her thinking. "Don't you cry, missus; you be proud! You were standing in his mind, the idea of you, as if it was now and years ago both at once—and at the same time there was another you in the place where he was headed for and he could see you there, too. You—" He stopped, fumbling for words. "People see things different ways. The you he saw in the new place was the most beautiful woman in the world, but she was all made of colors and shapes that came together like a painting, and the colors and shapes were what he felt. I could feel him in a sort of ecstasy because the colors and shapes were still you though they kept changing all the time as if the painting was never finished. But it was real as if that is what you really are. Not just you but the terrific joy of loving, painting love where bodies and words weren't enough to say it. They were his way of saying love as nobody else could say it be-cause nobody else was exactly him. And he felt guilty because he was pulled between you in the world and you that his love saw. I could feel all this."

I was afraid Mother would crumble, but she sat straight up with a little smile on her face as if she knew it all, and I saw that

I had never understood how much this mundane, undemonstrative pair loved each other.

Frankie nodded at me. "You were there, too, not as bright as your ma but there all the time. You were a bit different, sort of squarer. More macho. I suppose that's how you seemed to him because your colors and shapes were all hard-edged, but soft in the middle so he could reach in and know you. You be proud, too!"

I wasn't proud; I was wretched. He had painted his love, year after year, and I all unable to see it.

"There were other people but I didn't know who they were, except they were people he loved. And don't forget that while I saw his mind he saw mine, so we were each in two worlds at once. They were like actual worlds but separate, not touching. And his mind jibbed at what he saw forming up in mine. It shocked him and his shock hit me, too, so that my own vision closed back around me."

I thought this must have the moment when Dad reacted on the table. Straight after that, Frankie had gone into his convulsion. What he was telling us must have happened in just a few seconds of real time.

"I didn't have a chance to shut it out. There was a furnace, but it was in a big open mouth like an idol's jaws and I was falling into it, falling and falling, and all the time little kids were passing through my hands. They were all Johnnie. That is, they were me really, but as I looked in their faces they would change into strangers, not Johnnie. They hung onto me, loading me down so I kept falling, but my hands stayed free to catch another Johnnie and seek him for my twin. Or maybe it was me I was looking for; it seemed to be the same thing. It was after . . . it seemed like hours . . . I saw the furnace was going to take me because I couldn't stop my searching and pawing. My mind started screaming because the furnace was my father's open mouth, hating and condemning and making sure that hell was a real place and I would be in it. Then Dr. Bentinck brought me back."

You might think there was nothing we could say to these outlandish visions, but instead we had an eruption of the outlandishly actual. Without apology, as if it was his right, the young boy spoke up, not in the voice of childhood with its confusions and resentments, but in the prissy, overeducated accent of the "classy" preacher. I still feel a shock of disbelief when I play back this part of the chip.

What the little monster said, in a cold tone of laying down the law, was, "The doctor of minds soothes wounds but cannot heal them, for forgiveness is not in his power. Frankie lived life in sin and will requite it in fire."

Neither Bentinck nor the father showed surprise; Bentinck seemed to watch our reactions. Young Mr. Gregg, who must have encountered grotesques enough in legal life, examined the boy as if considering him for a specimen jar. Mother, inexpressibly shocked, sat still with her eyes on her hands.

With silence stretching, I said, because I could not help myself, "With you for a brother he must have had punishment enough by now."

The boy turned uninterested eyes on me and said dismissively, "I am not his brother."

"Then who are you? A sightseer of sick confessions?"

"I am Jesus."

He said it simply, without flourish. I found myself scratching idiotically for an explanation and concluding vaguely that it was not an uncommon name among Spanish-speaking people. But Mother took an outraged breath to ask Bentinck why the brat should be party to a supremely private exchange.

"He is in his fashion a member of the household. He is the elder Mr. Devalera's ward. I could not exclude him but hoped he would have the social sense to keep quiet. Since he has interfered"—he shrugged—"take it that we have had an interlude for clowning and can now return to our proper business."

Neither Devalera nor the boy reacted to the insult.

"If a point must be labored," Bentinck went on, "it is that Mr. Devalera is a lay preacher, fundamentalist in the most basic sense, who shouts fire and brimstone to delighted pagans from a soapbox on the Yarra bank on Sundays. He, like the mother, never forgave his son for the death of the twin, which, in view of the boy's later activities, he saw as a crime of demonic possession. Frankie's vision was obvious symbolism from which he has now been set free."

Contempt did not touch the graven statue by the tea trolley. He sat, entire in himself, steadfast in brute belief in the righteousness of his judgment, impregnable.

It was awhile before Mother collected herself to speak directly to Frankie. She could not control a tremor as she attempted the question crying out for answer.

"I suppose you could not see . . ." and could not finish it. How to ask a man in Hellmouth had he noticed what happened to her husband?

Frankie smiled at her. "But I could. I did. Why else are you here? I told you we each knew what the other felt and thought. Thought and experience there were open, not private and owned but—well . . . there. Dr. Bentinck talks about collective unconscious and maybe there's an answer there somewhere."

Bentinck snapped at him with gravelly irritation. "You misunderstand the term. Jung applied it to species intuitions and shared basic mental characteristics, such as self-preservation, the sexual urge. He did not postulate a never-never land of intuitively apprehended experience."

Mother reacted to his irritation. "But it exists! You saw it in your monitoring helmet, didn't you?"

"Nothing is seen in the monitoring helmet; it only measures the strength and flux of electrical flow."

Mother, always at sea with technicalities, was obstinate. "Yet you are told that this place of collective sharing exists?"

Bentinck's answer was careful. "Something took place that contradicts both knowledge and theory. I cannot discuss what I do not understand."

Mother claimed the last word. "Then you have study to occupy you for some time to come."

Frankie put an end to it, speaking loudly across them. "Anyway, I know where Brian went." For a moment he had trouble with words but it was through his desire not to hurt where he tried to heal. At last he said baldly, "You won't wake him."

Mother bowed her head for the third time that morning, this time in acceptance. I think she guessed what had happened.

"Mrs. Warlock, he joined his loved ones. What I mean is, he joined the happiness and love he had fashioned out of his loved ones, all the shapes and colors, the perfection of them. He pulled his mind tight around him. His body can't reach him. It might be that he couldn't come back if he wanted. And, anyway, who would want to come back from heaven?"

3

Good question: Who would want to?

And on that neatly dramatic inquiry the statement ended, with the appended signature, Steven Parry Warlock.

Peculiar!

Could it be that the police had, in view of the bizarre circumstances of Warlock's condition (sleep? coma? suspended animation?), required an eyewitness report (and there might be others on file) in case of future complications (lawsuits, accusations of professional incompetence, and so on) and Steven Warlock had supplied one? His report, read into the boxcoder, had the fluency of a written declaration and his dramatic taste had dictated the upbeat ending. He had given an acceptable (sort of) explanation of the circumstances and perhaps considered that enough.

Well, it made a change from the usual soulless dreariness of the file room.

So, what was to be required of me? Something to do with the thirty-four-year-old peccadillos of Frankie Devalera? Hardly.

Another query knocked less urgently at my mind. Just a matter of curiosity: What had prompted (or alerted) Connor's interest in the dead file in the first place?

Surely not some deferred legal complications; those might interest the Legal Section but not the administration of day-to-day police work.

I gathered the sheets together and patted them on the desk to even the edges—and by sheer chance the light fell on them at an angle that caught a small spot in the upper right-hand corner of the top sheet, like a glaze mark. It was not the mark itself that caught my attention but the position of it; that place was reserved for a particular item of information on file documents.

I held it to the light and made out, with difficulty, an almost invisible "C1." The document had been copied, on the File Vault printer, by someone who could not risk smuggling a large enough camera into the vault and had sought to disguise the theft by taking out the "copy" mark imposed automatically by the printer; he had used a fluid eraser and dried it off with cloth, probably his handkerchief—and in the process had flattened the paper fibers sufficiently to catch my stray glance.

Who?

In thirty years, any number of possibilities. The copier might well be dead by now. There was no time to ponder; I was due in Connor's office.

I reported, dead on the hour, to the office where Connor studied a file with complete absorption, his insulting back not quite fully turned to me. I did not speak; he knew damned well I was there.

Don't be misled by my personal dislike; he was, quirks and all, an efficient super with a pretty well faultless record. When he was ready he barked, "Questions?"

Prepared for his game playing, I answered while his mouth was still closing, "The document has been copied, possibly more than once, and the identification number erased."

"Ah, you noticed."

By accident and the grace of God, yes. "When was this discovered, sir? And by whom?"

"By me, this morning, when I sent for the file. Never consulted in thirty-four years."

"Makes it hard," I said.

The point was this: the job of file manager was one of Connor's administrative training ploys—a sensible one if you know anything of filing and reference complications. The position was rotated among junior constables every six months (with a trained civilian clerk keeping them out of real trouble), which meant that there would have been twenty or so during Connor's tenure—any of them could have made the copy or copies (but why?); otherwise, only Connor and the supervising clerk had key-and-code physical access to the File Vault. Mentioning that would have gained me only a suspicious glare and a mental note to repay impertinence.

"Any clue to who or why, sir?"

"None. Ideas?"

"Only that the file contains information with meaning not apparent to casual scrutiny but may have value for somebody with additional knowledge."

"So why not take the file itself? Why risk being caught using the copier?"

"That would leave a visible gap in the register, showing it out as soon as it left the shelf. The copier could be used one sheet at a time." An empty slot signalled itself automatically to the master file.

As though that mysteriously satisfied him, he changed direction. "What do you know about Warlock?"

Machine gun Q & A can be wearing. (But it keeps the lazy buggers on their toes, begod!)

"Only what is in the statement." But I had made a fast foray into Crime Files on my way to Connor and was able to add, "None of the people named in the statement, except Devalera, has a record, and he's been clean since his 2035 arrest."

He knew that, switched again. "Do you follow the newscasts?"

DOWN THERE IN DARKNESS

Every copper followed them. At a reasonable venture I said, "Not the Arts segments." Art criticism made me feel ignorant, and art news was for trendies.

Connor said, "Warlock is still alive. Still asleep."

Was he, indeed? I waited.

"That hypnotherapist, Bentinck, will attempt to revive him. Tomorrow."

Connections began to surface at last. But why Bentinck? I pointed out, "Graves was Warlock's psych."

"Dead." With that Connor stepped out of whatever character he was playing and spoke his longest sentence to date. "There's a dogfight over the custody of Warlock's unsold paintings and it might be that some pressure has been put on Bentinck to make his attempt at this time."

"Dogfight, sir?"

"You should try to stay abreast of matters of public interest."

We all dreamed of murdering Connor at some stage of our service. He continued an explanation probably researched at high speed that same morning. Nothing so impressive as awesome mastery of the facts!

"When Warlock went into his state of . . . call it suspension . . . he had been preparing an exhibition and had some thirty canvases available. His agent—feller name of Elfrey—claimed the right to exhibit and market them under the terms of their mutual contract, but Mrs. Warlock wouldn't have it. She even threatened to shoot him if he tried to take the pictures out of the studio. That landed her in court for a lecture and a binding over, but her lawyers managed to get an injunction against sale or exhibition and she was granted custody. The legal reasoning was that since the planned exhibition had not been finalized, or even the exact canvases selected, the artist's wishes were not known. He may, for instance, have had plans to retouch some of them and to retain others for his own purposes. Since he was—and is—technically alive, it was held that no decision be made on his behalf while there was a possibility of his return to full consciousness. The wife was not in financial need, so there was no necessity to sell. All that happened back in 2038, so now the eighty-year-old Mrs. Warlock is sitting on a fortune in paint, agent Elfrey has waited thirty-two years to get his twenty percent claws on the bonanza, and Bentinck is about to try rousing Rip van Winkle. There it stands."

It promised to be a caterwauling of geriatrics over a man who, if Devalera had reported correctly, would not thank them for dragging him back from Nirvana or wherever. With all that locked-up money pleading for release, a few people (of whom the tax inspector would be a baying frontrunner) would give not a damn for Warlock's rights and miseries.

I asked, "Has resuscitation been tried since Graves died?"

"No. There was no funding for ratbag fringe research once the forties depression closed in. Mrs. Warlock and her son were left with an expensive upkeep responsibility, which they seem to have carried without complaint. Bentinck comes into it after all this time because he claims to have fresh ideas about cerebral interconnections and wants to try again. Or that's his story." He held a portentous pause before getting to the point a less theatrical mind would have made at the outset. "You will be present at the attempt."

A touch of the mildly macabre would be a break from routine. "To do what, sir?"

Connor told me, "Be undercover as a ward orderly, assisting Bentinck." And then, with a meaningless smile, "You've played the role before."

At least he had the good taste not to say, "During the Beltane affair." I had to ask again, "What or who will I be looking out for?"

"Hard to say. See who's there. And why they're there. Mostly why."

A fishing trip; a sniffer job. "Specialists, I imagine. Maybe Mrs. Warlock and son. Any idea of others?"

Spread hands and raised shoulders signaled, "It's all yours Ostrov." The bastard had no intention of telling me. Why? I picked up the son's statement. "I'd better look over this again."

"Return it to me, here, when you've done with it."

Why not to the Files Clerk? (Because Connor had abstracted

it himself?) That harried trainee possibly did not know of its existence among the ancient, unconsulted thousands, much less that it had been pilfered and pillaged.

There was one more matter, a suspicious matter I had saved for last. From the door, I said, "I'm rostered off tomorrow."

"I know that." No "Sorry, but this is important."

"Do I report in and out?"

"No. Stay away from the station. Then report only to me—tomorrow night, on a tight line. Vid Bentinck for your instructions; he'll be expecting you to call."

Bloody ham! Also a bloody good super who had to be forgiven his flourishes.

He had one more flourish for me. "Bear in mind that if Bentinck succeeds in rousing Warlock, your orderly duties may be subsumed in keeping watch over a confused man for a few days, until he feels capable of dealing with a considerably changed world."

He knew but did not add that this duty also I had performed before, with Beltane's father. It was clear that these were my qualifications for the job—as well as some other reasons that needed thinking over.

Back at my desk I thought about Connor. That tomorrow was my free day was a stroke of fortune that had allowed him to so arrange matters that only Bentinck and our two selves would be aware of my fancy dress surveillance. Nor need any record of the assignment appear in station files, since I would not be reporting in. He was playing a private game outside the rules and probably had some other puppet investigating the Dead File theft, under some similar wrap.

Did it matter? It did. My further promotion, perhaps my job itself, might hang on Connor's success and my silence.

The matter of the unrecorded overtime involved did not worry me. Connor, when you discounted his posturing, was a fair-minded man; he would find a way of finagling the payment into the Ostrov credit account.

Curious about Bentinck, I checked the psych's vid number and was about to call, then changed my mind. Any call made to or from the station would be automatically recorded, and I had a perverse instinct to bar Connor's prying where I could; if the man became sufficiently frustrated, he might open a chink into his personal interest in Warlock . . . or Bentinck . . . or some player whose name had not yet surfaced. My call would be made later, away from the station.

I settled to reread the statement but in the end was no further enlightened.

My question was still unanswered: Why had Connor called for the Warlock file? And what was his interest in the Bentinck experiment? He expected something to happen—but what?

4

It was mostly my fault if dinner that night was a half hour of monosyllables and silences on my part, with the Warlock affair crowding the forefront of my mind. My mum and my dad, Bill, knew that great change had overtaken me in the past year. They could hardly have avoided the evidence of altered behavior but they knew nothing of the experience behind it; they were the last people to whom I could have confessed a lifetime of distrust and half-contemptuous irritation with them. Neither could I speak of my altered feelings; Psych Section's panacea did not include the gift of open contrition, which would have embarrassed my parents as much as myself.

After the meal I said I wanted to use the vid, and neither pointed out that I had a two-meter police-issue screen in my bedroom. They never queried what I did; sometimes I wished they would, but their love made no demands. The point of using the family screen was that calls from my police set would be recorded at the station. Tapping into the larger living room wallscreen was feasible but would require procedures and approvals that I suspected Connor would not be willing to undertake; the smell of secrecy was rank.

Did it matter? Probably not. My attitude, at bottom, was simple suspicion of petty surveillance while I worked more or less in the dark.

I called Bentinck's number and he answered at once from a blank screen, as though he had been sitting over it, waiting. His voice offered a single word, "Who?"

I couldn't tell whether he was being careful or merely ill-mannered. Perhaps some pressure had been put on him. I identified myself and his very deep, clear voice asked, "Are you the man with orderly training?"

"You could call it that. Enough for routine work."

The screen lightened on a tall, lantern-jawed man who leaned on the edge of a table, peering into his screen as if he might thrust his head right through it for a closer view. At first I did not realize that he was searching our living room to be sure I was alone. Kitchen noises told me where Mum had gone, but Bill was sitting in an armchair on a level with the screen; Bentinck would be unable to see him and there was no reason why Bill should not hear what we said. I had trusted his silence before and not regretted it.

Bentinck seemed younger than the seventyish man I had expected; despite gray hair he seemed only middle-aged. But then, he might have had juvenation treatment before the government cracked down on those long-life procedures that were so blatantly at odds with the pressures of overpopulation and underemployment.

He asked, a mite too blankly, as if he didn't care one way or the other, "Are you recording?" and I lied routinely, "No. Should I?," while my belt chip saved every word. He did not know much about the police.

He answered, "Suit yourself," after a hesitation a fraction too long. Another one with a private hand to play?

He stood back from his table and waited, as though it was up to me to make the running, so I asked, "Where and when?"

His reply, however, was crisp and definite. "Demo Room Eight-C in the Bio-Psych Complex. Ten hundred hours." When I said nothing he added, "I will bring an orderly's overall for you."

That had to be prevented. "Thanks, but no, Doctor. I'll supply my own. Then there'll be no problem of poor fitting." If he was surprised he did not show it. "Also, I'll need accreditation if I'm to enter the complex without declaring a police connection."

"I will bring it."

Whatever Bentinck's qualifications and life experience, he was no conspirator. "Again, no thanks. We should not be seen together, exchanging papers or parcels. To your audience I must be a complex orderly, anonymous and unnoticeable. You'll go in the front while I use the staff entrance."

"We can meet—"

I interrupted him. On the job it is I who have my way. "Please send the accreditation to me here, by public messenger, tonight." I gave him the address.

His expressionless stare recalled Steven Warlock's description of him; he seemed blank enough to begin fading from notice at any moment. But he asked, "Do you insist?"

"For reasons of security I must."

"Very well. Has your orderly persona a name other than Detective Sergeant Ostrov?"

Did I detect the beginning of a twinkle in—no, not his eye, but his voice. I told him, "Harry."

"Is there anything further?"

There was a great deal but it would have to wait. "No."

"Then, goodnight to you, Harry."

He switched off. If economical speech from an immobile face was the measure of the man, his patients must have found him unnerving. Perhaps it was just an analyst's professional gambit. But, was he an analyst? His description as hypnotherapist placed him on the less respectable rump of a psych fraternity that held divided opinions about the technique.

As I cleared my screen, Bill said, "Undercover stuff, eh?" He was hopelessly romantic about my mostly plodding job, loving nothing better than harmless confidences about details of crime that did not reach the newscast spruikers. I gave him a large, slow wink, enough for the moment.

Now I needed Gus Kostakis. For a moment I hesitated to involve him in something whose parameters I was unsure of, but I needed a swift course in at least the superficial aspects of the Warlock oeuvre, and Gus could provide it in nontechnical language that would not leave me floundering among impasto, quattrocento, and neosurrealism. I would pay for it by having to keep his inquisitiveness flattered and satisfied until the job was finished, but I knew nobody who could keep a stiller tongue than that peculiar man, and I suppose there could have been few more mismatched pairs than Gus and myself. I was, then, the product of a highly technical education and a home that preserved the social niceties of the wealthy Minders rather than a working copper milieu, while Gus had gained most of his life-knowledge as a street kid, was apt to behave with the tentative manners of one never sure whether or not he did the correct thing, lived rather too intimately with a world of private fantasies, and spoke with a flat Australian wide-vowel accent that caused Mum actual pain. She did not approve of Gus as a friend for her boy and could not understand my affection for him, but treated him with a terrifying courtesy that sometimes reduced him to whispers.

The reason I needed him at this late juncture was that he had, improbably but actually, grown up in the dream of becoming an artist. It was something he had wanted as only a street kid could want a moon forever out of reach, but he had been forced to recognize that he possessed neither the technical gift nor the creative perception to be more than a hack designer. Rather than settle for what he saw as a shameful second best he had turned his back on longing and become a property guard in a private security firm. What he had preserved from his disappointment was an encyclopedic knowledge of painting.

So I vidded him, told him what I wanted, and all he said was, "On me way. See y'in half an hour."

Dad brightened; he prized Gus's tales of lowlife above vid-shows and diamonds. Mum said nothing, prepared to disapprove in silence.

When he arrived, long and angular and smelling unabashedly of sweat from the humidity outside, he dumped a bag of equipment on the floor while he complained that he had to be on duty at midnight. His security firm (the same whose government contract had been terminated for its failure, along with my own failure, to prevent Beltane's suicide) was scratching for work and he would not risk being a minute late on the job. All this was mixed in with his greeting to my parents, poured out in the gutter accent of a man whose education had stopped dead at age eleven, when a bankrupt government cut funding of schools to a point where only the brilliant or the privileged had any hope of making a full life for themselves.

I asked, "What have you got?"

Fitting a single chip into the vid repro, he said, "All the Warlock stuff that hasn't been exhibited."

Mum sat up slightly; like Gus, she was familiar with the Warlock story, as any art lover would be. My own appreciation of paintings stopped short somewhere around the beginning of the twentieth century; so much work after that required detailed understanding of technical and historical development that clarification, if and when it came, hardly repaid the effort.

I asked how he came by such stuff and thereby revealed my ignorance of the commonplace.

"Bought it, of course. Old Mrs. Warlock covers costs by selling repros, and they ain't all that expensive. It's only the originals she won't let anybody see. So what's all this about?"

I told him of the resuscitation attempt and cautioned him to keep his trap shut about it until the newscasts carried the story. He shrugged, "So what?," but Mum and Bill paid rapt attention for various reasons.

"What," I told him, "is that I will be doing a nursemaid job on the man if he wakes up. If I'm to be up to the knees in apprehensionist art for a week or two, I should at least know what it is when I talk to him."

Dad only grinned and Mum looked at me with quizzical interest; she knew my limits of appreciation. Gus said, "Does your super give a good mark for trying? Harry, you wouldn't understand if Warlock painted a shithouse and it fell on you." He glanced warily at Mum and decided it was too late for apologies. "I'll show you some of the simple stuff, but I'm warnin' you, if you try to talk to him about it you'll sound like a blind bat goin' squeak squeak."

There's no friend like the outspoken one who lays it on the line and sees no reason for you to get upset about it. Better than being lied to, he would say, and by the rules of the game it was also my right to upset him. If I could.

I fixed on an unfamiliar projector he lifted out of the bag. "That's a pretty expensive piece of equipment, Gus."

"So?"

"What did you use for money?"

He set his narrow face into offended dignity. "It was given to me by an appreciative client."

"What did he appreciate? Your silence about certain items found on his premises in the course of your duties?"

"Harry, you know one rat don't rat on another rat."

I called myself an honest copper in those days, but what can anyone do with a man who trusts him utterly? Dad choked on a laugh and I didn't dare look at Mum.

There were two of the projectors; he fixed one on each side of the vidscreen frame and switched in the screen. A tiny flash of color expanded from the center of the screen as if rushing toward us until it almost filled the view.

"This one's called *Fulfilment*. Seminal stuff, I reckon."

Mum gave him a side glance of surprise at the offhand remark, having never suspected this side of him. He circuited in the two laser projectors and they performed the trick I had seen before but never did understand. Visually, it was as if the lasers picked the painting off the screen and held it in midair, in a 3-D presentation so real that the rough surface of the paint seemed touchable.

"Exact size. Two hundred and ninety centimeters by two hundred and ten."

I could have stared at it for the rest of the week and made little of it. At first glance it was just a red-gold curved line on a background of various shades of white—rough white, smooth white, dull white, white with the barest hints of subliminal color and, in the lower left-hand corner, a single amorphous spread of brilliantly reflective white behind which the colored line plunged like a homing arrow. It took me some time to see that the plunging line was painted in different depths of red-gold, giving the impression of winding its way through forests of—of what? The splotched whites seemed to have no individual significances but I formed an impression of a pulsating ribbon threading its way through a maze of obstacles.

Yet, when I closed my eyes and then opened them, the painted surface was flat and lifeless.

Gus said, "You're lookin' all wrong. You won't get anywhere just starin' at it. Start on the right-hand side, where the red curve comes out from the heart of the splash of matte white, and follow it across the canvas."

I began to recognize something of what I was seeing. The red-gold curve was broad at its emergence and narrowing like a trailing ribbon moving farther and farther away, sneaking in and out of the white maze, never losing its seeking arc but penetrating deep into the canvas to swing behind a matte white ovoid, out again to pass in front of rough white surface like a boulder, and back and forth, receding and advancing but at the end plunging into the final brilliant white target of its quest, somehow distantly within the painting, so that I felt I could plunge my hand in and drag the moving ribbon back to the surface.

"Hazard stuff," I said, remembering the hypnotic paintings of Belinda Hazard a generation before. Famous as they were, I had never seen one of them; they had been called in when she died, and stacked away in some secret darkness as being a psychological risk to the viewer. It was said that you could quite literally lose yourself in a Hazard canvas and have to be brought forcibly back to reality.

Gus nodded. "Warlock's the only one to get anywhere near old Belinda's technique but he never caught the sort of effect they say she created. Probably didn't want to. That colored curve is in a lot of his paintings, the ones named for his wife. The critics call it Warlock's Ribbon. You can see why."

Could you? Maybe Mum could. Then, very simply, I did see. Warlock had painted his fate long before it came upon him; when he undertook the hypno-trial he knew damned well where his mind would be going. He had rendered his love as a wandering ribbon of himself, threading the maze of his own bewildered perceptions and finally lodging in the heart of his shining desire. Whether I had the parable right or wrong, I did not respond to the work; it was more like a diagram than a passionate affirmation. (But, then, I always thought the Mona Lisa a smirking housewife not worth wall space, much less the adoration of the ages. You are permitted to sneer.)

I said, "The bright splash is his wife. He was trying to paint his love."

"Not bad for a bloody philistine that wouldn't know Picasso from wallpaper. It's his love story, all right."

Mum had said not a word since greeting Gus. Now she spoke. "I don't see certainty in that sinuous line, Mr. Kostakis, only searching. And it ends hidden behind a brilliance more hopeful than definitive. It is a beautiful line but it pretends to more assuredness than the end justifies."

Gus surveyed her with cautious respect; he did not know of her sketching. "Others have thought like that, too, Mrs. Ostrov, but I think he was painting a way to the places inside himself where he thought he couldn't go."

She seemed about to argue but smiled instead. "In a few days we may be able to ask him. May we see the others?"

After that, Bill and I might as well not have been there. Gus, as art critic, was definitely "in," bluntness and coarseness all forgotten. We were treated to two hours of modern, experimental, highly allusive, and elusive painting, which meant almost nothing to me. What, for instance, could anyone but a fanatic make of a pale yellow nimbus across whose expanse paraded gears and tools and meaningless metal assemblies that seemed to fade in and out as I shifted my angle of vision, with somewhere inside their complexities a raw human heart painted with an astonishing realism that made the rest of the canvas look like lifeless diagrams. It was titled *Steven* and, frankly, Steven was welcome to that particular declaration of parental love. Mum, on the other hand, was awe-struck. She said, like a sigh, "Oh, that lucky boy."

The viewing dragged to its end and I had to admit that Warlock and I would have nothing to say to each other about his work. Mum and Gus, however, found each other suddenly and endlessly fascinating, devotees bridging all differences in love of their subject. Mum fussed over him as if he were some wealthy Minder strayed into our working-class stratum. Gus preened and made the most of it; I had hard work to move him to get to his shift on time.

I walked down the street with him to the hoverbus stop on the corner. The night was brutally hot still, and the households were all out in the air. Mum had once told me that there had been a time when, in such weather, children would cool themselves by playing under garden hoses, and it seemed to me that this must have been one of the dispensations of paradise. The Australian continent had always been short of water; now, with a bulging population, restrictions were applied simply by making the stuff too expensive to waste. Even at this hour there were still naked kids around but no hoses playing. And few gardens for them to play in. Most Wardies had vegetables growing in backyard plots, and prayed for rain.

People spoke to me as we passed, partly because most of them had forgiven me the social solecism of being a policeman, partly because they hoped a friendly word might be remembered in some encounter with the force.

I had been pondering a possible use for Gus's eternal desire to meddle, and now decided that there was one. I told him what I wanted, keeping my voice low. "Find a man called Frankie Devalera for me. Frankie, not Francis. He was a sewer rat once and possibly still is. He lived in Richmond."

"The boy chaser they gave the brain drain along with Warlock?" I should have known that Warlock's bizarre passing would have been vidnews fodder and that Gus's interest in Warlock would have made him familiar with the name.

"I don't want it known that I'm looking for him."

He nodded. "You mean you don't want your super to know you've got a private game on."

"Could be."

"If any other copper said that to me, I'd start smellin' out what the racket was." He waited for me to take the bait, then gave in with a sigh. "What do I do? Strongarm the poor bastard?"

"No. Fix an appointment for me to meet him. Not at his place or mine. Somewhere public and by accident."

"Could take a couple of days."

"Good enough."

He turned his axhead of a nose on me, quizzing. Gus's besetting sin was an inability to mind his own business; he always suspected a story behind the story. "Couldn't tell me at home? Reckon you're bugged?"

"Could be." It could also have been that suspicion and uncertainty had roused paranoia in me, but precautions were never wasted in the Information Age.

"And that's all you tell me."

"For now. I don't want you chopped off at the knees for knowing too much."

"My knees are all right; worry about your own."

He had an idea that I shouldn't be allowed out alone but stood in permanent need of a nursemaid—namely Gus.

When I returned home, wondering why Bentinck's accreditation hadn't arrived, Mum had decided that it was a crying shame that a man of Gus's natural instincts had been given no chance to develop them. I said I knew that very well but that she had had to find it out for herself. The implied accusation of class-consciousness didn't go down too well but she contended herself with observing that anyone with a genuine appreciation of art couldn't be all bad, and I refrained from mentioning some of the forgers and dealers in the state rehabilitation centers.

At a few minutes to midnight, when Mum and Bill had gone to bed, the accreditation arrived. I opened the front door, not on a messenger but on Bentinck himself. Over his shoulder I saw the blunt shape of a hovercar and revised my estimate of his professional standing—upwards. Displaying no government logo, it was a private car, placing him well in the Minder income bracket. I surmised a clientele among the wealthy and the important, those who publicized their psych appointments to reassure the Wardies and the jobless that their interests were being looked after by intelligences maintained in what they called "running order." The Wardies and the jobless called it "lost from real," and meant it. Bentinck was taller than the screen image had let me think, as tall as myself and lean rather than thin. Nor did his skin show the slight but unnatural smoothness that marks the juvenated body. He must have been only in his twenties when Warlock went visiting in closed realms.

I said, with enough emphasis to let him know I meant it, "I expected a messenger service."

He shrugged and held out an envelope, without speaking. I took it and he would have left in silence if I had not followed him to the gate. He bowed slightly as I let him through and I leaned close enough to say quietly, "I have a question. May we sit in your car for a moment?"

Without change of expression and scarcely a movement of his lips he murmured, "Not there."

So his car was bugged. He was under surveillance and aware of it. So it was not that doubtful quantity, Ostrov, whom Connor was watching to estimate his performance, but Bentinck, to—to what?

No, not Connor. Bentinck would not admit that to another policeman. So, who?

I said, "Let's take a turn up the street." The neighbors were mostly in bed now; in any case, none of the locals were likely to recognize Bentinck.

When we had moved a safe distance, I asked, "Who's watching you?"

The question startled him. "Don't you know?" His voice held all the emotional response he withheld from his face.

"No. Who?"

"I don't know, either. My car has been tampered with. A mechanic found the device accidentally." I could believe that; the pickup could be a single chip, insect-sized, buried in the upholstery. "I thought the police. I have left it in place rather than alert the listener that I am aware. I am simply careful in my speech."

That was good sense. "What would they be hoping to pick up?"

His shoulders rose and fell. "Political gossip, perhaps. I have parliamentary clients."

"Nothing to do with Warlock?"

"Why should it be? Who cares about that ancient mistake, save those who made it? And his wife."

"Elfrey, the agent. And Steven Warlock."

"Steven drowned in a swimming fatality some months ago. What has Elfrey to gain from chance conversations?"

"Somebody has."

He gestured impatiently. "You had a question."

"This: Did you ask for police assistance at tomorrow's work?"

"I did not. Has your Superintendent Connor told you nothing? He arranged to meet me in a restaurant. There he told me that certain persons—unnamed—might wish to interfere with my work on Warlock, and that he had a suitable man to act as an anonymous watcher and, if necessary, to take preventive or protective action."

I felt like a nonswimmer pushed in at the deep end of the pool by some consciousless japer, curious as to whether or not I'd float. I said, "We're both in the dark."

Whatever was in progress lay between Connor's spider and

some unknown fly. We turned back toward the car and Bentinck said, "I also have a question."

"Go ahead."

"Orderly overalls are made in three sizes, not like ward coats that should fit properly. I would have brought you the largest size. What advantage has your personal fitting?"

"It takes pictures and listens to what is said."

He smiled briefly, as if a small light shone and winked out. "Such excellent tailoring!"

That was all; between us, a total lack of constructive information. He entered his hovercar and whirred off down the now silent street. And that was the unsatisfactory end of the first day.

5

The Psycho-Biological Complex was located on the northern edge of the city, out past Broadmeadows and the homes of the Minders who, as a group, preferred to live away from the dullness of Wardie surroundings and the very physical menace of the slums of the unwashed jobless.

In spite of its name the complex was a simply designed single building, six spokes radiating from an administrative center. Lawns filled the spaces between spokes; flowerbeds nestled against walls; trees surrounded the whole area. There were advantages in being a scientist serving the government—clear air, the scent of clean earth, freedom from the crowds that packed even the quietest streets, absence of the eternal roaring background of the city. These were pleasures whose reality transcended the noisebound imagination. Their existence brought home, like a hammer on the senses, the truth of the human condition on a spawning, fecund planet where food, shelter, and resignation were the only measures of existence for three quarters of its people.

It was a world where a middle-ranking policeman, living in a crumbling, century-old house in a moribund suburb, was counted a successful man.

I know I thought myself not too badly off. Adapting to our circumstances, we fail to see that we are demeaned by them. That's the history of the average man and at bottom I was average. Lucky but average.

When I presented my accreditation at the staff entrance, the doorkeeper said to some lounging offsider, "Fer Chri' sake! This bloody Bentinck brings 'is own orderly! Our personnel not good enough fer 'is 'ighness!" He jerked a thumb in no particular direction. "In yer go, Mr. Bloody Ostrov!"

That was one of the nastiness of herd solidarity, the consciousness of petty power and the petty urge to declare it—and to scream for the cops if challenged. It irritated sufficiently for me not to ask directions, so I wasted a quarter of an hour finding the correct wing and the rooms where Bentinck worked.

He was checking electronic gear on a wheeled operating table when I entered and he only nodded and indicated another door. I went through to a small room with cupboards and a shower recess, put on the overall I had brought from home, and returned to Bentinck, who fixed his gaze not on me but on the overall for a few seconds, and said, "I suppose questions would not be answered. The garment seems perfectly normal."

"It's meant to."

And questions would not be answered. The overall was a development of a creation of Arthur Hazard, one of the Nursery Children who were already forgotten by the public and remembered only by the research scientists who carried on their work. Briefly: The cotton was interwoven with hair-thin receptors that recorded sight and sound within a considerable radius and stored them in molecular code. The circuits were powered by body heat and there was literally nothing to be seen save under a microscope. The spysuits were illegal under the citizen's right to privacy code but most senior police sooner or later acquired one, in one under-cover costume or another. Once information existed, you could always invent the means of how it was obtained. And risk your job if you were caught.

I asked, "What do I do?"

"Warlock will be brought in shortly. You will push in the table with him ready on it. Then stand by. If he spasms or fights when coming to wakefulness, you must immediately take hold to prevent him falling or damaging himself. Do you know how to handle a threshing patient?"

"Yes."

"Connor says you are strong."

"Strong enough."

"Otherwise, you have no duty save your private commitment, whatever that may be."

I asked, "Will any unusual spectators be present? I mean, other than scientists?"

"Some."

"Mrs. Warlock?"

He showed a flicker of surprise at the question. "Good God, no! She has too much sense. She's over eighty and physically fallen apart, while he is still the outward fifty-two that went into his dreams. The meeting would be unbearable for both."

I had not imagined an unaging Warlock. This awakening took on an unexpectedly sour tone. The old woman's devotion could be repaid in bitter fashion, but at least she had no illusions about it. His reaction might be plain misery.

"What others?"

"I will introduce them to the assembly, if need be. Your prying-eye suit can listen and record their faces. Is it recording me now?"

"With body heat power it can't stop until I take it off. You should behave as though you don't know of its existence." He snorted contempt. "After all, Doctor, it may discover the answers that puzzle you also."

I could only pray that this dressing room was not bugged. My detector was quiet, but those with knowledge and money could outfox the systems.

Bentinck nodded and turned back to his gear and in a few minutes his checking-over seemed complete. He said, "He should be here at any moment now," with no particular sign of interest, as though miracles were all in the day's work.

Remembering Steven's description, I saw that a board at the head of the table held the dials and vertical meters of the telltales, and the small, shallow cap that could be held to the skull by padded arms; some improvement had superseded the studded helmet of the thirties.

Warlock was delivered without fuss on a trolley pushed by a complex orderly who assisted me in transferring the body (hard then to think of it otherwise) to the operating table, and left at once. For no good reason I had expected to handle something like a cadaver, cold and stiff, but of course he was supple and warm; his chest expanded and contracted, very slightly, with minimal breathing. He was as Steven had written of him, small-boned, slightly overweight, unmuscular, and with a little round pot belly. Everything about him seemed utterly normal save the marks of intravenous feeding on his arms. He was just a man in his fifties, comfortably asleep.

"Hasn't he aged at all, Doctor?"

"Why should he have? There has been no physical activity to trigger the aging processes."

The deadpan delivery brushed my question away as ignorantly pointless, but I asked, "Isn't some part of aging caused by progressive error in cell replacement?"

He treated me to a silent survey before he said, as though he had thought it over and come to a decision, "Yes, but there are ways of obviating that. We did not want so unique a specimen to deteriorate on our hands. Naturally."

Which meant that some small part of the illegal juvenation processes had been called on for more than thirty years. Paid for by the wife and son? And, perhaps, Bentinck? He had been honest with me simply because I had reached the conclusion for myself, and the larger matter was big enough to minimize—but not wholly excuse—the illegality. Still, it might make a small weapon (moral blackmail its proper name) for use if circumstances demanded.

I asked, changing the subject and not, I think, fooling him at all, "Shouldn't we strap him down if spasming is possible?"

"No. The reactions could be more powerful than you would expect of a small man. Against restraints, he could damage himself." He smiled faintly. "We must trust in your muscle."

I didn't doubt my power to hold him; there wasn't much of him.

Bentinck indicated the door to the demonstration room. "Take him in, please."

I looked down again on the chubby features of the artist whose unlikely power of passion had taken him literally out of this world. At a guess, I would have placed him as some librarian's fetch-and-carry drudge, who had had his grand passion early in life and now found it easier to turn over and sleep than follow the once a week erotic ritual whose climax was only the prelude to obscure disappointment and a sense of loss. Most self-portraits by artists (Rembrandt's gloriously excepted) show striking features to best advantage. Warlock's, if ever he made the attempt, could only make you wonder why he bothered. Perhaps all the others were a little suspect also.

I pushed the table through the door and found myself in a small theater whose semicircular auditorium might have seated a hundred students for lectures, but there were no more than thirty people to occupy the lower arcs of seats. And three others, behind and quite deliberately separate from the main body—two together and the third a little apart. My targets, surely. After the first sweeping glance I did not look at them again. The overall could do the work.

As I approached the center of the demonstration space Bentinck said, "That will do, Harry." I locked the wheels and moved myself out of the way. Bentinck placed a chair at the end of the table, where he would have a full view of the telltales behind Warlock's head, and sat down.

I saw that he had put on a skullcap identical with that provided for Warlock. It seemed characteristic that he paid no attention to his murmuring audience but produced a transcutaneous syringe, already loaded, from a carrying tube in his pocket and checked its level. Then he adjusted the fit of his skullcap, plugged its single lead into the small computer control on the arm of his chair, and ran a quick series of tests.

Finished, he beckoned me and placed me by Warlock's side, a half pace away from him. He said quietly, "Watch his face. If there is any change of expression be ready to act at once. If he goes into spasm, hold him as tightly as possible. Try, if you can, to hold his head still while I inject directly into the neck artery." He placed a finger on the carotid. "There. Questions?"

"If I can't hold his head still?"

"Then any available spot will serve but the tranquilizer will take longer to operate and you will have to hold him that much longer."

"Understood."

Quietly he murmured, "Be sure that your intelligent suit captures the three at the rear of the rest."

"It already has."

He did not acknowledge the answer but turned to the audience with a colorless, "Good morning, ladies and gentlemen," and bowed cursorily to their murmured answer.

The whole speech went into police records when my overall was deloused for its information but it did not interest me to the point of rereading it later. The early part of it was introductory and I discovered that this unpublicized attempt at resuscitation was of global interest. A job that had been merely an unusual curiosity of policing assumed a new dimension of significance, and I speculated again on what hidden hand Connor fancied himself playing.

I could openly inspect a panel of hypnotherapists and brain specialists from a dozen countries, mostly American and Oriental with a sprinkling of British, German, and Russian, and it became obvious that they were divided into political groups of whom only a few on either side made cautious attempts at mingling. That was to be expected after the Beltane revelations had split the planet in two—the threatening and the threatened. It was wonder enough that they were prepared to sit in the same auditorium since the saying that science knows no boundaries of race or color had proved as hollow as the rest of our old wives tales. Some tried; one had to award marks for effort, but it was an uneasy effort that betrayed the fracture lines. There was, indeed, one blunt-faced black woman, from Zaire I think, who sat grimly alone, speaking to no one, creating space around her by forceful silence.

Bentinck introduced every one of them, and they seemed to know and appreciate the standing of each man and woman as the names were called. He went on to say, "I trust you have all familiarized yourselves with the explanatory chip provided with each vidcase. I will run quickly through the procedure and take any questions—"

He was interrupted by the American voice (or perhaps Canadian; I never could distinguish them) of a man saying, "I think you've missed out on some of those present, Dr. Bentinck. I for one am not familiar with the three gentlemen sitting behind us here."

All heads turned to observe and at last I could examine them openly.

They made a curious group. Only one could have mingled with the scientists and not seemed out of place. He was mildly dark-skinned like many of Mediterranean descent, but that meant nothing; the mixing of bloods and cultures at that time made clues to origins irrelevant. He was smartly dressed in Minder fashion, possibly the best turned out individual present, and he stared ahead, deliberately unresponsive to the heads turned to him.

Beside him sat a thin, sharp-nosed man of seventy or so, perhaps eighty, dressed in a suit a good two generations out of date, crying aloud his social position among the jobless, clinging to clothes bought as a young man and now worn only on special occasions. At home he probably wore make-do mockups from the charity groups. He also stared ahead but he was aware of himself as a misfit and uncomfortable with it.

The third man, fiftyish, sat at his ease, smiling as if enjoying his misfit status. His clothes proclaimed him Wardie, a working man, a manual wage-earner dressed in his Sunday best, tight T-shirt under short-arsed jacket, with pipestem trousers and flashy, calf-length plastic boots.

They were as incongruous a trio as ever could have attended a complex demonstration.

Bentinck's reference to them was a masterpiece of misdirection—or, as I thought, plain lies.

"I have not introduced these gentlemen because they are lay-persons who will not take part in our discussion. You are all familiar with the difficulty of obtaining funds for any but essential research, so you will understand that the matter of Mr. Warlock's psychosuspension lay unattended, save for simple preservation, for many years. I was able to obtain the necessary funds for the present project, of which resuscitation is only the first step, only when private persons took interest and financed the reopening of the failed experiment. The interested parties have requested that their own observers be present and, naturally, I have agreed."

And that was that. What valuable observations might be made by an age-relegated ancient and a grinning Wardie must have passed all audience comprehension, but they had been told, with bland evasion, to abandon curiosity and ask no questions.

Bentinck went on from where he had been interrupted. "I will run quickly through the procedure, then take any questions," and from there on he might have been reading from a script, never faltering over a word or the structure of a sentence. I noticed only that in description of the hypnoelectronic process some enthusiasm lightened his voice, as if that was the topic rather than the fate of a sleeping man. Most of it was couched in technical language outside my range—words like hypothalamus and hippocampus conveyed vague meaning, but cholinergic and dopaminergic systems, the amygdala and substantia nigra passed through my mind unabsorbed. When he had finished, there were few questions. His audience seemed to have done the recommended homework.

Then he came to the immediate action. "We do not know precisely where Warlock's consciousness persists in terms of cerebral structure; we do not so much as know if it exists still in terms relevant to our understanding. There is much argument about the nature of consciousness, with a strong psychological contingent insisting on the 'soul' as a fundamental but noncorporeal nexus. If that is so, we may find ourselves at the edge of discovery or at the blank wall of bafflement."

His balanced tone gave no clue to his personal opinion; they could accept the soul or shrug it away. I was not sure then that I understood what the word meant; it had featured in youthful imagination as a filmy thing that floated out from the body when you died, and my mostly agnostic thinking had made little progress since. "Basically," Bentinck said, "we have to attract the attention of a person who has retreated from contact with humanity. We have to gate-crash his isolation. Several methods suggest themselves and I have laid out a series of invasions of increasing sophistication, to be followed in sequence if the first fails. The invasion concerning us today is crude but simple in operation, being in essence no more than a noisy knocking on the door of his hermitage. Since isolation of the consciousness is based on total insulation of the neuron system from the sounds and tactile sensations of the physical body, an obvious approach is to remove the insulation and then to amplify these to a point whereat the consciousness can no longer ignore them. Warlock has ignored natural sensation for more than three decades; we will see if he can ignore them magnified to a condition of uproar in the brain."

Without fuss he fitted the skullcaps to Warlock's head and his own. "I propose to increase internal sensation to a point that to the waking mind would be unbearable—a condition tantamount to a maddeningly magnified tinnitis. He will or will not respond."

He sat, facing the telltales and asked, "Are you prepared, Harry?"

I nodded and stepped a half pace closer to the table.

"Watch his face for first signs."

I nodded again.

"Beginning now."

I could not see the telltales, so, as far as I was concerned, nothing seemed to be happening. I kept my eyes on that undistinguished face covering an anything but ordinary mind but found my thoughts straying for lack of focus. Those three financial "angels," for instance . . . two of whom wouldn't be able to raise a charity contribution between them . . . and the question of what significant information might lie unnoticed in Steven's statement . . . and who pressured Bentinck, and why . . .

I thought Warlock's face twitched.

I leaned over him and was sure that a muscle in his cheek fluttered.

I lifted my hands ready for action and Bentinck asked, "Movement?"

"A twitch."

Seconds passed while, I imagined, the man's internal sensations were progressively magnified.

Yet I was not ready for the suddenness of it.

He gave an animal roar and I had a fighting beast on my hands. That smallish, uncared-for, underdeveloped body exploded against me with a force that came close to knocking me off balance. I would not have credited such a change from limp inertia to total muscular activity if I had not now experienced it launched against me. He moved like a mechanical thing whose control systems had failed before a surge of power, activating every process, arms and legs shooting out and in and sideways, spine arching and bending back like a stretched bowstring, head beating against my own skull as I flung my weight on him to hold him down before I could find a grip on him. When finally I did, his body thumped under me, lifting me with him.

The whole incident may have lasted no more than seconds because Bentinck and his syringe had not reached us when Warlock relaxed as suddenly as he had sprung to life. He relaxed utterly. Only his chest moved to a stertorous breathing. That was natural; the insane display of absolute effort must have drained his muscles of oxygen.

When I released him, Bentinck raised his eyelids, checked his pulse, and searched for a dozen signs I could not read. He said, "He's gone back. He heard us . . . that is, I think he heard us . . ." For once he spoke like a troubled human being who gnawed on an enigma. "Or perhaps he heard nothing. It may have been the body that rebelled against outrageous messages fed to its sensory system."

He pondered the still face for a moment before turning to his muttering audience, and when he spoke his control was again complete. "This approach was not successful and probably cannot be. Further stimulation might cause both muscular and cerebral damage. Other possibilities must be explored. But not today. There must be a complete physical examination of the man before we proceed further. Meanwhile, I welcome comment."

They came down around the motionless Warlock like a pack of schoolgirls hoeing into a treat, noisy and pushing for position until professional manners asserted themselves and they broke into arguing groups. I followed little of what was being said around me but looked for the "angels," wondering what they made of it, and was intrigued to see the Minder type and the jobless man seated as they had been all along, talking with some urgency to each other and paying no attention to the scientific free-for-all at the operating table.

Looking for the Wardie, I found him standing almost next to me, on the edge of a group surrounding Bentinck; he was hovering and excited and intent on attracting attention but not to the point of barging through them. In any case, Bentinck was aware of him, once or twice looking at him interrogatively and away.

It was some time before he could free himself to give the Wardie his attention; then he led him away from the press and, damnably, away from me. I would have given a lot to have heard what they said to each other in undertones in the couple of minutes they were together. That the overall was recording was well enough, but I felt that something was being said that would shed light on Bentinck's actions and fears. (I was wrong, but working in a vacuum sharpens all suspicions.)

For God's sake, why should he make time, during a gathering of his peers, to listen to a layman—and a laborer at that? The scientists had allowed him to glide over the presence of strangers with a transparent lie about finance, letting him keep his counsel at a time when backing was hard to come by, but I could not. I needed information, any information, badly. I glanced quickly at the other pair of laymen and saw that they were as intent on Bentinck and his friend as I was.

Reading gesture and facial expression, I felt that a suggestion had been made and that Bentinck was in two minds about acceptance. I saw also something that surprised me—on Bentinck's face, momentarily, an expression of gentle, almost paternal affection.

The Wardie, apparently satisfied, faded through the throng of scientists to where the two other counterfeit "angels" sat apart. As before he did not join them but stayed a little aside, with but not of them.

As the questions and comments subsided I asked Bentinck if I should wheel Warlock out of the hall. I had noticed a couple of the scientist audience reaching hesitantly for the still form, as if they might boast afterwards of having touched the unholy altarpiece. He nodded and I pushed the table into the dressing room. Warlock lay immobile, wholly relaxed, unaware that his mind-free body had frightened seven varieties of hell out of his orderly attendant.

I laid a blanket over him and waited.

It took Bentinck half an hour to free himself from his arguing peers. He sweated with tension and wore a slight frown of irritation, in him an almost volcanic display of feeling. He said, as if it were my fault, "Half of them understand nothing; the rest just enough to commit elementary errors."

I suggested that that was the price of highly individual research and added, at his sour grin, "Is there anything more for me to do?"

"No. You can get dressed."

He sat on a bench, watching abstractedly as I stripped off the overall while I tried to think of a way of conveying meaning to him but not to some putative eavesdropper, human or electronic. His eyes focused hungrily on the overall as I folded it into a plastic carrycase.

He said abruptly, "You did well."

"Only just well enough."

"Quite well enough. Can you be free to assist again next Monday?"

Four days from this. And Connor had hinted at an ongoing involvement. "I think so."

"Thank you."

"Same duties?"

"I will brief you in time. The procedure will be different." He studied his bony hands awhile. "I will need a second hypnotherapist. That will raise no problems, but can your organization of freelancers provide a second orderly as strong and as capable as yourself?"

"Organization of freelancers" was a neat touch; such groups of casual workers did exist. I said, "Yes," knowing at once where my choice would fall, whether Connor approved or not.

"Good. I will write accreditations to cover both of you." He produced a notebook and wrote them on the spot, in longhand, which was common form for such disposable notes. "You can fill in the names."

I pocketed them and said, "I have a good man in mind. I'll let you know as soon as I can arrange it." That made the excuse for further contact. "Maybe Saturday or Sunday. This man will require an overall; he is not police."

If that surprised him he showed nothing, only nodded. "That's all now. I'll get a complex orderly to put Warlock to bed. Thank you for your assistance."

And that was that.

No answers to anything.

But at least the lines of communication were open.

6

I have forgotten the time lapse. All this happened a century ago and today's people can have little conception of the world of that time. They have read the books (hundreds of the dreary things) detailing the impact of the greenhouse effect and what it did to global weather patterns, recording the flood of over-population (some twelve billion infesting the planet when I was thirty years old) and what that did to living standards, the work ethic, and the availability of food and water—and what they in turn did to common morality—but telling little of the everyday details. Such details, for instance, as the ubiquitous overall.

The overall was, worldwide, the uniform of the workingman and -woman. Fashioned of molecular-bonded cloth, pretty well impervious to ordinary wear and tear, it was the mark of every Wardie who had a job. It was, in many cases, the only outer clothing he or she possessed; a skirt or jacket and trousers for leisurewear was the envied exception rather than the rule. The overalls were precious items, handed down from parent to offspring (employers provided them and charged exorbitant pay deductions) and the wearers guarded them with their lives. Literally with their lives; murder for possession of an overall was anything but uncommon among the jobless whose existences were an endless struggle for food, clothing, and shelter. And the jobless represented, after discounting the aged and the children, half of the population of the planet.

So, if this offers you a vision of a working class clinging with snarling desperation to its job and its overall, that is exactly right. Imagine it, further, living in protective groups, forever on guard against the horde of predatory Suss Wardies who subsisted on the basic handout from their strapped and helpless states. Imagine these last in lives of endless hungry scrounging, where dog ate dog without compassion or remorse, and families formed tiny islands of alliance against a world prowling, ready to shred them for a coin or a mouthful.

We police, of course, had uniforms. But we had overalls, too, of various patterns, for disguise in the endless undercover war against smugglers, food raiders, kidnappers, forgers, and outright murder gangs—and any other criminal variety you can lay your tongue to, including a soulless trade in children for sex, any kind of sex, with ingenuities that defied rational psychology.

(Such things are not discussed in today's depopulated, superbly moral, sweep-it-under-the-carpet world—but they happened, you fools of paradise, they happened.)

And every policeman with ambition procured for himself, by hook or crook and mostly crook, a thoroughly wired overall such as I had worn at the complex. Authority, well aware of the problems, turned a blind eye. (Corruption in the force? Don't cite morality at me! We were all that preserved the semblance of social stability—and our own lives were cheap in the Suss world.)

So I was ready when on Friday morning Connor sent for me and made no bones about commandeering my overall.

"Come back in two hours," he said, and I didn't bother with questions at that point. Two hours was the time the electronics lab would take to delouse the garment and rough out a preliminary report.

When the time was up, and I presented myself at his office again, Connor tossed the rolled-up ball of my overall to me and said, "Cleared," meaning that all its recorded information had been erased by the lab. He added, "They haven't preserved a copy."

So, it seemed, the whole affair was private to myself, Connor, and some unnamed lab technician. I said, "I think I should know the reason for secrecy if I am to be of any real use."

"Yes." He looked as glum as if a tooth had begun to nag. "That will appear in a moment." Then, grudgingly, "Your time with Bentinck was productive," as if it really hurt him to say it. Meaning that he found it necessary to let me a little further into his confidence.

He turned over a photograph that had lain facedown on his desk. "Can you identify any of these?"

It was a blowup from my overall. I said, "Bentinck presented them as observers for the 'angels' who funded his resurrection act. I don't think anybody believed him—two of them are obvious Wardies—but you don't question a man protecting his privacy."

"The hell you don't!"

Quite so, but the illusion of the decencies had to be preserved.

"Too dangerous," I said, conniving with authority once the virtuous protest had been made. "Bentinck's car was bugged." I ran down the midnight conversation outside my house for him and he nodded sagely as if he understood the implications, which was more than I did.

He said, "The smartly dressed feller on the left is—or calls himself—the Pastor of Lambs in the Church of Universal Communication."

"Never heard of it. Just one more mushroom religion?"

The world was choked with them; the Minders giggled at them and called them the "Wardie cant fests," but attended their gatherings and supported them with ostentatious charity, having a little each way on hell or salvation.

"Well established," said Connor, "about twenty years old. The pastor's name is Ricardo Miraflores—or so he says—but he calls himself Jesus."

"The boy in Steven's statement, grown up to sit on the right hand of God? Chutzpah!"

"Plenty of that. Bentinck," he said abstractedly, as if it were just a throwaway line, "is a member of his church."

I caught the information and stowed it, without comment.

"The old gent with the fierce eyebrows and the fifty-year-old fashion jacket is Ewen Devalera, one-time hellfire preacher, member of Miraflores's church and father of the Frankie Devalera featured in the Warlock statement. The middle-aged man sitting a little apart is Frankie himself, also a member of Jesus' flock but looking, in your record of events, as if there's a small schism in progress.''

He stopped there and fixed me with a quizzical gaze so, like a primed robot, I asked the obvious, ''You think that Jesus' church has a hand in the copying of the Warlock document?''

''Ah, that,'' he said, as though it had slipped his mind. (Christ! but what an infuriating man, forever in character at center stage.) ''I suppose you have given some thought to the document itself.''

Of course I had; he didn't really take me for an idiot. ''First, the statement is not a regular police statement; it's far too smooth, without halts and stumbles and repetitions. It was read from a prepared statement directly into a voxcode setup of the time, probably in response to a police request for an eyewitness account of the affair in case of later developments. There may be other accounts but they would lack the final meeting with Devalera. Since Steven is dead, we might try his wife for additional details.''

''Steven never married his Helen; perhaps she tired of waiting. Eventually he married a strapping blond who claims to know nothing of the document.''

''Mrs. Warlock, Steven's mother?''

''I haven't got around to her yet. You might care to try.''

It was an order. ''Today?''

''In your own time, Harry. I don't want any unaccounted-for absence on your worktime record.''

Why, oh why? ''Absence? How about next Monday? I'm to be with Bentinck.''

''I imagine you'll be taken ill that day. Hmm?''

Yes, I could be sick as a dog on Monday.

A few questions and answers rounded off the interview, with little revealed on either side.

As I left he made a parting remark, in full character, dramatic to the last.

''The Church of Universal Communication is a wealthy institution, far too wealthy to be dependent on its Wardie congregation for support. What rich tithes could it command from such as our Constable Jarvis, who is a member, a Lamb of Pastor Jesus?''

Devious bastard! Billy Jarvis, only three months in the station, was occupied in doing his stint as trainee records clerk. He had personal access to the records vault.

So the Church of Universal Communication—strange name—must be investigated. Quietly, with caution—and without involving Connor, without leaving any filed records, without leaving traces of an investigation whose point I could not determine.

Much as I disliked Connor, I did not believe him corrupt. There was nothing for it—as yet—but to proceed in the half dark, observing the half understood and trying to make sense of it.

Connor had said that my overall had been cleared. Since the laboratory did not make copies unless requested, this meant that his private copy was the only one extant.

Except, that is, mine.

I had unloaded the entire "take" onto replay storage the previous day because there was a very pertinent time during the proceeding when I had been unable to observe Bentinck's audience because I had been fully engaged in restraining Warlock, and it had occurred to me that the reactions of the Devaleras and Miraflores (Jesus, indeed!) might possibly be revealing.

Making the replay chip had needed only the touch of a finger but making sense of the stored material required endless patience. Remember that every inch of the overall was recording sight and sound from every angle in a full three hundred and sixty degrees; the resulting strip was an incoherence of audio-visual montage, back and front and sides all together, complicated by the wearer's movements and the multiple foldings of the cloth in consequence of them. The Police Laboratory had analytical computers to sort and cohere sound and image at blinding speed; I had only memory and a reasonable idea of what section of the overall would hold what I wanted.

So I had sat that night at my bedroom screen, patiently replaying segments painfully extracted from chaos. I reckoned that during my struggle with Warlock the sections exposed to the audience would have been my upper arms and shoulders; it took me three hours to clear them from the surrounding clutter, but at the end of that time I had clear pictures and a headache.

Frankie Devalera, who had gone down into the depths of the mind with Warlock, watched my wrestling with the sleeper with a fierce concentration until at the end he relaxed in clear disappointment. His father sat still, betraying nothing. "Jesus" Miraflores wore throughout an expression of something more than expectation, almost a readiness to explode in an exultant celebration— then, when Bentinck used his injector on Warlock, he collapsed momentarily into evident despair before resuming a determinedly placid mien. The Pastor of Universal Communication seemed to have lost a vital communicant. Or, perhaps, communicator. But of what?

The remainder of the audience displayed close interest—and there had certainly been an interlude of melodrama and promise to rouse them—with the single exception of one woman who rose to her feet with hands clenched before her (in their concentration nobody seemed to notice her), but she did not appear to be watching the table where I struggled to hold Warlock down. Her gaze was fixed somewhere to my right, her expression one I could only interpret as triumphant complicity. She seemed young, somewhere in the mid-twenties, to be part of such a brainstorm of scientists, but there is no age limitation on intellect. I lost sight of her as Bentinck moved in front of me to inject his tranquilizer and when next I picked up her image she was composed and calm.

It took me another half hour to find the visual that connected her with Bentinck. There was a moment during Warlock's convulsion when his glance crossed with hers and he looked immediately away in plain anger that had in it a measure of contempt.

I took a still-picture extract of her complicity and his contempt.

Seeing there was still time to contact Gus before he began his night shift, I vidded him at home and told him I needed him on Monday morning.

He asked, "When do you think I sleep?" but had that avid look in his eye that welcomed involvement in matters that were none of his business. I told him what was required of him and promised that Bentinck would provide a laboratory overall.

When I had finished, he told me that he had set me up the meeting I had wanted with Frankie Devalera.

Frankie, he said, was willing to talk to an undercover cop—which meant that I was either on to a good, revealing contact or about to be led up a garden path.

Then he told me how the meeting was to be set up and I had that little chill at the back of the neck that warns of something nasty waiting in the works.

Or it may have been simply that second thoughts had suggested that I needed more knowledge of the background before I homed in on the sewer rat, and Gus had moved too fast for my indecision to be resolved.

7

I had not given Gus any special instructions as to how the meeting should be set up; he knew the undercover routines as well as I did.

You must realize that the twenty-first century was the Age of Information, an age that began triumphantly with the gathering and storage of data worldwide and its almost immediate availability to all—via the network at first known as the superhighway and later, contemptuously, as the snitchline. Technology outsmarted itself, not for the first time; electronics coupled with microengineering to create systems whereby personal privacy became impossible. Big business, having the resources to command research and patents, was first in the field to belabor the public with the inescapability of "intimate advertising"; I was born too late to suffer that plague, which eventually collapsed when the research that had initiated it reduced all manufacturing to automation, transport to electronic guidance systems, shopping to selective button-pushing, and all manual labor to the sphere of high-speed robotics. The Dancing Thirties went out in despair as jobs vanished and, after this "recession" (as the term was) never returned.

As seemed inevitable in conditions of poverty, the birth rate increased in defiance of governmental efforts, but the children did not die in their early years as in their great-great-grandfathers' time. World population exploded by the tens of millions each year and concentration on artifact research gave way to food production on a scale that only vast automatic networks could handle, spelling the end of crop and cattle farming by individuals. So the world was fed—with a diet carefully measured to keep its population alive to an average ninety or so years in a state of health that previous generations, overfed and ignorant or contemptuous of intelligent diet, could never have aspired to.

So the rich, who controlled the means of production and became the ruling class by inevitable progression, were comparatively few in number and wealthy beyond avarice. They dwelt in enclaves, under guard, and traveled only under guard. (Not that killing a few would have solved any problems; their administrative expertise was an essential factor in the economy and the fact is that they worked long, driven, harassed hours for their privileges and freedoms.) Under their dispensation the sciences withered; there was little money for research and none at all for the huge projects of the previous years that had swallowed sums equal to the incomes of whole states in the interest of "pure" research.

If there was little progress between the disastrous thirties and my policing in the sixties, there was a distinct regression in the condition of the jobless Wardies. Their living conditions were primitive for lack of the home equipment that was no longer in production and that they could not in any case have afforded; too many of them had no homes but lived on the streets, summer and winter.

The result was a spreading of dog-eat-dog criminality that the children grew up to recognize as underclass morality, while their parents tended to gather in interdependent groups that supported each other while baring their fangs at outsiders. And outside yet intermingled with them were the true predators, the ruthless who preyed on rich and poor alike, with for weapons the legacy of the great information explosion, the snitchlines.

The secret of all successful planning is intelligence, up-to-date and constantly updated. The police knew it, the criminal-minded knew it, and the predators knew it—and the superhighway of intellectual freedom became a battleground between the gatherers of information essential to the running of a planet bankrupted by its own fecundity and the ingenuity of the hackers intent on collecting every smidgin that might be turned to plunder or blackmail.

Existence was a battle between surveillance and evasion. Evading the operators of the snitchlines was in the long run nearly impossible ("information was born free" proclaimed the hackers of the old 1990s and gave no thought to its victims) but there were ways and means of managing a short private exchange, even in the open street—at the right time and place.

Gus, born to the streets, knew the acts and the angles.

Let him tell it.

What Harry wanted me to do was not so hard and he could have done it hisself if it wasn't that he looks like a copper whereas I look like any ordinary piece of shit you find around the streets. Don't get me wrong; I can put on a bit of style when the job calls for it, but the Wardies can smell a copper two blocks away while with me they only smell the old familiar shortage-of-water.

Anyway, I got Frankie Devalera's home address and workplace from the public directory and dressed down to sewer-rat level (mainly a matter of looking as if your overall needs a wash), which was a mistake because when I watched him leave home in the morning he was all clean-and-ironed and his cap badge told me he'd come upstairs from the drains and been upped to a staff job. He'd be too noticeable talking to someone off the shitheap. I had to go home and clean meself up and catch a bit of sleep and try to tap him on his way from work.

I picked him up as he left work in the late afternoon, only this time I was up a class or two and carrying a workman's holdall. I wanted to tap him in a crowded street, where it's easier to be private. (When you do a job for Harry it's best to reckon somebody else will be interested, and take a few precautions.) His place was in Richmond, so I hoped he'd go through the Bridge Road Shopping Centre to buy some home necessity.

And that's what he did. You can be lucky.

At that hour the road was crowded with Wardies going on and off shift. Overalls everywhere in every color of dull and drab. I reckoned that anybody mixed up in copper business might be tailed and I followed him for quite a bit, looking for hangers-on and seeing nobody I could nail for a snake. Frankie seemed clean, though in that crowd you could never be sure.

I moved up close, right behind him, so when he stopped to look in the window of a Ration Distribution Center I naturally cannoned into him and dropped my holdall. Of course it fell on Frankie's feet, didn't it? And sprung open and let some small tools fall out so that he bent to help me pick them up, saying, "Sorry mate," and me saying, "No, it was my fault," with both of us scrabbling for tools on the footpath, our heads well below the level of any tracker with a directional earpiece, and shielded by the crowding passersby.

I says, right into his ear, "Got a message."

He was an old sewer rat, all right, all right, whatever his job was now. And streetwise, with it. He never even blinked, just looked at me to sum up whether involvement by a stranger meant trouble, made up his mind fast that he'd better know what brewed and, still picking up spilled tools, says, "Hearing you."

"Copper wants to see you."

I thought that might put the wind up him but he only looks puzzled and says, "Why? I'm thirty years clean."

"Warlock."

That stopped him. But he recovered fast, never even hesitated

handing me the tools. I could see Harry was definitely on to something here. Frankie says, "Go on."

I finish dropping stuff into the holdall, snap it shut, and tell
him, "Where? When? You name it."

He stood up and turned to the Distribution Center with his
face close to the glass and I knew I had shocked him enough to
make him think about electronic ears. The old sewer rat hadn't
forgot the simple ploys and I matched his stand so both of us
talked straight to the glass. That way our words would rebound
slightly distorted and the surrounding crowd noise would help to
interfere with any earpiece reception. Not a perfect cover but useful.

He says, "What's he want?"

"He don't tell me. Undercover." "Undercover" would be interpreted as "He only wants info, no arrest."

Frankie says quickly, "Warlock's dangerous stuff," and I can
hear he's edgy.

"So you don't play?" I make it sound like he's digging his own
grave if that's the way of it.

He hesitates and I can see him thinking better a deal of some
kind than get arrested—because then the excavation would really
dig him out. He had to decide fast.

In the end he says, "Wardie café two blocks along. Blue Rose.
Sunday, eleven o'clock."

"Got it."

"How do I know him?"

"He'll know you. See ya!"

We went our ways and as far as I could tell nobody was interested in us that shouldn't be.

I could trust Gus's account; he had an accurate memory for dia-
logue. All I had learned was that Frankie was streetwise and fast
to pick up a cue and make a decision.

I had asked for it; now I had no idea what to do with it. Events
had moved in a wholly unrevealing way to leave me no clue to

what might be gained from the man—except the titillating fragment of a thought that the Warlock business was dangerous. Which already seemed plain.

I pondered possibilities while I waited for Sunday, and came up with nothing useful. When the time arrived to stop pondering and think about interrogation I dressed in a gray overall, good enough for a clerical worker, not too shabby and not quite "Sunday best"—and fully wired—and set out for Bridge Street.

The Blue Rose was every bit the Wardie café Frankie had said it was. Ten minutes before time I walked past without stopping, taking it in as seedy without being actually dirty, holding a dozen tables and nearly empty at this pre-lunch hour of a Sunday. What accounted for Frankie's choice of venue, I decided, was the blare of cheap music crashing through its door, a racket to deafen eavesdroppers.

He was not yet there. I strolled a couple of blocks and returned, to catch sight of him now in the farthest corner of the café; the only other customers were, expectably, by the street window.

The smell of jostling thousands never entirely leaves the streets but inside the buildings it seemed to cling, as though walls and fittings absorbed it. It hit me hard as I entered the Blue Rose, but in my workingman character I could not afford to notice it.

I called Frankie's name above the blast of sound, to establish my reason for joining him, and he responded with a grin and a wave of the hand, playing his part. I drew coffee at the tap range and took the chair beside him, where we could speak directly into each other's ears; the lack of a warning tingle in the nape of my neck signaled that he was not wired and no bug was fixed close enough to matter. (But no detection system was ever perfect; it was the chance that had to be taken. I had no reason to suspect electronic wizardry in a group of religious Wardies.)

At close acquaintance he seemed a very ordinary man of average height, on the thin side but with the thickened hands and fingers of a laborer, his hair showing the first shadows of gray. His ordinariness and the dull disinterest of his gaze made it difficult to see him as the once young man hungry for an identity, expressed in grubby fiddling with boys.

He said at once, just softly enough for me to hear, "I know you. The orderly. You really a copper? Got ID?"

I showed him, quickly, just enough for him to recognize the rank but not the name, and he asked, "Does Bentinck know you're a copper?"

I had to answer at once, with no time to weigh possible danger to Bentinck. Frankie, with a clean record through thirty years and whose only crime seemed to have been amenable to treatment had, I thought, to be trusted. "Yes, but I was wished on him. He didn't ask for me."

That might save Bentinck, in some small fashion, if his bug-listeners were alerted by Frankie, who at once asked the obvious question. "Like that, is it? How much do you know?"

His face gave nothing away.

"Nothing. My super knows something but he doesn't tell me."

"So what do you want?"

"Who bugged Bentinck's car and why, for a start?"

"Don't know but I can guess."

"So guess."

"Nothing for nothing. Why did you pick me for a nark?"

That was a question whose answer I hadn't even formulated for myself. Curiosity, perhaps, about the details of his experience with Warlock. Or maybe the circumstance—peculiar when you think about it—that of all the people in Steven Warlock's document he was the one who emerged as knowing his mind and talking ordinary sense.

I said, more or less at random, "Because you know Bentinck. I've read Steven Warlock's account of your electrohypnosis session—"

"What account? Didn't know he left one. But then, I never saw him again after him and his mum came to see me and Dad."

"He dictated one for the police. We're drawn in because someone copied it and smuggled the copy out of the Police File library. We want to know why—and who for."

For the first time his face showed an expression, puzzlement. "I'd reckon Jesus bugged the Doc's car because he doesn't trust him much, but I can't help you with the rest. Who'd need the file? And what for?"

Indeed, who would? Another hypnotist, interested in technique? But the account had no technical content. Another scientist in a related discipline hunting for a clue to some research of his own?

I remembered. "There was a woman present at the attempted revival the other day—thirtyish, dark-haired, a faintly aboriginal cast of face but fairly light skin, could be a third-generation mixture. I saw her looking at Bentinck after Warlock played up. Not like a visiting scientist, more as if they knew each other and there was something unsaid between them. Know her?"

He nodded. "Her name's Wishart. I don't know what she was doing there; she's in genetics. I suppose Bentinck would know her. She talks a lot to Jesus."

At last some cross-connections appeared. But what to make of them? I should ask Connor but—if he reran the lab tape of my overall he would see that I could not have been watching her at that juncture and would deduce that I had copied the readout and was keeping my own counsel about some aspects of the investigation. Best to let that ride for the moment.

I asked, "Local woman?"

"Yes."

"A member of your church?"

"An affiliate." I thought his eyes showed a wary flicker.

It was time for a more direct approach, to remind him that he had put himself in my hands. "Is she part of the danger you spoke of to my contact?"

For a while he was silent and uncomfortable, twisting his coffee cup around on its saucer, his eyes looking inward. At last he said, "That was careless of me."

I agreed, "Of course it was. You were startled and said the first thing in your mind—the truth."

He shrugged, neither yes nor no.

DOWN THERE IN DARKNESS

"What is the danger, Frankie?"

Instead of answering, he went to the tap range and refilled his coffee cup, sat down again, and said, "I'm afraid. They're capable of killing."

Afraid? Possibly he was but neither voice nor face confirmed it; he was fully in control of himself.

"We can protect you." We always say that and always it rings hollow. The entire force could not protect a man marked for death by an intelligent antagonist.

He said, "Like hell you can," and, surprisingly, grinned in my face, the wide open, friendly grin of a man too world-wise to care.

"Just the same you want to talk. That's why you made the slip of the tongue with my man. Your real need was showing."

"Cop psychology now?" He was amused. "Tell you what, copper—I'll think about it and tell you tomorrow. That is, if you'll be assisting Bentinck tomorrow—and if I decide I want to tell you."

"I will be there but contact could be difficult. I'd find it hard to talk to someone in the audience."

He was surprised. "Hasn't Bentinck told you what's doing? I won't be in the audience. I'm going down in the dark after Warlock to try and get with him like I did before. To try to bring him back with me. So I'll be seeing you right close-up."

And he got up and walked out, leaving his fresh coffee undrunk. I decided against calling him back; I read him as a man who stuck to his decisions. Finishing my coffee, I wondered what the Wishart woman, a geneticist, would find interesting in Warlock or electrohypnosis. And whether Connor had noticed her presence. And had kept the information to himself. And if so, why?

And, more importantly, who or what was dangerous?

8

Gus had been working a weekend shift from midnight to eight in the morning, and on Monday he came to my place for breakfast and to clean up and shave, while he complained that he should be sleeping. Then, without a break, he asked what we would be doing at the complex.

When I told him, he wanted to know was that all. "Just hold the bugger down?"

"If necessary. We don't really know what can happen. And you being there will remind Frankie there is more than one person interested in what he has to say."

"Maybe whoever the 'danger' is has told him what to say by now. You should have held on to him."

"Charged him? With what? Taken him to the nearest station just to have him clam up and make us let him go?"

"Could have held him on suspicion."

Like most Wardies, Gus suspected the police of finding underhanded ways of doing as they pleased with the helpless suspect, whereas we were in fact bound hand and foot by legalities. I won't pretend there weren't shortcuts and sharp tricks, but in a case as nebulous as Frankie's it was best to be circumspect. A willing nark was the best nark.

I didn't argue with Gus; instead, I vidded the station and alerted the On-Clock that I would not be in, having a medical appointment. Gus listened suspiciously to the deviousness and was openly curious when I told him we would travel by public transport rather than vid up a police car.

"Real undercover, eh?"

His feeling for covert drama was roused but it would not affect his efficiency in a crisis. Not that I expected a crisis; at this stage all I wanted and hoped for was information.

Mum gave us breakfast with an air of disapproval because I gave no explanation of Gus's presence, while Dad preserved the secret smile of one on the fringe of state secrets. Then we went out, a couple of overalled workmen, to travel by bus to the complex.

In the dressing room, Frankie was there before us, seated naked on his operating table trolley with its cargo of telltales and looking pretty fit for his age. He grinned in recognition of me and nodded at Gus. "Cops one and two," he said.

"Cop one only," I said, leaving him to wonder if more than the police were involved in investigating him. At the same time I wondered if any bugs had been added to the room since our last session. My detector was silent but it was possible to coat an entire room in a clear lacquer that would pick up sound and picture and relay them by fiber cable to a distant recorder.

Frankie gave Gus a speculative stare, shrugged, and pointed to a white overall lying on the trolley. "Bentinck left this for the assistant," he said.

Gus told him, "That's me," and stripped off his work overall. I did the same; I had carried my wired version in a bag.

A complex orderly came in wheeling the unconscious, naked Warlock, looking as though he would dearly have liked to ask about his exotic cargo if our blank faces had not discouraged him.

When he had gone, Gus bent over Warlock with his thin, pointed features fixed in bemused awe, as if at the advent of deity, and I wondered not for the first time what went on in that romantic but most practical head. And at the stature of an artist whose works were to me so baffling.

Frankie glanced at Warlock, said, "Hasn't changed much, has he?" and then, to me, "Well, copper, no questions?"

"Are you prepared to answer them?"

He looked doubtfully at Gus, shrugged again, and said, "I reckon so." Then he added, "We can talk here. They haven't had time to get at this place. No excuse to get workmen in."

That was a bonus. I asked immediately, "Who's the danger man?"

"First, Jesus—at least I think so. And behind him, Wishart."

"Who's Wishart? That geneticist woman in the audience?"

"She's only representing her grandfather—the man with the string of biology labs." His name meant nothing to me. I was much more interested in the placid way in which Frankie said, in an all-in-the-day's-work sort of voice, "You'll have to look after me, you know. They'll use truth drugs on me if you don't keep me close."

He held my eyes with a little half-smile, a man sure of himself—or, at any rate, a man whose mind was made up and not to be changed. "All right," I said. "Full protection,"—and prayed that Connor would agree.

"This is my only chance to talk in full insulation; I might never get another one. I even combed a bug out of my hair this morning. We're all watched."

I wanted to ask, "Who's we?," but Bentinck came in with another man in white, middle-aged and slightly overweight, and introduced him with no waste of words. "Ostrov, this is Dr. Reilly, who will be monitoring Mr. Devalera. And this is your additional orderly, is he?"

Gus held out his hand to be shaken. "Gus Kostakis, Doctor."

Bentinck took his hand briefly. "Do you know what is required of you?"

"Harry's explained it."

Reilly had been scrutinizing Gus's droop-shouldered, angular figure, and he asked, "Is he strong enough? After your account of Warlock's spasms . . ."

I said, "He'll handle Frankie all right, but why not strap them down?"

Bentinck looked at me as he thought me inane. "You wrestled with Warlock, didn't you? Strap him down and he might break his own bones."

True; you can miss the obvious on another man's territory.

Frankie grinned at Gus and said, "It isn't me being dragged back from heaven. I promise to come quietly."

But Gus didn't know the reference and merely looked sour. Bentinck, probably distrusting an amateur's instruction, told him minutely what was expected of him and Gus only nodded. He never trusted himself to speak much in educated company, though in many fields his special knowledge could lose them.

Bentinck consulted his watch, said, "Bring in the tables; we might as well get on with it," and went out. We followed, with our subjects on the tables into the anteroom, and through it to the lecture hall.

I did not pay too much attention to his opening remarks because I was searching the rows for the Wishart woman. She was at the back, as before, and not paying much heed to Bentinck, as though he said only what she had heard before. Old man Devalera and "Jesus" Miraflores were seated apart, as before, and I wondered fruitlessly what was her connection with them and with Frankie's "danger," until some of Bentinck's words penetrated and I thought I had better listen.

Frankie's role in the recovery, it seemed, was to make contact in the nebulous and basically indescribable fashion I had found in Steven's account, to argue or persuade the man to return to consciousness, or, failing that, to bring back news of Warlock's mental condition or anything else—vague stuff, this—that might assist the effort at resuscitation. In all honesty, I couldn't see why a man in the "heaven" of his own wish-fulfillment should desire to tear himself loose. Nirvana is Nirvana and total bliss.

But—what had caused the physical eruption on the other occasion? A purely physiological reaction of some kind? Was that possible without some form of mental collusion? I felt a little like someone lost in an old melodrama, in "regions man is not meant to know."

Then Bentinck seemed to have finished his introduction. He turned to Gus and myself, asked, "Ready?" and we nodded, and he and Reilly put on their control helmets.

GEORGE TURNER

Gus and I stood at our tables, and the routine of isolating Frankie from all sensory influences began. He seemed calm enough, even winked at Gus in an early stage and was fully relaxed. But, then, he had had thirty years of Bentinck and must have developed trust in him.

Reilly spoke. "Isolation is complete."

I looked closely at Warlock as Bentinck said, "We will wait two minutes before attempting—"

We didn't, because already Gus was fighting a yelling, terrified, maniacal Frankie who appeared to be trying to run as if the devils of hell were after him.

My man was quiet, motionless.

Gus had his work cut out holding Frankie, who seemed to be in a state of utterly desperate terror. I could not risk going to help him in case Warlock should also cut loose. Reilly watched in dismay, not daring to interfere, but Bentinck kept his eyes on Warlock.

Expectably, Frankie collapsed suddenly, crying on Gus's chest while Gus patted him like a puzzled nanny. At any rate, the man had come completely out of sensory isolation.

The assembled scientists remained in their seats, fascinated but well-behaved where a street crowd would have surged around the tables and probably overturned them.

Reilly moved to examine the distraught Frankie while Bentinck asked Gus, "Is he all right?"

Frankie recovered sufficiently to say in a strangled voice, "Never again, Doc, never! He can rot there before I go back down."

Bentinck's expression, fleetingly, registered an unexpected you'll-do-as-you're-bloody-well-told.

Then, while I tried to relate that to the muddle of circumstances, Warlock stirred, took a huge rasping breath, raised himself on his elbows and, in a voice creaking with disuse said, "God, I'm stiff!"

I sprang to hold him but he pushed me away. "I'm not a bloody cripple. I can look after myself."

He levered himself upright with difficulty, frowning at the effort. Thirty years of isometric exercise had not smoothed every joint of the body, but it had worked better than I would have anticipated.

Warlock looked around him. "We're in a different room. Who are these people?" He caught sight of Reilly. "Who's he?"

While in the rest of the hall you could have heard the proverbial pin drop, Frankie screamed at him, "You've waked up, you silly bastard! After thir—"

But by then Bentinck had a hand over his mouth.

Warlock asked, "So who's that? Why have we shifted, Dr. Bentinck? And where's Dr. Graves?" He pointed at Frankie. "He looks like—" And there he stopped, peering uncertainly.

Something in the nature of a sigh, a little hiss as of breath exhaled, came from the watching scientists, but they knew better than to speak.

Bentinck said to him, quietly, "You have been in isolation longer than we intended. You will want a while to reorient your thinking. The orderly"—he jerked his head at me—"will wheel you into the next room while you recover."

"Recover!" He glared at Bentinck as though the man had affronted him. "It all made no sense! Well, some things did—and then they didn't. I'll have to sort it all out." Still angry, he pointed at me. "He's new, too. And who's all this bloody great crowd? There was only a handful!"

Bentinck said to me, below his breath, "For God's sake get him out of here," and I shifted Warlock quickly into the anteroom with him asking questions all the way.

As we moved off, the scientist audience broke into speech as if a barrier had been broken—not the loud speech of an undisciplined crowd but a quiet passing of question and guesswork. I heard Bentinck ask something of Frankie and thought I heard him answer what sounded like, "my father's mouth."

Then we passed inside. Reilly came after us.

Warlock sat up with his legs dangling over the side of the table. "Go to sleep in one place and wake up in another. It's confusing.

And where's Frankie? He went under with me, didn't he?''

I wasn't sure what I should or should not answer and looked to Reilly, who said, "He'll be along later."

"Not the bad fellow they said of him. I saw quite a bit—" He hesitated, unsure of his own meaning. "That is, I had an experience of him . . ." His voice trailed off. After a moment he said, "I need different words for it." And lapsed into silence.

Reilly said, "Don't try until you are ready," but he might have spoken to a stone. Warlock was deep in his private puzzlement.

We sat quietly, with nothing useful to say to each other—until Reilly muttered, "What the devil is he telling them out there?"

It seemed an age before Bentinck appeared, with a babble of what sounded like discontent behind him, followed by a lowering Frankie and Gus pushing the trolley. Bentinck said to Reilly, "I've done what I could; I've promised them individual audio-visual tapes of the interrogation when it is completed, but they aren't satisfied."

Reilly exploded, "Nor would I be! Some of these people are from Europe and Asia. They have a right to at least a question-and-answer session for their trouble."

Bentinck's pervasive calm seemed on the verge of deserting him. He said, "I know, I know, but it mustn't happen until we find out what has taken place with these men. Frankie's statement raises queries that need answering."

"Statement? What statement?"

"He found himself falling into his father's jaws—as at the moment of his first awakening."

"Well?"

Warlock spoke harshly. "So did I."

Frankie said sullenly, "It was same as the first time, only worse."

I couldn't see any meaning to this but Warlock asked, "You mean this is Frankie? More likely his father."

It would be hard to imagine a man more at a loss to understand what was being said and implied around him. He looked into all our faces in a species of growing fear, suddenly aware of his world's familiarity radically, unsubtly changing its shape and sound. He cried out, "What's happened to you, Frankie?"

Frankie made a gesture of impotent appeal to Bentinck, who nodded helplessly, his plans for gentle breaking of the news in ruin.

"I've just grown a bit older, that's all." He put out a tentative hand and took Warlock's wrist. "It's been a while since—I mean, they couldn't wake you up."

Warlock stared at him distrustfully and pointed to Bentinck. "He hasn't grown older."

"He's had juvenation. I don't think they had that in your day."

"My day?" He pushed Frankie's hand away. "What do you mean by my day? I was in isolation for a few minutes, that's all, so what are you talking about?"

He was trying for an angry shout but his voice cracked.

Frankie said miserably, "It was more. It was thirty-four years."

Warlock didn't take it in, only regarded Frankie as someone trying to make a fool of him.

"Minutes," he insisted and turned to Bentinck. "Minutes, wasn't it?"

Bentinck shook his head. "It was thirty-four years."

Warlock said in a stifled voice, "You bloody fool hypnotist," and fainted. I caught him as he began to slip from the table, but it was only a shock effect, almost immediately over. He stood, leaning on my arm and panting like a winded runner.

When he could speak, he said, "Millie! My wife!"

Bentinck made a gesture of frightened helplessness; he had planned revelation to lead gently into the necessary truths but the event had defeated him.

Warlock's voice was harsh, even menacing as he asked, "Has she died?"

Bentinck shook his head. "She is a very old lady, but still in good health." He hesitated, then took the plunge. "She thought that under the circumstances it was better she should not attend your wakening."

Warlock shouted, "Why?," outraged and aggressive. Then, realizing the truth, "Did she imagine I wouldn't—"

His eyes filled with tears and he clung to me. In his misery he would have clung to anyone, unrecognizing, this man plucked from an eternal heaven.

For a long moment we were all frozen in the acute embarrassment of a situation without precedent.

Then the door opened and the man who called himself Jesus strode into the room.

The Pastor of Lambs, the Only Begotten Son, looked ordinary enough to a practicing atheist, something of a fifty-year-old businessman who kept a good table and beat his wife only in moderation.

Behind him came the elder Devalera, carrying himself with that composure that covers the uneasiness of a man in turmoil.

And, behind him again, came the Wishart woman, the geneticist whose interest in an electrohypnotized artist needed explanation. Seen close-up she was attractive, most attractive in what my copper's mind recognized as a purely sensuous fashion that had nothing to do with a fairly ordinary face and figure. A sensuous scientist? Well, we live and learn. And first I must learn what embroiled her interest in a deeply sleeping artist.

I felt, at last, that with this eruption of principals, events might begin to move. Even Connor's involvement might appear. After days of fumbling in the dark I sensed the breaking of a little light, but what broke most plainly was a sense of tension in Bentinck and Frankie. Perhaps Frankie's "danger" was about to manifest.

"Jesus" Miraflores came ten paces into the room and halted, taking us all in with the stare of a man accustomed to authority. That sat badly on him because his walk was the rolling amble of a man with fat thighs and slightly knock-knees; he looked, I thought, like an insulted schoolmaster.

And he behaved like one. He pointed a thick finger at Frankie and said, in a voice of controlled outrage, "Get dressed at once. Your nudity is obscene!"

It was at least a revealing introduction to the morality of the

Church of Whatever-it-was Communication, and I noted a fleeting smile on the face of the Wishart woman. She was not one of the gulled flock.

Frankie glanced at Bentinck, who nodded.

Miraflores looked over Warlock with a positively episcopal disapproval. "And take him with you."

Warlock came out of my support with an agility at odds with his signs of collapse. He seemed to be a man of fast changes and reactions. He snarled—and I mean snarled—"Who's this shithead?"

It was not the language I expected of a serious artist but I hadn't had much acquaintance with the breed.

Miraflores said grandly (I can't describe his tone any other way), "I am your Sponsor." You could hear the capital "S." Then, with a switch to world-weary courtesy, "Please get dressed."

Warlock turned to Bentinck. "I want to see my wife. And my son."

Miraflores answered for the hypnotist. "Mrs. Warlock will be brought to you"—and he hesitated a bare flicker—"soon." Then, with crass brutality, "Your son, Steven, was drowned in a boating accident."

Warlock grabbed for my arm again, crying out, "My Stevie!"

The fool of a man surveyed him impassively and the elder Devalera said, "In God's name, have a little pity!," but the fool answered, "God gives and God takes and it is for us to bear reality."

The faintest trace of a grimace disturbed the Wishart woman's face.

I said to Warlock, "Let's get out of this," as I urged him toward the dressing room and signaled Frankie and Gus to come with us.

Bentinck said in a shaken voice, "Mr. Warlock's clothes are in a locker inside. I had them sent for."

In the dressing room Warlock sat on one of the forms and buried his face in his hands. It was hard to imagine the shocking awakening of a man who thought he had been absent from the world for only a few minutes, and I confess I didn't try to imagine it. It couldn't be taken in all at once; he must, I thought, be in a state of acute mental shock wherein realization trickled only slowly to the refusing brain.

I found the clothes that must be his—shirt and underwear, socks and shoes, and a jacket and trousers beautifully tailored in a style and cut nobody today would remember—and laid them beside him. He did not look at them.

Gus asked, "Who's that lot that came in behind us?"

I explained quietly to him while Frankie dressed rapidly, watching us all the time, and Warlock sat in his miserable abstraction. At the end I said, "I think they're Frankie's 'danger.' "

"Some of it," Frankie said and went to Warlock and put an arm around his shoulders. "Better get dressed, mate."

"I want my wife."

I told him, "I'll take you to her soon. But you'll have to put some clothes on first."

"You'll take me? Who are you?"

I said at random, "I'm the bloke detailed to look after you."

"And who's the fat bastard that talks like a ringmaster?"

"Try to forget him. He doesn't matter. I'll be taking you out of here."

Frankie said, "He matters. Never forget it."

Warlock began to dress, taking his time.

After a while Frankie said, "If you take him out, you've got to take me, too."

I hadn't envisioned snapping Frankie up under his priestly master's nose, but I had given my word and my parents brought me up to be old-fashioned about that.

He said, "They've got Steven's account. Now they want Brian's to add to mine."

"Why?"

"Take me out and I'll tell you. And you can believe that it's important."

"Tell me now."

"No time. It'll take hours to make you believe it."

I had to decide on the spot—and be a laughingstock if the whole affair turned out to be fairy floss. But Bentinck and Frankie were frightened men and I needed to know why.

"All right," I said, "I'll take you out."

He nodded, satisfied, and relaxed so completely as to surprise me at the extent of his tension; he had not been merely frightened but terrified. To be honest, I had not taken this affair, despite its bizarre aspects and Connor's curious interest, too seriously; in the back of my mind had been the expectation that in the end it would show up as a financial scam of some kind, probably involving church funds and Warlock's pictures. Even the bugging of individuals was par for the plotting of amateurs as their intrigue reached the quarrelling stage and their plan began to fall apart.

In Frankie's patent retreat into dependence on my given word, the almost despairing scrambling for needed cover, I saw his "danger" as real and present, something other than a falling-out of petty crims. I surely would "take him out"—and scrape him clean of everything he had to give.

Gus picked that moment to ask, in the injured tone that suggests I keep secrets from him, "What goes on, Harry?"

I could only tell him, "I'm buggered if I know," while part of my mind wondered what could be the significance of comparing Steven's account with those of Frankie and Warlock.

Then Warlock said, "I'm ready. Now you can take me to see my wife. Is she somewhere near?"

I answered, since his aggressive tone needed an answer, "No, she's at home."

Probably. I hoped she was.

Then we all went out into the anteroom.

We were in time to hear the voice of "Jesus" Miraflores raised in most unecclesiastical choler—plain bad temper, in fact. He stood in the middle of the room hands on hips, chin out-thrust, and face scarlet with anger.

The elder Devalera appeared not at all the puritanical evangelist of Steven's account but stood against the wall, anxiously wringing clasped hands with an air of wishing himself elsewhere. The Wishart woman had seated herself a little behind the Pastor of Lambs and out of his line of sight. She seemed hugely amused by whatever was going on and was vastly more attractive with the addition of a smile.

What we heard sounded like the culmination of a tirade, with a furious Jesus at full bore, yelling, "I'll not have you resisting my authority! It is I who will decide who is to receive transcripts of the debriefing and I will not put up with pussyfooting delays on pseudopsychological grounds—delays that I suspect are designed to allow you to make unsupervised copies of Warlock's statement!"

Bentinck stood half the room distant from the blast, absorbing it with a doggedly mulish expression at odds with his professional calm.

He said, in a quiet, determined voice, "What you call 'pussyfooting delays' are designed to allow the two subjects to settle their minds after what has been a patently disturbing episode for both of them. We need recollection in tranquility and properly relaxing surroundings, not a confused outpouring of impressions."

Plump little lord Jesus saw us come in and made an effort to control his voice; it emerged now as a choking rasp. "The Church of Universal Communication is the abode of tranquility, Doctor. I remind you also that my church has funded this work of resuscitation from the outset and has a right of decision in the disposal of its results." (I caught a glimpse of amazed surprise on the face of Dr. Wishart, instantly suppressed, and promised myself some investigation of the "funding.") "That being so, we will take our leave together with Mr. Warlock and Mr. Devalera—you also, I must assume, if you wish to oversee the debriefing."

With a hint of desperation Bentinck said, "You are interfering beyond your expertise. Nor am I satisfied that funding gives you any right of decision or even that your claim to total funding is justified."

Miraflores reacted as if a pet kitten had clawed him, but Warlock preempted whatever might have been his riposte. He said, "I don't know who this overbearing churchman may be but I am not bound by his imagined rights and from this place I am going immediately home to my wife."

Miraflores rounded on him, almost spitting at this fresh defiance. "You have no home! Twelve months ago Mrs. Warlock placed you in the care of the Church of Universal Communication. We have supported you and tended you during that time and brought you back to consciousness. In moral terms we own your total cooperation."

"Moral terms? I'll see my wife, then we'll consider morality." He waved at me. "This gentleman has offered to see me home. Later on I will get in touch with you. Perhaps. Meanwhile, I feel my debt is to Dr. Bentinck." He smiled brightly. "I don't understand what's going on here but it seems a fine kerfuffle over what has been to me just a few minutes' sleep." He frowned. "Well, perhaps unconsciousness." He seemed to reconsider. "Maybe not quite that. Perhaps I need some of Dr. Bentinck's recollection in tranquility." He became aware of us hanging on his words, and muttered, "It was confusing—I need to think."

Bentinck said softly, a confident victor, "I agree that Mr. Warlock's family duty comes first. And that he needs time to think."

Miraflores breathed deeply and recovered his calm (save for a promise of rage in his eyes); after all, he could scarcely snatch a resisting Warlock and run with him.

With stiff grace he conceded. "Mr. Warlock, I will look forward to hearing from you very soon—if possible, during this same day. Frankie, Dr. Bentinck, we will leave now; I will take you in my car."

The concluding offer sounded almost like a threat.

Frankie said, "I'm not coming with you," in the dead level tone of a frightened but determined man. And he looked straight at me.

I had had no time to decide how I was extricate Frankie from whatever toil meshed him. While I thought about it, Miraflores said, "Don't be silly, man; we'll drop you at home." He sounded mild and friendly but there was steel in it.

I prepared myself for a speech, not knowing how it would develop or end. "I must take over at this point. Dr. Bentinck did not know when he hired two orderlies from the pool that one of them would be a policeman, undercover." That, I thought, would leave Bentinck free of any suspicion he might be under. "I am Detective Sergeant Ostrov." I produced my ID and nobody uttered a word.

Miraflores seemed carved in stone and the lingering smile vanished from Dr. Wishart's face. Only Warlock shrugged at one more proof that he had emerged into a mad, mad world. "I must take Mr. Frankie Devalera in charge and have him accompany me to the nearest police station."

They were all silent, making nothing of my interruption, until old man Devalera, who had not so far spoken a word, asked, "But why? Why? What has he done?"

What, indeed? The father had a right to an answer.

"We've had an eye on him for some time." I had an inspiration. "There have been complaints of offenses against children." I suppose it was an obvious thought, to resurrect Frankie's old trouble, but I realized immediately that I could scarcely have chosen worse.

Old Devalera collapsed against the wall and cried out, "Dear God, no! No, no!"

Frankie said, "It's not true, Dad! It hasn't happened at all. They're only suspicious because of the old affair."

Thinking frantically, I had succeeded in reopening an ancient can of worms. But it was done now and I could get my man out. Then I saw that there was a further gain to be had. I said to Bentinck, "I would be glad if you would also accompany us; I understand you had previous contact with Mr. Devalera's condition and may be able to give valuable advice."

DOWN THERE IN DARKNESS

Bentinck's face was inscrutable as he answered—I think "suave-ly" would be the word for it—"Of course, Detective Sergeant."

"And Mr. Warlock must go to his wife. She will no doubt be surprised to have him returned to her in a police car."

It would be entertaining to know what passed through Mira-flores's mind as he saw his three major pieces swept from his board. But—what the devil did he want with them, anyway?

In a whitefaced silence he disengaged old Devalera roughly from his son's protesting arms and literally pushed him out of the room. Dr. Wishart left more slowly, her face a puzzlement.

When we were alone, Frankie said, "You could have picked a better reason. The old man's shattered."

"Sorry," I told him—and I was sorry, "but on the spur of the moment, I couldn't." I turned to Bentinck, who wore a thin smile that I interpreted as pleasure.

"Where's the nearest vid? I have to ring my station for a car."

Gus said, "Drop me home first. I have to get some sleep, you know."

"Don't you want to hear the debriefing?"

That shut him up; he wouldn't have missed it for worlds.

I, on the other hand, was not so sure of my welcome from Connor. I might well have sprung my batch of informants before his time was ripe.

9

In the police hovercar they kept quiet, even Gus, who must have been bursting with questions; each of the others had enough to think over and possibly to fear. I broke silence once to ask Ben-tinck, "Is Dr. Reilly a member of your church?" and he shook his head. Reilly had disappeared without farewells, probably glad to escape the drama and snarling—and maybe talk to reporters.

At the station I seated them all in the waiting room under the eye of the desk clerk.

Then I went to Connor to make my report.

When I was done he said, "Harry, you've either blown the investigation completely or cracked it wide open. The alarm is out to that damned church now and there'll be an instant scattering of rats. God thank you or forgive you—whichever." He managed, simultaneously, to seem harassed, stern, and greedily expectant; I merely wished I could safely point out that this was his own damned fool fault for not briefing me properly in the first place, for playing games with official information and being in general a devious bastard.

He grumbled on as though it hurt him. "Find Constable Jarvis on the File Desk or in the File Room and bring him here. We might as well shake the cocktail a little harder." As I went out he added, still morosely, "You'd better vid Mrs. Warlock and get her down here," and, with a world-weary smile, "for a welcome home party."

I detoured through the waiting room and said to Warlock, "I'm going to vid your wife," and he answered at once, "Don't!"

To my querying silence he explained, "I've had some time to think. She will be eighty-one and there will have been all sorts of changes." He made a little, irresolute flutter of the hands. "I need to think it out."

He was afraid of seeing, facing the reality of an old woman. So, in his circumstance, would I have been.

The others said nothing; I went in search of Jarvis and found him at his desk, disconsolately sorting file folders and info-chips for a dozen detectives and departments. He was only a youngster, perhaps nineteen and on his first posting. I said, "Super Connor wants to see you," and grinned with pleasure for the interruption. "And don't be too happy in advance."

I marched him into Connor's office where he stood properly at attention while the super arranged his features in I-regret-that-

I-must-do-this mode and held the pose to the thin edge of discomfort. His tableaux tended to hold long after the director had shouted, Cut!, but he reduced Jarvis to squirming apprehension.

At last he said, "On Monday of last week you made four copies of File 292-33A-2036."

Jarvis's face did not change but his stiff attention relaxed as though a ramrod had been removed from his spine. He seemed less like a man caught out than one suddenly readied for battle. He said nothing.

"You have not been long on the File Desk, Constable Jarvis, but long enough to know that the copier automatically records all transactions made on it and the time of the transaction. No other personnel used the copier during that shift." He waited, in something approaching quizzical mode. "Well?"

Jarvis nodded slightly. "I didn't think it would be noticed."

The reply was offhand, close to contemptuous. Connor chose to ignore it but explained elaborately, "Because record search is commonly made for a specific file and nobody notices the surrounding lists of material? It was your misfortune that I had use for the file and observed that it had been copied and the copy-numbers erased. Rather amateurishly erased. To whom did you pass the copies?"

Jarvis remained silent.

"To Mr. Miraflores, known to his flock as 'Jesus'?" That shook Jarvis a little. "I have some interest in this little lord Jesus, to the point of having attended one of his services—where I observed your presence in the congregation."

I could have throttled him for not giving me all this before.

Jarvis seemed to realize all at once that his career in the force was over and all his restraint was simple habit. He stood easy, let out a long breath, and allowed himself a cheeky smile. In a mocking Suss whine he said, "You've got me cold, guv."

Connor matched him with the friendly survey of a hungering shark as he summoned a sergeant. "Cold as the very little fish that in fact you are, and ripe for interrogation by piranhas." To the entering sergeant he said sunnily, "Place Constable Jarvis in detention in an incommunicado cell. A charge will be proferred within the statutory period."

Jarvis was led out and Connor remarked to the air, "You have questions, Harry?"

"Around a dozen or so, but one for starters: What was your interest, in the first place, in the Warlock file?"

That was broad enough to require detail in the response.

Connor looked pleased. "You haven't forgotten how to go for the throat, have you, Harry?"

Compliments, yet? Watch out for diversions, Harry! But what I got was fairly short and to the point. And something of a stunner.

Connor said moodily, as if revealing a secret of the soul, "I have an interest in art, with a particular bent toward the work of Brian Warlock." He expected, perhaps, that I'd go off into a laughing fit: Old super-plod haunting art galleries for his kicks! I contrived to look sympathetic and understanding. (You see by now that any dealing with Connor smelled of drama, with characterizations shifting at high speed.)

"So I followed the accounts of Mrs. Warlock's legal battles and was intrigued to read of another attempt at the painter's resuscitation. I was more intrigued to see among the names of international scientists to be present that of Valda Wishart, who is a geneticist."

"The part-Koori girl?"

"Quartercaste. Could pass for white. You noticed her? Why?"

"She seemed to know Bentinck better than just casually."

"Quite. I haven't had time to get to her yet."

He leaned back in his chair, clasped his hands behind his head, and said with deep satisfaction, "But you will find time, Harry, much time." He leaned forward to impress a point. "What does a geneticist want with a cult leader and a hypnotherapist?"

"I've wondered."

"Pursue the wonder, Harry. She is the granddaughter of Abel Wishart, founder of Wishart Biological Laboratories—who still lives, hale and hearty, after at least one legal juvenation process and possibly another, less legal."

He was beginning to get on my nerves. I said, "So what?," with less than respect for his histrionics.

"Abel Wishart is one of the transglobal group who developed the Devil's Flu."

You might think that the Wishart name should have rung a bell in my mind, but there had been so many involved—not only scientists but politicians, military personnel, ambassadorial staffs, and secret agents of every breed—that their names dissolved in a single phrase, the "White World Conspiracy." The wonder was that the thing had not been blown open by the weight of numbers involved, but they had probably played the cell game wherein each group knew a little but only a few knew the master plan. It had taken Beltane's brutal broadcast and suicide to alert the stunned planet.

What mattered immediately was that Connor had spotted the connection and I had not.

As for the Devil's Flu, that was the name dreamed up by the Wardies of the world for the contraceptive disease whose unleashing on the planet had been preempted by Beltane's broadcast before he shot himself. Simple mention of the thing was still enough to arouse shudders in a world accustomed to ongoing starvation and horror; the mere knowledge that it could exist was warning of an ax poised over the neck of the race. That it still existed as formulae in the heads of certain people—and nobody knew certainly which people—was part of the human intellectual ambience and fearfully accepted as such. Already it had ceased to be a staple of conversation; it was just one more image of mortality.

Still, I could see no connection and said so.

"No? Then let's see what your group of frightened men have to say. Have we enough chairs? I think so. Bring them in, Harry."

10

It would be useless and confusing to attempt to detail the confessions and declarations of the next hour. In the long run only a few matters were clarified and they did not add up to a plain total; we ended with a few facts and no overall view. That we achieved that much was due to Connor's ability to home-in on essentials and I sourly had to admit his efficiency when the character acting was set aside.

He began by pointing a finger at Gus and asking, "Who is this one?"

The question was for me but Gus answered for himself, "I'm Gus Kostakis and I'm a security agent." I could have strangled him when he added smugly, "Detective Sergeant Ostrov gets me to help him now and then."

"Does he, now? Detective Sergeant Ostrov was an intelligent man, once."

I said, before Gus could start mayhem with a smart comeback, "I needed assistance and by your instruction could not call on members of the force. Mr. Kostakis gave me valuable help in the case of Premier Beltane."

"And now he knows all you know?"

"With respect, sir, that amounts to precious little and he is wholly trustworthy with information."

"That's to be seen. If he isn't, God help you because I will not."

He turned to Frankie. "Mr. Devalera, you have stated that you wish to give evidence of some kind."

Frankie said stoutly, "In return for protection."

"That's to be seen. Your request will be considered in relation to the nature of the statement."

"Will murder do you?"

"If you can prove it."

"I can't, but I'm frightened of being next now I've come here."

Warlock's eyes wandered from face to face with the distracted gaze of a man wakened into a madhouse, while Gus swallowed revelation with a relish for more to come.

But Bentinck interjected, in a tone of frozen dismissal, "Nonsense, Frankie. There has been no murder."

It was the tone of a master to a schoolboy, intended to shoot down contradiction out of hand, but Frankie would have none of it.

"What about the kurdaitcha man? Stabbed between the vestry and his home! And anybody else who stood up to Jesus—"

Like a man demented, Bentinck passed from cold self-possession to instant bellowing rage, standing and shouting down into Frankie's face. Frankie matched him yell for yell, neither of them intelligible, both of them red-faced and out of control. The unfortunate Warlock, who had been seated between them, got up and positioned himself against the wall, bewildered and shaking.

Connor waited with an expression of amused inquiry until they ran down in a hoarse, inimical breathing. "That's much better," he said, "and not totally unproductive. The mention of kurdaitcha raises a hint of connectivity. Eh, Dr. Bentinck? And I think Mr. Warlock can safely sit down again."

He might have explained then what a kurdaitcha man was but he changed the subject completely. Or so it seemed at the time.

"Now, Dr. Bentinck. In spite of the immediate past performance, I understand that you are here to shepherd Mr. Warlock and Mr. Devalera through their debriefing sessions. So, why not begin?"

All three of them protested at once, and again Connor waited for them to exhaust themselves.

"Quite so. I have read Steven Warlock's statement and realize there may be some mental confusion. Still, we must make a start somewhere. Should we begin with a cup of tea while we all rock back to equilibrium? Then we will retire to an interview room and begin trying to make some sense of these disagreements—because the clue to them lies in this central activity, I think. I know, Dr. Bentinck, that this will be only in the nature of a preliminary debriefing and that your full study will come later, but now that the police are involved they must be fed some crumbs. Don't you agree?"

Bentinck glared.

"Tea," Connor ordered comfortably into his desk intervox.

As a social event, tea was a disaster. Bentinck and Frankie behaved like total strangers to each other while Gus tried to talk to Connor about art. Connor, after some initial surprise, was sufficiently interested to take a cautious part but Warlock, asked some abstruse question about meaning, grunted, "Whatever you think," and ignored them. Conversation wound down to bare politenesses. As a relaxation exercise it achieved nothing and I think we were all relieved when Connor shepherded us out to the interview room.

I saw that he had thought about Gus's participation and decided against sending him away at this point, possibly thinking he might have something useful to add, more likely because it might be unwise to dismiss him with a headful of unanswered questions. He could be muzzled afterwards.

He ordered extra chairs brought in and seated his interviewees in a semicircle with himself facing them and me beside him.

He did not activate the recording voxcoder.

Which meant that he relied on my wired overall for later study of the proceedings. And that nothing of the next hours would be found in police files.

The complete record would have been a nightmare for any investigator trying to read it.

The trouble with Warlock's account of what had happened to him was that it had a beginning and an end and only an indecipherable middle. What had happened in the thirty-four years of sleep—which had seemed to him only a matter of minutes— appeared to be a monstrous montage of ideas, memories, emotions, and bodiless thoughts, all inchoate and beating at an un-comprehending mind with no defense and no hiding place to escape them.

It was the fascinated Bentinck who eventually realized, in a vague fashion, some possibility of what had occurred and made suggestions that Warlock embraced like a drowning man—or like a near-mad man seeing possible sense in his flustered brain.

Frankie's story was more straightforward though with prob-lematic elements of its own. Strangely, its central figure was his father—a monster of a man whom his son's story treated with the gentleness of a nurse. He seemed actually to love the old brute.

When it was at last all done Connor said to me, "I'll have your overall, Harry."

I had badly wanted a chance to copy the recording and study it at leisure, but I handed it over without much grace. He took it, in full knowledge of my frustration, and had it sent up to the lab. I would have to do with that undependable mishmash, memory.

So I will reproduce here, as best I can, what went on down there in the darkness of two minds. If I scramble for words and stumble over clarity it is because only the two "sleepers" could adequately express what they saw and felt and experienced. If such expression is possible.

At the beginning, Frankie rehearsed rapidly the story of what had happened in his first experience of electronic hypnosis, thirty-four years earlier. "Because," he said, "I reckon it has a bearing on what happened today."

The rehearsal was little different from Steven Warlock's ac-count save that he dwelt much more heavily on the vision of his father's mouth as Hellgate. "I can't create it in words. I didn't really see it because I didn't really see anything. Down there wasn't like a place where you stand and look out. It all happens in your mind—right inside you. Everything is inside you. You aren't aware of anything except inside yourself."

(From there on he—and later Warlock—hesitated and stumbled over words in the effort to render intelligible an experience beyond simple coping in language. Metaphor helped a little but in the end led to more confusion of meaning. What follows is a condensation of their statements for clarity's sake—if clarity is possible.)

He was desperate in his attempt to present to us a picture of a happening without form or substance, of an awareness outside the senses. I had some feeling for what he tried to get across—I suppose each of us did, in his own way—but retreated from the attempt to visualize the purely mental, the thing that was inside the brain on its own utterly personal terms.

Only Warlock nodded understanding.

"So I didn't actually see my dad's mouth gaping to swallow me but I knew that's what it was, and I knew that if I fell all the way into it that would be the end of my mind. Forever. But Dr. Bentinck pulled me out, or maybe I pulled myself out in sheer fright."

Bentinck said in his usual colorless voice, "Your body was still acting normally. Your fear was great enough to overcome the isolation. It may have been coincidence that my recall whistle sounded at that point. How long did it seem to you that you were under hypnosis?"

"Two or three minutes."

Yet Warlock's years had seemed—or so he had declared—to take no time at all.

Bentinck made no comment, said only, "Go on to the next experience."

"The second time was different. I went into isolation with Brian on my mind because I had to look for him and try in some way to get to him. But he wasn't there. I was looking for him in a way, but when he wasn't there I didn't know how to look. Like I said before I couldn't use my eyes because there wasn't any sight. Then I became aware of people. I think this didn't happen the first time because the nearest mind to me was Brian's and anyway I was intent as well on my own project. At any rate, in the—the emptiness, I felt Dr. Bentinck's mind close to me in some way and the pastor in the audience and Miss Wishart, but those two weren't interested in me, they were concentrated on Brian. There were people all around but they weren't important; just the scientists, I suppose, looking on. And my father. He was thinking of me—with love, the sort of love he never showed for me in his life. And he was crying. How can I tell you? His heart was crying."

He stopped, at a loss. No one spoke. After a while he went on. "I've looked after the old bastard all these years and never knew what he felt. If only he could have said, even once . . . It was like being swamped in love. It was all around me, swallowing me just the way his vengeful mouth had opened for me before, and the two things came together in my mind and all I had was the sense of being—how can I put it?—engulfed. All the love and all the holy vengeance, together, and me sinking in it like something I could never escape from and all I could think of was waking up before I drowned. Then I did wake up and this man was holding me down and I think I was screaming."

Gus said, like a self-satisfied alligator, "You had a fair head of steam up; stretched me a bit, you did. But no harm done."

Bentinck was less satisfied. "You made no contact at all with Mr. Warlock?"

"Not a bit. I was wholly taken up with my dad."

Bentinck swung on Warlock. "Then what brought you back to consciousness?"

Warlock seemed to think about it. At last he decided, "I suppose you could say at bottom Frankie did."

I had a sickening feeling that Warlock was about to complicate the threads of experience past unraveling. No reason had yet appeared to suggest why Miraflores should want to assert a moral right (based on some exotic sacred law of his own devising?) to custody of Warlock, even less why Frankie should chatter about murder of a kurdaitcha man, whatever he might be. We were rapidly approaching "ghoulies an' gaisties," table rapping and Dream Time.

"That was part of it," Warlock said, "but it isn't easy to sort out. Everything happening at the same time—I'll never make you see that. But it wasn't so at first. At first I was just going down in the dark. Not like Frankie. He seems to have felt things emotionally and had no sensual input, whereas I am a visual artist and perhaps I reacted visually. Even his father's gaping mouth was lifted from my mind—I think. It was my visualization of Frankie's idea of the old man's rage that gave him the sight of it."

This promised to become unintelligible, but Connor was paying the close attention of a chela to a guru while Gus showed open-mouthed wonder—but Gus's childlike streak was always ready and waiting. Frankie nodded as if it made sudden sense, explaining some aspect he had failed to grasp, while Bentinck wore what I suspected was his therapist's face of passive acceptance before blandly making all plain.

"But at first it was just blackness and falling. Not really falling but a sensation of falling. Falling down my own mind, perhaps. I could feel Frankie there and see his mind full of stuff about little boys who all seemed to be himself, and a mirror of himself as a child. And his father's face like vengeance incarnate. Then it was as if I fell deeper into my own mind, right into the thing I was supposed to be searching for—and there it was. Call it artistic expression if you like and if that means anything to you—it doesn't mean much to me. Only words. I was in a place. I don't know what place. Just a place full of light and color and form, all moving and changing shape and meaning. It was my wife and my son and all sorts of people I've loved. Frankie seems to have seen them as people with bodies and faces because that was the only way he could translate my feeling into a form he could understand, but for me it was the vision I always dreamed of getting on canvas, the perfect expression of people, not what they look like but what they really are to someone who cares—the perfect painting of my love for them. I know I'm not making it clear but it's the best I can do. I could have stayed there forever, examining my own art. For that's what it amounted to—the selfishness of my own perfection. Because even love is a final possessive selfishness, isn't it?"

I remember thinking, That's Brian Warlock seeing himself, but all people aren't introverted artists; they might see differently. Then, again, perhaps he was right . . .

"I might have been held there, looking at myself so to speak, but Frankie was intruding. His mind was howling. I don't mean making a sound but making the feeling of it. Absolute terror and panic. I was absorbed but his fear encroached so badly that I looked at his mind—that is, I contacted . . . or just paid attention to . . . or became aware of him . . . I don't know how to express it—to see what bothered him and try to shut it out. I saw a great head, blood-red with rage and vengeance, drawing him down into its throat. I knew it wasn't real, only a creation of his mind, and in some way—perhaps from his mind—I knew the monstrous thing was his father. As he told you, our minds were open to each other. I don't mean telepathy, because there were other minds around, too, but not so clear, more as if they were farther away. But with Frankie it was like being in two minds at once. Then he vanished; his whole mind simply blanked out and I was alone except for the murmur of other minds at a distance. I didn't know where he had gone."

"Back to real life," Frankie told him in a hard, strangled voice. "I rolled off the table and broke my shoulder and a couple of ribs."

Bentinck said, "Shut up, Frankie. Mr. Warlock, how long did all this seem to take?"

"Hard to say. A few minutes, I suppose. A bit longer than it takes to tell it."

"But you retained a definite sense of time passing?"

"Up till then, yes."

Bentinck sat back, apparently satisfied.

Warlock continued, "The next part is harder to put into words. I was still with my visions of form and color but I had a sense of more behind them, as if there was a deeper truth to find—and I still had this falling sensation—and I wanted to know what it was. Remember I'd had psychologists poking this need to know into my head until I couldn't ignore it had I wanted to. So I fell—further into my mind, I suppose—and saw what might have been the answer but I didn't understand what it meant and still don't.

Besides, I was past stopping to look. I can't describe it; it was as if there was an end and I reached it. As if, as if . . . That's how it all seems. Can you grasp the idea of pure thinking without pictures or words or even ideas relating to each other? It was like being wide open and having perceptions pour into me. Everything at once."

He paused and into his silence Bentinck dropped an emotionless, colorless question. "Perceptions of what?"

"I said—everything. I meant 'everything.' And all at once. The—the place—was full of thought. There was nothing else, nothing to see or experience but the bombardment of minds. I knew they were minds, or even thoughts without minds, so many of them that they could have been all of human thinking since thinking began. Maybe longer. There were thoughts there so self-centered and stark that they could have been the ideas of animals, pure greed or defensiveness or the expulsion at birth, and others so complex as to be meaningless to me. They came from the past and the present and just sometimes I caught hints of what they were but they were all mixed together in a great combined yell. Hardly anything came through that made connection. Anyway, they weren't people from the past, only their ideas, their thoughts. And they slid into each other and joined and separated."

He stopped again, then said, "I'm not making any sense, am I? I don't think I can. I'm not capable . . ."

Bentinck said, "It doesn't matter. You have tried. You can think about it and find better words. How long did this phase seem to last?"

"I told you it was everything at once. There wasn't any time." Warlock began to sound surly, like a man who has done his best and knows he has failed. "I mean time didn't exist there. It might have been an age or a couple of seconds; there was no way of telling. It just happened. It wasn't a phase; it was an instant of total perception of all things at once. And then I came back."

"After thirty-four years! What brought you back?"

Warlock made a helpless gesture. "I'm not sure. It had to do with Frankie."

"Before that. You had a muscular fit on the table four days ago, before waking."

Warlock nodded. "There was a thing happened but I can't tell when. There was no time there, only an instant of happening. There was a thought down there, mixed up with all the other perceptions, but strong as though it made an effort to come through to me—to me especially because all the other perceptions were simply there, in existence for anyone to pick up. There was an Australian aboriginal. I don't mean that I saw him, only that I knew what he was in the—the uproar of thought. He brought with him the red image of Frankie's father and was forcing my mind into the gulf of its throat. It was a vision of rage and vengeance but had no meaning for me. It terrified me and I had the urge to escape but there was no place for flight. That may have been when my body reacted, but I don't know; there was no orientation in time, no then or now or when. Perhaps I shifted back a little way then, because I suddenly had Frankie's mind with me again and he was struggling to escape the red mouth and I struggled too, because his terror engulfed me. There was noise around me and a strong light in my eyes and I came to. Frankie was fighting with the orderly here and I was in a strange place."

11

What to make of it all? For myself, I made nothing, save for some idea of an instantaneous dream in the second before waking. Frankie seemed thoughtful but unsure of his thoughts and Connor bemused, but Gus, my good friend and repository of miscellaneous garbage, was swelling with an idea.

"There was a bloke last century said thoughts never get lost. He did experiments with rats—"

What shook me, shook all of us, I think, was not that Bentinck shut up a gabbling amateur but the violence of the shutting. He yelled at Gus from a face contorted with anger, "Don't peddle that discredited rubbish to me, you ignorant Wardie ratbag!"

I had never before seen a man actually tremble with fury, but Bentinck did. The fit lasted only a moment but it was an electrifying sight in that small room, and it was, I thought, a fury with a touch of fear behind it, as though a nerve had been exposed, a rage out of all proportion to its cause. And "ignorant Wardie ratbag" had had a shock effect; in that day of extreme social distinctions and equally extreme tenderness of feelings a careful person did not use terms to another that bared an intellectual and class-inferiority distinction so frankly.

I fancied for a moment that Gus would hit him, but he had nous enough to swallow his temper and study his shoes. Then Bentinck took charge of his brain and body, to say, "I'm sorry, Mr. . . . ," and floundered because he could not remember Gus's name. He repeated, "I'm sorry, but I hear so much of these ancient, discredited ideas in my professional life."

And the moment passed. But I remembered the fear behind the outburst and determined to quiz Gus's memory at the first opportunity.

Connor, with regal imperturbability, suggested, "Perhaps you could give us your ideas about these recollections, Doctor."

Bentinck shook his head. "It will require some consideration. A snap judgment is out of the question. The time element alone . . ." He let it trail off.

"Very well, Doctor—some time for thought. Could I have your preliminary ideas in, say, two days?"

But Bentinck had recovered himself. "No, you could not. Science is not handed out by the bagful for easy consumption and I'll have nothing to say until I am sure that what I say is right and backed by facts."

I expected Connor to try to pin him down to a time but he let it ride. "Then I must make do with Mr. Devalera's suspicions of murder. He will remain. The rest of you may go about your business. Detective Sergeant Ostrov, you can escort Mr. Warlock to his home."

Bentinck protested, "Frankie has passed through a traumatic interlude today. I should be on hand to support and interpret."

"I had imagined Mr. Warlock would be your immediate care."

"He would be if your detective had not interfered. I will now have to depend on Warlock's goodwill to remain in contact with me."

Connor offered a bright smile. "Yes, you will, won't you? Go home, Doctor; you've finished here. Go home and ponder today's results." The smile faded. "Or report to your Pastor of Lambs. Perhaps he will find it worth his while to visit me. Or not."

Bentinck's face had shown some animation, a little but not much. Now, as Connor chose to prod him, it faded back to its uncommunicating norm.

He made no answer. He simply walked out.

"Wondering," Connor said, "how much I really know."

"Which is?" I suggested.

"As much as yourself. I suspect something—but what? We must ask Frankie what his worries are. They may be revealing."

He turned to Gus. "You had best go home. You should not have been recruited in the first place."

"But I was. Me and Harry—"

"I know about you and Harry. Go home, man; keep your mouth shut and your head down."

Gus wheedled, "If there's anything I can do—"

"Go home! If a detective gets his silly head blown off, that's in the line of duty; if you get hurt it could cost me my job."

Gus went in silence, wearing the look of a deprived child who sees the forbidden candy in the selfish grasp of another.

Connor addressed Warlock. "Now that you've spilled some of your load, are you ready to see your wife?"

Warlock took his time about answering. At last he said, "As ready as I'll ever be. At least she'll give me something to eat."

Connor, taken aback, began to apologize and Warlock waved

him to be quiet. "Maybe when I see her I'll have more time to think if my mouth's full."

What do you say to that kind of remark? Connor recovered sufficiently to tell me to take a car and see the man home. "We'll let Devalera stew for an hour until you come back."

My "sick" day was developing overtime proportions but I couldn't complain that it was dull. As we went to book out a hover-car the only thing Warlock said, in a tone of tired puzzlement, was, "I can't realize that my Stevie's dead."

12

It turned out that the Warlock home was not far from the Psych-Bio Complex, in what might be called upper-middle-class Melbourne—a condition well beyond my means but without quite the sprawling opulence of the Minder sectors. It seemed that in his day (that I had to remind myself antedated mine by two generations) he had been a more successful artist than my ignorance had imagined. He was a man who had reached his height in the Dancing Thirties, when people spent as though money were made in heaven and rained down on a verdant earth.

His home was a brick-and-timber period piece from the middle-twentieth century, comfortably placed on the "quarter acre block" described as the ideal of the time.

I'd have given ten years of my lifespan for its comfortable spaciousness.

We pulled up at the grass verge of the footpath and Warlock said, almost under his breath, "Hasn't changed much," and then, like a disappointed complaint, "Those sunblinds are new."

He sat, making no move to get out.

I nudged him gently. "Would you like me to go in first?"

He nodded. He was crying. So, in his place, I might have been, in fear of such a meeting.

The path to the front porch ran between smoothly trimmed lawns and stands of roses, red, white, and golden yellow, and there was no bell on the door, only an old-fashioned iron knocker that I banged a couple of times uncertainly, unsure of the "olde worlde" protocol. Feet sounded softly inside, a chain rattled in disengagement and the door opened a crack through which I was examined by suspicious gray eyes.

"Who are you?" The voice was ungracious and I realized that I was in, instead of uniform, a Wardie work overall I had drawn from store when Connor commandeered mine.

I held out my ID for her to see as I said, "Detective Sergeant Ostrov, madam."

She opened the door wide and I saw that she was slender and gray-haired and blessed with the agelessness that comes to some women and just a few men in the late years of their lives, but at sight of my ID her face fell apart into age and foreboding and she plucked at her lips with thin, trembling fingers.

She whispered, "Is it Brian? My husband? Why do they send a policeman? What has happened to him? Dr. Bentinck was so sure . . ."

Is it part of our rotting world that the appearance of a policeman means disaster and fear? I said, "He's alive and well and awake." The enormous relief in her had me leaning to support her as I gabbled some nonsense about, "Tired and a bit stiff; probably needs a rest," but she pushed me aside with sudden strength.

"Where is he? Is the doctor holding him?"

"He is here, with me. In the car."

"Then why—?" Her face altered again and the whole weight of her years flooded into the expression of her dread. "Has it all—changed him? In some way?"

I tried for a cheerful note and probably sounded like an idiot. "No, the silly man's just nervous because it's been such a long time."

"Nervous!" It was a cry of outrage. Then she looked down at her wrinkled hands and spidery fingers and felt at the skin of her cheeks and neck. "Yes, a long time."

I heard the gate creak as it opened and I turned to see that the painter had braved his nerves to come to the house with the lingering steps of a truant boy. She brushed by me to run down the path like an excited girl.

They did not kiss but flung their arms about each other and stood cheek to cheek in the avenue of roses, swaying together like young lovers in ecstasy.

It was time for me to leave. I went across the lawn rather than disturb them—though I fancy they would not have noticed me—but still was able to hear one of those exchanges that remain with you.

She said, "I'm sorry I've grown old, dear." It was a tiny, tremulous phrase, alive with apprehension.

And he gave the reply that nobody else could have done, "What is 'old'? I paint you, not skin and bone."

In God's name, what did he see when he looked at her? She was a fairly ordinary woman who had, I thought, never been a really pretty one, but he saw a reality beyond the flesh, a reality for his eyes alone. With a shiver for the man who had "seen" so many things down there in darkness, I wondered for a crazy moment if he could see a soul.

That led, in the intricate, hidden way of mental association, to the possible reason for "Jesus" Miraflores's foolish attempt to assert a moral right to the custody of Warlock. I suspected we had not heard the last of that piece of silly desperation.

13

When I got back to Connor's office Frankie was sitting there, silently bored stiff. I guessed Connor had been, for whatever reason (perhaps a softening-up process, perhaps no more than a simple disinclination to talk) giving him the "too busy for chatter" treatment, but when I entered he asked cheerfully, "How went the meeting between youth and crabbed age?"

With the surprise and wonder of it still on me, I was not inclined to match his lightness. "Better than I feared or expected."

Before he could dig for more that I was not prepared to give, Frankie asked, "Don't you even care, Superintendent?"

Connor studied him as an odd specimen before he said, "No, I don't suppose I do; I am simply interested in an unusual human problem. Should I therefore assume an air of muted awe or smarmy solicitude? We deal in practical matters here and there's little room for emotional response. So let us be practical." He glanced quickly at me and I activated the voxcode on the wall, priming it to record and print out the proceedings. "Why are you here?"

"Hasn't the D told you?"

"You tell me."

"He promised me police protection."

Connor toyed with a pencil—and with Frankie. "Detective Sergeant Ostrov had no authority to make such a promise. However, he used a serious charge, which he admits to be baseless, in order to bring you here. Why, Sergeant?"

"I need to know what he has to tell."

"And what have you to tell, Mr. Devalera? Aside from the matter of an illusory protection there is your duty as a citizen to reveal factual information relevant to the investigations of the police."

"Get stuffed," Frankie said. "You're a bag of wind. I'll talk to the D."

(Good for you, Frankie!)

Connor was unshaken. "Who has promised more than he can deliver. Who are you afraid of?"

Frankie stayed mulishly silent.

"The probability seems to be that you fear some members of the Church of Universal Communication; in an outburst earlier you mentioned murder to Dr. Bentinck—who is a member of that church—and will no doubt, in spite of my forbidding, relay the information to others. So they will know—possibly already know—that you will be explaining that mention to us."

"I want protection."

"Earn it."

I could understand why Connor did not want to commit himself. Murder was all too easy a crime in a city dominated by the warrens of the Suss Wardies and where electronic detection methods made hiding nearly impossible from those who could command the necessary equipment; even the addition of a false name could be traced to its cut-off point. Police protection was a precarious promise at best and an incredibly expensive one to carry out. I admit that we made such promises and in honesty tried to keep them, but they were vaporous stuff. (And in the backs of all our minds was the appalling population surplus and the blind fact that every death by our failure was to the advantage of the planet.) And who am I to criticize Connor for backing away from an almost worthless promise made by a man—me—who in his heart knew the minuscule value of it?

Frankie was aware of all this. Everybody was. So it must be an urgent affair that caused him to fight for even so doubtful a protection.

"Once it is known that you are here," said Connor, "your vulnerability is exposed to the church. Say what you have to say and we will do our best for you. We pay for value received."

In a pre-debased coinage.

Frankie was caught and knew it; whether he spoke or not he was caught. I could only hope that his statement would sway Connor toward protection.

Connor waited long enough to underscore his point, then moved to business. "I don't read you as a religious man. What is your connection with Miraflores's church?"

"Just a parishioner." The three words made a slow, unwilling submission to necessity.

Connor was brusque. "Nonsense, man! I have read Steven Warlock's statement to the police, so I know that Miraflores was a member of your household as a boy."

"Okay, but I don't know anything about the statement. You know about my time in prison, and what for?"

"Yes. A psychological aberration. Since no recurrence is recorded I assume you were treated successfully. By Dr. Bentinck. Is it relevant?"

"Yes." He had made up his mind and was answering easily now. "My father was—still is—a religious nut. I'm an atheist, whatever that means, but my father was one of the Independent Salvationists—that's what they called themselves back then—used to preach hellfire and brimstone with all the other food cranks and political ratbags on the Yarra bank. He was ashamed of me, of course, but he loved me in his crazy way and when I got jailed he must have missed me because he adopted this Holy Joe of a kid. I don't know where he got him—I didn't want to know because it surely wasn't legal—but he just about fell in love with him and his Bible talk, and when the little bugger claimed to be Jesus the old man fell for it like a revelation. I don't know whether the kid believed it himself or was just squeezing his grip on a home and free meals, but he had brains, and even in his teens he started gathering disciples. He was a dab hand with people, could manipulate them like a con artist, and he soon got a couple of Minder women behind him with the funds to found the church. He consecrated my old man a bishop, would you believe? I joined the church to keep an eye on Dad because I was worried about the money collections and the possibility of him getting into trouble about the way it was spent without any accounting or audits, just as young Jesus willed. The young fellow didn't believe I was genuine but I think he reckoned it best to have me where he could see whatever I might be up to—which wasn't much because I just watched and worried about him or Dad making some damn fool mistake. Also, he was interested in the electrohypnosis experiment and kept asking me about it as if I might remember some important fact that would give him a clue to whatever was in his mind about it. Then he got on to Bentinck."

Frankie paused, eyeing us speculatively. Connor waited.

"Can you see Bentinck as a hanger-on of a shonky religion?

GEORGE TURNER

Can you? I never did. Still, Jesus recruited him a couple of years back and he came every Sunday to the service, but it always seemed to me he was under pressure. I remembered him, of course, and after thirty years he didn't look any different. Juvenation job, of course. But when?''

A moot question. Juvenation treatment, which could add decades to a normal life, had been outlawed in 2041, worldwide, as part of the antipopulation movement, but money could always find a way. The rejuvenating process, which shaved years off an aging body, was easily detected but juvenation, by the "antisenescence hormone" method when applied to a young body could only be suspected until too many years of youthfulness made it obvious. After so much time there was no way of proving when the operation took place.

"I reckoned it was blackmail, that Bentinck had had a hormone job after the legal cutoff and Jesus had some way of proving it. He wanted Bentinck to revive Warlock and either he provided the funding or got it somewhere—maybe from Wishart.''

Connor said softly, "Ah!''

"He's close with Valda Wishart but I don't know what her interest is. She doesn't attend the church. The other one he got on to was Steven Warlock. That was just about the time Valda turned up. Jesus recruited Steven to the church and kept questioning him about his father and me. Valda was in on that, too, very interested. I think Steven woke up to something he wasn't intended to know, because they killed him. He wasn't drowned in the river as it was reported; it was done somewhere else and they dumped the body in the river after.''

Connor asked sharply, "Can you prove that?''

"No, but I worked it out. There were a lot of little things that added up.''

Connor's sigh would have fanned a bushfire. "We'll come back to it. Go on.''

"The next one Jesus got hold of was Jimmy Gordon. He was an aboriginal but I don't know his tribal name. He was supposed to be a kurdaitcha man—a sort of magician, talking with spirits and all that.''

"Not quite," Connor said, and gave one of his displays of odd knowledge (for the benefit of the voxcode, I suspected). "The kurdaitcha is, factually, a pair of shoes made of emu feathers and pointed at both ends to deceive a tracker as to the direction taken. By association the word means generally a 'trickster.' Or it may mean simply 'evil.' There are variant forms of the word in different tribes with different meanings and attributes attached to them. Sometimes it translates roughly as a magician or a man with special powers, such as the ability to make spiritual journeys outside the body or communicate at a distance, perhaps even to contact the spirits of native legend, who are very real beings to the tribal aborigine. You shouted at Dr. Bentinck that your kurdaitcha man was murdered. Explain."

Frankie hesitated like a man unsure of himself. "I don't know where Jesus got hold of him and he didn't become a member of the church, but he had him in with me for questioning about what he saw and heard in trance states. Valda sat in on these sessions, too. Jesus should have known better because the aboriginal adepts, or whatever they call themselves, never reveal such secrets except to others who have been formally initiated into the knowledge—and especially not to a woman. Even I know that much. Anyway, Jimmy wouldn't talk. He was pretty dignified about it, just refusing to break tribal law, but Jesus was just about out of his mind at someone refusing him what he wanted. I knew he had a maniac ego and a foul temper out of sight of the congregation but now he behaved like a lunatic—threatened Jimmy with all the seven hells and eternal torments, as though he really believed in that junk. Jimmy listened and told him quietly that he was an evil man who deserved a pointing. I think he meant a pointing of the bone. They say that if a magician 'points the bone' at you, you go into a decline and die. What hit me was that Jesus took that seriously; he really believed he was under some kind of psychological threat. Jimmy walked out on him, wanting nothing more to do with him, and Jesus watched him go with a sort of rage and terror on his face. He screamed at all of us to go away, to leave him alone. Well, Jimmy never reached home that night. Early-shift Wardies found him in the gutter a mile away with stab wounds back and front."

He stopped abruptly. Connor said nothing but punched up the Murder file on his desk screen. "Unsolved."

Only one of hundreds in the course of a year.

He continued reading. "Richmond; a mile or so from your church. The body was discovered last Thursday morning—on the morning of the first attempt to rouse Warlock. You knew this at the time, Mr. Devalera?"

"Yes."

"So it was on your mind during the revival procedure?"

"Very much so. I was sure Jesus was responsible—that he had sent somebody after Jimmy—and his interest in the experiment was becoming sinister. Dangerous."

"And Warlock claims an aboriginal presence was connected with the terror that awakened him. Was he, perhaps, aware of your thinking? You were close-by, with Gordon on your mind, and your mind is one with which he is in a sense familiar."

"But he didn't wake till four days later."

"I realize it, but time seems to be a variable component of his dreaming." A peculiar expression flitted across Connor's face, as if he had fathered a thought too incredible to entertain. He repeated, as if to banish it, "Dreaming!" Then, in a normal tone, he said, "I take it you think the unconsecrated Reverend Ricardo Miraflores had Gordon murdered?"

"He believed his life was in danger. You should have seen his face."

"We can't arrest him for his face, Mr. Devalera. Is his face and a rather dubious threat all you have to offer? That and a theory about the death of Steven Warlock?"

Frankie said stubbornly, "I've seen him in anger and in fear and I'm sure there are wicked things going on in that church. When he wants something he'll stop at nothing. I'm afraid of him.

I want him stopped but I'm afraid for my own life since the sergeant arrested me."

"I'm sure you are. Possibly with reason. Switch off the voxcode, Harry." I did so. "Mr. Devalera, I'm going to take you with us while Detective Sergeant Ostrov and I visit Mr. Warlock. He should have recovered from his transports of joy by now, sufficiently to realize he must answer more questions than he will find welcome. Tell me, Mr. Devalera, have you heard of morphic resonance?"

"No."

"Harry?"

"No, sir."

"No? Well, it's an old forgotten business, but I keep thinking of that aborigine in Warlock's vision—or in his 'apprehension,' of whatever kind. Let's be on our way before common sense rejects the thing out of hand."

14

Warlock came to the door, all animosity and rejection, ready to tell any caller to go to hell. I could hardly blame him. At sight of the three of us he held his temper with a surly "Can't I be free of people for an hour? What do you want?"

Connor was placatory. "I understand, Mr. Warlock. You need privacy, naturally enough, but a matter has come up that needs immediate attention." He was all contrition and gentlemanly smarm. A great actor had been lost to the soap opera tradition. "I assure you we will take only a few minutes of your time. May we come in?"

Warlock stood holding the door, hating all of us, till he said grudgingly, "I hope it is as important you say," and I wondered what Connor would have done if he had slammed it in our faces.

But he stood aside and ushered us down the passage to the drawing room.

"It's the bloody police, dear," he said to his wife while I took in the table, set with used plates, cups, and saucers. After all the drama they had settled down to a cosy cup of tea! Mrs. Warlock rose to greet us.

Warlock made introductions and she played the gracious hostess, save that to Frankie she said with distinct disapproval, "Mr. Devalera and I have met previously."

Warlock said hastily, "That was all long ago. Please sit down, gentlemen. Now what can I do for you, Superintendent?"

Connor went straight into it. "You will have gathered that some criminal activities have attended your awakening and are under investigation."

"Yes, but I don't know what has been going on and I don't think I want to know."

"I sympathize, but a man has been murdered and a section of your statement may have some relevance."

Warlock studied the super as if he had proposed a fantasy. "How could it? If you need interpretation you might try Bentinck."

"No, sir. It concerns something sighted around about the moment of your awakening."

"I explained to you that I was in darkness."

"Nevertheless, you received impressions of various sorts. Not with the eyes, if I have understood you correctly, but directly to the brain, just as the surround of murmuring thoughts impinged directly on your mind. Does that express it?"

"Near enough." His bad temper had subsided into watchful grumpiness.

"I am interested in the aboriginal who seems to have brought the Hellmouth vision. How did you identify him as such if you did not see him?"

Warlock said slowly, "I didn't see him because there was no seeing in that place, only knowledge of what things were and what thinking took place."

"What things were? Could it be that the mind took things in

without activating the senses—but storing them in the same way?"

Warlock closed his eyes and after a few seconds said, "Millie, do you have paper and a charcoal pencil?"

She said placidly, "Of course. The studio and everything in it is ready for you to take up work again."

She had never doubted his return. My spine crawled at the thought of that ghostly waiting.

She left the room and returned with pencil and sketchbook. Warlock took them silently and with the sketchbook on his knees made a couple of sweeping strokes to outline a face. More carefully he filled in features. The whole drawing took him about three minutes.

When it was done he gazed at it for a little while in puzzlement before handing it to Connor. "It's crude, more like a cartoon, but it's a drawing of something I never consciously saw."

Connor handed it to Frankie. "Know him?"

Frankie's hand shook as he took it. "It's Jimmy Gordon."

Warlock said, "There was a feeling of anger and blood. Blood all over him."

Connor was exultant. "Indeed there was, and he used Devalera's memories to wake you. It sounds very much as if he gave you a considerable fright in order to send you scurrying for safety in the only direction you knew—back to full consciousness."

Warlock didn't much like the "scurrying for safety" description and he answered only a surly, "That seems to fit."

"But why did he do it?"

"He'd been killed, hadn't he? I suppose he wanted somebody to know."

"Mr. Warlock, you didn't tell us this before. Why not?"

Warlock glowered. "You had me there for two hours trying to make sense of what had happened to me. I told you the main things and you and Bentinck between you kept on questioning—mostly questions I couldn't answer because I just didn't know what anything meant, and that includes half the questions. Do you think I told every detail of what happened in my mind? There were a million things! It was like having the history of everybody stuffed into your brain in a single big block of impression. I didn't know what was relevant and what wasn't. I could talk for a week and keep remembering new details; I probably will when Bentinck starts wringing me dry."

If Warlock was telling the truth (and why should he not?) the real wonder was that he had escaped with a sane mind. The bombardment of information was unimaginable. I could only suppose that the overloaded brain had shut out everything but the strongest impressions.

If Connor sympathized he was not in caring mode.

"Who killed him? Did he tell you?"

Warlock snarled at him, "Nobody told me anything. All I received were thoughts. He was thinking about Jesus, if that makes any sense."

"Indeed it does, Mr. Warlock; indeed it does." He had what he had come for and stood up to go. "You've been very helpful, sir, though it's not the kind of evidence acceptable in a courtroom. We'll try to leave you alone for a couple of days. Good afternoon, Mrs. Warlock."

He led us out in an undignified hurry. As we piled into the hovercar he said, "We must see that the news gets to little Jesus. And tell him death was too late to prevent the bone pointing, shall we? Then we'll see how holy orders stack up against tribal ritual."

Frankie said, "You don't believe in that stuff, do you?"

"Wrong question. Ask, does Miraflores believe in it?"

15

An Incommunicado Remand Cell (in copper talk, a "blindhole") was a desolate room, soundproofed and solitary in every fashion, furnished with bed, table, clotheshooks, toilet, shower stall, and a bell for summoning a warder—a cell built for the preservation of valuable and vulnerable prisoners. Even the surveillance cameras were removed; in that age of technological virtuosity they could be tapped by interested parties to identify and even flash messages to the inmate. Only an elaborate routine of peephole inspection allowed certainty that he or she was still alive; food was served and dishes removed by a closely supervised wall dispenser. Nevertheless invasions of one kind or another had occurred and on two occasions in thirty years or so inmates had been killed by those requiring their silence. It was a time when murder was commonplace; respect for life was not a prime commandment in a world wherein the vast bulk of population had no hope of rising out of Suss poverty and nurtured little morality beyond self-preservation. Even those of us who saw ourselves as conventionally moral had enough of the pervading steel in our souls to accept the status quo and lose no sleep over it; things were as they were and all we could do was deal with them on their own terms.

It is no doubt wrong of me to regard today's tranquil citizenry, living virtually crimeless lives in Wishart's flat, dull Garden of Eden, with impatience and some disdain. God knows I have no call to criticize righteousness but I confess to a hankering for the life in our old labyrinthine cities with the leaven of alert watchfulness for danger.

Be that as it may, Frankie was happy to embrace his safe solitude. "No electronic snoopery?" he asked, and on being assured, said, "Now we can talk the real stuff."

He sounded chipper, insouciant, a Wardie streetboy on top of the world, but as I turned from shutting the door behind us I saw in his face an instant of destruction before he caught my eye on him and resumed the mask of self-possession. But I had seen the depth of his haunting; he was afraid, and had been since he had made up his mind to talk. He was still afraid because he knew the fragility of any defense against ruthlessness.

But he had made his play and must live with it, so we sat ourselves on the bed, on each side of him, to talk "the real stuff" while I made notes in that outdated mode, shorthand, which—in my personal version, at any rate—few could read.

Connor asked straightaway, "What is your position in Miraflores's church?"

Frankie answered, "None. Member, parishioner, dogsbody. You asked me that before."

Connor sighed at a backward pupil. "And received an answer full of omissions. Now I ask it again, expecting better. How does a simple parishioner come to suspect dark deeds in high places? By way, perhaps, of the father bishop?"

Frankie appeared to suffer a moment of internal argument before he made a grudging answer. "I didn't want to drag Dad into it."

"A laudable son! Now let's have the extended version of the story."

"All right, then. Jesus hates me from the guts up, but I'm useful to him. You'll have my history, so you'll know I came out of jail in 'thirty-six. Well, I got home to find Dad had adopted this ratbag kid with a big idea of himself and I wasn't happy about it, but Dad fell for the new messiah stuff and was up to the ears in preaching the new gospel. I treated the kid like a joke and the young bastard called down hellfire on me after death. It wasn't a happy house. He was only nineteen when he started campaigning for a big congregation and the Jesus stuff really took off. He was top of the pops for the rich Minder bitches and at twenty-two he had his church and Dad became a sort of icon because he did the preaching while the young feller ministered—that's his word—to the private souls of the members with money and influence. He was a bloody good businessman, the young feller.

"Well, he created Dad a sort of bishop, head of the pulpit side while Jesus did the promotional work. Jesus got himself a holy manse where he could operate in private but Dad was a natural-born anchorite or whatever, so we stayed in our house with me working to keep him. The congregation saw him for a real holy man. Then he had a mild stroke and finished up a bit rocky on his pins and started getting forgetful to the point where people would see there was something missing. So I had to look after him, even standing behind him in the pulpit in some vestments Jesus dreamed up, and prompting him in whispers.

"Dad wouldn't let anybody else do it and the messiah just had to put up with me because the members thought Dad was right next to him in holiness. For me it meant being on duty at all hours, with the sewage job and everything. I suppose I could have walked out on him, but after all he's still the dad and, well, I didn't want strangers getting at him.

"Besides, he tells me things. I don't mean he drops secrets but he says things without remembering what else he's said some other time, and I put two and two together and come up with conclusions about things—like where a lot of the church's money goes."

He paused as if he had reached a point of significance.

Connor obliged. "Unnumbered bank accounts, perhaps?"

"Some. But a lot goes to labs owned by the Wishart group."

He paused again. More significance.

Connor asked, "And?"

"I've looked Wishart up—vid files and such."

"And?"

"He had something to do with the Devil's Flu. Not a nice man. I wouldn't reckon he goes to church much."

"Quite," said Connor, "and, that being so, let us talk about murder."

"The abo bloke?"

" 'Abo' is a prohibited term. In Victoria the approved description is 'Koori.' "

Connor's voice was tight with disapproval; it was not a part of his act. Words like "wog," "nigger," and "abo" were a social no-no, even subjects for defamation actions, but few people made much fuss about them and the Suss Wardies used worse. I looked across at Connor, wondering was there perhaps some Koori in his lineage, but if so it was not obvious; plenty of people sported the odd Koori in the bloodline (and in truth there are almost no pure-blooded races on the planet) but it was a mite old-fashioned to be uptight about it—unless you were Minder with class affectations, which a serving police officer certainly was not.

Frankie also seemed surprised but he said, straightfaced, "All right, Koori, then."

Connor relaxed. "I was not thinking of Mr. Gordon's death so much as that of Steven Warlock."

"I can't prove anything about him."

"But you suspect. Why?"

"Well, Jesus was always asking about the hypnosis experiment right from the first time he heard about it as a kid at home, fascinated by it. Some of his dislike of me was because I wouldn't discuss it with him. Why should I give such a private experience to a nosy kid? He tried to pump Bentinck but the doctor brushed him off, too. He had some fancy idea about people being able to communicate below the level of ordinary thought."

"As a boy he thought that?"

"No; that came later."

"And the fact is that in your first trial, you and Warlock did communicate by thought."

Frankie shook his head. "No, no. We were sort of aware of each other's ideas and visions but we weren't passing messages or anything like that."

"And, later on, Miraflores called his. . . . establishment . . . the Church of Universal Communication."

"What about it?"

"I am trying to fathom the nature of his interest. Did he ever mention morphic resonance?"

"You asked that before, too, and I told you no."

"Are you absolutely sure he never mentioned it?"

"Not that I ever heard. What's the connection?"

"Something that Detective Sergeant Ostrov's friend, Kostakis, had started to say when Dr. Bentinck shouted him down. Quite savagely. Let us return to Steven Warlock."

I remembered that Gus had begun to say something about rats running mazes, some jewel of strangeness his magpie mind had lighted on and preserved and produced in time to have it crushed at first hearing. Bentinck had done more than simply reduce him to silence—he had exploded in a passion of destruction. I had put it down to nerves and tension; now I saw that I had missed a possible clue.

"Morphic resonance." A term to remember and pursue.

Frankie said, "I didn't suspect anything about Steven until the abo—the Koori—was knifed, and then maybe it was because I knew about the church funds going to places the accounts body knew nothing about and I was ready to suspect Jesus—he's a fake from the feet up and absolutely self-centered. All right, I grant he looked after Dad, but that's the only good thing I can say of him. He's cold-minded and cold-blooded and I reckon he's capable of murder."

He ended on a defensive note, not so sure now he had been forced to put vague suspicion into words.

"Steven Warlock," Connor prompted.

"There was a meeting the night before Steven died. It was held in the holy manse. Steven was there and Dr. Bentinck and Dad and myself—all the people that had been present when I told Mrs. Warlock what had happened to Brian under hypnosis, thirty years before. Except Mrs. Warlock herself and her lawyer. Jesus was insisting that we knew more than we had told him, even though he had himself been present and he had tried to question my memory a dozen times. Bentinck tried to calm him but he just switched his attack to the doctor, saying he knew more than he let on. In the end he lost his temper—he always did when he was crossed—and swore he would have Bentinck resuscitate Warlock. Steven said he certainly would not and he would make damned sure Mrs. Warlock would not give permission for anything to be done under Jesus' authority, because he didn't understand the man's interest in the matter and thought it was just a way of publicizing his church and making money. Steven was a member of the church but he had kept a mind of his own. Jesus screamed at him that he would go to the law to have Warlock placed in Bentinck's control on grounds of unskilled and incompetent amateur attention and Steven replied that if he tried it he would find himself under investigation for misappropriation of church funds. I don't know how he got on to that—it might have been just a guess or maybe he heard something or just worked out that there was more money than ever got accounted for—but it sent Jesus into a real screaming fit. Steven just walked out on him, with Jesus yelling after him that he would do as he was told while Dad and Bentinck tried to calm him down.

"And the next day Steven was pulled out of the river, but there was no water in his lungs. Or that's what the local talk claimed—that he was smothered somewhere and put in the water with weights. Just another unsolved murder."

"Not a skerrick of proof to ascribe guilt," Connor said.

"But the thing is, he never got to see his mother, who had custody of the sleeping body. And straightaway Bentinck got on to her and got her permission to try to wake him, saying he had got private funding to make the attempt."

Connor spread his hands. "It's tempting but it doesn't make a case. If, for instance, we knew why Miraflores so badly wanted the body wakened . . . it happens I may have an idea about it." My ears pricked up at that but he went on another tack. "Have you anything to add to your account of Gordon's death?"

"Only what I told you: he walked out on Jesus and by morning he was dead."

"Two acts of defiance followed immediately by two deaths." He turned to me with a happy smile. "And you, Harry, have snatched Warlock from his grasp. Another act of defiance!"

I was not to be baited on that count. "He won't worry over me; he'll be planning to get Warlock back."

"True. I shall arrange total surveillance for Mr. Warlock, who will have enough on his plate without a demented preacher clamoring at his heels." He stood up. "Thank you, Mr. Devalera; you will be safe here for a few days. Your mere presence in our hands should cause anxious ripples in the holy manse—particularly when we question your father's knowledge of church finances."

Frankie looked troubled. "Go easy on the old man," he said. "He's a sort of holy innocent."

Connor smiled his predatory smile. "I believe you. We will suck him dry with indirect and subtle questions, shall we not? Come along, Harry; we have thinking to do."

Our thinking didn't amount to much beyond arranging surveillance for the Warlock household that, since they lived in an outer district, had to be done through another station—twenty-four-hour camera oversight and a tail every time one of them left the house.

Once that was attended to, I had a question that had puzzled me: the matter of Frankie's vision of the Koori.

"Warlock sees him in his mental world or whatever the place is, on the morning of his murder, and gets enough of a shock to nearly pull him out of stasis; he fought like a demon before he fell back into sleep. Yet Frankie gets the vision four days later just as Warlock received it, and it wakes him up in a fighting fit without doing more than bring Warlock somehow into consciousness. It doesn't make much sense."

"It does if you accept that time does not exist in the mental universe. In the perception of Warlock and the Koori, Gordon, the two events happened simultaneously—Warlock passed the Koori's outrage to Frankie who at the same time completed Warlock's awakening."

I had to suppose he was right although I found it difficult to visualize events in a timeless universe.

In any case, I had no better suggestion and contented myself with the complaint that my "day off" had stretched itself into some ten hours' overtime. Connor, mindful of expenses, said he would have me rostered off the next day while he considered what, if any, action he could take against Miraflores. "It might be best," he concluded, "to let the holy faker make the next move."

I said that he might not be all faker, that the thing had begun too early in his life not to have some spark of genuine delusion.

"Once upon a time," Connor agreed, "but I think God has

bowed to Mammon as the possibilities for profit expanded. My main problem is his interest in morphic resonance. Why, Harry, why?"

Having no answer, I called it a day and headed for home.

As I was heading out I was paged for a vidcall. It was Gus, saying, "Come home quick!"

It had to be urgent; Gus was no ditherer.

In those days I lived in South Melbourne, fairly handy to my station at that time, and I got off the hoverbus at my street corner to see Gus waiting on the footpath.

While I still wondered what the devil might be wrong, he almost shouted at me, "Christ, but I didn't know what to do for the best."

Only an upset Gus raised his voice.

"What's happened?"

"I got home from your cop shop when it struck me I ought to tell you about morphic resonance. That's what Bentinck shut me up about in Connor's office."

I hated to tell him that Connor already knew of it. I expected him to be crestfallen but he brushed it aside.

"That don't matter now. I come back, meaning to wait in your place for you to come home, maybe have a yarn with Mrs. Ostrov, but I was about fifty meters off when a hovercar passed me and pulled up at your house and two fellers got out and went to your door. The car didn't wait but done a U-turn and come back past me, so I saw who was driving. It was Bentinck."

I think I went cold with fright for my mum and dad at home alone. "How long ago?"

"About twenty minutes."

"Did Bentinck see you?"

"Not to recognize. Back in my regular overall and with a hat on, he wouldn't notice. He didn't look at me. I waited to get a better look at the other two but your old man let them in after a bit of talk and I waited to see see what happened. It didn't look good but I knew you could look after yourself. Then I thought what if you aren't home yet? And them still inside. So I got on the corner vid and called you.''

2.

GUS KOSTAKIS

16

This is where Harry stopped writing. He stopped because (or so I reckon) this is where the thing that was going to happen next hit him so hard that he has never got over it. When it came to recording it, he just wasn't capable. He couldn't go on.

Think about what he wrote up to now and you'll see what I mean. He could see other people and write what they were like but when he tried to see hisself it was as if he couldn't bear to look too close. You don't get any real idea of the man behind the face.

Seems to me this began in Premier Beltane's office when the premier had Nguyen hit us both with his truth drug and then he asked us questions. You may have read about this already (if the book still exists in the New Age) but Nguyen's drug was one that reached to the bottom of the mind, to the real dregs, bypassing all the "intellectual" bullshit and the silly "beliefs" imposed by life in an artificial society and getting down to the dirty sludge where a man hides all the fears and hates and greeds he never admits even to hisself.

The premier asked us things that got down to what we really thought of human beings and how to treat them. When we recovered and gradually got back memory of how we had answered and how the answers showed us up as real shit, at first I think we didn't credit what it all meant. Then the premier shot hisself and the uproar kept us both busy for a couple of days, but after that the meaning of the questioning began to sink in and both of us went into the horrors at seeing what really powered our stinking souls.

It took a long time of psychiatric treatment to get us back to something like normal, with Harry looking after me like a baby. The psychs said that in the sewer depths of their minds everybody had lousy reactions and civilization was as much as anything a process of keeping the reins on basic instinct.

Well, maybe, but I still think there are natural good people in the world.

Anyways, I rocked back to an ordinary life in the end, maybe because I never had a big opinion of myself. I always knew I was second rate, with big ideas and no real brains.

But Harry never could live properly with hisself after that experience. It was more as though he mistrusted hisself, was always worrying over his real motive for doing anything, as though something sneaky and rotten had to lie behind what seemed honorable and right. He used to talk to me about it a little (after all I was his closest friend and had been through the same gut-rotting experience) but not much. It was like he would never get over seeing hisself down in the dark of truth.

Anyways, I think that's why he stopped writing—because the things that happened he didn't trust hisself to see straight.

But in the long run you can only report what happened, no matter what you think about it, so that's why I take it up—to leave a record of what happened before the arguments start and the lies and "folklore" set in.

I'm no writer and I don't even speak proper English but I've corrected everything as best I can and asked Sammy to help me when I wasn't sure.

It'd be easier talking to a voxcoder but there's no voxcoders anymore and no power to run them even if there was. People make paper but it's hard to get enough to do a lot of writing.

Still, here goes!

17

Harry was half out of his mind, thinking of the two old folks alone with a couple of thugs that must have come from the Jesus feller. He didn't show much but I know the signs in him and no matter what he was feeling it didn't stop him thinking and deciding.

He said as calm as if it was some routine job, "I'll go around the back of the house. Give me a minute's start and then knock at the front. Whoever answers, play it by ear."

Play it by ear—that's trust for you! I said, "I'm not carrying." I never carried a gun off the job. Harry always carried because his job didn't always stop when he clocked off.

He said, "No matter. They don't know you; you're just some caller," and he was off running for the back lane behind his place.

So here was defenseless me going into action against the Church of Universal Communication and all its angels.

I strolled down the street, taking it slow to give Harry time to get into position for whatever he had in mind, then knocked on the Ostrov door.

Nothing happened. I just waited, knowing there was at least four people inside but nobody answering. I knocked again with the same result. Not a sound from the house except a bit of vid-music.

I didn't like that at all and automatically I began Doc Nguyen's concentration exercise. It was something he taught me in the early days of my guard job at the Premier's Lodge, a method of channeling physical strength and mental concentration into a sort of explosive effort.

(The doc was later executed for treason against the state; I got to know some really special people back then.)

After a while there was a sort of thump from inside. Like a body falling, I thought. So I belted hard on the door, to cause an added distraction if nothing else.

What it caused was a long silence. So I belted on the door again and called out, "Police here!"

To tell the truth, although I was psyching up to full concentration on whatever action might be necessary, a part of my mind was hoping that the intruders would take fright and scarper out the back door. I was afraid that it was Harry who had taken a fall and I was on my own.

But I got a result. Footsteps came down the passage and the door opened a crack and a man put his face to it.

He looked pretty doubtfully at my overall and said, "Police, you reckon? You got ID?"

I put my left hand to my inside pocket as if I was going to produce it and, like I hoped, his eyes followed my hand. It gave me just the extra half second to push his face back inside and bash the door open against him. As he fell back I followed him in, put my other hand under his jaw and lifted him off the floor and just threw him away. The concentration lets you do that sort of thing though you pay for it in the letdown later.

I heard his head crack against the wall and it was the crack of breaking bone. I thought. Oh fuck, I've killed the bastard, and had a little vision of trial and time in jail.

But mostly my mind was on the feller's mate, who wasn't in sight, and on the fact that lifting and throwing a man of about a hundred K, one-handed, had taken most of the preparation out of me and I needed a little time to psych up again. Time I didn't have, because there was another of them and I didn't know where.

I began to pussyfoot down the passage. There was a bedroom on the right and I took a quick look in. Nobody. Nothing for it but to continue on down to the lounge room. There wasn't a sound in the place.

The first thing I saw in the lounge room was Harry, on his

face, out like a light. Entry by the back door hadn't got him any profit. There was a mark on the side of his neck, a red circle where a transcutaneous syringe had been pressed hard against the flesh, beginning to fade already. I turned him over, watching all around like a nervous cat, and saw he was still breathing.

I had seen those syringes in action—on myself and him—in Premier Beltane's office. There had been a different brew in this one but the thought of them made me feel sick.

Then I saw Harry's mum and dad, sitting on the couch as if they watched the vidscreen. They had their backs to me but I knew at once they were dead. There's something collapsed and empty about someone dead; you can tell. I shook them but it made no difference to their loose limbs and dropped jaws. Their necks were broken.

The vidscreen had no picture but it was playing some quiet music, I don't know what. I thought what this would do to Harry; it would shatter his reserve wide open. In these last months they had become the center of his life, as if to make up for the offhand way he had treated them before the questioning under Nguyen's drug had made him question hisself as well.

All the time I was watching for the other feller and hoping he had taken fright at the noise in the passage and scarpered out the back way. I went through into Harry's bedroom. Nobody there. Then the kitchen and bathroom.

Nobody. The only other door opened on to the backyard.

I yanked it open fast, expecting him to be up against the outer wall, one side or the other.

But he was standing on the doorstep, syringe at full arm's stretch and pointed at my face, and the sight of the thing sparked a panic in me. It reminded me of Nguyen and the shameful result of the injection he had spurted into me, and I hit out at the syringe instead of at the man. His hand smashed against the doorframe and he cried out in pain but didn't let go of the thing, and then he came at me like a bolting madman.

Like a bloody idiot I went to grab at him instead of the syringe and at about a meter's distance he emptied the thing full in my face. I hit him then fair in the throat and he went down choking. The stuff in the syringe wasn't pressed home properly but it spread like a cloud around my eyes and nose and mouth with a smell like incense and a taste like pepper. I hung on to the door, all at once weak as a kitten, trying to blow the stuff off me, but it was in my lungs already and I felt my hands slipping down the wood.

And that was it. Lights out.

18

Waking up was horrible. I was sick to the stomach and my head ached like the brains were trying to bust out through the skull; there was a sort of aftertaste of pepper in my mouth and I felt as if my whole body was swinging in circles. Whatever was in that syringe hit every way at once.

I laid quiet because my body didn't feel capable of much else and partly because there were voices nearby and some little bit of sense told me to lay still and listen. At first they were just voices, a light one making protesting noises and a dark bass one being contemptuous, but they made no sense through the sick uproar in my head and guts.

But after a while the swinging sensation died down and the sick stomach got quiet and I began to hear properly and I recognized the light voice as belonging to Jesus Miraflores and making the same sort of outraged noises as in the anteroom of the complex lecture room when Harry stopped him from taking Warlock away. Being kidnapped by his Church of Whatever-it-was did nothing to cheer me up; I didn't know much about him but the bits Harry had told me didn't add up to nice.

I didn't know the other voice but it was deep and dark and rumbling to some order as it told Little Jesus he was ten kinds of a bloody lunatic who shouldn't be let off his lead rope. "A policeman, by God! They protect their own, you fool! A missing policeman is not some nameless Wardie left dead in a gutter. That Commissioner Connor will loose every hound in his pack on a trail that leads directly to you!"

Jesus said like a sulky kid, "He won't be found."

"You underestimate the police! And who is this other man? Another policeman?"

Jesus was spitting angry. "His interference was fortuitous but I would have sought him out in any case because Bentinck claims that he knows about morphic resonance."

The bass voice snorted at him, "So might any literate idiot with an interest in astrology or occultism or the prophecies of Nostradamus. The world is awash with mystic numskulls blathering metaphysics."

I won't claim I've got all these statements word-accurate though my memory's trained for it. For a start, the bass man had a Minder accent as thick as clotted cream and he chose his words like a programmed machine and used them better than I ever could, but I think you can get the idea of how he sounded.

After him Little Jesus sounded like garbage. Raging garbage if you like, as he said, half choking, "You will live to eat those words, doctor. The resonance is reality; the physical world is only a preparation."

Mentally I had written him off as a classy con man with both hands grabbing for big Minder cash (plus whatever coins the Wardies might come up with, just for sweeteners) but that last bit sounded like the real thing, as if he'd got trapped on his own flypaper.

Then a new voice came in, a woman's voice, quite close to me. Right alongside me, in fact, close enough for a breath of some kind of Minder perfume to penetrate the peppery sting in my nose.

What she said was, "Granddad, I think you should keep an open mind on this. I am impressed by what I've seen and when we get Warlock's firsthand account, and Devalera's, I feel you will be also."

"Granddad" was not buying soft soap though he didn't sound

so snooty addressing his granddaughter, pointing out that Deva-lera was in detention and Warlock's name would surely become big vidnews in the next twenty-four hours. "With two witnesses about to be posted missing as soon as their absence is noticed, any further interest in the matter could be suicidal."

I remembered Jesus saying, They won't be found, and started to wonder what he had meant. Something final? My guts gave an extra churn.

He began talking again, protesting that he needed Warlock, but I didn't listen too hard because I was busy trying to open my eyes just the barest crack, wanting to see where I was and how many people were about. Even that little effort shot a bolt through my head and the light was painful. What I saw was the lass with the perfume, and of course she had to be leaning over me, staring into my face.

She said, "This one's awake," which I reckoned meant Harry was here, too. I opened my eyes properly as she carried on, "He got only a passing lungful."

If I had the hangover of only a passing lungful, Harry's reaction to a full dose would be a disaster.

I took in the girl's face as she smiled slightly into mine. She was the silent one who had come into Bentinck's anteroom with Jesus when he made his play for Warlock. At close range I could see at once the trace of aboriginal blood in her, which was pretty common at that time though not among Minders, who were trying to distance themselves from "common" folk with all sorts of little discriminations and delicate differences. Her granddad, or maybe his dad, had played around before the social gap opened up. Just the same, she was a good looker who could have passed for white among them that didn't know what to look for.

I didn't say anything but turned my head to see the others. I seemed to be lying on a table, with Harry next to me asleep and looking like a corpse, in a room without any other furniture. A sort of purposeless spare room. Jesus was saying something I didn't listen to because I was intent on the feller with the bass voice.

I knew him at once—Wishart of Wishart Laboratories.

I should have recognized that voice because I had seen and heard him on the newsvids, but I would never have connected him with this second-rate church scam. Wishart Laboratories was worldwide, with labs and dependent manufacturing businesses all over as well as money in projects that had nothing to do with science. If it made money, he had a bit of it. It was said, on the downside, that his labs had a nasty connection with the Devil's Flu, but I didn't know whether that was true or not.

On the newsvids, where they shoot carefully to make the big names look impressive, he always seemed a big, powerful man but in fact he was only middle height and not much different from the ordinary feller in the street. But his voice had the pitch of power in it. He looked about forty or so but it was common knowledge that he had had a juvenation while it was still legal; my guess was that he had snagged another one under the counter since then because he had to be coming up on eighty.

Aside from all that, I was betting Connor didn't know there was another Wishart in Australia—the really big one, whose administrative center was in New Guinea. What for? Almost at once I got the answer.

Wishart was saying, "My granddaughter called me urgently and I came. All I find here is a mess that I will leave you, Mr. Miraflores, to clean up as best you can. I am not interested in the myth of morphic resonance and I think that you, Valda, had better dissociate yourself from the Warlock business. My interest was purely in the phenomenon of his failure to age over some thirty years and that promises to be submerged in an ugly kidnapping scandal."

Jesus only glowered while I wondered with no comfort at all what form his "cleaning up" might take, but Valda was sticking to her guns. "Granddad, you should speak to Dr. Bentinck first, hear his story of what was said in Connor's office, particularly what Devalera had to say about seeing Gordon. That's why I called you."

I wondered what time of night it might be. Wishart could have made the trip from New Guinea in a couple of hours; it could be still short of midnight. If it mattered. Or if indeed I mattered; no-body was paying any attention to me. Jesus was fuming and mut-tering, Valda was badgering Granddad, and he was eyeing her with a sort of grudging trust.

At last he said, "Very well; bring Bentinck." Now he seemed to become aware of me. "Why is he here?"

Jesus said, with the annoyance of a man hampered by having to deal with fools. "He blundered into the Ostrov kidnapping. It was best to bring him also for his knowledge of morphic reso-nance."

Wishart turned to me. "Tell me what you know."

I made an effort to sit up and my head nearly exploded.

I lay back again but Wishart grabbed me under the arms and pulled me into sitting position with my legs dangling over the edge of the table. "Talk," he said.

With guts writhing and head splitting I made the effort to spill my little scrap of knowledge before they decided to force it out of me. "There was a feller back in the 1990s—can't remember his name—who did some experiments with rats in mazes and saw that other rats, later on, did the same tests quicker than the first lot. And a third lot quicker again, like as if the trick was passed on to them. He tried it out with human beings doing crossword puzzles and found the same thing. The first lot took ordinary time but after that the teams doing the same puzzle got it out faster and faster. So he worked out this idea about thought being preserved like in a sort of pool and we tap into it unconsciously. It sounded to me like that was what Bentinck was talking about. I heard about it on a vidshow about old ideas being passed over."

I was happy to shut up after all that and let my head throb with no interruption.

Wishart said, "Useless knowledge for the bug-eyed public to lick over and create fantasies."

But Valda, bless her, looked in my eyes and said, "This man is suffering."

Jesus shrugged. "Effect of the somnolent."

"You have no counteractive?"

Jesus' stare at the girl held no liking and a sullen irritation as if he made up his mind how important she was in his scheme of things. Important enough, I reckoned to have her female whims attended to, because he reached into his inside coat pocket for a tablet pack and tipped a white pill into his hand.

He came up alongside me and said, "What more do you know about the resonance?" He sounded impatient, as if I was really a waste of time.

"Me? Nothing. It was just a thing I'd heard about. Trivia stuff, like."

"But Ostrov told you something."

"Not me, mister. I was just called in to do a strongarm job, holding Frankie down."

"But you were present at Connor's meeting afterwards."

With my eyes on that white pill I said, "I heard what Bentinck and Frankie and Warlock said, but I reckon the doctor told you all that, didn't he?"

Wishart said, "For God's sake give the poor bastard his pill. You're wasting time on him."

Jesus tossed the thing at me and turned away. I swallowed it down and waited for it to work, my head still exploding and my guts sick as a dog.

Wishart asked Jesus, "Did you record Bentinck's statement to you?"

"Of course."

"I'd better hear it since Valda thinks it important. I doubt that Ostrov matters anymore than this one."

"It will be morning before he wakes. He took a full dose. His importance to me is that he probably knows what alerted Connor to Warlock's importance to the church and what is planned by the police."

Wishart was contemptuous. "Don't you think your two ill-conceived killings sufficient of an alert? That he is investigating you should be information enough to caution you. You'd better get rid of these two at the first opportunity. Now let me hear the Bentinck statement."

"The vox is in the next room."

Valda said urgently, "Granddad, the implications of what happened are enough to change the world."

Granddad was unimpressed. "The changing of the world is already in hand. It would be better done without complications."

Then they went out. No "Bye for now" or "See you later." Jesus slammed the door behind them and a key turned on the other side.

They left the light on, which was just as well because there was no window in the room. I was left to contemplate Harry sleeping beside me.

And the slight easing of my head and guts as the pill did its work.

And just what "getting rid of us" entailed.

And what changing of the world was "already in hand."

And if you think I was being the ice-cool security man calculating the situation and planning how to get out, I wasn't. Oh, I could've took the three of them by surprise, all boots and fury—that's if they weren't carrying any weapons to shoot my brains out. Also, I hadn't a blind mole's idea where I was. Also, taking some ninety kilos of Harry with me had its problems.

I didn't have a real thought in my head. Only a lot of questions with nasty answers. I concentrated on feeling good as my head stopped thumping and my stomach stopped trying to climb up into my throat—and felt queasy again as I thought how Sally would be vidding around trying to find where I was and why I hadn't come home for dinner. She'd be saying, "The bastard's got some bitch in to," when the truth was I was a true and loving husband—well, there'd been a couple of slips . . .

I must have gone to sleep lying on the table, because Jesus and the Wisharts were back with me and talking as if I wasn't there.

Jesus was saying, "A power failure is easily rigged, or a fault in preparation, something not noticed until decay sets in."

Granddad Wishart was sharp and irritable. "You have the

imagination of a moron." However big Jesus was in his own eyes, he was shit in Wishart's. "You might as well leave them lying in the street for Connor to find. Do the police ever inspect the cryo chambers?"

"No. Why should they?"

"Someone must. There are laws governing standards of up-keep."

Jesus was sounding mutinous now. "There are twice-daily technical inspections by cryogenic experts and electrical trades-men."

"And these inspectors are your employees?"

"Certainly. Cryogenic preservation is by contract between the church and the preservee. There is no government supervision."

"And your inspectors are members of your church?"

"Indeed they are."

"And will not question the addition of two new preservees?"

Jesus took time to answer. At last he said, "It can be so ar-ranged."

And so it was well on the way to being "so arranged" that Gus and Harry would end up in frozen sleep. And I saw no way of stopping it. There was no sign that anybody cared if I had any thoughts about it.

19

That Jesus' church had a cryogenic annex was common knowl-edge in the sense that all the main churches had them. You people seem to think that back in our time—that is, me and Harry's time—there was no reason for cryo preservation, that most of it was for sick people looking forward to a time when there'd be cures found for them. (There were a few ratbags who just wanted to see the marvels of the future, silly shits.) You think,

Cures for what, because the doctors had it all under control, didn't they?

No, they didn't. What you don't know about the past would fill a lot of books. You haven't a clue about overpopulation and the effect it had on every minute of life. You know about it but you don't realize it.

The biggest thing was feeding the world. By about 2020 the food scientists had the game pretty well in hand with year-round fertility of crops, artificial vitamins and meat grown in two-ton stacks in factories. And of course every success in the food labs put more pressure on the birth rate. The fact is that no government ever succeeded in controlling that. Clandestine birth was big business in most Wardie enclaves and parliaments couldn't argue food shortage when there was enough for everyone—well, nearly enough. Some countries even encouraged birthing to provide soldiers to fight their endless border wars!

That might have worked if it hadn't been for the big Tokyo earthquake that destroyed the city just before I was born. Since it toppled the stock exchange, that rocked the financial world down to its ankles. Then with damage running into trillions of dollars, Japan, which had been the big lender to nations with budget problems, started calling in its debts, and that started the recession we never recovered from. With the first need being to feed and house people and warm them in winter and sewer their wastes, bankrupted governments cut down on public expenses—like education, for instance. After a single generation of education cuts there weren't enough professional men, like doctors and engineers, to service the public. I learned to read and write and figure from my folks, who weren't all that good at it theirselves; I never went to school much.

As for science, all that was encouraged was what a government thought necessary, which half the time meant weapons research, and only the youngers with big IQs got the training even for that.

As the population increased the people spread over the countryside and crops disappeared; more and more food came from factories with genetic techniques forced to their limit. What mattered more was that the forests disappeared, 'specially the rain forests. Scientists knew back in the 1900s that the rain forests were breeding grounds for bacteria and viruses, ever since the HIV started up and spread through everyone. Well, as the rain forests disappeared the bugs—particularly the viruses—mutated and got into the people living in the cleared spaces, almost as if they were ready and waiting for them, and since most of them were new to a science that by now couldn't cope with new stuff, they played bloody hell with the human immune system. The doctors couldn't cope because by then nobody much was doing new science. (There were some big conglomerates like Wishart Laboratories but they were mostly doing government work and had to train their own researchers from childhood up.)

The worst was the gradual-debility viruses, the ones that didn't show up for years so that people didn't know they had them. Then they'd go into slow breakdown with soft bones or brain troubles or gland disorders or fading senses. There were so many of them that the hospitals couldn't cope and they had to be treated at home.

Well the Minders, who copped the viral attacks like anybody else, took to putting their incurables into cryo sleep in the hope there'd be better times ahead when they could be put back into action.

How the churches got into the act I don't really know (except perhaps nobody else, certainly not the governments, wanted cryos on their hands with the constant supervision needed) but they did. Maybe nobody else cared.

They talked for quite a bit but I didn't pay a lot of attention to them because my head was full of Sally and my kid and the chances of making a break for it and a fair load of plain funk. Still, I was building up for a Nguyen strength-and-speed effort but not making much of a job of it because my mind was too distracted; it takes concentration to do it properly.

All the same, when Jesus turned his head to me and barked

like a sergeant major, "You! Take your clothes off!" I was up and running for the door without even thinking about it.

What I ran up against was Wishart with a syringe pointing at my face and I skidded to a halt with the blunt end of the thing inches from me. "Back," he said, "to the table."

He didn't bark like the other one; his arrogance was the certainty that I'd do as I was told. And I did, because Valda was hefting a syringe, too, and so was Jesus, and one of them was sure to get me even if I broke Wishart's neck.

"Now," said Jesus as if he was really the man in charge though he plainly wasn't, "get your clothes off." He raised his voice and called out, "Vox Three!" That was an activating signal to a communication setup.

Somebody, somewhere, answered, "Three on-line," and Jesus said to the air, "Two trolleys to Six," and some goon at the other end repeated the message and signed off.

There was nothing for it but to play along and strip off and hope for the best, so I took off my shoes and socks and unbuttoned my shirt, making a slow job of it, not only to gain whatever time there might usefully be but because I don't like parading naked, especially in front of a woman. I'm no prude but the fact is that I'm no sight for sore eyes in the altogether. I've got thin bones and although there's a bit of muscle on them the effect is all knobs and angles, and long, skinny legs with size thirteen feet.

I left my underpants till last but Wishart gestured and said, "Off," and Valda sniggered—actually sniggered like a schoolgirl— and said, "I think I recognize one of my own."

I was leaning against the table and Wishart too was examining me with a sort of lazy interest while I realized what Valda meant. "Grandmother," I said. "Same as you."

"Not the same. I'm Wuywurung. You have the desert shape."

Like her, I don't show much color from my aboriginal grandmother, but she had spotted the distinctive build correctly. "Wahlpiri," I said and she nodded.

The Wahlpiri are a desert tribe from the Northern Territory area, around Alice Springs, which makes me a proper multicultural mixture—Greek, Norwegian, Wahlpiri, and probably a couple more if the truth's known about a world where the races were mixed like a drunk's cocktail and "nationality" only meant where you were born. Grandma's genes had skipped a generation (my old man was shortish and stocky) to gather in me, because I had all the physical characteristics of the desert tribes—the long slender bones and broad chest, the thin, long-muscled flanks and flat, narrow calves, all the distinguishing features of the desert breeds, built for distance trekking rather than strength. That was no doubt right for desert survival but in a southern city it made me feel naked, like a collection of knobs and sticks.

Valda said, "He could be useful, Granddad. He's young enough for breeding."

Granddad was dismissive. "Too much dilution of the strain." He looked at her with a kind of satirical grin.

"You could run a transfer probability test if you think it worthwhile."

"Oh, I will."

There seemed to be an undercurrent in her voice, as if more was intended than actually said, but it was to be a long time before I found out what that exchange meant.

Then the men in white overalls came in, pushing hospital trolleys, and I saw fate closing in on me with not a thing I could do.

At the same time, on the table behind me Harry began to snore softly and Valda said, "He's coming out of it."

Wishart gestured to the orderly, who produced a syringe—an ordinary needlepoint job this time—rolled up Harry's sleeve and punched it into a vein. In this place everybody seemed ready for action. Then his mate approached me.

I pulled back, calling out, "What're you going to do?" Only I'm afraid I was losing control by then and I heard it come out as a Suss Wardie gutter squeak—"Wotcha gunta dew?"

"Just put you to sleep," the feller with the syringe said. He grabbed for my arm and I pushed him away so hard he staggered back and fell on his arse.

Wishart said, "Whoever you are, you should not have knocked

on the Ostrovs' door and seen so much. The clerical gentleman here would have had you killed but I was able to convince him that too many bodies were already associated with his scriptural teaching. So you and your policeman friend must go into retreat for a time."

The orderly was on his feet and looking unpleasant. I said quickly, "How long?," and Wishart hesitated as if that was a thing he hadn't thought about. He shrugged.

I was that desperate by then that I whined, "I've got a wife and kid," as though that would make a difference to anything.

Wishart nodded, I'll swear with a real sympathy. "The price of calling at the wrong house at the wrong time."

Then both the orderlies were on me at once and I was struggling and yelling like a mad thing, but the needle went into me and they stood back while I slid to the floor glaring with rage now that rage could do nothing. I remember cursing them for all the bastards uncastrated and uncrucified and in the middle of it Valda saying, "The poor man!," and then me starting to cry with despair.

And then nothing.

20

W aking up was slow, cloudy, like coming out of a dream. In fact I think it started with dreams though I can't remember any of them; I never could remember dreams once I woke up.

After a while I knew I was awake but still tired and not wanting to move. I didn't open my eyes but just lay on my back listening to someone breathing alongside me. Harry? I wanted to make sure but the effort was too much.

In the end I did open them, like forcing up a pair of creaking shutters, and I was on my back staring at a white ceiling with old paint starting to strip off it. It was only a small room and sunlight came in through a window somewhere behind and on my right.

I wanted to see if Harry was with me but turning my head brought on that creaking feeling, as if I had laid too long in one position, and I stopped trying. But the person beside me said, "Oh, you're awake," as if she'd just noticed and was in a flurry about it.

She stood up and leaned over me. She was only a kid, about eighteen or so, with the kind of accent you hear from someone trying to imitate Minder speech, prissy and affected. She was in a nurse's overall but I'd never seen a nurse before in an overall with mends and patches and streaks of rust or something that wouldn't come out with washing.

"Lie still," she said, as if I had ideas about doing anything else. "I'll get the doctor."

She went away and I drifted back into sleep.

The next time I woke was different, as if I'd been injected with some real get-up-and-go (as in fact I had) and I was ready to run ten K and take on a heavyweight. I just opened my eyes and sat up.

I was still in the same room but instead of the nurse, Valda Wishart was standing over me. She was in a white overall but hers was a new, clean one. Aside from that there was something different about her that I couldn't place at first.

Then I placed it, and with my heart in my mouth I said, "You've got older."

I don't know what she'd expected but not that and she hesitated like somebody looking for an excuse, and in the end said, "Only a few years."

I hadn't really inspected her all that closely before but I insisted, "How many?"

She said, "Oh, six or seven. I don't remember exactly."

"Christ! I've got a wife and kid!"

She simply looked startled as if that had never occurred to her. There was only a sheet over me; I pushed it back and swung my legs out of bed and saw that I was naked.

She said quickly, "You can't leave here yet."

Well, something had changed; before, I couldn't leave at all. "When?"

"Soon. There are some tests to be made. We don't want you relapsing into a coma."

She smiled and rested her hand casually, oh so casually, on my knee.

"Can I see my wife?"

"Not right away."

The hand slipped up along my thigh and I thought this could be encouraged if there was some tactical gain to be made from it. It seemed the game had changed, but I didn't know the new rules yet and any little advantage was worth considering.

Then she withdrew the touch abruptly, as if some fresh thing had come to mind. She said, "I'll tell Granddad you're ready to see him," and simply walked out. The door clicked behind her.

I tried it at once, but it was locked.

The window was barred, so there was no immediate way out. Besides, I had no clothes. I thought in a panic about Sally and how she would have got on without my wages coming in. She would have got the Suss but that only meant bare subsistence; she would hate the bastard who had run out on her. I loved her in the sense that people living together form bonds that take the place of the love you started out with, but in fact we hadn't got on all that well for some years; what I felt was a sort of guilt at letting her fall from Wardie into real Suss. Something had changed to make them revive me, but what? Did Sally know I still existed? And young Jared, who would be nearly grown up now?

I put them both from my mind, deliberately, forcing out the brittle ache.

Instead I thought of all the things I should have asked Valda, but my mind had been empty of everything but being alive and the worry about Sally. I was surprised at being alive at all; I had really thought that needle in my arm signaled the end of me, yet here I was, bouncing with health and feeling good as a lottery winner. I looked myself over and saw nothing to concern me, nothing much gained or lost. There was no mirror in the room but I felt my face; somebody had shaved me.

The room was bare of everything but the bed, a chair, a desk, and a bed table with a piss bottle on it.

Wondering where I was, I went to the window and saw at once that the bars were only recently put in. For my benefit? Looking out, I knew at once where I was—not in some church cryo annex but in the Psycho-Biological Complex. There was no mistaking the four-square building style with the two visible arms radiating from the center. After all, I had been there only this morning. Well, whenever . . .

Then I wasn't so sure. Instead of lawn there was long grass with the neglected look of wasteland and the flowerbeds were gone. I thought perhaps this was the back part of the building, which would look exactly the same as the front except that the show gardens had not been laid out here, maybe to save money. There were houses in the distance, along the roadway, but I hadn't paid attention to them, not enough to recognize them. I slid the window up and put my face to the bars to get the direction of the sun but it seemed to be about overhead and told me nothing.

Then the silence hit me, the absolute stillness of the place. It was as if there was nobody at all in the building. And there was no traffic on the roadway. And most of all the sound of the city was missing, that dull roar you're so used to that you don't hear it till it goes away.

Familiar things gone—in seven years?

Before I had time to panic the door opened and a young feller came in. He was maybe in his middle twenties and his overall was like the nurse's, patched and stained. He saw me at the window and stopped dead, blushing furiously.

Then he looked away from my nakedness and said in a prim, disapproving voice, "Could you please cover yourself decently?"

It was hard to credit my ears. In the summer heat—and it

surely felt like summer—people were only too glad to strip off once they got inside out of the UV. His embarrassment embarrassed me, like I'd been caught having a scratch in front of a Minder lady, so I sat on the bed and pulled the sheet over me to cover whatever troubled him. A real product of the nursery nannies, this one!

Once I was "decent" (a word, I found out later, used to mean keeping "the privates" covered, but was well out of date, the sort of snooty attitude only practiced by the most classy Minders) he sat hisself at the bed table and produced a wad of paper held together by a wooden clip.

"Now," he said, all brisk efficiency with the offending bits and pieces out of sight, "your full name, please."

I told him, "Ignatius Twigglebottom."

He gave me a look that didn't belong on any nanny's boy and said quietly, "Don't fuck me about."

It sounded like the words were all right to use so long as he wasn't faced up with the real thing. It also sounded like he meant it. He was nothing to be frightened of but I reckoned I was on the wrong end of the game and better play along for the moment.

"Gustavus Reginald Kostakis."

He checked with one of his bits of paper, then wrote it on his top sheet. "Quite a mixture."

"Blame my parents."

"Quite. Your age?"

"Dunno. I've been out of circulation." I wasn't all that trusting of Valda.

"True," he said, "so tell me your date of birth."

"Second of September, 2032. What's the date today?"

"The thirteenth of February."

"Year?"

Instead of answering he took a tape measure out of his pocket. "I'll need a few measurements for preliminary genetic typing."

I insisted. "What year?" and this time I was really starting to worry.

He said, "Neck, chest, and arms first," and got up to lean over me with the tape.

I pulled him down on top of me and growled, "The year!," but under the overall he was strong as an ox and dragged free as easy as you like and hissed at me, "Don't try it, man!"

I don't know what might have happened next because I wasn't anymore in a take-it-easy mood, but the door opened and an old man came in, followed by Valda.

He said, "Behave yourself, Kostakis!," like somebody used to commanding. It somehow brought me to caution.

The sound of real authority, I suppose. He sat hisself on the side of the bed and waved my notetaker out of the way.

"It seems that the softly-softly approach is not working with you."

He was really old, wrinkled and stooped with age, but I had a feeling I had seen him somewhere before. "I only asked this bastard the date and he wouldn't tell me."

"He has his orders."

"You tell me?"

He looked at me a long while before he said, with a curious note of disgusted impatience, "You have been in cryo-suspension for a hundred years. Your world has vanished."

I know I thought, Sally! And the boy! They'll be dead.

Then all the universe crashed around me and my mind blanked out.

21

From the private notes of Samuel Johns, scribe.

I was shocked by the sudden brutality of the Dr. Supreme's reve-lation to the resuscitee. It contradicted all our social training in consideration of the feelings of others and appeared to me as driven by an irritable impatience, but not being a member of a scientific discipline I had no moral right of objection. However, I noted that Dr. Valda Wishart was also disturbed, though she said nothing.

The effect on the resuscitee I may describe as horrendous. His mouth gaped open in what seemed to be disbelief and he stared at the Dr. Supreme with the gaze of one deprived of intelligence. Then, in an instant, he became maniacal. With face distorted he took the Dr. Supreme by the throat and would no doubt have murdered the old man if I had not intervened and chopped him severely enough on the biceps of both arms to induce a momentary paralysis, sufficient to allow me to set him back on the bed, where he lay in a sudden blankness as though control of both mind and body had been relinquished.

Dr. Valda Wishart said to the Dr. Supreme, "That was cruel. And deliberate."

He smiled at her in an unpleasant fashion, said, "You've got what you wanted," and walked out of the room, apparently unperturbed by the resuscitee's attack.

Dr. Valda stayed looking down on the man and, as if absently, stroking his leg with her fingertips.

After a while he seemed to rouse from his collapse and said to her, "Stop that. Get away from me."

She stopped the stroking as if caught in a misdemeanor, frowned at her thoughts, and went away, leaving me alone with him.

After some time he asked, "What's your name?"

I told him and he commented, "Tough boy," intending it, I think, as a compliment.

("... intending it, I think, as a compliment." I must consider the validity of such personal comment, remembering always that I am recording history. This assignment must be regarded as important, since it will be read and weighed by my seniors and may have some effect on my future prospects. I will need to consider carefully the matter of inclusion and exclusion when I pen the final version for submission to records. Shall I, for instance, offer an interpretation of Dr. Valda's caress of the resuscitee's thigh or a comment on the Dr. Supreme's apparent brutality? Is history in the eye of the beholder? Or must it be regarded only as a glacial record of facts? Or am I simply nervous of the reactions of the doctors to my personal observations?)

Kostakis lay still and silent. At last I noticed that he was weeping, with eyes wide open. Disturbed, thinking he must be in shock after the Dr. Supreme's revelation, I laid down my pad, but he noticed the movement and said, "I had a wife. And a young son."

It was not a dramatic statement or a cry of misery, only forlorn.

Some time passed and the tears dried; his rather kindly face took on a grim, foreboding expression. He asked, "What about Harry?," but I did not know who Harry might be.

Later he asked, "What's all the writing for? Hasn't the complex got voxcodes?"

"Complex"? "Voxcodes"? I could only shake my head, uncomprehending. I will inquire of these things from the older men, but they are reticent about the past, even the recent past. They tend to fend off inquiry with the slogan that haunts and taunts my generation, "History begins with you."

I told him, "Whatever these things may have been, they have vanished in the regeneration."

He turned his head now, to stare at me in a fashion I can interpret only as a species of puzzled horror, and said, explosively, a word that sounded like "Kraist!"—an expletive I have not encountered before. I should note here that he speaks in the loose manner we normally use only for joking or to shock or attract attention. Also he has an unpleasant, indescribable accent in his speech, as though all the words originate in the very front of his mouth. One hesitates to believe it characteristic of his time.

22

When the old man said a hundred years I believed him because I suddenly knew who he was. He had changed but
his ugly, impatient way of speaking hadn't. It was Wishart, grown
old in spite of all the juvenation treatment the whispers said he'd
had, but the voice was the one that had snapped at Jesus.

But that was only by the way when I thought of Sally and the
boy. Everything lost forever. Then I had a mental blackout when
maybe I said things or maybe not. Then I remember the writer
feller saying something about no more voxcodes and that simple
thing shocked the hell out of me because I remembered the silence of this busy building, the grass and weeds growing outside,
the everlasting growling of the city that had stopped, and put them
all together into a scare like the end of the world. And this feller
writing, pages and pages, on and on. Nobody wrote much, not
even signatures when thumbprints could be vidded; lots of Susses
didn't know how.

I had loss like a huge hole inside me. Not just Sally and the
boy . . . they had to be fought down and put away because they
had to be come to terms with later, when my mind could cope in
some kind of calmness. For now they had to be just part of the
life that had gone past me and could no way come back.

My mind wasn't big enough, so it ran for cover.

I swung my feet out of the bed and stood up. The Wisharts
had gone and only the scribbler was with me. He put his pad
down, watching me, ready to come the strongarm if he had to,
but I said, "It's all right. I've had the fright and it's over."

He said, "I regret having had to apply a necessary violence."

He actually talked like that, making everything sound formal
like a Minders' dinner party, but I knew he could talk another way

when he wanted; I had heard him. My arms ached a bit from his "necessary violence."

I wandered over to the window again while he looked away from my nakedness but must have decided against complaining about what seemed natural to me. I looked out at the tall weeds and grass and saw years and years of neglect.

"No traffic sounds. It's as if the city's gone dead."

He nodded. "Nobody lives there anymore. Except, that is, some old people who cling to their homes for, I suppose, sentimental reasons." He added, as if retailing a curiosity, "They grow vegetables and keep cows and dig wells." He smiled and shook his head, wondering.

Wells? "Have they got electricity?"

"Some may have old solar panels that are still in operating order but I think not many."

"Sewage?" He looked as if it was a new word. "For carrying away the shit."

That seemed to be a distasteful word. He said a bit coolly, "They dig their jakes, like anybody else."

And that was a new word for me. I tried again. "What happened to the city?"

"It died as the people died."

As if I really ought to know all about that, though in fact it was a stunner that surged through my guts. I managed to ask, "Died? What of? A plague?"

He looked uncomfortable, as if I'd caught him out in what he ought to know but didn't. "We do not dwell much on prehistory. Ours is the New Age."

There was pride there; you could hear the capital letters. He was beginning to sound as if the whole shebang had gone up in a smoking bonfire and he was here to wave a flag over the ruins.

In the end he said, "You had best ask the Dr. Supreme."

"Boy, but that's some title! You mean Wishart? Can you get him for me?"

"I can ask him to see you. Please wait."

He went out.

When he came back, he said, "The Dr. Supreme is a man with many responsibilities. He will see you when time permits."

Seemed my waking up wasn't really a big deal, just a chore to be fitted in. It was time to inquire the obvious: "Are all the sleepers being brought back?"

"Only yourself and one other, a man named Ostrov."

My heart leapt a bit at that but I only asked, "Why us?"

"I am not privy to the doctor's reasons."

Not high enough in the pecking order. "What happens to the rest?"

"I understand that they died as their solar cells or other instruments were damaged or otherwise nullified. I was too young to take an interest in their passing. Besides, it is a matter of prehistory, and relegated."

Oh, the dustbin of history! I felt like a dug-up dinosaur. But if so many had been allowed to rot, the survival of Harry and me must have been planned ahead. I tried a shot in the dark: "Have you heard of Jesus Miraflores? Is he still around?"

At a hundred-and-fifty odd? In this carnival of odd bods it was worth asking.

"I do not know the name."

"Or Brian Warlock? Heard of him?"

"No."

Why, then, should Wishart be interested in me and Harry? I had a replay of Valda's fingers playing across my not-all-that-muscular thigh and maybe her fantasy of some new sex thrill—having it off with prehistory—but that hardly seemed worth so much trouble for a scraggy specimen like me. Harry, now, had muscles from ankles to ears . . . It still didn't seem likely.

The boy said, "I must write up my notes of this conversation while it is fresh in mind."

Politely, Shut up while I concentrate. So I did.

There wasn't all that much I could ask a feller who hadn't majored in prehistory. So I got back on the bed and laid still and tried not to think about Sally and young Jared.

•   •   •

The old man came back sooner than I expected, slamming the door behind him and grinding to a halt like a bad-tempered terrier, sticking his face into mine.

"What do you want?"

"Some answers," says I, sitting up and giving him the steady eyeball.

He said, "Sammy can tell you all you need to know for the present."

"You mean your boy here? Sounds like his marks in prehistory ain't all that good for questions like, What happened to all the people?"

He snapped at me, "That's a longer story than I have time for." Sort of grudgingly, he added, "Later." Then, "What else do you want to know?"

I said, "I reckon I know you from before. You're Doc Wishart that gave Jesus his telling off way back when. What happened? You run out of juvenation pills or whatever?"

For a minute I thought he might hit me, then he took hold of hisself and started being ordinary human. "The juvenation process has limitations. Cellular recovery fails eventually. There is no immortality. I survived three treatments and am now a hundred and sixty-seven years old. That's miracle enough."

I thought about granddaughter Valda. She looked about thirty-five, maybe ten years on what I remembered as if it was yesterday. Maybe she was on her last treatment, too. I asked, "What about Jesus? And Dr. Bentinck?"

"Dead, both dead. Bentinck murdered Miraflores and died in jail serving a life term for the crime. They were of no importance in the world."

He didn't say that contemptuously, more as if it was what any ordinary person would think. Could be he was right but I wondered what "important" might mean to him.

"And all the people in cryo?"

"There was no future for them. They wanted impossible cures and were mostly aged or mentally debilitated. The new world would have no place for them."

"So this new world just pulled the plug on them?"

He made a wiping-off gesture. "It was expedient. And intelligent."

And past. And forgotten. The new world had to start clean. It began to seem a chilly world. "All except me and Harry."

"Harry? Do you mean Ian Ostrov?"

"He liked to be called Harry. Is he around?"

"Not yet. He will be revived when I have time. It is a lengthy process."

I supposed you couldn't just thaw 'em out and let 'em loose. "Why us two?"

He thought awhile about that and finally said, "That was at my granddaughter's request. It ties in with one of her genetic projects. She will wish to give her own explanation."

A genetic project and fingers caressing my thigh. It sounded like some pretty practical experimenting.

The Dr. Supreme went off on a new tack. "Your lab tests are all satisfactory; there's no reason you shouldn't get outside for a while. Take it easy for a day or two, There may be some mutated bacteria or viruses you haven't been exposed to in the past, but nothing that can't be easily handled."

And with that he went away—small interruption expeditiously handled, patient pacified.

"Sammy, I need some clothes."

"One moment, please." He finished making his notes of the conversation with Wishart and put down the pad. "Your clothing has been preserved."

And he, too, went away.

I was alone.

I sat on the bed and cried like a baby. Because I was a baby, newborn into a strange place where I was "prehistory."

I cried for Sally and the boy. I cried for everything I knew, even for the disgusting, crowded, stinking civilization that was the only one I had.

Sammy came back. I wiped my eyes at the sound of him at the door. He saw me, of course, and his face showed a flicker of distress, but he said nothing, which was just as well; you can't offer sympathy for wipeout.

He had my clothes over his arm, the overall and underwear I had worn a hundred years back, all clean and pressed and ready to wear. He laid them on the bed, each item separate and spread out, and stood looking at them as if they were special. They were certainly different from his own patched and scruffy overall, which looked like it was made from cotton or wool or some such instead of the long-wearing threads in mine.

He said, wistfully, "You wore new clothes that day."

"No. I had that overall for years."

"Without a tear, a worn patch!" He was incredulous.

I told him it was made of cross-linked fibrene and would last for years but he'd never heard of the stuff and asked me where it was grown. I tried to explain chemical fibers to him, drawn in a single thread as long as you wanted but he only looked bemused. After a lot of misunderstanding it turned out that these people had only wool and cotton for cloth-making and had only heard of artificial fibers as some vague thing that had been forgotten. "Prehistory" began to take on real meaning.

He explained that clothing was scarce and had to be looked after because the changeover from handlooms to steam-powered machinery was only recent and production was still limited.

You could have blown me away with a quick spit. Steam power!

And that might not last too long, he said, because all the construction metal was reclaimed from the deserted cities and the techniques of mining had now to be relearned and taught to the people.

But what about the solar power panels, the hydroelectricity, the . . .

It made no sense. I pointed to the electric light globe over my head. "What runs that?"

"There is a machine in the basement, run on oil. The fuel is very precious and reserved for the Dr. Supreme and his laboratories. That also will soon be exhausted."

The Dr. Supreme title really seemed to have meaning.

It began to sound as if the whole world was lining up for a fresh start; it couldn't be just Australia that was back to kindergarten.

I came back to the question he had evaded before. "What killed all the people?"

He began, "I told you before—"

And I interrupted him with a real bullying yell: "You told me fuck-all! What happened to them?"

I expected resistance, even violence, but he surprised me by saying, almost submissively, "I don't know."

"I think you do."

He changed gears again, suddenly poking his face into mine and screaming at me, "Stop trying to make a fool of me! I don't well know! Now shut your yammering trap and leave me alone."

I said, all placid and calm, "Well, it's nice to know you can talk like a real human being. I reckon I like you better that way."

At once he was back to starch and whalebone. "I apologize for the outburst. We scribes are trained in English usage and expected to maintain it, but one cannot wholly abandon one's early practices. As to your question, there are old men's whispers that the young cannot avoid hearing, but these are garbled and contradictory. We have never been told the facts."

Oh my, my! Here was an artificial product molded to fit his niche. "Old men's whispers," eh? Well, at least it was obvious that somebody was in charge and running things. On the general lines of an infants' school—obey your betters and don't ask awkward questions because you won't get told. I let it drop and turned to my clothes.

Overall, singlet, underpants, shoes, socks, broad-brimmed sun hat. "Will I be able to get a change for when these have to be washed?"

He hesitated. "You should ask Dr. Valda. Usually one must order and wait one's turn. Your case may require favored treatment." He sounded resentful and I couldn't blame him when he said, "In most cases we wash and dry our garments overnight."

Real short commons! Sounded like a new world starting from scratch. "And when do we eat?"

Actually I wasn't hungry and thought I'd likely been doctored to be up-to-date on meals with intravenous feeding and what-have-you.

"Morning and evening," he said and I thought it best not to ask about the menu. Gruel and rusks, maybe, with bread and jam on Sundays?

I started putting on my clothes. I saw that the shoes instead of being stiff and cracked with time had been looked after and kept soft. And my pockets had the same things I had started out with—handkerchief, notebook and pen, security company ID, pocket comb, and some small change. The notebook paper was not stiff or browned at the edges; somebody had looked after things.

"My watch is missing."

That watch had cost me a packet, scrimped together by saving a little bit of every pay; it was a Security Special, twenty-four-hour digital with current date and personal alarm and here-I-am guidance system. Radiation-powered, it should still be going—if somebody hadn't pinched it.

Nobody had. Sammy had it on his table and handed it over, plainly curious but asking no questions. I clamped it on my wrist and didn't try to explain the impossible.

Dressed, I felt like a million dollars. Well, half a million; there was a considerable wash of doubt whether I would like this not-so-brave new world.

"What say we take a look around outside?"

Sammy shook his head. "That is not within my orders. I can ask Dr. Valda."

"Do that, mate."

He came back after a little time. "Dr. Valda says she will escort you in a short while."

She would? I had some close personal questions for her.

23

I gathered she had more important things on board than running after me, because she took her time in showing up and said no beg pardon when she did, only "You look quite the gentleman in your clothes."

I was a bit browned off with waiting so I said, "I'm no bloody gentleman."

It must have sounded like a warning because she said, "There are no Minders here, Wardie, and nobody carries a gun or a knife."

"That makes it paradise?"

I could see Sammy tensing up to interfere if it got rough. I might teach him a thing or three about violence but I realized getting testy would take me nowhere and, anyway, Valda took the question seriously. "Not yet. We're still beginning. Perhaps one day."

"Nice, but this day I'd just like to look around."

"So you shall." She said to Sammy, "We shan't be long; there's no need for you to come."

All stiff and formal, he protested, "My order, Dr. Valda, is to accompany Mr. Kostakis at all times and take notes."

"I'll fill you in if there's anything worthwhile."

He didn't like that but it seemed he had to accept her authority. "Come on, Gus."

And so we stepped out into a long corridor, just a passage

lined with doors. It was lit with dim bulbs—about seventy watts I guessed—so the generator was working up enough light to see by. There was no dust, so somebody was doing the cleaning.

The next thing I noticed was an ache in my thighs and calf muscles. Valda said, "You must expect that. You've had massage but isometric exercise appliances are no longer available. We'll take it slowly."

Then the silence hit me again. "The place is quiet."

"It's mostly unused except for our labs and a few rooms opened up for your revival. Your friend, Ostrov, is in one of them."

"Can I see him?"

"Not yet. He is still in cryo-suspension and we don't want to risk disturbing the temperature level. The machinery is more or less cobbled together for the purpose." I hobbled along beside her until at a cross passage she said, "There's nothing here for you to see; we'll go outside," and turned down it to a doorway.

We went out and right away I knew one thing had not changed—the weather. It was sweat-hot, I reckoned about forty-five Celsius. Maybe more.

There was a path down to the fence about half a K distant but it hadn't been used in a long while. The long grass on each side had been cut away but you could see where it had pushed up and cracked the concrete. There was a smell in the air, a smell of things growing, but more than that an absence of smell; there was no city smell, that mixture of fuel and smog and mass human sweat that you only recognize when it goes away.

And there was the silence, as if we two were alone in the world.

Just to break the quiet I said, "You ought to wear a hat out here."

"I'm melanoma immune."

Something new, something discovered after my time. (Now that was a hell of a way to think of my life while I still lived it!) "You are? Well that's one way of beating the ozone hole."

"You don't beat a global catastrophe; you adapt to it. My skin immunity is vaccine-induced, but the new generations are developing genetic protection. Haven't you observed Sammy's dark coloring?"

"Not all that dark. Could be Mediterranean or a touch of Koori. You wouldn't notice it back then."

"Back then? I had forgotten. It's been a long time."

I think that was when the lapse of time really hit me. Suddenly, I felt like someone in a dream, not taking part in the new world but looking at it through a window, refusing to believe that what I saw was real but not able to wake up.

Morning would come and I would hear the roar of the city and pull on my stained and dirty overall and go out into the stinking streets . . .

Except that I wouldn't. The view through my eyes was real and my aching bones were making heavy weather of a stroll in another universe.

I heard Valda say, "Steady!" as she caught my arm. "Are you unwell?"

"No; I just saw the ghosts of twelve billion people."

She glanced at me but was silent.

I tried again. "What happened to them? War? Plague? What?"

"You had best ask my grandfather. In the end the question is for him to answer."

"I'm getting fed to the teeth of asking questions and being told to ask somebody else."

She said hesitantly, "This one has emotional overtones; my answer could be a distortion. I will tell Granddad he must talk to you."

"Thanks a lot!" I was getting pretty snotty over all the evasions. "But Granddad says you have to talk to me about why Harry and me was saved out of all the cryo people left to die in their iceboxes. He said it was your idea."

"Yes, it was." She frowned, like somebody working out the best way to broach a touchy subject, and I remembered her fingers at my thigh. "The idea originated when I saw you both stripped in preparation for hiding you in the cryo-suspension vaults. I observed certain physical characteristics in you that interested me."

She added quickly, "As a biologist, that is," and I thought, Not quite quick enough, lady. "So I took DNA samples and had your genetic records searched. Only three generations had been recorded at that time but they showed the dominant factors I was looking for and old birth certificates confirmed the genealogy."

"Back to a black great-grandpa—an Australian aborigine?"

"Yes."

"What's interesting about him?"

"The dominance of his strain in your physical makeup."

"You mean the big chest and skinny legs?"

"Those and other things. The splayed nose, shape of the skull; many small indications."

"I been told before that I strip like a white abo."

"More accurately, like an aborigine of the desert tribes of Central Australia."

"And Great-grandpa has passed it all on?"

"Indeed."

I began to see a little light on those caressing fingers, but I asked, "And what has Harry got to stir a biologist?"

"Mainly the bones and physical proportions of a naturally powerful man passed to him by both sides through several generations."

"A muscle-man for the ladies, eh?"

She gave me a disgusted look. Just as I was getting ready to put in another goad, she said, "For the right, carefully chosen ladies."

I got the smell of a genetics program; it fitted well into Sammy's New Age talk, so I asked, "You got plans for my coupling, too?"

She said briefly, "Yes."

"Like my great-granddad to your granny or whatever she was? Keeping the abo strain alive?"

She snapped, "There are aboriginals enough to fill that role."

"Just the same, I remember the fingers stroking my thigh while the lady stared into the distance as if it was by accident."

She looked not exactly angry, more like a kid caught with his fingers in the jam and wondering what excuse to make.

All of a sudden I was mad angry at the stupid impudence of her idea; the vision of Sally, lost and gone, flooded my mind, and I yelled at her, "You fucking bitch! I want a real woman, not a bloody science-hag a century old!"

I suppose it was over the top but you've got to keep in mind that I was all the time trying to come to terms with change enough to shake anyone off his perch.

And my leg muscles were starting to ache after walking only a couple of hundred meters. Add all things together and they still don't excuse my insulting her that way.

She said only, "That's another thing I had forgotten—the simmering ill-temper of the Wardie streets and the unfettered expression of it."

Full marks to her for self-possession, but I wasn't in any mood to apologize and I kept walking and saying nothing.

When she was ready she said, "Ova and sperm will be obtained by laboratory staff, so your chastity will be untarnished."

That made me feel nasty again. "What if I don't want to contribute spunk? You can't take it by force."

"Of course we can." With a sharp edge to her voice she mused, "It could be said that for all practical purposes we own you. You could run away but where would you run? Only to people who would return you to us as soon as they recognized your unfamiliarity with the present world."

Just a laboratory rat; that was me. "All right, so I apologize. My legs are aching and I want to go back and sit down and contemplate being a tribal forefather."

We returned in silence and she went back to her lab.

Sammy was at once all over me, wanting to know what we had talked about, for his interminable notes. I told him in detail and he was properly scandalized; I gathered I had insulted a minor goddess.

When he had done disapproving he told me he would take me to see Wishart at four o'clock.

That was two hours away so I said I'd like something to read, but it seemed there were few books in the complex, in which only a few rooms had been opened for the doctor's use. Nevertheless he went on a hunt around and found, in some forgotten corner, of all things a thumbed and tattered copy of *Alice in Wonderland.*

I had never read it but I did now and it seemed to me an only slightly exaggerated picture of the goings on in the real world.

24

Sammy ushered me into the doctor's office and shut the door. He motioned me to be seated in front of the desk and sat himself down in a corner with his notepad. Wishart said, "I am a busy man but can give you an hour for explanations."

I cocked a thumb at Sammy. "Why does he have to write it all down?"

"Because records of history are important for the preservation of truth and you and Ostrov are items in the history of the New Age."

I put forth an objection that had puzzled me earlier. "But he can't write fast enough to take down conversations."

"He can. The method is called shorthand. It is centuries old but fell into disuse in the Electronic Age."

I promised myself a look at Sammy's pad later on; the idea sounded useful. But for now there were other things to find out. "You let all the other cryos die but after a hundred years you suddenly decided me and Harry were useful for something."

Wishart shook his head. "No. The decision to preserve both of you was taken a century ago. Briefly, when you were stripped for cryo-preparation, my granddaughter, who is a genetic biologist, observed certain physiological traits in you—notably the body shape. She consulted the genetic records so easily available at the time to trace the history of those traits in your genealogy and found that you were suitable for a project that was only a possibility in both our heads at the time. It might be said that the co-incidence solidified the idea in our minds. It then remained only to preserve you until the time was available to make a beginning—now."

Perhaps I should have felt important; in fact I felt like a rat on the experiment bench, with Wishart removed from any emotional involvement as he explained my circumstances to me with just the number of words. He had an hour to spare and was using it without wasting a sentence.

"And I don't have any say in your plans?"

"We could use coercion, but to what end? We require some sperm. In return we will fit you into a place in this new society, guaranteeing food and necessities. What say do you need?"

Put so plainly, I didn't need any say. Still, he shouldn't have it all his own way. "Harry might think different."

"Ostrov?"

"Yes. Keep in mind that the last thing he saw back then was his parents with their necks broke, and you was one who had something to do with it."

He said like someone accused of a misdemeanor, like traveling on a bodgy bus ticket, "But I had nothing to do with it; I recall very clearly being affronted by Miraflores's ineptitude in arranging a kidnapping that by accident included you. I would never have countenenced such action."

"Try telling Harry that! To him you'll all be one group of crims without a soul between the lot of you. You're much the same to me, but at least my wife and kid weren't murdered. Keep that in mind, too."

He took time out for thought, as if such matters hadn't occurred to him. Which they possibly hadn't across the gap of years. Time turns complicated situations into a memory where only your own point of view sticks out.

At last he said, "I had no hand in the killings or the kidnappings, but once they were done it was necessary that you two should disappear before the police should trace you. I could not afford to be linked with a man of Miraflores's stamp.''

"I couldn't work out why you were there anyway."

"My granddaughter had a bee in her bonnet about morphic resonance; she still has. I came to Melbourne because she called me. It was as well I was there to take charge of that mad churchman's muddle. It was fitting that he should eventually be murdered for his criminal pains.''

That seemed to satisfy him as a summing up of the whole schemozzle. It's all a matter of the point of view, isn't it? I wondered what Sammy's "historical notes" would read like.

Wishart continued calmly, as if some minor preliminaries had been settled, "I brought you here to bring you up-to-date on social change so that you will have some understanding of what you see here.''

Perhaps personal tragedies really didn't affect him; maybe he was so old that he had seen it all and no longer gave a cheap fuck what people did to one another. At any rate, he was into his potted history and I listened.

"The world of your time, already overloaded with twelve billion people and showing little sign of a population leveling out, was ripe for culling. Those in power advocated it privately but dared not make an open declaration of their stance while the gap between rich and poor was so great and had become unbridgable in any foreseeable future; any cull would surely be of the mass poor. Technological improvement had ground to a halt due to the immense cost of basic research that only governments possessed the resources to back, but were prevented by the increasing cost of maintaining a population thrown idle by that same technology with its dependence on total automation. Ultimately the Suss Wardies became the main bulk of the people, unable to afford the product of the factories, which went into decline. Food was also a problem as forests and grazing lands were polluted and overrun by housing; even solar plants delivering cheap power covered vast acreages. The ozone holes killed off plankton with UV radiation in the upper strata of the southern oceans and, since plankton was the bottom of the predatory food chain, the abundance of all seafood was affected. I assume you were aware of all this."

It came out in a continuous spout, as if he had it all worked out before he started, every sentence exactly in place—and not one sentence with a hint of feeling in it. Come to think of it, the only spontaneous feelings I had seen in him was his spats of bad temper. It made an orderly mind seem not such a good thing to have.

I told him, while he frowned at my interruption, that we didn't think that much about it and weren't even sure that the rest of the world was as bad off as ourselfs. We were all too much concerned with scratching a living and I meant really scratching; the lives of the Suss Wardies didn't bear thinking about, so we didn't think about them except as people to keep away from.

He said then as if he was explaining to the class dunce, "I was simply presenting the evidence that in a species incapable of restraining natural growth a cull was inevitable."

"We knew that; we used to make sick jokes about it. We knew it was real after Premier Beltane broadcast his speech about the Devil's Flu. We never knew who was responsible for making that virus for cutting off birthing but your name was bandied about as maybe one of the gang."

"Indeed it was." says he, calm as you please. "Its final form was designed and produced in my laboratories. The form that was the subject of Beltane's broadcast was imperfect and unused and its only consequence was to divide the planet into mutually suspicious nations prepared for war. Something more insidious was needed, a form that could be produced privately in a single laboratory, without the collaboration of the consortium of nations with a conscience-haunted premier for its weakest link. The clue was provided by the so-called AIDS virus, which had been eradicated some sixty years earlier. It was a virus communicated between human beings by sexual congress or by direct blood contact."

He paused as if for my reaction, but I had never heard of a disease called AIDS. Before my time. But in terms of my reaction that didn't count. What counted was the matter-of-fact way he talked about killing off most of the human race. It should have freezed my blood, but it didn't; I just sat there and soaked it in as though it was some sort of made-up story, with me interested in how it turned out. I hadn't actually seen the outside world yet and I had nothing real to relate to; I didn't feel involved. I suppose the fact is that what had happened was too big to take in all at once and I just listened with my silly mouth open like a kid with a fairy story.

"The AIDS virus had an incubation period of from two to five or six years before its effects showed. It also had a considerable ability to mutate. One early theory was that its latent period was a period of mutation until it achieved the form that allowed it to attack the body. This was a part of the truth, a part that engaged the attention of my researchers. They reasoned that if a virus— which is a fairly primitive aggregate—could be programmed to pass through a planned series of mutations before its final and effective form appeared, and without the initial common cold with which our original virus announced its presence, it could lurk undetected in the human system for a determinable number of years." He broke off to ask, "Do you understand this?"

Yes, I did. Most people knew at least the simple facts about viruses after the Beltane broadcast sank in.

"My laboratory eventually produced a true lentivirus with a mutation period of ten to twelve years. In other words it could be disseminated widely by way of sexual congress, lie in wait undetected until it attained final form, and then emerge to totally inhibit human reproduction. Humanity would cull itself by simple inability to create progeny. The Wishart virus would lie in wait until its time came, then strike with universal effect. It could be disseminated in water systems, even in prevailing winds, and human promiscuity would do the rest. There was, of course, a drawback. Destruction of the entire race would be a pointless exercise; there must be a residue to build anew. It was here that a fresh factor entered the work—how to leave not only a residue but a desirable residue."

Meaning how to pick the best. "The best" meaning people

who thought the same way as hisself. Funny how do-gooders always had the same idea of perfection.

Well, I had a surprise coming to me.

Wishart said, "Basically, the human population problem was caused by technological progress overtaking available resources; the planet was destroyed, ecologically, in order to feed the demand for artifacts. On the other hand, primitive races lived on what was immediately present for hunting, gathering, and adapting. This placed automatic limits on population before growing medical expertise eliminated most childhood deaths and extended the life expectation. It became obvious that a return to recognition of natural limits imposed by availability of resources was required."

"Obvious" to who? If it was "obvious" to Wishart, did that make it the way to go? But it made a sort of sense while nobody was present to argue against it. A sort of ice-blooded sense.

"The phasing out of human numbers would automatically phase out also the technological civilization for lack of a workforce to sustain it."

I began to see how big his "phasing out" would be—big enough to make the world primitive, to put it back in the starting blocks. But it hadn't quite wound down, had it? The complex was still here. Maybe the race was still only half on the way to self-destruction.

I heard all this with my mind at a remove from reality, as if I listened to a lecture about people on some other planet. I knew it was all true but I hadn't come to terms with it yet. The real guts of me wasn't reacting; it was too big.

Wishart changed tack. "You possibly did not fully understand that Wishart Laboratories, in your time, was a planet-wide organization with a dozen research branches in a dozen countries. They were biological institutes, funded in part by independently wealthy Minders dreaming of immortality and perfect health when the inevitable social breakdown occurred from sheer overloading, but the greatest financial support came from the independent churches whose idiosyncratic beliefs attracted a Minder class with little to occupy the intellect but their own futures. Wishart's founded the Cryogenic Preservation Utility, employing methods superior to past practices, and supplied the techniques to the more successful churches, which supplied their own columbaria and paid Wishart's well for the privilege—and, as with your Miraflores, lined their ecclesiastical pockets. Even the few peddling genuine if stupid beliefs were able to discover biblical justification for raw greed.''

I had never really known whether I believed in God or not, but hearing Wishart dispose of the whole caboodle in one sentence made me a bit queasy.

"Wishart's also supplied curative and palliative measures for various complaints, measures that were genuinely effective and gained a huge market. I tell you this so you will understand that the laboratories were immensely wealthy and so able to fund an enormous project—genetic selection of the racial strains best fitted to occupy the future planet.''

I was properly impressed by the idea of a single organization—probably just a single man—with the resources to take on what a collusion of whole countries had failed to bring off. And I was more than merely impressed as he told how he went about it—I was staggered.

"The first necessity was a vaccine with which to isolate those selected to continue propagation of the race. With the resources of a dozen major laboratories on call, that was achieved quickly; it was, after all, a fairly simple inhibition of the virus's ability to mutate, a genetic rearrangement.''

Simple? Sure, if the man said so. I was well out of my depth.

"The actual selection of those to be vaccinated was in essence uncomplicated but required the deployment of a considerable research force whose members were unaware of the end use of their labor. At that time only I knew it. I created a research project requiring an examination of the DNA records of all the world's children under the age of ten. These records had been taken and computer-stored by all governments over some fifty years—in fact from the time those governments realized what control such rec-

ords afforded them over the lives of men. The possibilities of informed manipulation were limitless; that they were in the hands
of self-seeking bureaucrats was a misfortune; that they could be
consulted by an organization as powerful as Wishart Laboratories
was a gift requiring little more than a request. The planet, after
the idiot revelations of Beltane, was divided into rival camps of
suspicion, more or less the white races versus all other colors, but
our laboratories straddled frontiers and languages and we encountered little opposition to our project of surveying the entire
world juvenile population, to make projections of mental growth
and locate undesirable strains on a basis of heredity, caste, intellectual ambience, and a dozen other statistical red herrings."

The voice was almost without inflection; deliberate sentences
spilled out with the easy perfection of a brain untroubled by emotions. There was a temptation to take it in one ear and out the
other; I had to concentrate.

"Some one and a half billion records were extracted for study
of genetic suitability for propagation of the species. Race and color
were ignored. The true demographic distribution was not by na-
tion but by environmental suitability; physical types could be divided into geographically based groups characterized roughly as
coastal-dwellers, plainsmen, mountainmen, tropical foresters, and
so on. Throughout human evolution each of these environments
had shaped its inhabitants into forms suitable to their survival.
Mountain-dwellers developed powerful muscles on small, light
skeletons for scaling and carrying; tropical types developed epi-
dermal melanin for protection against solar UV radiation, and so
on for hunting plainsmen, cold-climate dwellers, and others. It was
necessary that all these physical types be preserved in order that
all habitats should be provided for." He broke off suddenly to ask,
"Do you follow?," with a frown suggesting that my brain might
not be up to it.

Sure I followed: a place for everyone and everyone in his
Wishart-decided place. All for the best in the best of all possible
worlds, hurrah, hurrah! But I only said, "Yes."

"With the historic intermingling of types the issue of suitability had been lost from the human consciousness; it was essential that it be regained for the redistribution of population. Mingling would take place eventually, but for the initial stages of remastering the planet by a numerically reduced species it was necessary that properly adapted types be selected. Hence the intense study of children who would be sexually efficient in some twenty years' time. From some one and a half billion scanned, approximately fifty thousand were selected for vaccination on the basis of chromosomal characteristics that could be manipulated through two or three generations to reproduce the various environmental ideals. All were, of course, pinpointed as to location and identification. And all were inoculated, under a variety of excuses, with the antiviral vaccine. The preparation was complete.

"So then," he said—and it was a real throwaway line, delivered as if it didn't matter a damn—"we launched the contraceptive virus into the atmosphere and water systems."

Just like that! No fanfare, no overture and beginners. Just a quiet private ceremony at Wishart Labs. A modest drink and a toast to the boss?

"The presence of a new virus was detected, naturally, but Wishart Laboratories was able to demonstrate its harmlessness as merely another parasite on the human physiology. There were suspicions, of course; the capacity for mutation was detected but not its end result, and interest slackened. Governments had little money for any but urgent research and few institutions had the Wishart access to funds. There were twenty years to wait until the last child was born under what might be called the old dispensation." There was the slightest trace of self-satisfaction in his voice, like the job was finished at last and he could relax and put his feet up, as he added, "That occurred in 2098 and only our vaccinated selectees, now sexually mature, remained to generate the new humanity."

So now I knew, and so what? It was done, over, and the brave new world was waving its spunky little cocks at the jump-start of new history. And it seemed I had a part to play in this ratbag vaudeville. With Valda in charge?

197

Wishart had another comment. "Strangely, there were a few who escaped the virus. In the early 'nineties the south Russians built the first ship designed to cruise to the stars and find other planets for Earth to colonize, and two years later the Western Alliance, probably in no more than a spirit of competition, launched a similar ship, the *Search*. God only knows what the pinbrains hoped to discover out there, and they have never returned. One must hope they are not infesting some helpless planet with their ravaging sperm and ova."

One might hope, too, that they would not come home to find the trash heap of half a million years of evolution.

But Wishart had more to spill in his peculiarly spiritless account of mass sterilization. "There is nothing to be gained from an examination of mass hysteria and futility. The presence of a core of fertile men and women was soon discovered and the distribution of their semen and ova demonstrated to be unavailing. It was time for the education of the new humanity to be undertaken. This was the province, mainly, of my granddaughter. I will leave her to explain it to you."

There he simply stopped speaking. He had said his piece. He didn't even ask, "Any questions?"

In Sammy's corner the scratch and stipple of his pen stopped dead. I felt they were both waiting for me to say something. Did Wishart expect I'd kiss his hand and proclaim him saviour of the race? Or just burst into tears? Or maybe throw some kind of tantrum and curse him to the shithouse?

But my only feeling was that I had listened to a lecture about events that didn't seem to touch me personally because they were weird like a vidshow, a virtual reality job that wasn't really there. I had listened to something monstrous told in the way a second-rate instructor would deliver a not all that interesting lecture to a dull class.

I just didn't react. Maybe I would, later on as it seeped into me.

What I said was, "I'm getting hungry. What time's dinner?"

25

Wishart's astonished silence scalded the air as Sammy took
me back to the room I was beginning to think of as my cell.

Sammy was furious with me. In the cell he exploded, "What
possessed you to treat the Dr. Supreme so? He gave his precious
time to your instruction and you wiped it away like rubbish!"

"Precious time?" In my empty-minded confusion I had behaved like a dolt and now this "Dr. Supreme" stuff stuck in my
overloaded gullet. "Who the hell does he think he is? God's bloody
mouthpiece?"

Stiff as a board, Sammy told me, "He is the most revered person in this world."

"The man who all on his revered own destroyed it?"

Sammy's reply was like ice down my back. "He destroyed only
the reproductive insanity eroding a world plundering resources
and returning nothing. There was no cull, no assassination; people
lived their time and died in due course." Then, with the sound of
irrefutable truth, he said, "We of the Third Generation feel no guilt
for an act of necessity; that we are the benefactors is neither a
responsibility nor a burden."

I reckoned he had been taught it as a child, had it repeated
and repeated to him until doubt couldn't be even thought of. Wishart had built hisself a world with its back turned on its past and
he, God's mouthpiece, dribbled excuses.

God's scribbling servant, with that matter closed, said, "We
will eat in half an hour."

We ate in another room, a replica of the others I had seen
except that instead of a bed or a desk it housed a table and four
chairs. That other people existed in the so-silent building was

proved when a tired old codger—a relic of "pre-history" by the look of him—wheeled in a trolley with table settings and food, set them out, and shuffled back to wherever he came from. I put him at about eighty-plus.

I said, "About time he was put out to grass, isn't it?"

Sammy said, "In a world with much to be done, everyone is employed while he is physically capable."

It sounded like another instilled-in-childhood line.

Then Valda and Wishart came in. He gave me a cheesed-off, disgusted look but Valda flashed me a little secret smile as if she had heard of my fox-paw with Grandpa and was highly amused.

I had been wondering if austerity included food but there was plenty to eat. We wolfed it down in silence until just to break the strain I held up a chunk of meat on my fork and asked, "This is kangaroo, isn't it?"

Wishart didn't seem to have heard but Sammy said a short, "Yes."

Valda was more forthcoming. "The countryside is swarming with them. The best way to keep them down is to shoot and eat them. They devastate the pastures now that the rabbits have been eliminated."

I was about to suggest electric fences but remembered there was no big power generator.

Instead, before the silence could set in again, I said, "Dr. Wishart, when are you going to revive Harry Ostrov?"

He answered without looking at me, "Soon. When I have time." A couple of mouthfuls later he asked, "Is it of importance to you?"

"Sure it is. I'd like someone of my own kind to talk to."

He was affronted. "We are not barbarians."

I wasn't going to let him brush me off. "No, but to me you're foreigners and I have to learn the language." Then I said what was on my mind. "I've been thinking about your virus story and how Harry might take it. I reckon you should leave me to tell it to him."

He looked interested at last. "Why?"

"Because he's a different man from me and will see it a different way—and because the last thing in his memory will be the sight of his mother and father with their necks broke by a couple of your thugs." His remoteness scraped my patience to the point where a jab at his self-satisfaction seemed in order. "He won't take kindly to them dying for your holy new order."

It was wasted; he finished chewing a mouthful before he said, "I was not responsible for their deaths and made it plain that I found Miraflores's reaction to the police danger clumsy and unnecessary. Nor is the new order holy; it can do without God until such time as it creates a metaphysic of its own. Which I suppose it eventually will, since man seems unable to persist without a concept of transcendence. As for Ostrov, I accept your suggestion; I don't wish to have to deal with emotional contortion. Samuel's presence will guard against factual errors on your part."

It all rolled out, accurate and complete, from an orderly mind whose frosty control unhinged my temper. "You never had a feeling in your life, did you!"

Wishart continued eating. Sammy said, in one of his moments of unstarchy speech, "Insult the doctor again and I'll wipe your mouth clean."

Valda stopped eating and looked expectant. I said, "You could try it, scribbler," and began preparing myself for a concentrated strength exercise, ready to do him—or anyone—some real harm so long as it relieved the anger in me.

But Wishart said, "No, Samuel. Mr. Kostakis's own feelings are in turmoil and some unreasonableness is to be expected. And you, Mr. Kostakis, must accept the inevitable strangeness of your surroundings because there is no going back. Time remains immutable." He smiled, actually smiled, as if a thought could touch him. "You are how old? Thirty-two or-three? Young enough to adapt and perhaps find some consolation in the prospect of fathering a branch of history to come."

I couldn't help glancing at Valda—and at once the ghost of Sally rushed in. There was nothing unattractive about Valda but I had to remember that time, like Wishart said, was immutable, and the ghost had to be put down as part of the price of the new world.

I didn't say anything during the rest of the meal and didn't listen to much of the others' talk. The "father of a new race" stuff reached me as part of a dream that had got out of hand, and I became a bit depressed and moody.

When Sammy and I returned to the cell he said in his more relaxed tone of voice, "Your muscles will be tight for a day or two; I can give you a massage. So far there has been no time."

It was true I ached a bit and my calves and thighs had not fully recovered from the walk with Valda; I felt I was creaking faintly all over. I said, "Go ahead, feller," and stripped off my overall; I thought I'd better keep my underpants on to spare his blushes. The bed's mattress was firm enough to make a rubdown table.

He also stripped down for the job and showed a solid, very muscular frame when the disguising overall was off, solid enough to make you think twice about taking him on unless you had a trick or two up the sleeve.

As a masseur he had been well trained by someone. "The oil smells," he said in apology (and it did), "but there will be a shower after." I stopped worrying about oils or showers as his very expert palms and fingers teased and probed and I lapsed into the somnolence a good rubdown can bring on. When he had done I could have wished him to go on forever but he hurried me out to a shower room where lukewarm water took the oil smell off me and I felt my limbs were floating on the air.

He hurried me through that, explaining that rainwater was collected on the roof and the supply was limited. He kept his eyes averted the whole time while I wondered who had set sexual morality back a century or two in the bright new dawn. Then we went back to the cell.

Valda was waiting there.

It was time to update some more of my education, she said. So I sat on the bed while she prowled up and down, snatching words out of the air like a cat chasing a ball around the room. She didn't have Grandpa's practiced lecture style but was a sight easier to listen to.

And Sammy took shorthand notes.

"Grandad took you up to 2098, when the virus was disseminated, but he felt you hadn't taken in what he told you."

"I hadn't," I told her, "and I still haven't. I heard it all and I know what he meant and maybe I didn't seem too intelligent about it, but how would you feel about being told your whole world, everything you were used to, had gone for good and you could like it or else? It's a fairy story. And now you're going to put some more to it."

She nodded. "I understand that, but Granddad has had many years of people listening to what he says as if it were law, and from the start he was never one to suffer fools gladly."

"The fool thanks you," says I, but she ignored it and dived in to what she had to tell.

Her pacing the cell gave me a chance to look at her from all directions and I found myself deciding she was a looker, no matter the little bits of Koori inheritance showing in the nostrils and the long, slender fingers and just a little bit in the skin color. In fact they added rather than took away from her good looks. I began to think about her in bed and reckoned there was a lot to be said for it. And if Sally stayed quiet in my mind—well, there had been times when I slipped off the straight and narrow. Maybe cooperation in fathering a new strain wouldn't be that much of a chore.

I had wandered off the track and came around to hear her saying that ". . . of course there were pockets of people who for one reason or another had remained immune for various reasons. Mainly solitary desert or arctic types and even a few who seemed to possess a natural physical immunity. Granddad worried about them as imperfections in his overall vision but I saw them as variations in a too restrictive gene pool. With careful supervision they could add useful traits, even form crossover types for strains too closely wedded to a single ambience. For instance, he had not provided for desert-dwellers, whom he thought unnecessary, whereas I saw their natural advantages as plus values. Their small bones and narrow build provide large areas for perspiration, their muscular structure leans to stamina and endurance rather than unnecessary brute strength, and their natural coloration protects against sunlight."

I saw where we were heading in that description of me (though I don't show much color) and couldn't resist a little jab at the vision of perfect humanity: "They're the kind that make good soldiers."

She stopped as if I had used a dirty word. Perhaps I had. "We are not planning to include warfare in the training of people adapted to their environments."

"You should," I told her. "You and Granddad aren't going to last forever and sooner or later the kids in your playground will discover the fun of bloodying each other's noses. Anyway, you can't train the whole world the way you want it to go."

She stopped pacing to give me a frustrated look, and said, "I am here to tell you what is being done," but I thought I caught a little hint of uncertainty.

She began pacing again as if that helped her to concentrate, and I was thinking that she did herself no favor by wearing that baggy overall that concealed the shape of her figure. I could tell she was thin, or at least thinnish, which suited me all right, but I had to imagine the rest.

She said, "The sudden cutting off of propagation caused at first consternation, then something close to panic. The work of the mutated virus was detected easily enough but could not be reversed."

That was history in a nutshell. I tried to imagine it but it was too big. I could only come up with puzzlement and despair, leaders trying to preserve order potency while the small people looked in fright to the end of their world, and the lunatic fringe of "revelation" preachers scared them even sillier with talk of God's vengeance. And then the make-it-a-party types who were going to have a wild time while they still lasted, and against them the face-the-end-with-dignity brigade carrying on as courageous ladies and gentlemen should while civilization fell to bits around them. Maybe senseless wars and outbreaks of crime. Maybe anything you could think of.

"The discovery of isolated groups still able to produce children had a calming effect at first, then generated a backlash of resentment—a 'why them and not me' reaction. Some of the children were actually killed by the deranged or simply resentful, but generally common sense prevailed and extraordinary efforts were made for their preservation. They were, quite literally, guarded day and night when it was discovered that their progenerative abilities were unharmed. In fact the virus had reached its determined final mutation and died with its hosts."

History was racing past me at a hell of a belt, and it seemed this was only a fast run over the background because suddenly Valda switched to what she plainly thought was the real stuff.

"All of this had been predictable in outline and Dr. Wishart had prepared against it. From his production laboratories around the world he had gathered a like-minded group believing, as he did, that the culling of humanity was inevitable and best carried out by those who could plan a new civilization. They were dedicated and of course secret. They were men and women of conviction, not bought by promises of personal sexual potency; their lines would be extinguished with themselves. They believed in what they were doing."

My thought was that any crackpot with a dream can find a following, even among scientists whose brains are supposed to be logical. Wishart's ideas weren't all that far from the rantings of the salvationists—destroy the sinners and let the perfect people take over!

And then I thought about how in my own time the idea of the cull was always in the air and everybody knew in his heart that populations would have to die off or starve. I didn't get to think Wishart's idea was the right one but I had a hopeless feeling that he only got in first before something even nastier happened. And, come to think of it, he hadn't killed anybody like the racists or bloody conquerors would have, just let them die of old age or whatever. What he did wasn't right but it wasn't outright cruel either. I began to feel confused about right and wrong, good and bad, but mostly I felt it was wrong for one man to make the decision for everybody.

No matter what I thought, Valda carried on explaining, not offering any opinions, just saying what happened. "Sixty-two years have passed since the last child of what we think of as the Final Generation was born, and most of them are dead; only a few aging women and a smaller number of men still exist in the outskirts of the old cities. They are looked after; they will soon be gone, but they paid for their old-age comfort with service to the New Age."

She stopped her restless walk to look hard at me as if she was summing up whether or not I had enough brains to follow what was coming.

"I can give you only a compacted idea of the nature of the changes that occurred. At first there was only small everyday change, and that mainly psychological, as the impact of a reduced future became apparent with only some fifty thousand human beings known to have the ability to carry on the race. The old died off and the middle-aged became the old—and eventually the New Children became the focus of attention. I will come to them soon. Meanwhile the financial structure of the world collapsed—not all at once but quickly enough for the end to be obvious. With twenty years of deaths replaced only by a minuscule number of births, and an aging workforce, demand for nonessentials dwindled and attention became concentrated on necessities.

"Now the people of the Wishart plan began to be heard. They began by laying out an elaborate plan for individual survival as the mass culture fell apart. Briefly, it featured a gradual return to the land as population fell, factories closed, and services vanished. People, the plan said, must become self-sufficient, grow their own food, absorb their own wastes, establish their own networks of communication, develop their own small centers of education for the new young. And, perhaps most of all, they must preserve the science and cultural philosophy of the race against the time when new populations would have developed sufficiently to recover and use it.

"Granddad had had half a lifetime to study the method of propagating his teaching and he simply appropriated the noise and something of the style of the revivalist churches, which were flourishing, save only that his men and women addressed not the masses but the intellectuals and sober minds who did not follow where the mob led. His people preached to governments and leaders of every genre and made impact simply because they preached the simple common sense of everyday life backed by scientific knowledge of the most productive aspects of grassroots methodology. His people charted the gradual breakdown of the next two generations and showed how each collapse could be countered by intelligent anticipation.

"In truth he had nothing to offer that thinking minds across the planet had not worked out in one fashion or another, but he had an organization across the planet to push it. Also, he chose the moment when the first realization of disaster was losing its force and people were looking for a leader with something simple and understandable to say to them. In the end it turned out not so simple as all the ramifications of his future developed, but by then the 'revivalist' rhetoric he used on the masses was working."

She paused as if she was going to make some maybe doubtful point, then made it anyway. "I suppose it would be true to say that Granddad had learned and used the manipulative techniques of the swayers of the masses, but it is also true that he offered hope and a practical outcome. There were those who disagreed with details of his ideas but his organization, unleashed in every major country, took both intellectuals and the mob with it."

I said, "You mean he shouted loudest and to the most people."

Sammy's pencil stopped in disapproval. Valda said frigidly, "That is what I mean."

"I'm only an old Wardie," I explained. "We called things by their right names."

I only meant to warn her she wasn't dealing with an idiot and I could translate what she said in my own terms, but she gave me the sort of glare a Minder would give an uppity butler. I gathered she had clout in whatever today's society turned out to be and wasn't used to corrections. Bad mark, Gus!

She continued on, a mite stolidly, "Dr. Wishart's first concern was the education of the small but vitally important young. They and their parents were moved out of the cities and congregated in groups of half a dozen families, where they lived as self-contained communities, learning self-sufficiency from first principles. The children were little problem, being barely contaminated by their dying cultures; their parents, accustomed to amenities, were rarely competent in practical pursuits, and large groups of aging tradesmen, rural workers, and teachers had to be devoted to educating the young. The education was intensive but thorough and by the year 2140 the first generation was ready and able to pass essential knowledge to their own children."

A cram course in basic living, delivered by experts! The poor little buggers must have been hammered from wake-up to drop-dead.

"This was as well because the teaching pool was shrinking. This had been anticipated but the reality was dismaying. The older generation died off comparatively quickly as production of supportive drugs dried up, food supplies became restricted, medical practitioners became unable to support the workload as diagnostic machinery ceased production and increasing power failures made many operations impossible."

. . . And as their middle-aged offspring gave up the struggle to keep the old turds alive. My own overcrowded world was already pretty pragmatic about life, death, and tender care, but I reckoned I'd best keep that comment to myself.

"As the workforce aged and food production became more basic, so the national amenities began to break down. Transport collapsed as solar collectors and motors became irreplaceable and the breeding of carthorses flourished. People left the cities in order to find space to produce food when everyone must look to his own living."

I tried to imagine it but the sheer magnitude of galloping changes made it impossible. I could only come up with a vision of families with pack animals and loaded carts streaming outward from dark and empty streets, on a starvation diet, the old ones dropping in their tracks and maybe left there, the young ones clinging to possessions and eyeing every stranger with defensive suspicion . . . the sewage systems breaking down, the air filled with fecal stink, disease creeping at peoples' heels . . . and the water pipes rusting unmended . . . and the thieving and looting and murdering . . .

Did Wishart, with his dream of some new Garden of Eden, foresee the chaos and destruction his act would bring? A man born to Minder status, never suffering the realities of basic subsistence, might well have seen his grand persuasion leading the people to hail his ideas as the bright way forward—until communications broke down as power plants lost their workers and their supplies, and replacement parts for the universal vids dried up, and the dying race was left without even news beyond the doings of a nearest neighbor . . .

I must have missed something in a moment of confused vision because Valda was saying, "It was essential that the Wishart Laboratories should operate as long as possible in order to oversee and guide the new generations. Solar grids were established from the beginning, with replacements stored and an inter-lab vid network set up."

And, I would bet, with all Wishart scientists and technicians given juvenation treatments as long as doctors trained in the outlawed technique still existed. And with storerooms loaded with all the stuff that helps to make life worth living. And telling themselves they were on a great crusade to save humanity from itself and so they must be kept fit so as to stand above the ruck and keep the New Age well in hand and doing as it was told.

I was getting angry and that wouldn't do. I had to discover

what was, not start spitting and cursing over how it got that way. Besides, there was a little voice in the back of my mind saying that the population had had to come down one way or another and maybe Wishart's way was as good as any. And another voice was saying, "Who's this bastard to be telling the whole world what to do?!"

"There was very little resentment of the New Generation or their parents. We had expected more, even the fury of the condemned, but the tendency quickly turned to a form of reverence boosted by religion. The various churches of Our Last Days extolled them as God's preserved, and religion took great hold as the masses looked for comfort. Granddad's teachers of course made the most of this attitude, encouraging it. It created an opportunity to separate the New Generation from the mob and gather them in educational enclaves."

I was never religious myself but this cold-blooded account of seizing opportunity stirred the dregs of belief in me and I actually found myself thinking that an affronted God might have something in store for Wishart.

That thought surprised me so much that I lost a bit of Valda's lesson in wondering at myself.

And, after all, this was in her past—over, done with—and only the fanatic nurses mental attitudes forever. Whatever her feeling, the fact was behind her and getting further away every day.

"Our teachers were well trained but their numbers decreased with time and the first of the New Generation became the tutors of the second, able to pass on not only an ideal theory of living but the actual practice of it. By the Third Generation basic production was so well in hand that we were able to educate beyond what were once called the three Rs and open the brighter minds to the possibilities of science and the arts. We encouraged early procreation and Samuel here is already a father to sons and daughters of the Fourth Generation."

I thought of Sammy as a father, with his surface primness that covered a possibility of violence. There was discipline in him. Was sexual strictness passed on in the name of civilization? What sort of life did the kids have?

Valda was saying, "The time is here for the new generations to inherit their world. We have done what we could but there are few of us left and most of those are aged. The resources for juvenation no longer exists—I was among the last to be treated—and the laboratories have for the greater part exhausted their research stores. The young ones are on their own now. The museums and libraries have been preserved and all the knowledge of the past is there when they are ready for it."

She stopped abruptly, as if there was no more to be said. I had a million questions in my head, to be sorted out, but not a comment that wouldn't sound ignorant and silly. The only thing I could think of was to ask, "When can I see for myself?"

Valda and Sammy exchanged glances and he asked, "Can you ride a horse?"

I had seen a stuffed one in a museum once. "No."

"Then you will have to walk. Are you too stiff to walk a distance?"

Yes, I was, but I could put up with it I reckoned. I wanted to see. "I can walk."

He looked doubtful but said, "A massage in the morning could help. I can accompany you tomorrow."

"It's a deal," I said to Valda, "Thanks for the lesson. There's questions but I'd like to sleep on it."

26

There's a lot to be said for a massage. With a good masseur you drift off on clouds and come to afterwards feeling like a joker in the pack. So I was raring to go on my walk around old Melbourne, and off we went about nine o'clock in the morning, me in my clean century-old overall and Sam in his patched and mended one.

We went out the back gate of the complex, crossed a cracked-up road—it was eerie crossing a road with not a car or truck in sight or any sound of one—and were straightaway in the middle of a housing sector. It was the kind of surrounding I recognized almost like coming home—small, four-roomed brick houses, all cheap-built on much the same plan with a tiny garden and back-yard. These were the houses of Wardies with jobs. We called ourselves "middle class" so we weren't confused with the Suss Wardies who had no income and lived on scavenging and government handouts in big concrete towers like pushed-up rabbit warrens. I could see a couple of the old towers in the distance.

Well, all that was history, and Melbourne—and, I supposed, every other city and town everywhere—was dead and empty like a "dig," and maybe one day Sammy's archaeologist great-great-grandchildren would turn it all over to see how the old bastards lived.

For now, the houses were run-down and skeletal, their little gardens overgrown with long grass and thistles. A lot of them had glass and window frames missing and even doors, but most noticeable was that roofs were open to the weather where tiles and roofing sheets and rain gutters had been taken away. Waste not, want not was today's watchphrase, I reckoned. Couldn't blame them.

We walked down the street on a footpath of tumbled blocks of paving busted open by the pressure of growing weeds, past wooden fences rotted by time or kicked in by forgotten vandals, and over everything lay the silence like a thing you could feel. Sammy never said a word, as if he was leaving me to my dead.

And it was a city of the dead—

Except that suddenly somebody was there.

She was an old woman, old enough to have been born before Wishart's plague took hold. She was lined and gray-haired and black—pure Koori black, rare enough in the southern states where generations of mixed blood had just about eliminated the tribal strains.

She leaned over the gate of her house, and the house itself was in perfect condition—well, as near perfect as could be after half a century or more of amateur upkeep. It had its windows intact and roof complete and the garden was planted with hydrangea at the front of the house and roses along the fence.

Her face opened in a big smile as we approached and she said, "Hello, Sammy." A male voice echoed her. I had not noticed him, another full-blood Koori, in the shadow of the doorway.

Sammy answered, "Hello, Emily; hello, Bill," and introduced me: "This is Gus Kostakis. Meet Mr. and Mrs. Gordon."

The name should have registered with me but didn't; from way back most aboriginals had taken Australian names, ostensibly because their tribal names—like, say, Ebatarinja or Pinchinjarra—were too awkward for us locals. Privately I thought it was to do with pride, with keeping a distance between their culture and ours, because they used the real names among themselves. Nobody had observed race distinction since the early twenty-first century, let alone looked down on them like in the old days (they gave us an equal run in the intellectual stakes anyway), but they had tribal lore and secrets they kept to their own company and conversation, things that were no business of "whitey" unless he was initiated. Initiation happened more often than you might think because they didn't observe any race barrier and never had, but the initiated ones kept the secrets. All sorts of stuff leaked out of course, like spirits haunting sacred places or kurdaitja men flying through the air on vengeance trips, but that was just humbug for kids; the real tribal lore they kept close and secret and even the anthropologists knew little about it.

We exchanged some empty words about the weather. Then we moved on. I felt that their eyes followed us—no, followed me—down the street.

I asked Sammy, "Are there a lot like them, old people clinging to the old places?"

"Quite a few. I cannot quote numbers and in a few years they will be gone. Building a civilization is for the young and these are too old to care for tomorrow."

"They're looked after?"

"They are supplied with basic necessities but in the main they look after each other. The Gordons, for instance, keep a few cows in the complex grounds and supply milk to families nearby."

"I was thinking of health, medical care."

He was quiet so long I thought he was ignoring me but after a while, when he had thought it out, he said, "Such care, as you knew it, has passed with time. The techniques I have read of, whereby obscure complaints were diagnosed and treated by radiant machinery, and synthetic drugs maintained the dying in the very teeth of death, are gone by because in the smaller world there is no one to manufacture them. There are doctors but their practice is limited mainly to advice and the care of physical strains and breakages. They advise on diet and exercise, two of the commoner factors in illness, and on the application of the Great Herbal."

All this came out with the familiar Sammy precision; I could literally hear the capitals of the last two words. I had to query something so plainly marked with pride.

The Great Herbal, it appeared, was a compendium of all the drugs that could be extracted, by relatively simple methods that anybody could employ, from locally growing plants. Wishart Laboratories, he told me, had been for half a century examining and testing the products of plants from every quarter of the globe and had compiled a vast volume of cures and palliatives available to every community. Literally thousands of remedies unknown to the past were available today for the simple gathering and preparation; the rarer plants were grown in herbariums by specialist gardeners and made available at need. Even the common cold, he said, was under control. And every man and woman was taught first aid from the age of eight.

I had a confused vision of Grandma's remedies and broken bones treated by Boy Scouts.

"It seems we have enough for our needs and in time will have more, but our medicine has limits at present. The incurable die in such comfort as can be managed; those in irremediable pain are assisted to die."

It was hard to get used to his super-orderly mind dripping words in exactly right sentences but at least I got proper answers to my questions.

After a while I asked another one, making it a sort of curiosity ploy. "You're not making any notes today."

He said, "No, I am not."

Just that. I could make what I liked of it.

Then he added a little. "Exchange of pleasantries with the Gordons scarcely seems noteworthy, do you think? Or do you not?"

His expectant sideways glance said he wanted a reply and with it the reply slipped into place in my head.

"Are they Gordon's children?"

"Bill is his grandson. A kurdaitcha, like his grandfather."

I was surprised that he knew the word; the aboriginal tongues, dying out in my day, were studies for scholars. I only knew it because I read a lot and have a magpie mind for odd bits of information.

I said, "A mumbo-jumbo man."

"You think so?"

It was my turn to look sideways and wonder at that question from down-to-earth, factual Sammy. "I wanted to know what you think."

"I think there are more things in heaven and earth than—than we know about."

Shakespeare, even if he tailed off at the end of the quote! I like the old bard; he was a brainy bugger.

"Could be," I said, and played a long shot in the dark, straight off the tongue before I should have second careful thoughts. "But Dr. Wishart wouldn't be interested in things like that when he checks your notes. He doesn't go for the flimflam stuff. Just as well to leave it out."

"Yes."

That sounded like a cut-off point, signaling "Enough for now."

We continued our walk down the ruined street but there was

nothing fresh to see. We passed another neatly maintained house where a shifted curtain said we were observed, but a lifeless residential street wrapped in silence and lined with gutted shacks was only a reminder that yesterday was just bloody yesterday. Dead as a doornail.

At the first twinge of an ache in my bones I suggested we go back.

As we passed the Gordon house again they were not in sight but Sammy said, "You might call on these people when you have time. They would be interested in a firsthand account of the Warlock awakening and what followed."

"You know about that?"

He said, a mite carefully I thought, "I know what they know. And Dr. Valda has told me of it."

It seemed yesterday was with us still. I reckoned Wishart wouldn't much approve of that, and said so.

Sammy nodded. "He has a thoroughly practical mind. It does not include"—he smiled—"mumbo-jumbo." Later on he said, "I must write up my notes for the day. So far, nothing of interest."

I had not exactly been admitted to a secret but the limits of confidence had been pointed out. And I liked the hint of Sammy with a private life outside the complex.

The walk hadn't tired me much or stiffened the muscles, but Sammy gave me another rubdown and shower. Then he broke the seal on what he said was a presterilized kit and produced a thing like an old-fashioned condom from before the suppressor-pill days but with a little clear plastic bulb at the end of it, and told me—with stiff-voiced delicacy—that Dr. Valda wanted a sperm sample. After providing some, I was to squeeze the tips of the bulb closed, insert it in a metal tube (which was nearly too cold to handle) for delivery to the lab, and dispose of the rubber that, I gathered, was designed to prevent contamination by my dirty hands.

Ah, well, back to teenage pleasures! So Valda was seriously in business with her father-of-the-new-strain project! I couldn't raise much enthusiasm for the idea of myself as sire to a laboratory-based family tree but it could lead—I hoped—to more practical carnal connections later on. It doesn't take much to raise a man's expectations, does it?

I went to the bathroom. When I had done, Sammy took the tube in gloved hands, checked that it was stoppered, and carried it away.

I couldn't resist a call to his departing back, "There goes the real future, a jack-off from the past."

He didn't even break stride, only slammed the door hard.

27

That night, after a dinner that Wishart scoffed down in a pre-occupied silence (planning some more future for his wrecked world?) while the rest of us had little to say, Sammy escorted me back to the cell, said "Goodnight," and left. I didn't know where he slept or how he passed his spare time, and didn't then care. Caring came later.

I tried reading one of the ancient novels Sammy had rooted out from somewhere, but I was too accustomed to lying back watching vidprint with its continuous flow; the business of sitting up and holding the thing and turning pages upset my concentration and I gave up the effort. Instead I took a shower and went back to sit on the bed.

I had plenty to think about but not enough current knowledge to make useful sense, so I stripped off and lay down. The night was warm and a single sheet—a sort of thick flannelette rather than linen—was cover enough; I could always sleep at a moment's notice and I dropped off thinking I must quiz Sammy about a change of underwear.

I woke up when the door opened and closed and the light

came on. It was Valda. She said, "I didn't think you'd be asleep so early. I want to tell you what will be done with the sperm you supplied." No "Beg pardon" or "Sorry to disturb you," just straight to business. "After all, the product will be your children and mine."

I doubted if I'd feel like that about them; "product," as in a batch of whatever from a—a battery hen with a chained cock. I pushed the sheet aside and sat on the side of the bed. She didn't blush or come all over virginal. Why should she? She'd had plenty of previous sight of what I had to offer. I asked, "How many you counting on?"

"I have thirty ova in cryo."

"Too many for the gene pool."

She looked a bit surprised; she had probably forgotten that back in the days of family-size regulation such things were common small talk.

"Not at all. There will be controlled differentiation. Remember that we are selecting for specific traits. My grandmother was a Wahlpiri woman from the Northern Territory; your grandfather was from the Western Desert though which tribe is uncertain, but he had the necessary genes and has passed them to you. Those genes and supporting traits will be preserved in each child, but others will be manipulated to provide gene-pool variety."

"You mean you'll take some out and put others in?"

"Heavens, no! I don't expect you to be educated in genetics, but that could be disastrous. Genes act in groups as well as in dominant effects; introducing a new gene could produce changes unwanted and even dangerous. We propose only to manipulate some chromosomal groups to allow variation in dominant and recessive traits outside the main factors defining essential characteristics of the desert strain. Can you follow that?"

Sort of. All to be the same in essence but different in details; different enough to allow interbreeding. I nodded.

She continued, "This will be delicate precision work and there will be failures, but I think not many."

"And the end result will be like breeding back to the body types of the aboriginal side of both our grands?"

"Yes."

"And they'll look like me?"

"And like me. Don't forget me."

I remembered the fingers on my thighs and reckoned I could push my luck a bit. I said, "I'm not forgetting you at all, but I don't know what you look like."

I really didn't know; you can't see shape properly in an overall. She didn't go on with any shy smile stuff, just kicked off her slippers and started to unbutton. (That was one advantage we had in the old days—I supposed nobody had time now to make things like zips.)

When she stepped out of the overall she had nothing on underneath. I thought, A real Girl Guide—prepared. For whatever. And John Thomas gave a restless stir.

She had the desert tribes' body all right, the female version of my own with the wide hips and load-carrying shoulders and the legs that looked long because they were narrow with the long-fiber endurance muscles.

I said, "It isn't fair, leaving it all to some lab assistant with a test tube," and by then John Thomas was standing up and sniffing the air.

For answer she put her hands on my shoulders, leaned forward and kissed me and I grabbed at her like a starving ape. Sally never had a chance to protest.

Afterwards I said, "Sammy would be shocked out of his mind if he came in now."

"No, he'd just pretend not to see."

I explained about his looking away from nakedness. "What's wrong with the human body? Are all the new folks like that?"

"More or less." It appeared that this was an aspect of the breeding plan that was calculated to preserve useful physical

strains by mating like types on a fairly rigid plan. Wishart had spoken of mountain types and forest types and so on and it seemed
that these youngsters of Sammy's generation were disciplined in
their sex lives, guided to mate with those selected for them. Part
of their indoctrination—or that's what it seemed like to me—was
a no-no attitude to promiscuous sex and a shying away from dis-
tracting items like genitals. The remaining operative labs, she said,
were experimenting with a sort of tailored pheromone designed
to react only to each individual's generic type. It all sounded like
sex by numbers and no fun at all, but I was to remember it in aces
and eights at the end.

Well, you live and learn, and every activity in this age seemed
to lead to a lesson of some kind. I wondered what Sammy's home
life was like.

Then, casually, she got up and dressed and left me.

Definitely a business relationship.

28

Don't get the wrong idea about relations between Valda and
me; that first night wasn't the beginning of any great love
affair. In fact, I'm not too sure what the right idea might be. Put
it that we were good friends who liked the occasional roll in the
hay. It seemed she was a very busy girl with her laboratory work,
which she hardly ever talked about unless I asked her—and when
I asked I didn't understand all that much of her answers—and sex
with a willing partner was more a relaxation and a winding down
than an emotional commitment.

That was all right with me; I didn't want an emotional commitment. The shock of being suddenly and forever cut off from
Sally was an undercurrent in my head that I tried not to dwell on
because dwelling would get me nowhere—except maybe a crying

jag and a hatred of Wishart and all his work. And hatred is no way to begin a new life. And beginning new life was what I was doing, wasn't I?

I don't want to write much about it because "gone forever" is exactly that. You either give in and spend your days howling for the past like a dog on a rubbish dump or you bury it deep and concentrate on the now. Take it that Valda and I each got what we wanted—or needed or whatever—without making a fuss about it.

When I came to think about it, and about the opportunities available in a very strictly monogamous society (or so I thought it was then) I supposed she didn't have all that many targets to choose from. So maybe I was just plain lucky.

In the morning, as we came back from breakfast—a meal designed to carry you all day, which was hard for a tea-and-toast man to get used to—Sammy said, "You'll have to learn to ride a horse. Otherwise you'll see nothing."

Horses and pack mules were, it seemed, big business these days, the only locomotion business. (Plans and texts and blueprints of cars and trains and planes were all preserved in boarded-over libraries and museums, waiting for some future technological penny to drop!)

There were thirty odd horses in a bay of one of the complex wings and the sight of them frightened the living daylights out of me. I hadn't realized they were so big and I couldn't see myself in control of one of the snorting things, and Sammy gave one of his rare laughs as he urged me to some unwilling patting of flanks and stroking of noses. At any rate, none of them tried to bite me or trample me underfoot and after a while he picked one out—a very docile mare, he said to my timid doubts—and put a saddle on her.

I was expected to climb onto the beast. He gave me a demonstration of flinging a leg over from the stirrup, as I learned to call it, and urged me to copy him. I'll draw a veil over the rest of the morning. There's no way to tell how he practically lifted me on board the bloody thing, which stood absolutely still while I climbed all over its back like a gasping grampus, and retain a grain of dignity. I had to get on and off a dozen times before he was satisfied that I could scramble up unaided, and that was only the beginning of a routine of voice commands mixed in with rump pats and knee pressures as the horse and I padded slowly out into the ocean of long grass.

Fortunately the horse knew more than I did about the way to do things and was willing to amble placidly until I got the procedures right. Sammy's information that most kids learned to ride at age five or six did nothing for my pride, but at last it was over for the day and he was complimenting me on my progress. I could have killed him.

I was stiff and sore and certain that my arse and back were a mass of bruises.

Once inside, I demanded massage and got it, accompanied by the big grin of the triumphant torturer.

But I have to admit that after a few days I began to look forward to riding lessons and became quite friendly with Cleo, who would come up behind me and nibble my ear.

Then the day came when Sammy said, as if it was nothing special, "I thought we might say hello to the Gordons," and we rode off down the empty, wrecked, silent street.

Nobody hung over the garden gate this time as we tethered the horses to the picket fence the front door opened and Bill sung out to us to come in. I got the feeling this was prearranged.

Their house was more comfortably crowded with furniture than my home had ever been, and I supposed looting had been the order of the day as householders died without issue and their belongings were free game for firstcomers. The Gordons were a bit ceremonious (perhaps because I was a stranger) and served us tea and some homemade biscuits while we talked polite nonsense, but I noticed right away that Sammy dropped his stiff way of talking with them, while they were educated people who spoke better English than me with my Wardie snarl of an accent.

When the teacups were cleared away Mrs. Gordon left the room and did not come back. There was a space of silence until Bill raised his eyebrows at Sammy, who nodded him to proceed, and he said to me without any preamble, "I am what you white people call a kurdaitcha. That is, a spell-caster, a player of rituals for the credulous and a general humbug who wields some power over those fearing his capacities. Is that how you see me?"

What I saw was a white-haired, genial eighty-year-old transformed without effort into a man of status and some authority and moving to his own ground of expertise, and wanting a quick answer with no time for evasions, so I said right away, "A little bit but not altogether. I reckon you might know a thing or two—psychological stuff that really works, like pointing the bone."

"Yes? The bone?" It was a demand and I had no genuine knowledge; I had to think fast.

"A witch doctor fella points the bone, naming the bloke who is to die. He makes sure the bloke hears about it and because the poor bugger believes in witch doctor powers he makes no effort to live, just gives up and dies. Must say I've never seen a case investigated."

"Why should you? A black man dies for no apparent reason. His relatives shrug and say, 'The bone was pointed.' Pointed by whom? No answer. Do they not know or do they fear to speak, fear they may also die for breaking tribal gunmarl or, as you say, taboo. So the investigation is at a dead end. Besides, nobody advertises such a death. Sufficient unto the day is the evil thereof is white man's wisdom—and most praiseworthy. But the one you call witch doctor is a koradji, not kurdaitcha."

"So tell me what a kurdaitcha really is."

He said bluntly, "No. That knowledge is for initiates."

"Which don't include white men."

"You are not a white man; Sammy tells me you have mixed blood."

"After a few generations so does everybody everywhere."

He smiled pure winter. "So why make the distinction in your mind?"

"Habit," I said, trying to be honest while my brain asked questions about underlying racism and didn't know the answers. My drop of Koori didn't rankle in me; I'd never tried to hide it though it wasn't obvious, but I always thought of myself as white, automatically.

Bill said, "Aborigines populated this land for about sixty thousand years before they saw their first white men and were thereafter hunted close to extinction by them, but they never made the distinction between one kind of human and another. From the earliest years of white invasion there were tribes who took in white men, mostly escaped convicts, and treated them as their own. There was the famous Buckley, in the nineteenth century, who lived with a Koori tribe for thirty years and even forgot his own language." He leaned forward a little. "So it would not be impossible for a white man to undergo initiation."

I wondered for a moment if he was making me some kind of offer. In return for what? But he changed tack suddenly. "I am told that you knew Brian Warlock."

"For one day."

"But in the course of that day you heard his version of the events concerning his experience of sensory suppression."

"That's so."

"We would like to know what he told you."

Old strategist Gus didn't miss that opening. "Who's 'we'?"

"The kurdaitcha."

"And what's their interest?"

He hesitated, and told a lie. He wasn't good with concealing body language and to a trained operator the falsehood stood out—but not the reason for it. He said, "My grandfather was murdered by a renegade priest because of Warlock's knowledge. We need to know why."

Okay, I thought, but I want something in return. But what did I want or need that he could give? I had to temporize. "If I tell you, will you answer some questions for me?"

"That will depend on the nature of your questions. I cannot reveal tribal or kurdaitcha secrets." He said it without emphasis, almost as a throwaway that scarcely needed saying at all.

I knew that was a barrier that couldn't be talked or bribed away. On the other hand, there was no good reason why I should refuse him a secondhand account, even if I knew what I wanted in return. I became aware of Sammy, notepad on knee, pencil poised waiting, and I wondered who would be the recipient of these notes; certainly not Wishart. And if not Wishart, who? And to what end? Wheels within wheels, eh?

"All right," I said, and gave Kurdaitcha Bill what he wanted while Sammy took shorthand. I had never really tried to sort it in my mind and it wasn't easy, being mainly what Warlock had said in Connor's office but with bits Harry had told me mixed in with what had happened in the lecture hall and with what Frankie Devalera had had to say. It wasn't easy to make straight sense of it all but Bill seemed able to sort it out and never interrupted me.

When I had finished he asked a few questions to pin down people's exact words as far as I could remember and then said, "Thank you, but you tell me nothing new."

"You knew all this stuff?"

"Of course. Warlock talked, in the end unstoppably, but his story never varied; unfortunately for his final reputation he branched into metaphysical theory and was laughed at for his wild ideas. I have written copies of much of his outpouring, taken from news files and written down as the power sources for vid replay failed. Devalera had the good sense to be quiet about what was beyond his understanding and left no public record. Connor likewise."

"Bentinck and Miraflores?"

"Jesus Miraflores had reason to be silent and in any case was soon dead. Bentinck died in jail serving a life term for his murder; he said nothing."

"And the kurdaitcha connection?"

"The experiment in sensory suppression penetrated much that we held secret. I can only speak of it now because there are aging folk who remember the scandal of the Church of Universal Communication and the Warlock affair. What is known even to a few is no secret." That seemed to tie it all up until he asked, "Have you a question I may answer?"

May. Yes, I had.

"I don't understand about your grandfather waking Warlock and Frankie. The no-time business is hard enough to stomach, but why should he frighten them into life?"

Bill considered that quite awhile. At last he said, "That was an accidental effect. In his dying moments my ancestor uttered a great cry directed to such kurdaitcha as might be near enough to hear, a cry of such power as to be heard in real time by the sleepers. They did not see his face but the essential spirit of the man. My ancestor wanted his murder known by his people."

I thought that made as much sense as I was liable to get. "He wanted to be revenged? Could they fix that? Did they have people in Melbourne?"

Bill smiled at my simplicity. "Why in Melbourne? Why a direct action? Bentinck cut Miraflores's throat and justice was done." He raised his voice to call his wife, "I think we would like some more tea."

The session was over. I was not to satisfy curiosity about action at a distance. The remainder of the visit was social chit-chat.

Sammy and I rode back mostly in silence. He seemed to sense that I was doing some thinking and left me to it.

I surely was thinking. About old man Gordon's big shout in his death throes reaching out to the tribal magicians . . . telepathy? I didn't believe in that stuff; there was no part of the brain provided for it.

What, then? (Assuming that old Bill's talk wasn't just flimflam.)

I wondered about morphic resonance and the way Bentinck had shut me up when I mentioned it. And about those experiments back in the twentieth century with rats running mazes and people doing crossword puzzles that other people had worked out before them, and the more that did them the faster they were able to solve them. It was as if there was a reservoir of thoughts that those working on the same problem could tap into, unconsciously, so the more people that worked on it the faster they got it out.

That tied in with Warlock's account of a huge sea of thought he could only make small sense of.

Now, if the kurdaitcha had some way of tapping into that without Bentinck's machinery, sort of fading out the body activities by concentration or meditation or even some drug, they might have been able to hear old Gordon's "shout" through all the mess. (A real big shout might account for Frankie hearing it days later, but this no-time business needed a better brain than mine.) If they heard him and whatever information the shout held, that might have put them straight on to Miraflores. And if they could "hear" (for want of a better word) Bentinck's fear and hatred of his boss, could they have worked on his mind to cause him to cut the bastard's throat?

We were turning into the complex as I explained all this to Sammy, trying it out to see how it sounded to somebody else.

All he said was, "Perhaps. Please keep it to yourself."

3.

SAMUEL JOHNS

29

My name is Samuel Johns. I am twenty-eight years of age. I am a farmer but also occasionally employed as Overseer/Stenographer of Historical Records in the state of Victoria, in Australia. At the time of writing I am on secondment to the Dr. Supreme of Wishart Laboratories in the Melbourne area, where my present assignment is the recording of the circumstances and results of the the resuscitation of Gustavus Kostakis and Ian ("Harry") Ostrov, cryo-sleepers from the previous century.

Certain other duties concerning these men also devolve on me, duties unspecified by the Dr. Supreme, who tends to rely on staff to make their own infrastructural arrangements, and which make me general guardian, guide, and secondary tutor to them. The colloquial term, "dogsbody," may be apt. It is this amorphous situation that has allowed me to exercise some influence on their introduction to the twenty-second century, and it is the outcome of this small influence that has dictated the compilation of this account as distinct from the official historical record.

I propose to deal, with some frankness, with matters secret and sacred to the Koori inhabitants of this country and for this reason the manuscript must itself remain private. I am writing for a posterity in whose time the presently sacred matters will have become the common knowledge of the people.

The matters I refer to may be subsumed under the general

heading of morphic resonance, a forgotten offshoot of meta-physical theory that gave rise to some passing interest—and a criminal scandal, as well as the cryo-suspension of Kostakis and Ostrov—early in the last century. The documents concerning the theory and the scandal lie safely in one of the sealed libraries in the ruins of Melbourne, but their contents are familiar to the tribal kurdaitcha men, of whom I am one.

This last statement requires some explanation. I was reared in New Warburton, a settlement some fifty kilometers out of Melbourne that was also the gathering center of the remnants of the aboriginal tribe of the Wuywurung. Few of those remained after the fierce cull of the Dr. Supreme and most of those were half- or quarterbreeds who preferred tribal association to that of the pure white—though the people who called themselves "white" were by then the products of an inheritance too garbled for resolution by nationality.

The point I wish to make is that the aboriginals never at any time discriminated on the ground of skin color (though they them-selves suffered savagely at times from the white people who con-sidered them an inferior species) and on several well-attested occasions actually received willing whites into their tribes. So you will understand that I, a white child, growing up on a market gar-den with a number of black children of my own age, became in-timate with them and, when my parents died in a flooding of the Yarra River, was received by a half-breed couple who took me in as a foster son.

At the age of puberty I was happily initiated and inducted into the Wuywurung tribe and to the responsibilities of manhood in the yulang ring. Later, when certain of my juvenile curiosities and arcane interests attracted the attention of some tribal elders, I was instructed in various matters and eventually reached kurdaitja status as an adult. Most of these "matters" relate to magic ritual, which is of extreme secrecy, but others are of great practical sig-nificance. I shall not write of either. It is sufficient that the kur-daitcha are often regarded as malignant (and possibly some of them are) and this reputation keeps their genuine preoccupations from prying eyes.

As a youngster this ordination into an ethos parallel with but different from my earlier upbringing made little impression on me; I think I regarded it on the level of membership of a secret society, a level at which I was party to all sorts of exotic information consisting mainly of the hereditary tales on which the Koori laws and ethics are based. Later, as I realized that I was being prepared for kurdaitcha status, some sense of a split mentality gave me uneasiness, particularly with regard to the sacred secrecy aspects of the preparation; there was now a part of my life that could be revealed only to other initiates.

I could reconcile my special knowledge only by regarding it as a course of instruction to be relegated to the back of my mind and never used, like an archaeologist treasuring to himself the whereabouts of some rare "dig" to which he alone has access.

Whether or not the Wuywurung knew of my divided attitude I cannot say; I practiced such duties as were required of me—mainly matters benefiting the tribe—to their satisfaction and avoided any use of the more arcane "private" instruction. Whether or not the State Area Councils are aware of my involvement I do not know. I think not. After all, no great amount of my time was taken up and white–Koori relationships were commonplace in our social upbringing; the tendency was for Koori to merge into the general population and abandon tribal allegiances, except among a few groups who quite fiercely maintained the traditions of their ancient past while assimilating what appealed to them of the New Age. At any rate, it was with the blessing of the state that I married a Koori woman of the Wuywurung whose breeding DNA matched satisfactorily with my own, and continued my studies at the newly established university.

Since I displayed linguistic and writing skills, the state found me suitable employment, and so it was that Dr. Wishart one day detached me temporarily for his private service. The Dr. Supreme no longer takes any direct part in government—the various world communities run their own social systems, subject only to the strict guidance of the genetic charts—but who and what he wants he obtains without question.

I have great respect for the Dr. Wishart who built our present world, but privately I must acknowledge that he has grown old and that attitudes have hardened in his mind. I have heard Gus Kostakis's account of the doctor's appearance in the purlieus of the disgusting poseur, Miraflores, and may reasonably date his opposition to the theory of morphic resonance from the time of his realization of the nature of that man's greedy criminality; he put the matter from his mind as a monstrous perversion of psychological practice and has refused to countenance it since.

This is a shortcoming in him but one he will not see exposed in his lifetime. The resonance exists. I am a kurdaitcha—I know.

While the Dr. Supreme refuses to countenance the concept of morphic resonance, refuses even to read Steven Warlock's statement (long ago abstracted from files and copied and studied by kurdaitcha men), the same is not true of his granddaughter, Dr. Valda, who finds the subject enthralling and would encourage study of it if suitable investigators could be found.

Found they will be but not by her. It is men's business. Tribal women have ceremonies and rituals exclusive to them, barred from the knowledge of men as male business is barred to women, and morphic resonance is not a field for women. The white component of my tribalism sees this separation of interests as a hindrance to real progress in any form, but it would be more than my welfare is worth to attempt to interfere; tribal justice is swift and inflexible and delivered more often than our white men's legal system suspects.

Meanwhile there are kurdaitcha who understand what happened to Warlock and discuss among themselves the nature of the white man's machinery that made his extreme vision possible. Their problem is how to achieve the same penetration by purely psychological means, since all Bentinck's paraphernalia has vanished. In any case, they would not know how to use it. It is a problem for generations to come. When it is solved the very nature of humanity will alter forever.

It is enough for the present that I am a man of two lives. They are separate; they do not conflict.

Now I must consider Gus.

In his overall, Gus Kostakis is long and gangling, but the clothing is deceptive. He is in fact deep-chested, narrow-hipped, and long-legged with the stringy but very capable musculature persistent in the line from his single Koori ancestor. I see clearly why Dr. Valda selected him as one of the fathers of her projected Desert Genetic; that she selected herself as his founding partner is another matter, one of personal taste manifesting in private encounters aside from laboratory requirements.

Their attachment forms a wry commentary on sexual preference. Who can tell where the lightning will strike? (I understand that Dr. Wishart plans to regularize this particular lightning to further the maintenance of his plan for genetic suitability among later generations, a plan that envisages coupling decided by some form of pheromonal selectivity. This I lack biological training to understand, but for once I have some doubt of the doctor's aim; it seems to me that with Forest, Mountain, Tropical, and now Desert Genetics we have sufficient restriction of choice, sufficient regimentation.) For Dr. Valda the lightning has struck, as it seems to me, peculiarly, for while she is not in my eyes a physically attractive woman, she has an undeniably brilliant brain whereas Gus has the intellect of a half-educated guttersnipe.

His narrow face is contradicted by the full lips and distended nose of the Koori, his brown eyes regard the world with a stare of perpetual surprise, and he exhibits an air of general laziness that conceals a disconcerting stamina and fluidity of movement. He claims to have had only the minimum available education of his time but is astonishingly well read—no, smatteringly read on a whole compost heap of subjects. He appears to have a considerable knowledge of the art and artists of the past but only a hen's pecking of almost anything else; he seems to have gathered, from omnivorous reading, an entry into most subjects but mastery of none, so that he can surprise with instant familiarity some abstruse or academic subject and the next moment be dumbfounded by some simple extension of it. His comments on this age are often penetrating and just as often informed by a comfortably "folksy" unwisdom that drives Wishart to furious silence, and causes me to give laborious explanations of the modern outlook, which are received with patient scepticism.

Yet I like the man very well and suspect the presence of a competent brain behind the fluff of talk, perhaps one of which to be wary. And I must confess to some envy of his writing style. It is all ill-spelled and ill-constructed (he accepts correction with a child's eagerness to know better) but loose and flowing, while descriptively accurate and in an unself-conscious fashion reflective of his personality. I wish I could acquire some of it, but I have been too damnably well trained.

He will continue his narrative and it will have some future value, but it has come to the edge of matters he does not and cannot be permitted to understand. Some future reader will find my parallel version of the facts a necessary filling-in of Gus's writing.

30

Now: The matter of the morphic resonance.

The aboriginal Australians have been on the continent for sixty thousand years, long enough to make them the oldest homogeneous culture on earth, long enough to have developed several hundred languages and dialects while maintaining their root traditions. They have developed a tribal system based on living with the land rather than simply inhabiting it, so that everything is used but nothing is destroyed—a far cry from the culture of greed and ruthless development practiced by our own Last Generations.

As an isolated culture living in comparatively small tribal units, it is understandable that they did not develop the art of writing; it needed large, concentrated populations with increasingly complicated interactions to produce it in the outside world, and that (so the books tell us) only in comparatively recent times. Yet, having no maps, they developed the "song lines" that, connecting geographical features with one another, guided the traveler unerringly over the whole eight million square kilometers of the continent. Also, they developed a legal system that, though founded on crude "payback" justice, was understood and generally followed throughout the land. And their traditional tales, representing history, passed orally from generation to generation, showed a remarkably cohesive descent (despite regional variations) for a people inhabiting hill and forest and shoreline and even the inhospitable desert at the land's heart.

Invading Westerners found them savage and totally unsophisticated and treated them, with the typical Western brutality of the nineteenth century, as an underclass to be exploited and, if turbulent, massacred. Some two hundred years passed before the white masters of Australia realized that they were "assimilating" and, in the process, coming close to wiping out a deeply spiritual and deeply thoughtful society. Even so, when the tide turned in favor of preservation of native culture the good-hearted investigators, the eager professors, the shiny-eyed book writers were unable to see the culture through Koori eyes. They compared the hereditary history with the folk tales of the rest of the world, found creation myths and generation myths and rite of passage myths, and saw that these were universal in human experience; they equated them with current knowledge and failed to observe the significant differences.

As an example, they failed to see that tales of the kurdaitcha as vengeful people, bent on outrage and harm, represented only the exploits of the few and made cautionary tales for those in need of them. They did not see that the accounts of spirit vengeance, of out-of-body visitations and the like, were the tribal expressions of spiritual thinking, that even the kurdaitcha's back-to-front shoes, presented as attempts to frustrate a pursuing enemy, were symbols of a dual-natured world.

It will not do to categorize the kurdaitcha as sweet-natured philosophers—after all, they are human first and subject to human failing—but there are those among them who have thought deeply over the centuries. They had never heard of morphic resonance but in our present day they knew its spiritual manifestations and had a better conception of its implications than even Warlock, who had glimpsed the ultimate depth without understanding it.

I do not write here of all kurdaitcha as students of metaphysics and the occult. Only a few pondered the problems of communication with the dead, which was until recently the angle of contemplation commonly adopted, and those few became an almost vanishing few as Wishart's virus enveloped the planet. Still the knowledge and fearful apprehension of the life-beyond-man persisted and was handed on to those judged worthy, a secret within the kurdaitcha secrets. Among the tribal aboriginals nothing is ever lost.

It was Bill Gordon who taught me all I knew of the resonance, the life-beyond.

Old Bill, now in his eighties, was born in the closing years of the Last Generation and was one of the few tribal aboriginals (who rarely came to the cities) to receive a full classical education. He became what was called a Doctor of Letters in the closing years of such distinctions, a noted poet and writer of essays on ethics and on the Wishart future when the nature of that became plain. In his old age he continued to circulate poems among those who remembered him.

His tribal life never impinged on his public persona. Only

some philosophic and contemplative equals, and a few pupils, were aware of his kurdaitcha status.

I went to see Bill on the night that Gus engaged in—dalliance? fornication? is there a properly expressive word for it?—with Dr. Valda. I said I had come to talk men's business and his wife at once left the room. There could be no question of her listening at the door in the hope of hearing secret communications; men's business is men's business and women's is women's. This is the tribal practice, bequeathed through God alone (if he exists) knows how many generations, and I have often thought privately that it should be abandoned in the New Age, but the tribals cling with love to their ancient culture and would be abusively resentful of a suggestion of change.

Yet it was change that was in my mind as I sat down in the old man's lounge room and said tentatively, "I have been thinking of morphic resonance."

"Of the life-beyond," he said flatly. It was a contradiction.

However, I had used the technical term deliberately. "Of the machinery used by Bentinck to free Warlock's mind for self-contemplation."

"Ah, the machinery. And?"

He was attentive and politely interested, but I knew that he had no love for the fact that white science had bypassed the Koori's need for intense inward searching to achieve what the experimenter had plumbed in a single trial.

I said, "It could possibly be reconstructed while the generators still exist to power it."

He cocked his head on one side like an alerted bird but made no answer.

I continued, "The patent office files still exist, sealed for the use of far future generations. An appeal to the council in session would see us granted a search permit; also, there will almost certainly be a detailed plan and description in the archives. The Council—"

Head still cocked, he interrupted me. "Ah, yes, the Council.

How many tribal Koori have seats on the Council?"

I knew what was to come now, but it was not a time for retreat. "Two."

"Two among forty-seven Councillors. Considering the sparseness of the aboriginal population, that is a quite respectable number. But not a significant number. The appeal would surely be granted and I don't doubt that the machine could be found or duplicated. But to what end? What new thing will be loosed on the world?"

"Knowledge."

"Ah, that! The life-beyond is known. What more can Dr. Bentinck's machine tell us?"

"It can reveal what lies in the darkness."

"Given time and dedicated minds, the darkness will be pierced and its confusions understood."

It was more or less the resistance I had anticipated. I persisted. "Time and minds, Bill? How many kurdaitcha adept in search for the life-beyond are still alive? There never were many. Now, perhaps three or four in the whole continent. Perhaps fewer."

"Enough to pass on knowledge."

"To whom? Few of the assimilated people care about such things; they are citizens, not tribals, and their interests are the interests of their neighbors. Assimilation has shifted them away from their culture. They look to the laboratories and the genetic guidelines to plot their futures. The tribal culture is the concern of the tribals, and their numbers shrink by the year; among them, how many are kurdaitcha? And among kurdaitcha, how many are willing to face the desert training only to pursue a mystery? The machinery could make investigation open to trained minds of all the genera."

He knew the picture in my mind—the silent desert, the absence of life, of sound, of movement, the utter loneliness of the self in a shutting out even of the conception of loneliness itself. The intensity of the deliberate shutting out. The freeing of the mind from the trapping of the body. The arrival at a state where even the mind vanished from its own consciousness, where only receptiveness looked into the chaos of thought.

I had never fancied the grueling training of my mind into such selflessness and I knew that Bill had gone only a little way and put it aside as too demanding of a life given to poetry.

He asked with, I think, genuine curiosity, "To what end? Knowledge? Only that? Knowledge to be disbursed to the many, to hoi polloi, to the mob, for popular misuse and greater confusion than already cloaks men's minds?"

His curiosity was, for my thinking, to be balanced against his derision. "We knew," I insisted, "that Warlock proceeded more deeply into the darkness than any kurdaitcha has done. Kostakis's statement confirms it. Warlock penetrated a region where a great maelstrom of human thought lies waiting."

"So? In all his years of contemplation he merely observed the maelstrom, making nothing of it, bringing back with him not a single breath of your 'knowledge.' And in his appreciation the time passed almost instantaneously. Little wonder that his glimpse of the world's thinking yielded nothing—if what he chanced on was indeed the world's thinking. Then, too, it required the mental outrage of my dying grandfather to shock him back to the world of men. Send another after Warlock and who will return the explorer to life?"

I had thought of these things and was ready for him—after a fashion. "Others, men of intellect knowing what they will encounter, will be able to penetrate the darkness and eventually understand what it holds. Means will be found of restoring them to consciousness. A thousand generations of kurdaitcha have never so much as seen the true darkness whereas a scientist's machinery has revealed its existence."

"Therefore the darkness must be lightened for all humanity?"

"Do the kurdaitcha of the life-beyond seek the knowledge for purely selfish ends?" A flicker of anger on old Bill's face suggested the question had a barb of truth. "What do they hope to find as reward of a lifetime of self-contemplation?"

He hesitated a long while, then said, "They hope to find the Dream Time."

The Dream Time—in aboriginal belief the cradle of creation, the putting together of land and sky and water by the great creation spirits, the birth of man at their hands and the source of all man's dreaming down the ages. Not only man's dreaming but the dreaming of the birds, the lizards, the kangaroo, and all created things.

I said, "So you believe as my thinking leads me to believe, that the darkness holds all the thinking of man and beast since time began, that we can find there the spirit of the world preserved in a place beyond time."

He tensed like an animal startled by a threatening sound, and relaxed only slowly into an uneasy calm, as though my shot in the dark—it had been no more than that—had raised an ugly wind of passage.

Then he said, with a perfectly blank face, "Your teaching binds you to silence. Your thinking can be tested only by a lifetime of self-denial and inward communion. This conversation must remain private. Forever."

That was the end. It was more than a reminder of tribal obligation. It was a threat.

I made my way back to the complex in slow thoughtfulness. I had expected a hearing from Bill, almost certainly to be followed by a negation of my ideas, but a negation expressed in terms of sympathetic recognition of my white man's need to exploit opportunity in so original a field. I had badly underestimated his attachment to the tribal beliefs of his Wuywurung ancestors. He was one of the few tribals who had taken university education to its limits and I saw now that I had made the error of bracketing him with myself as a man of two minds, one of which recognized the spiritual values of his tribe yet remained conscious of their logical shortcomings, while the other appreciated the possibilities latent in the utterly different drives of the white majority. My error revealed him as a man deeply imbued by the ethics and mores of the culture of his birth.

So much for the "multiculturalism" on which we prided our-selves, for our acceptance of all human beings as equals without consideration of skin color or physique or ancestry or heritage. My black foster parents had not made me Wuywurung except in the assumption of a cultural duality that gave way instinctively to a white viewpoint, and Bill's education had reacted instinctively against what he could see only as an attack on the beliefs in which he had been born and reared. It probably did not matter to him whether or not my argument made sense; what counted was my assault on a thousand generations of order, behavior, and tribal law.

He had uttered no direct threat but only a blind fool could have disregarded the implicit menace. For him, my idea of for-malizing an investigation was dead and buried by his opposition.

31

Understand, please, that Bill Gordon's opposition was not trib-ally based; there were no tribal secrets or privacies involved. "Kurdaitcha" is a term describing the practices of individuals of various tribes, only a very few of whom were involved in the men-tal and physical rigors of pursuing the life-beyond, and even these few did not form a coherent group. That they would resent public discussion of their secrets was certain, but kurdaitcha had a gen-erally evil reputation among tribals, who would be unlikely to offer them support.

So, though I understood and in some degree respected Bill Gordon's stance, I was not much awed by it. After a night's sleep, I determined to approach Dr. Valda.

This was more easily determined than done; she was heavily involved in Dr. Wishart's genetic planning, requiring as it did the directing of several generations of sexual relations designed to preserve essential features of each genetic line while avoiding close interbreeding and passing of undesirable characteristics. (It was work for the computers, of which only a few remained; they broke down in time, and replacement parts were no longer available.) Hers is demanding work and several days passed before I found opportunity for audience. What determined me to seek her help was her belief in the Bentinck work and her refusal of the Dr. Supreme's blunt dismissal of it. (I think that he felt shamed by his financial involvement with the greed-driven Miraflores and the brutal outcome of the man's machinations, and wished to put the entire unsavory business from his mind; behind his autocratic behavior lurked the same psychological weaknesses as those of every man.)

She received my ideas with interest, particularly about the work of the twentieth-century investigators, of which I was surprised to discover she had not heard. Indeed I had heard of them myself only from the grab-bag memory of Gus Kostakis. These men charted the success of teams of rats running mazes, finding that each successive team ran the course more successfully than the previous one. They tested these results on humans with crossword puzzles (some manner of popular word game) and again found that each successive team completed the test more quickly than the last.

"It was as though," I said, "each fresh group plucked out of the air, as it were, some residue of instruction from the previous group—as though thought persisted beyond the moment of thinking and could be picked up by minds in a state of great concentration. It appears to have been a fragmentary transmission, with the puzzlers snatching at bits floating by. Then Kostakis told me of Warlock speaking of what seemed to be a vast accumulation of human thought accessible to the mind of a person literally shut out from his own body—save that he was unable to make sense of a flood of information spilling, undifferentiated, into his brain."

I paused for her comment, fearful of having pushed extrapolation too far, but she said, "I talked with people at the time who had reached a similar conclusion." One sees her youthfulness and tends to forget the effect of juvenation—an eerie business. "The affair was forgotten in the pressures of simply staying alive in Warlock's time. What prompts you to raise it now?"

"The likelihood that the plans of Bentinck's machine exist somewhere among the sealed records, perhaps in the patent files. Perhaps the machine itself, somewhere preserved."

She considered that a long while. "And then?"

"Why, then," I said, "we may repeat the experiment with the advantage of knowing what we will encounter and perhaps be more able to extract value than poor unprepared Warlock."

"Value?" Dr. Valda had been infected, over the years, by a little of the scientist's arrogance and it was displayed in the hint of mockery tainting that one word. "What do you need so badly to know, Sammy? Yesterday's thinking evolved today's certainties. It is outdated. Do we need to rake over the garbage heaps of the past?"

Nettled, I replied that much constructive thinking may have been lost and could be recovered.

She smiled. "And we should emulate the archaeologists, collecting shards of broken pottery and inspecting the ashes of prehistoric campfires in the hope of confirming the existence of some local custom? I have always thought archaeology a fringe pursuit for the decoration of history. Poring over ancient thought seems an extension of the same."

That was too outrageous and I realized that I was being goaded to an answer. In truth, I had been filled with the excitement of the project rather than any rationale; it was time for me to collect my thoughts. In desperation I said, more or less forming the idea as I spoke, "If the history of human thought can be unraveled it may be possible to detect future trends and anticipate them. To detect dead ends of logic. Even to see logic itself as a system blowing to a wind of fashion and so provide it with new parameters."

I stopped because I was not sure that I made good sense, but she nodded and applauded, "Good. Good. Excellent, Sammy."

I should have been wholly pleased but pleasure was soured

by the note of schoolmistress praise, as though I had merely reached an end she had attained before me. I was reminded of my status as a laboratory servant. I was aware of her night foray with Gus, had in fact predicted the assault, and wondered did she give herself princess airs as she condescended to such a commoner as he.

Then she surprised me with complete cooperation. She said, "It will require permission from the Area Council."

"Why?"

"If archives are to be unsealed and searched a squad of special archivists must be assembled and the work overseen, particularly the handling of documents, by a preserver panel. Nothing can be damaged or mislaid."

In the enthusiasm of an idea I had not considered daily facts.

She continued more thoughtfully, "That could occupy three weeks or a month while petition is made and slow consideration given."

With this turn my mind was racing ahead of her. "Then the Council's decision will be published in the broadsheets."

"Yes, and I promise you full credit for the proposal."

The last thing I wanted. I may have sounded a little desperate as I protested that I did not want my part in the affair publicized, because she gave me a silent stare of suspicion as though she speculated on there being more here than met the eye.

She asked simply, "Why?", in a tone that demanded an answer.

And I told her why. I told her of the kurdaitcha and their contemplative explorations and of the "professional" secrecy enjoined on their fellows, including myself.

Naturally enough, she protested, "But we will only prove and justify their work!"

So I was obliged to explain to her the tribal rules regarding special secrecies. I had to explain that there could be retribution for the breaker of "magic" secrets and that Bill Gordon had warned me against disclosure.

How much credence she placed in my words I could not easily discern because she was plainly ignorant of tribal law and found it grotesque, but at least she appreciated that a threat had been implied and should be heeded. She agreed in the end that my participation should go unmentioned, but I felt that her agreement was in the nature of a sop to a troubled child, that she had detected me in mental confusion and thought the less of me for it.

Ours is a time when racial differences go unnoticed, so it happens that our aboriginal folk are now a very small fraction of the population and scattered over all the vast area of the country. Where a few are gathered together, as on the edges of the old Melbourne ruin, they keep their counsel about tribal matters and are regarded rather in the nature of a sect than as the guardians of an ancient tradition. Where they choose to be close-mouthed about what are essentially private matters, why should anyone question them? And so, since the Last Generation, some knowledge and understanding have been lost in the superficial fusion of cultures. Little wonder that Dr. Valda failed to appreciate that I walked a social tightrope where a slip might be paid for in ostracism of myself and possibly of my family.

I may have been playing tit-for-tat when I reminded her that she would face opposition from the Dr. Supreme, whose total rejection of the theory of morphic resonance had in the past been expressed violently, but she shrugged the objection away.

She said, "He will not interfere with an Area Council decision. How can he?"

It was true that Dr. Wishart never interfered in social or governmental matters and that he held no office of any kind. Nonetheless, like most people, I suspected that a word from him would sway any council anywhere in the world, though I knew of no evidence that he had ever attempted it. He was revered.

Perhaps it showed in my face because she added, "What does he care about local decisions save to abide by them rather than cause friction? He creates the future; the present must legislate its own problems."

•   •   •

When she left me I had an exhilarating moment of having broken the tie between my two cultures. I had also some self-doubt in that I was unwilling to have it announced.

Strangely, the act that rose most persistently in my mind was that I had discussed male "magic" secrets with a woman. If revealed, this would be regarded as a most severe infringement of the gender demarcation. I had never heard of such a thing happening.

The sense of freedom from a system of social beliefs to which I had actually paid little more than lip service—a freedom-in-secret though it truly was—needed expression. I recorded the whole matter, not in the "historic" record I keep for the laboratory files, but in this private diary, to be preserved for the eyes of the future. Why should I not have my small niche in history?

4.

GUS KOSTAKIS

32

A few days after the visit to Bill Gordon, Wishart came into the cell looking as if he had a bad smell under his nose, and said to me where I sat on the bed, "I want your assistance," as if I'd tug the forelock and say, "Yes, sir, anything at all, sir."

Since I just stayed sitting and looking at him, he had to go on. "Ostrov should awaken soon and it might be as well if you are there to . . ." He hesitated. "For immediate company."

He had decided he didn't like me and he wouldn't climb down to say, He may wake up the hard way and better he take it out on you than me. But at least he had listened to my advice.

Sammy picked up his pad and stood but Wishart said, "Best leave them alone, Sam; Ostrov was taken at a traumatic moment. There is a concealed camera and an intercom you can use from the library."

He wasn't going to miss whatever fun there was, from a safe distance. Well, he was an old man and thought himself entitled to save his brittle bones.

He said, "You may have a wait, Mr. Kostakis. I don't know when he will wake. Probably within hours."

Then he went out. The king had spoken. I hadn't said a word.

Sammy interpreted my silence. "The doctor is very old and increasingly unwell."

"Doesn't excuse him behaving like a sergeant major."

Sammy asked, "What is a sergeant major?"

I said, "Forget it. Let's go."

He led me only a few doors down the passage and opened up a room the dead spit of my cell. Harry lay on the bed with a sheet over him. He looked just the same as ever.

Sammy said appreciatively, "He's a muscular man. One of my genetic, I would say." He went out and closed the door behind him. He had told me once that he was classified as Forest Genetic, meaning designed for hard work like tree felling and scrub clearance. He was a tad smaller than Harry but very muscular, so I suppose the classification fitted even for a stenographer.

I had nothing to do then except just be there. It seemed typical of Wishart arrangements, the I-say-and-you-do attitude, to leave me to stare at the wall while he went about other business. I dragged the chair to the side of the bed and sat down and looked Harry over. He looked to be in good nick so far as I could tell; he would have had plenty of feeding and isometric-style exercise to get him ready for the New Age—as if anything could really get you ready for it.

Then I had nothing to do. In the old days there would have been at least a small vidscreen for passing the time but in this year of our Lord there was no vid—or anything else to do besides count your fingers. I soon got tired of watching a sleeping man and did a few sitting-up exercises and got bored with that, too. Then I just sat for maybe an hour or more, until I saw a change.

What I saw was tears seeping from under his eyelids. The idea of Harry in tears was hard to come at—until I remembered what his last sight had been before he was laid out, and then I panicked a bit at the job of pacifying a man blind with rage and revenge.

It wasn't like that. He opened his eyes and saw me and said in a creaky voice, "They're both dead."

In a sort of quick gabble I said, "The ones that killed them are dead, too. So's Jesus and his rotten church."

He gazed at me blankly and I guessed I had said too much for him to take in all at once. After a bit he let out a long, soft, "Aaaaah . . ." that seemed to say it was good that way.

He wiped his eyes on the back of his hand and tried to sit up, and winced as bone and muscle protested. He took it gradually, puzzled by his resisting body, until he sat upright and asked, "Where's this?"

The creaky voice puzzled him, too, and he tried clearing his throat. Wishart or somebody had foreseen this and left a jug of water and a glass on the desk, so I poured a drink for him. It helped a bit because his voice was clearer as he repeated, "Where's this?"

I said, "The Bio Complex."

That brought a frown. "Why? Who brought us here? Bentinck?"

"No; he's dead, Harry. Listen, things have changed. We've both been in cryo-sleep." Best get it over quickly.

He repeated incredulously, "Cryo-sleep? Who did that? Why?"

His voice was stronger now but mine stuck in my throat as I tried to face up to explaining while no words came.

He grabbed me by the chin, asking, "What's up with you?" and I could only gape at him, it all seemed so complicated. "Who put us in cryo-sleep?"

I managed to say, "Dr. Wishart," and Harry asked, "Where the hell does he get into it?"

"It was his idea, so there'd be no bodies left for the police to find. He was afraid a dead cop would loose a big team investigation."

He nodded abstractedly and said, "So it would have." I knew his mind was on his dead parents and other things were automatic responses. "And how long have we been in sleep?"

I couldn't see any way to break it easily. I said, "A hundred years."

That got through to him, rocked him. He was quiet for a while, then got up, stretching his unused muscles, and did a couple of kneebends, gasping at the pain. Like a clown, I said, "Sammy will give you a rubdown; he's extra good."

He said, "Try to make sense, Gus. Start at the beginning."

So I did.

It took a long time, with me straining to get it right because I knew people elsewhere were listening in. When I came to how Wishart let his virus loose, Harry lifted his head to stare me in the face as I told how everybody died except the ones picked out to parent the New Age. It was as if he didn't believe me at first but in the end dropped his head again because he had to believe.

33

When I had finished—and he never interrupted me once, only nodded and breathed hard a few times—he got off the bed and went to the window to look out and just stood there, not saying anything. I reckoned he was stunned by the idea of so many people gone as if all history had never existed.

But when he was ready what he said was, "Grass is a bit long. Otherwise much the same."

I told him, "From this side, yes, but wait till you see Melbourne—houses with their roofs torn off and windows pulled out, grass and weeds busting up the footpaths and not a living thing in sight. Sammy taught me to ride a horse to get around on. There's no cars or electricity—except a few small petrol generators for Wishart's work."

He gave a thin smile. "Did you ever see a horse before? They bred them for racing. A Minder sport."

"No Minders now, Harry."

"Seems there's not much of anybody. This place is silent."

"That's soundproofing. There's thirty or more people working here for Wishart and Valda. Mostly for Valda. I think Wishart came here only to direct the job of bringing you and me out of cryo. His lab is somewhere else."

He seemed to be accepting the new setup, the whole idea of change in a way that was unreal. But then, he had the one-thing-at-a-time sort of mind that had made him a good copper.

Then Sammy came in, carrying Harry's clothes. While he laid them on the bed I said, "This is Sammy Johns. He looks after us and writes us up for some future history book. He writes in shorthand; you know what that is?"

"Yes." He looked over Sammy, sizing him up as if he had expected some sort of monster.

Sammy held out his hand, keeping his eyes away from the naked sexual apparatus, and said, "How do you do, Mr. Ostrov? I am sure you would like to get dressed."

Harry took the hand, smiling slightly at the primness, and dragged on his underwear while I thanked all our stars that the first hour had passed without an outburst.

He was in his cop overall when the door opened again and Valda came in with Wishart behind her. I introduced them to each other as formally as if they were guests at a party. It was as smooth as all mates together.

Until Harry blew it apart right away by greeting Wishart with the kind of smile that makes tigers back off, and saying, "It's an honor to meet the greatest mass-murderer since an asteroid put an end to the Jurassic. You make a real meal for a policeman."

It froze the room solid. It was my old Harry speaking, the copper on the job, calling some piece of guttershit by its right name.

Sammy, shocked and horrified, opened his mouth to say something but Wishart signaled him to shut up. He said, "Mr. Ostrov, the reason you are awake and present is to provide the more useful Mr. Kostakis with some company of his own time and ambience. For the rest, you are no longer a policeman and my position in the New Age is assured and unassailable. You'll do well to conform to present custom."

It was a judge's speech delivered to the prisoner at the bar.

"You mean," Harry said, "that the people here like you? I'm pretty adaptable but I have my limits."

I remember thinking that Wishart looked a very old man then, very frail. And white in the face because no man faces up easily to naked contempt. For a long moment he said nothing at all but when he spoke it was in a way that hit Harry where it hurt.

"I expected better, Mr. Ostrov. Many years ago I read your account of Premier Beltane's disastrous suicide, with some interest in your answers to questions put to you while under the influence of a truth drug. You displayed complete racial and ethnic intolerance and suggested that the virus be used to clean out all but a white-skinned, English-speaking world. I refined your ethnocentrism to create a planet whose ecological balance would in due course be restored with inhabitants more physically suited to the world that bore them. You should applaud."

He went out, a clear winner in that little spat. I didn't want to look at Harry because I had heard him say such things under Nguyen's drugging, but I also knew how his thinking had changed afterwards. His waking up was turning out very sick.

Valda broke the new silence by saying, "I didn't read the book. Did you say those things?"

It sounded like pure curiosity, not agreeing or condemning.

Harry answered her, with eyes like stones and voice to match, "You're Valda Wishart, aren't you? A mite older but still around after a couple of illegal rejuves. Yes, I said them. Beltane wanted to know what the common people thought and that's what he got. It's what comes out when the drug gets right to the bottom of your mind, to the real subconscious truth you don't admit even to yourself. He got other stuff out of me, too, stuff that nearly brought on a mental breakdown when I had to face up to it. I had to learn to clean my mind, to think about my real attitudes and do something about being properly human. Your grandfather doesn't know that part. And wouldn't give a tinker's curse if he did. Do you?"

It sounded like spitting in her face but she replied calmly enough, "I've no call to care what happened to your mind a century ago; what matters is that you are a survivor and must make the best you can of new circumstances."

He watched her quizzically, as if he was asking hisself what sort this one was.

She said awkwardly, like somebody treading treacherous ground, "I know you have awakened to dreadful last memories. I can only hope time will ease the pain."

"It won't."

Valda made one of those hopeless little gestures of someone who's done their best and knows it isn't good enough, and said, "I'll see you later; I hope you will adjust."

She left us. In the silence Sammy looked wistfully at the police uniform and tried to lighten the atmosphere, "It must have been fine to wear clothes so beautifully made to fit."

But Harry had his head down because he was crying. In the end he had loved his parents very much.

Suddenly I was angry with him, in the way you can only be angry with a friend. Hadn't I lost my wife and my son down in the pit of years, with no chance of ever knowing what had happened to them as two jobless nonentities among the world's billions, tossed on to the government Suss when their earner vanished without a trace? And hadn't I faced up to it? And here he was, drowning in regret for all the love he hadn't given his mum and dad when he had the chance. I wanted my mate back with me now, not a mass of evil-tempered self-pity. I felt deserted.

· I took his head up by the chin and snarled at him, "You think you're the only one that lost anybody? Under Nguyen's dose you talked about getting rid of the old and useless, didn't you? Wishart gave you what you wanted so face up to it!"

His tears stopped as if they had been blocked off. He looked up at me wooden-faced and then started a slow smile, not in a nice way but one that pinned me to the board. "Remember what you said under the drug, Gus? You said to kill all the people and leave only the beautiful animals to inherit the earth. It was the cry of the lonely, unwanted man. Now you have to leave me my little loneliness to be got over."

I felt like a cheap shit, remembering too well my mind opening like a howl of despair.

And there was Sammy—staring, troubled, ill at ease like a stranger caught peeking at privacy.

I sat beside Harry on the bed, said, "Sorry, mate," and he patted my knee, suddenly laughing at me.

That got it over. It was a matter that didn't have to be opened up again.

Harry became aware of Sammy's troubled gaze and said, "What's your name? Sam, is it? Well, Sam, I'd like something to eat; I missed my dinner at the century intersection."

I started to explain that this age ate only twice a day but Sammy interrupted me in his prim way, as if correction called for a special schoolmaster tone, "It is customary for those engaged in heavy physical labor to eat three times a day; I do so myself when on forest work. I will find something for Mr. Ostrov, to tide him till dinner."

He went out and Harry asked, "Does he always carry on like an old nanny?"

I thought it best to warn him. "No, and when he lets loose he sports a sort of karate chop like a blunt ax. I've felt it. Actually he's a good bloke. Be nice to him."

"Of course. As Wishart reminded me, I'm not a policeman anymore to make moral judgments about the population. But I think I could hand down verdict and sentence on that self-satisfied bag of old bones. And enjoy doing it."

Then Sammy came back with some fruit and bread rolls.

34

The Wisharts didn't come near us for days. (Except that Valda came to me occasionally at night but that wasn't strictly business. Call it friendly biology; it was too cool and practical to call a love affair.)

Sammy tut-tutted about Harry's performance with them and trotted out the old arguments that we knew backwards before he was a gleam in his daddy's eye—that the old world hadn't been able to produce enough food to feed itself (probably true with the population increase in the thirty years after Harry and I went to sleep), that the forests had nearly vanished and the arable land had been ruined by forced growth that drained the soil without putting anything back, that three quarters of the wild animal population had vanished or was endangered, leaving mostly cats and dogs, that farming the seas had polluted the oceans and poisoned the fish, that people lived in squalor because raw materials were running short, that the very air wasn't fit to breathe in the cities . . .

Harry listened to the finish and then said, "So killing the polluting bastards off was the right answer, was it?"

"Nobody was killed off. They were prevented from propagating."

"Leaving what? A few lousy thousands scattered around the earth, each group carefully tailored to flourish in a single environment. What happens when a group outgrows its bit of suitable land and begins looking over its neighbor's territory?"

Sammy's answer took both of us by surprise. "That is far in the future. There will no doubt be interbreeding then, but by then we will also have a technological civilization that can accommodate a greater spectrum of physiological types. All the old knowledge is preserved for our use as new pressures demand it."

See? All cut and dried, just waiting for the new generations to pick it up.

Harry said, "And when the tough mountainmen come down to the plains they'll come with guns in their hands, manufactured with your carefully preserved knowledge."

Sammy replied with the first sign of real anger I had seen in him. "There will be no wars! Our training is designed to eliminate such conflicts."

Harry laughed at him. "How about the Desert Genetic that Gus and the Wishart woman are creating between them? Big chests and slender limbs, long-stranded muscles made for strength and stamina, men created to withstand thirst and hunger and carry loads day and night without dropping! The perfect recipe for soldiers!

In time they'll own your world. Probably in bloody quick time, while the rest of you are remembering your pacifist training."

It was the hectoring tone that shut Sammy up, the sound of a man who doesn't mean to listen to any argument. He said, in the voice of a fed-up nursemaid, "You have wakened in a combative mood. You will understand more clearly when you have seen something of our people."

Harry shrugged, accepting the argument as closed, temporarily at any rate, but I wondered just when we would see "our people."

35

It seemed to fall to me in the next few days to keep Harry entertained, and that was hard going. There was literally nothing to do in the mostly silent complex. We wandered the corridors, finding mostly empty rooms, and met a few of the staff, mostly cooks and cleaners going about the business of looking after the Wisharts and their lab workers, but of the Wisharts themselves we saw nothing. We had served our purpose and were of no further interest.

Harry seemed smugly amused with the idea of waking up in a new civilization and finding practically nobody home, but he was reserved and taciturn. After their opening brush he got along well enough with Sammy, choosing to regard him as an interesting curiosity with Sammy returning the compliment. I was bored stiff.

I discovered that at some time in his boyhood Harry had learned to ride a horse and had even been out into the countryside, which to me was just a picture on a vidscreen. This inspired me to take a ride with him to Bill Gordon's place.

On the way he commented on the wrecking of what had been beautiful houses and said it was to be expected once the city was no use anymore. But he found the empty streets eerie and quoted some poetry I had never heard before: " 'Is there anybody there?' said the Traveler / Knocking on the moonlit door. And his horse in the silence champed the grasses / Of the forest's ferny floor. Well, there isn't anybody in—except the ghosts of a slaughtered civilization."

So that was still on his mind. It was the sort of thing I didn't want to dwell on, so I didn't answer.

At Bill's place we were received as if he expected us. He knew of Harry's existence and I guessed he had his gossips among the complex staff. He gave us tea and some biscuits and told Harry his interest in the morphic resonance theory and asked him to tell his story. And this Harry did, mainly out of courtesy, I think, to a very old man. His story was the same as mine, of course, only more detailed, but old Bill was very attentive.

Afterwards he talked about the last days of the past age and shepherded us out with an invitation to stop by any time we felt it; he didn't have many callers.

Well, it helped fill in the day.

It could have been coincidence that Sammy brought up the subject the next day, but later on I thought it must have been in his mind all along. What it amounted to was that he wanted Harry to write down the whole story of his connection with Warlock and Bentinck.

I think he expected Harry to say they knew enough and he couldn't be bothered but instead he listened while Sammy explained how it would be useful for the historical record, personal witness and all that. At the end he said he was willing to do it and that it would help him sort out his own ideas about the whole business.

But, he said, it was a pity he didn't have a copy of Steven Warlock's account of the first trial because there were details he wanted to check and, besides, that was the real beginning of the thing.

Sammy told him, "That document is available. Dr. Valda Wishart has a copy. I can borrow it for you."

Harry didn't hide his surprise. "Has she now? What's her interest?"

Sammy was a bit offhand in saying, "Oh, purely scientific, I imagine." I could have told him not to waste such sleight of tongue on an old-fashioned copper, but Harry didn't pursue it and Sammy hurried on to say he could supply plenty of writing materials.

Next morning he produced Steven Warlock's statement and Harry asked straightaway, "Where did this come from?"

It was a good question because the edges of the paper were yellow with oxidation well into the margins.

"Dr. Valda says she rescued it from the Miraflores church records when he was killed. She says it was copied by a renegade police constable."

Harry grinned like a hungry terrier and said, "Filing officer Jarvis's contribution to the history of the New Age!"

Then he got to work. And I mean work. It took him five days to write it to the point where he found his parents murdered—and that's where he couldn't bring himself to write the scene. That's the point where I took over to write up the last of our time with Jesus and Wishart and how I woke up in the here and now.

It was a sustained effort and it seemed to be more than simply boredom that drove him; I thought he had become really interested in the morphic resonance and wanted to make some sense of it.

I was in his cell with him when he handed the papers over to Sammy and asked him what he meant to do with them.

"I will read your history for my own interest and pass the account to Dr. Valda for preservation."

"For preservation? Or to look for clues? What does she want, Sammy? I asked before and you brushed it off. Why was she in Miraflores's church in the first place?"

I could almost see Sammy's mind tossing up private information and deciding that coming clean could do no harm. He said slowly, "Dr. Wishart financed the Miraflores church; Dr. Valda was there to audit the books for him, though I am not quite sure what that means because we do not use money. She was fascinated by the Warlock story and insisted that it heralded a wholly new development in human psychology. Dr. Wishart disagreed, categorizing it as nonsense. She might have studied it further but all her attention was soon taken up in preparing the heredity guides and charts for we folk of the new generation. Then you and Gus were revived for your genetic heritage and the whole matter of morphic resonance was revived with your story.''

"And now," Harry said, "the lady wants to dabble where Bentinck left off? How?''

Sammy hesitated over that, but finally said, "There are meditation techniques . . ." And then, as if what-the-hell-does-it-matter, "She plans to search the science museums to discover if Bentinck's apparatus survives.''

"And if it does?''

Unaccountably Sammy shivered. "Perhaps," he said, "we will see the Dream Time.''

"Dream Time?''

"In aboriginal myth, the time when all things began and the natural order was created.''

"But you don't believe in that stuff, do you? You don't look to have any abo blood.''

Sammy's face became as blank as if a slate had been wiped clean. He answered Harry, but only slowly and indirectly, "I was orphaned early and fostered by an aboriginal couple. I was given tribal initiation at puberty and some kurdaitcha learning. My wife is an aboriginal. Now I would like to read your manuscript.''

And he went away to wherever his place for being private was.

Valda came to me that night. Afterwards I asked if she had read Harry's story and she said she had.

"And?''

"He adds nothing new but there is a postscript I must talk to him about.''

"What is it?''

"He scribbled on the bottom of the last page that he has had time to think and a lot of contradictory things about morphic resonance are beginning to make sense. I will be very busy for a few days but I would like to hear his ideas."

"Before you get on to Bentinck's machinery?"

That made her frown. "Has Sammy told you that? It may come to nothing; the Area Council may refuse permission. The Council can be very conservative about preserved artifacts—if indeed the thing still exists."

I hoped it did; it promised some ongoing activities for the future.

36

A few days later Sammy had a surprise for us. We were to visit his village, some thirty K outside the edge of Melbourne, for a few days, "To see," in one of his few lapses into casual talk, "how the other half lives."

To Harry he added, "Dr. Valda finds your manuscript most pertinent, particularly the scribbled concluding note. She wishes to speak to you about it in a few days, when she is free."

Harry just grunted, unimpressed. He had not much time for Valda; to him she was just one more of the murder gang. So under the circumstances I could hardly have told him different; I didn't want him getting testy with me over my choice of entertainment.

We saddled up and made for the outer edge of the city. All we took was changes of socks and underwear; everything else would be laid on, Sammy said.

It took us an hour to clear the city at a fast trot and a very depressing hour it was; the closer we got to the edge the more looted and knocked about the houses seemed to be. I suppose they were the nearest for pillaging when people started moving out to make settlements. Then the houses stopped altogether and we were on a track winding through trees, Sammy leading us in front and Harry alongside me, looking glum as he had all the time since his waking.

The trees made me uneasy. I had never been into the countryside before and the forest silence was new and menacing. When I say silence I mean that there were sounds of birds and some sort of animals rustling through leaves and bushes but they only underlined the stillness, as if we were watched by life we couldn't see and couldn't guard against. It had to be all right, since Sammy wasn't worried, but to me having only trees around me was spooky.

I told Harry it was spooky but he only grinned and said I'd get used to it. It seemed he had had holidays when he was a nipper, when his folks had taken him into the forest preserves to see koalas and lyre birds and possums and such. That came of having well-off folks; I had never got out of the streets. For myself, I couldn't imagine people choosing to make themselves homes in this loneliness. But then, that was the way of everybody thousands of years ago and these New Age people were beginning from scratch, weren't they?

Then all of a sudden there were no more trees and we were riding between big fields, maybe a kilometer long and wide, grown all over with what I recognized from illustrations as wheat. I have to admit it looked nice and friendly with a little wind blowing through it. There were people working but I don't know what they were doing and halfway along the track there was quite a big timber house (most of it obviously filched from city places) with only a couple of young kids of four or five playing on the verandah. I supposed all the older family members were working in the field. Sammy greeted the kids by name and they yelled back at him but we didn't stop.

Harry seemed to perk up a bit at sight of the wheat and asked where they got their corn ground. "Where we're going," Sammy told him.

I remembered that he is Forest Genetic by their accounting

and asked him if this where he was bred to work. Yes, he was bred for hard farm work among other things, but these surrounding trees were only new growth, too young for foresting; we'd see the "old growth" forests when we got to the foot of the mountain, some of it hundreds of years old.

We passed another couple of farms and through gaps in the trees I began to catch sight of the mountain, which seemed close but not all that high.

Then, after about three hours of riding, we were suddenly at the settlement Sammy called a village—ten or twelve houses, all wide apart from one another, with lots of little kids playing in the dirt and looking happy with themselves and one another. We stopped at the first biggish house where a whole horde of youngsters flung themselves on Sammy as he dismounted, all calling out, "Daddy!"

It looked as if Daddy had been spreading himself around quite a bit, because only two of them were white and four were half-caste aboriginal, while two of the girls were unambiguously black. An aboriginal woman came running onto the verandah to throw her arms around Sammy in the sort of welcome home you only read about in books while he matched her in kiss and cuddle.

As we dismounted he brought her forward to introduce her, "My wife, Miriam," and she offered her hand to be shaken.

There was more to prim and proper Sammy than we had imagined. He counted off the children (to make sure they were all there, I suppose) and then named them as if he expected us to remember what name went with who. The whole spectacle caught us on the back foot because in our time there was a one-child law (which the Suss Wardies took not much notice of) in the effort to keep the population down; it was like being lost in a kindergarten.

Fortunately the kids weren't much interested in us and stayed outside when we entered the house.

There was nothing stark or primitive about Sammy's house; it was a sight better furnished than my old place had been, probably as good as Harry's but without the vid and electrical appliances. No switch lighting, of course, but there were lamps everywhere for nighttime, and Sammy or someone had filled each outer wall

with windows to let in the sun. All the furniture was old and getting worn but I reckoned he had done a good job of plundering
the old city.

We stayed there for near on three days and I must say I liked the
country life, though it might have got dreary after a while. And
maybe I wouldn't have liked the work schedules; the whole village
worked sunrise to sunset at the business of producing food that
(after they fed themselves) was transported to a central market
twenty K away and bartered for whatever else they wanted. The
barter system to work without much fuss or dickering and Harry
remarked that in old Melbourne it would have been a disaster.
"What the Suss gangs didn't pinch the Minders would have stock-
piled and everybody else would have starved."

It was night in the big lounge room, with all the kids sitting
around listening and not saying a word (quiet kids was a revelation; we wondered how the parents did it), when we tried to explain the money system to Miriam and Sammy and got ourselves
into such a muddle when they started questioning that I began to
wonder how it ever worked. Force of habit, perhaps. Like silent
kids.

And, speaking of kids, we got some insight into the new genetic system. After the kids had gone to bed Miriam Johns explained that the half-breed four of the family were hers and
Sammy's while the two white boys were his by another woman
she had never seen and the two black girls were hers by an aboriginal man whom he had never seen. It seemed this was a part of
the genetic plan Valda was always working on, having large families by different but genetically compatible partners and so spreading the DNA as widely and as quickly as possible. It seemed the
new generation was wholeheartedly into the biblical spiel to be
fruitful and multiply.

She showed us a chart that Valda had prepared (and apparently every family had a different one adapted to their particular
bloodlines) showing which families in the district were compatible

for mating. Little wonder that Valda was a busy woman keeping
track of who was rooting who in the whole country—or was it the
whole world?

I couldn't think how to ask Miriam about her reaction to fucking with strangers but Harry, who doesn't get so tangled in his
English as me, managed it without putting a word out of place.

It was all done by arrangement, Miriam said, not at all discom-
posed. The chart allowed a certain freedom of choice and the rest
was a matter of meeting and trying until the injection "took"—
and that could be reasonably guaranteed in fairly short order by
some techniques Valda had supplied. The usual practice was that
male issue were reared by the father and female by the mother,
which explained Sammy and Miriam's mixed bag. If their family
was a criterion, the system seemed to work; all the eight kids
showed every sign of growing into the same blocky, powerful-
bodied types as their parents.

To Harry's hints about possible emotional involvements Miriam answered (a tad shortly, I felt) that the extramarital partners
were always from distant villages or groups and the custom was
that they rarely met again; they performed a duty to the racial
necessity to explode the population as rationally but expeditiously
as possible and rarely discussed the matter. In fact she found
Harry's questioning uncomfortable and would as soon not discuss
it any further.

Sammy sat through all this without a word, a model of suffering in silence.

Later, when we were alone, Harry remarked that this was the
explanation of Sammy's sexual prudery, that the New Age kids
were probably indoctrinated from birth with a hands-off pseudo-
morality that worked by simply suppressing discussion and then,
at puberty, presenting sex as a social duty with prescribed boundaries and attitudes. "Only a race of preconditioned prudes could
bow to such regulation. Nineteenth-century morality with extramarital sex for a sweetener! How long do Wishart and his scientists
think that will last?"

About fifty years, I reckoned, with the population tripling or quadrupling every generation—and by then the Forest Genetic stock would be sufficiently established for loose breeding not to matter very much.

Living in the complex I had lost count of days and didn't realize that Sammy had brought us out on a Sunday, which was still observed as a sort of rest day. The Monday was very different.

First the kids all disappeared to school as soon as breakfast was over, and Sammy disappeared, too, carrying a weird-looking blade he said was a scythe and saying he had a community job to do and would be back for lunch. Lunch? It must be a hard-work job, requiring extra food.

"Hard enough," he agreed. "Come and watch when you feel like it."

Miriam also was busy, with a house to clean, clothes to wash, and some sewing and mending to do; later in the day she would go out to "help the women in the field." For the moment, it seemed, we would be best out of her way and finding our own entertainment. The dismissal was courteous but firm. To our timid offers of assistance she suggested that we could fill the cistern.

The "cistern" turned out to be an iron bathtub lifted from somewhere in the city, covered over with wooden slats and with a drainpipe fitted into the plughole. It had to be filled from a well at the bottom of the rear vegetable garden and it seemed to take an unconscionable time for two strong men to do the job—enough time for us to realize that poverty in old Melbourne had its advantages, like the ability to turn on a tap.

After that we went sightseeing.

The first sight we came to was right outside the house—the biggest wheatfield we had yet seen (I wouldn't even try an amateur's guess at the hectares), stretching along the riding path with dwellings much like Sammy's every hundred meters or so and in the other direction spreading like a golden ocean to the foot of the hills. There were about twenty men working in the field, roughly in a line with scythes like Sammy's, chopping down the wheat with a rhythmic swinging cut and keeping it up long after I would have needed a halt if only to wipe the sweat off. Behind them was a line of women tying the wheat stalks into bundles.

Beside me Harry said softly, "Back about five centuries to manpower, horses, and dirty water from the family well. That bastard has a lot to answer for."

I didn't have to ask who he meant; Harry had a dead set on Wishart and cursed him for every little thing that offended him. And practically everything offended him. He hadn't talked a lot since his waking, even to me, and his expression all the time said he expected nothing and was getting nothing. The Wisharts hardly noticed, much less spoke to him, leaving him to Sammy to sort out, all of which I suspected did nothing for his appreciation of the modern age.

At the moment I wasn't thinking of the past or present so much as the future. I was caught by the way these men all resembled one another. I don't mean in their faces, which were all different, but in their build. They had all stripped down to their singlets and undershorts, with big wide-brimmed hats to protect their shoulders from the high-UV sunlight, which hadn't cooled off much in the past century, and watching them at work was like watching a team of weightlifters exercising. If this was "genetic" breeding then Valda's tinkering had produced a line of axmen or blacksmiths or something like that. It was the first I had seen of her results in the mass and it was pretty impressive.

Sammy came over to us during one of their breaks and explained that the field was community owned and that one man and one woman from each household was responsible for its working and upkeep. Since his was the one household without grandparents, an additional hand had to be supplied during his professional absences, which caused some grumbling (his word) in the village but not enough to rouse trouble.

"Meaning," Harry said later, "that the poor bastards do what they're told and pretend to like it."

I tried to be reasonable. "If they're brought up to it they'd just accept it and let off a bit of steam now and then like we did in our time."

"But this crowd," he said, "is going downhill, not up."

At the time I didn't catch on fully to what he meant and I let it pass.

From the field we went a couple of Ks to the village proper. Since this was a farming village the houses were spread out around the central field, but there was a communal core at a crossroads (dirt roads for horse-drawn vehicles) with a few houses and three much larger buildings at their center—a sort of generalized workshop, a store, and a schoolhouse.

The workshop contained what Harry told me was a blacksmith's forge (I had never heard of anything like it) for the manufacture of small metal articles but really needed as much as anything for the regular shoeing of the horses. Since there were anything from six to ten horses in grass paddocks by each house this made sense even to my ignorance of country life, but there were no smiths on duty this day; a fairly elderly man (fiftyish—grandfather grade!) was pottering around on one of the carpentry benches beside the forge and told us that at harvest time every available man and woman turned out to get the essential job done. He seemed to know who we were—I suppose word-of-mouth travels fast in groups of this kind, same as with slum Wardies—but seemed surprised that we didn't understand this necessity. Harry said something about historical "Russian collectives" and history repeating itself but I didn't listen too hard; he had found something to grouse about in everything he saw since he had woken up.

The grandfather said he was excused from the harvesting because his "rheumatics" wouldn't let him swing a scythe. That made me wonder about some drawbacks to the New Age; rheumatism was something we had dealt with by injections and nobody had actually suffered from it, but here it just had to be put up with. I understood from things Sammy had said that there was a very extensive herbal pharmacopoeia being added to all the time, but we hadn't got around to talking about general health care, which I now thought must be primitive.

As we left the workshop I speculated on what might happen

if I fell off my horse and got badly scraped and cut up. "You'd get gangrene and die," Harry snapped, not at all in tune with this catch-as-catch-can universe.

The store was closed—everybody out on harvest—but the schoolroom buzzed with kids. We arrived just as they came out on a break, and there looked to be over a hundred of them from five years old to about fourteen, all of them sturdy little lumps like their parents and promising to grow into the same balls of muscle. Given about twenty families in the village, it was plain that propagation was a growth industry and, since most of the parents we had seen were in their twenties, population was still on the up and up. About 10 percent, I reckoned, showed Koori blood in more or less degree, so it seemed Valda had no inhibitions about race or color. And why should she? She had her own splash of the tar brush.

The kids released into the schoolyard were like kids everywhere at all times, a yelling mass that disintegrated rapidly into smaller yelling groups playing games much like the basic games kids have invented since we came out of the trees. It was hard to imagine them as the demure, polite, attentive listeners in Sammy's house. There was certainly a smart discipline at work somewhere.

Harry had a grousing snort for it: "For the kind of lives they're going to lead, they'll need it." I wished he'd get over his grumps and start to take things as they came.

The teachers—four men and four women—were all middle-aged except for one eighteen-year-old girl who seemed to be some sort of trainee. We had only about ten minutes before classes would start again so we didn't see much more than that there were eight classrooms, which seemed a lot for the age range until they told us that boys and girls were taught separately. They did not understand why that should surprise us and explained patiently that while basic lessons—meaning mostly the three Rs—were the same for both sexes, there were men's jobs and responsibilities and women's jobs and responsibilities, and preparation for their roles in life was necessarily different. We understood, did we not, that sexual paring began as soon as school studies were completed?

I saw suddenly why Sammy's four youngest were half-breeds, the issue of hisself and Miriam; the four oldest were white or black because they had been conceived before marriage. As a genetic duty. Valda's genetic mix was used to introduce youngsters to the sexual act as a social necessity; love (call it that) came later, with full-grown maturity—and the same strictly limited choice. Sammy's sexual primness made sudden sense; the kids were actually taught sexual avoidance save along the prescribed guidelines.

(Afterwards when I put this to Harry he grunted. "I give it one generation before her precious charts fall to pieces.")

We hadn't got very far with the teachers (who, like everybody else, seemed to know all about us) when the break was over and at the screech of a whistle the whole playground went quiet. This was high-order discipline and it made me uneasy; kids just shouldn't accept regimentation like that. The Wisharts were building a civilization in a hurry, granted, but I felt these kids were missing some of the freedom they ought to have before the real world closed in on them.

But what I thought didn't matter right then; school was in session and we were shepherded out. We left as the silent youngsters, in segregated sexes, filed back into their classrooms.

We got back to Sammy's place an hour later just as the harvesters were breaking for lunch.

37

The men with their scythes and the sheaf-making women went off to their homes on the edges of the field. The kids came in from school, noisy and hungry but going quiet when they entered the house. I wasn't all that sure that I approved of that much strictness; on the other hand, it didn't seem to restrain their instinct to yell and play when they got outside, and nobody tried to shush them then. Other times, other ways, I supposed, though later on I learned there was more to it than that.

We sat down to a warmed-over casserole of kangaroo meat and vegetables and Harry remarked that he preferred the old-style three meals a day.

"The two-meal habit," Sammy told him, "is practiced only by those in sedentary occupations. It arose during a period of food shortages when factories were closing, transport was chaotic, and the shift to farm production was still incomplete."

Harry said, "I love the way you encapsulate history in a couple of sentences, passing over a time of what must have been terrifying confusion and outright starvation."

"It was before my day," Sammy replied with a sort of mild disapproval, as if Harry really should know better. "As I understand it, once the implications of restricted birthing were absorbed by the governing authorities they were very successful in adapting public facilities to the needs of the many."

Harry gave that a sour grin. "Sounds like they faced disaster with the traditional stiff upper lip. Business as usual!"

Sammy wasn't pleased by it but he said stiffly, "It might well have been so."

"And the sedentary workers made a virtue of necessity and turned the two-meal habit into a distinction between the elite and the working classes. How society changes—right back into the same old order!"

Miriam interrupted to say, "Not quite, Harry. I'm told most of them carry a snack in their pocket to be wolfed on the sly."

"Then Sam has short-changed Gus and me in our frugal cells."

Sammy had the grace to look uncomfortable but said, "I do as I am ordered," and Harry had enough of the same to change the conversation.

All through this the kids kept up their own conversation in low tones that never drowned out their elders, but I had the impression that at the same time they weren't missing a word of what we said. Whatever the parents–kids situation really was, it apparently worked well in keeping both parties out of each other's hair.

With the meal over, everybody went back to school or to the field. We were left to watch or do whatever we liked.

Harry produced a notebook and pencil from his overall pocket and sat on the back porch, looking solemn and making some kind of notes while the *swish* of the scythes moved past us. The men worked in silence but behind them the women tying the sheaves chattered to one another; it was like watching a performance of some historical vidplay.

Because Harry had been bloody irritating ever since his waking, refusing to see good in anything, and because I reckoned there are limits to grieving, even for murdered parents, when it shows itself all the time as bullish bad temper, I said, "Don't you reckon it's time you snapped out of it and stopped picking shit at everything that's said or done?"

He stopped writing but didn't look at me. "I'm getting on your nerves, Gus?"

"You are that."

Still looking at his notes he said, "That's a pity when you're all I've got."

I told him, "Balls to that. There's nice people around here if you'd let yourself see them."

Softly he said, "All puppets dancing on Wishart strings. A world seen through Wishart-blinded eyes."

It was bad that he wouldn't look at me. He knew his attitude was wrong but he was determined to hold on to it like a mutinous kid; he wasn't ready to listen to anybody but I persisted, "Haven't you seen a worthwhile thing in this age?"

He thought about it and said, "Miriam's a good cook."

He was being impossible, so I left him to his notes and went across the field to where Sammy was working.

I watched him for a while and said I'd like to have a try at the mowing, "But you'll have to show me how you do it."

He wiped his sweaty forehead and grinned at me, for the first time looking really young and boyish, and said, "It's not for amateurs, Gus." But I insisted and he gave in and showed me how to grip the scythe and place the feet to get a steady swing. It didn't seem there was much to it except I swung the blade too high on the stalks and tried to cut with the end instead of the middle part and cut about six stalks of wheat instead of a thick batch and went at it like an axman instead of a harvester.

It seemed the thing was not to belt at it because the scythe was sharp enough to slice with its own weight, but to use a steady back-and-forth rhythm, cutting low to the ground and moving forward a step at each swing. I can't say I mastered it because I didn't but I soon raised a sweat and saw that moving a field was bloody hard work. I surely didn't envy the villagers their job and I saw why the build of the Forest Genetic was so well adapted to this kind of farm work; a whole day of it would have half killed me.

Sammy instructed me with a straight face and complimented me on "a good try" and gave me a pat on the shoulder I didn't earn, and sent me off sadder and wiser.

I spent the rest of the afternoon reading an old book I found on a shelf in Sammy's lounge room—a Holy Bible—something I'd heard of but never looked at, and unexpected in an atheist society. (It's peculiar, the way people seem to need some sort of "beyond" thing to cling to.) I read bits of the Old Testament. Hell, but they were a bloodthirsty lot the old Jews, or their God was. I began to understand old Miraflores's savage attitudes, speaking love from one side of his mouth and vengeance from the other. All very human. When you come to think of it, all human history is the story of a pack of ratbags murdering one another and then creating kids to take up the slack. It's a wonder we ever found time to get "civilized"—whatever that turns out to be.

It looked like the Wisharts had some kind of perfectionist dream in their screwed up way but I wouldn't bet on it getting anywhere. Harry's downbeat comments would probably all come true and the likely thing was that some fresh twist would throw all plans into the wastebasket.

I didn't know it, but the fresh twist was already in the plot and set to blow up a storm.

The first sign, though I couldn't recognize it at the time, was when a horseman pulled up at the house and dropped a letter in Sammy's mailbox. Good old Pony Express, I thought; vidplay history.

The next sign, again one I couldn't pick up, was when Miriam came in from the field early to cook the family tea. She looked worried and didn't seem to want to talk, but private troubles were not my business.

Then Sammy came home, all sweaty and stinking and ready for a bath, and saw the letter in the box. He read it and seemed at first surprised and then almost joyous at good news. With an almost childish pleasure he said, "Dr. Valda has been working behind-the-scenes and there has been a special meeting of the Area Council. Harry, Gus, you'll be interested in this: they have agreed to let us unseal the museums and search for the Bentinck isolation machinery. We must return to the complex in the morning."

Harry looked up from the note-making that had occupied him all afternoon and asked, "What the hell does she want that for?"

Sammy was amazed. "To activate it, of course! To discover the truths Bentinck and Warlock missed. To find out what really lies in the depths of the mind!"

Valda had told me that this was in the wind but I hadn't paid a lot of attention, wiping it off as a hunt to satisfy her curiosity. I thought the electronic setup had most likely been lost in the collapse of the Miraflores church. It hadn't occurred to me that it had historical and scientific value and would be stored somewhere.

I said, "The old Dr. Supreme won't approve. He thinks the whole morphic business is a psychological rat's nest."

"He won't interfere. He never interferes."

"He will if it takes her away from work he reckons is important."

Harry said suddenly, "It isn't a rat's nest and it's a damn sight more important than her genetic meddling, which will fall apart in a couple of generations. I've spent the afternoon going over all we learned about the isolation results and I've come up with a few ideas. I hope the machinery's been preserved. We need to have somebody try it out who actually knows what he is looking at down there."

Miriam chose that moment to call Sammy from inside and he said, "We must talk about it," as he went in.

Naturally I wanted to know what Harry had in mind but he only said he had more thinking to do and wasn't ready yet.

Nor was the subject discussed that night. Sammy and Miriam were very quiet through the mealtime and afterwards they went to their bedroom for some sort of private talk. It was apparent that something had happened and we weren't being told about it. The kids yakked among themselves but didn't seem to be aware of anything out of the ordinary.

In the morning we saddled up, said our farewells, and went off down the trail, none the wiser until I got tired of Sammy's long face and asked him what had happened to shut him up.

He rode on a bit before he reined in his horse and said, "I had better tell you." When we had stopped, facing him, he said, "A bone has been pointed."

Harry laughed; it was his first laugh in days and it was not a nice one. He asked, "At you?," and Sammy nodded with his face tight. Harry shook his head in exaggerated sorrow and said, "You don't take it seriously, do you?"

Sammy answered with steel in his voice. Right from the beginning he hadn't taken to Harry's silences and snappish put-down comments, and now his dislike showed in the way he chose his words and the cold way he spoke them. "As an orphan I was raised by aboriginal foster parents. At puberty I was initiated into the rites of manhood of the Wuywurung. I am a man of two minds, reared in a tribal tradition as a child and carrying in me the deep roots of childhood spiritual experience, then educated as a grown man in the hard-edged logic of the New Age. My two minds, Mr. Ostrov, have no distinct barrier dividing them.''

It was like a master to a servant. Harry flushed deep red and dropped his eyes, and I had never seen him do that for any man. He said, very subdued, ''Sorry; I didn't know. I beg your pardon.''

Sammy said, ''Granted,'' cold as ice. ''You have many opinions concerning the New Age but show little capacity to understand or appreciate. Open your mind's eyes, Mr. Ostrov; this is a new world. Better or worse than yours? I have no idea. But this one exists and yours does not.''

Harry said nothing at all and the silence grew uncomfortable. I said, ''Would somebody tell me what's going on?''

''Just some native nonsense, as Mr. Ostrov would have it.''

Harry said, ''I call it superstition but it will be real to whoever believes in it.'' He fixed Sammy with his eyes, hesitated a little, and then carried on. ''When a tribesman commits a special crime, like breaking a taboo or perhaps revealing a tribal secret, the local koradji—a sort of magician or witch doctor—can punish him by going through a 'pointing the bone' ceremony. The man doesn't have to be there but the idea is that once the bone has been pointed he will die by losing the will to live. Right, Sam?''

''In outline near enough, Harry.'' It sounded as if Harry was forgiven. ''But is it just superstition?''

Harry said seriously, ''I think so. I don't know of any authenticated case of a victim dying but I can see how it might happen. The koradji points the bone; the victim may be miles away but news of the pointing soon gets to him—his enemies make sure it does. He can beg mercy and maybe the koradji will lift the spell or, if the magician will not, he can just go away and probably refuse food and die of hopelessness.''

''So, if he believes, then he's a dead man.''

''Could be. But, Sam, have you ever known a real case?''

''No, Harry, never. But news travels on the wind and I have had my warning. You will have noticed a number of aborigines among the villagers—to be exact, two full-bloods and three half-breeds. They whispered it to Miriam in the wheat field and she brought it home with her last night. The children will know by now; their school friends will be agog with the tale. For the sake of the children and Miriam I will have to seek out the koradji and suffer some payment for what I may have done. So you see, Harry, it does not matter what I do or do not believe; while others believe, I must follow protocol. Many Koori have abandoned tribal practice and traditional ways but those who follow tribal ways live their lives bound by law, ritual and ceremony, and beliefs older than the whole of white civilization.''

I had some idea of the truth of this from talking to city Koori in my own day, but in the name of good sense I had to protest, "But who is the enemy? Who called in the koradji?''

Sammy smiled. "Who indeed? The man in emu-feather shoes who disguises his passage? He will show himself in time.''

Harry asked, "Is the reason you decided to get back to the complex today because the isolation machinery was found? Because you have some idea who to look for?''

"Yes.''

"Can we be of any help?''

Now that was a big concession from Harry with a snout on the world. Perhaps he had a better idea than me of how serious the thing might be. My thought then was that Sammy would do some sort of kowtow to the koradji and the thing would blow over. Storm in a teacup.

"Thank you, but I think not.'' He smacked his heels into his horse's flanks and we started off again in a slow canter, and got back to the complex in the middle of the day.

38

We were gathered in my cell drinking mugs of the local coffee (not a bad brew, trekked down from Queensland) when Valda came in saying, "I heard you were back. Did you get my letter, Sam?"

Sammy said, "Yes, Doctor," while he poured her some coffee. "I imagine it was your influence that induced the Council to meet so quickly."

She sat herself on the end of my bed, saying a bit smugly, "I don't like to pull weight in local affairs but this did seem important; with a dozen or more venues to be searched, the sooner we start, the better."

"Of course. The vote was unanimous?"

"Bar one. Old Bert Mutawali didn't vote against, but he abstained."

"The other Koori member of the Council approved?"

"Yes. I don't know what got into Bert; the white members were enthusiastic about the idea and he usually goes with the majority, but he sat there looking like a disapproving nanny."

Sammy said lightly, "He's tribal from the Ganay region; you never know when the tribals will come up with some little reservation."

He said it lightly enough but I had the feeling he had caught something on the wing.

"It might have had to do with you, Sam. I know you preferred not to be involved, but Mutawali asked if Bill Gordon had discussed the matter with you and I had to admit that he knew about it. I gather Bert knew about Gordon's murder by Miraflores."

It wasn't always easy to gauge the true reaction behind Sammy's careful, unemotional words but I sensed a stiffness in his answer, an anger unexpressed. "He knew. Bill Gordon is Ganay, so they all know. It is tribal history."

"I hope I didn't put my foot in it. Did I?"

"Not at all, Doctor."

Suavity itself! But I could almost see his mind putting connections together and getting no joy there.

"So now all we have to do," said Valda, "is find the apparatus. I have a group selected and they will begin the search tomorrow. Then we need a suitable subject to test the isolation effect, and that may prove more difficult. Who or what makes a suitable subject?"

In the silence while we contemplated the resurrection of that bloodstained experiment, Harry dropped an answer.

"Me," he said.

Valda was startled and then exasperated. She had argued for his resuscitation and for her pains had acquired a raging, insulting radical who had no good to say for any part of her New Age. She said shortly, "It is not a cops and robbers exploit for yesterday's policeman."

Harry was standing by the window with the light on his face showing the distant expression that came when he was planning something. I expected him to bristle at her but he only shook his head and said, "Detective, not policeman. We learned to think, you know; it was a big help in staying alive."

"To think as criminals think. I would prefer a psychologist."

"In short supply today, I imagine, and at best only trained in Utopian dreams. But I actually talked with the people who had the isolation experience, only weeks ago in my recollection, laid hands on their struggling bodies and listened to their attempts to find words for what they saw down there in the darkness. I have good professional recall for words and tones and it is all very clear in my mind. I have done some thinking in these last few days—police-type thinking if you like, Doctor, but still the product of neurons sifting facts and possibilities—and have reached some conclusions. Warlock and Devalera went in without preparation and came out puzzled and confused, but the fact is that many of their confusions can be resolved. I would go prepared, knowing what to expect and with ideas to be tested against the reality."

Valda heard him out, even a bit respectfully. It's marvelous how somebody speaking good English gets a hearing; if I had tried to say what Harry did it would have sounded like a shill with the thimble and pea trick.

But all she said was, "First we have to find the apparatus."

When she came to me a couple of nights later I tried to put in a word for Harry. "He's no slouch, Valda; his brain really works. You want to listen to what he has to say."

"He says inimical, stupid things."

"He says things that get your back up but that doesn't make him always wrong."

"You agree with him, do you?"

Just like a woman, sidetracking a man! "Sometimes. Your New Age isn't heaven with all the angels singing."

"You, too!"

Aw, hell, the way they twist you! "Forget it."

"Oh, no," she said, "if he makes sense I'll listen."

Try and untangle that!

39

I had half expected Harry and me to be called on to aid in the search for Bentinck's apparatus—after all, we knew what it looked like—but nobody even mentioned us. I was left to talk to Sammy and go for rambles around the old suburbs. I rode right into the center one day, to where the tall buildings kept the streets in shadow; all the shop windows had been smashed in by looters;

weeds pushed up through the footpaths and the only sound was birds. It was eerie like the feeling of ghosts around and I didn't stay.

Harry stayed in his own cell, writing his story on paper Sammy supplied, until he came to the point where I had to take over.

All he said was, "You do it. I can't."

Then he shut himself away altogether for two days. I don't know what went on in his head but I feel he was regretting more than his parents, maybe reviewing his whole life the way a man will when the past is suddenly cut off and only today remains, and you have to decide what sort of real person will live through it. I know. I'd had to do it.

When he came out he was still quiet but more nearly human, not snarling quite so hard at everything he saw and heard.

Meanwhile I got on with the story, with Sammy helping out when the sentences got too tangled. It made something to do and in the end I got really interested in sorting out my own reactions to the New Age; I decided that it was a pretty queer setup but not all that unpleasant, but there were a lot of questions that needed answering.

I thought about leaving out my nights with Valda. I'm no gentleman but I thought she might object. Then I found out that Sammy knew all about us and it seemed everybody else did, too—so, what the hell! And so much for Sammy's sexual prudery!

That was one of the things I asked Valda about: Why, for instance, were the sexes segregated in school?

Well, now—they had settled the old "women's lib" argument by deciding that where women's abilities were the same as a man's, then a woman should compete on an equal basis with men. If she could do the job, why shouldn't she? About half the makeup of the Area Councils were elected women and women dominated in teaching and clerical work; men on the whole took on the more physical work, which made some sense in a fairly primitive society. After all, you had to recognize the sexual differences as well as the equalities.

It was in the home that the sexual lines were drawn, and this was where Valda's genetic program had its influence. Part of it depended on the necessity to spread the genetic stock as widely as possible in a small population, to avoid inbreeding at all costs. And so the kids were sexually educated to have their first contacts, as soon as they finished their schooling, with partners selected for them from another village. They were taught (believe it or not, and I took a while to swallow it) to regard these premarital couplings as a state duty having nothing to do with mutual attraction. I thought it must be like picking up a floozy on the street corner—wham, bam, thank you, ma'am—but it was not that way at all.

The education saw to that.

What in fact happened was surrounded with ritual and a sense of occasion. The couple was introduced at a party mostly composed of their teenage peers (with their schoolteachers presiding!) and bedded down to the encouraging noises of their friends outside. It seemed Dr. Valda had found and distributed means of ensuring pregnancy at first try and there were very few repeat performances needed; it was unlikely that the partners would ever see each other again since the villages were usually picked for being a fair way apart.

This seemed to be why the students were segregated—to prepare the sexes for their unemotional introduction to the facts of life, each with regard to his and her own needs and responsibilities.

It seemed to me a mite narrow and restrictive, a good way to kill romance stone dead, but it seemed that the old serpent raised its head in due time and true love eventually found its way—with a family ready-made and more to come, keeping up the numbers. At least the couple came to marriage with plenty of experience, if only in the pursuit of genetic variety.

As for Sammy's sexual straitlacing, it seemed to be a general thing pumped into the kids in their school years, a learned way that became a habit. I suppose it made some sense in a society regulated by genetic charts but I wondered how much hanky-panky went on while they waited for the wheat to ripen. Those nineteenth-century moral Victorians were a horny lot behind their shocked faces, weren't they? Human nature gets its way in the long run. Sammy disapproved when he read this paragraph but only frowned with no comment. But Harry said, "Two generations should see things loosen up and by then it won't matter. With families eight and ten strong there'll be variation to spare."

I queried Valda about it and she agreed that two or three generations should see the loosening of the artificial constraints and that by then the genetic groups, here and in other specialized areas, should be firmly established.

"However," she said, "you and I won't be here to see the world outcome." I said something about her being so devoted to this business and she answered, "It is the only thing I care about. The only thing."

Which put me in my place as casual relief—though to be honest it was a two-way arrangement of friendly convenience. Anyway, a man can't compete with dedication.

She gave one of those little can't-help-it sighs and said, "How I'd love to have two hundred years—or even one hundred—to see how things turn out."

I knew how they'd turn out though I wasn't going to say it; they'd build cities and rediscover technology and chase each other in and out of bed while her precious genetic framework fell to pieces and humans kept on being human. In the end it all comes down to genitals, not genetics.

40

I don't know how many people Valda recruited to search the museums, but she pressed into service a lot of the healthy old folks still squatting in the city. They did the job willingly. I hung around the museums, trying to look useful but not doing much, and was surprised at how much the Wisharts were respected. Nobody questioned their right to ask for and receive assistance; they just bucked in and did what was wanted. I found that they were familiar with the Wishart plans for the New Age and firmly believed they were good plans; digging further, I discovered that their belief went right back to the First Generation of the New Age, to the teachers trained by the Wisharts to spread their social and moral and sexual doctrines. It was ingrained and accepted as the way of life should be lived, while the Wisharts and their staff of teachers filled the roles of gurus with a monopoly on wisdom that nobody questioned.

I had to respect the old Dr. Supreme for pulling off one of the greatest con jobs in history, for creating his own private population of suckers and then leading them by the nose to his private version of human destiny. It was totally awesome.

Meanwhile, the army of human ants burrowed in the museums and found not a skerrick of the Bentinck gear. Ten days went by and Valda was getting a mite pensive, fearing it might have been destroyed. Then somebody had one of those ideas so obvious that nobody had thought of it—how about trying the huge basement storerooms of the complex, so big and so full of crated, nailed-up junk that even the human ants might quail at the task?

The stuff was there. It took five days to locate, but one afternoon some panting old geezer came to Harry and me saying they thought they had the Bentinck gear and would we come down and identify it?

It was the real thing and in prime condition as far as we could tell.

We went back upstairs and broke the news first to Sammy, who professed to be pleased in his po-faced way but didn't do any dance of delight. In fact he didn't try to look pleased at all.

He had been looking a bit down for some days, as if something was eating at him, and I asked as an offhand joke if the pointed bone was getting him down. He gave me a glare of such raging hatred that I apologized, which is not a thing I often do.

When we left him to look for Valda and give her the news, Harry said in the corridor outside, "We'd better do some thinking about Sammy. You may have put your finger on it."

I wasn't much impressed and I said, "There's nothing we can do if he's frightened by the old mumbo-jumbo."

"We can ask."

"Not me. He was ready to kill me."

"Because you treated it as a joke."

So we went back into the cell and fronted Sammy, and Harry asked, "You can tell us it's none of our business, but why was the bone pointed?"

Sammy turned from the window where he had been staring at the outside, and agreed. "It is most surely none of your business. It is a tribal matter, involving secrecy."

Then he went on, in the tone of a man confessing, shrugging a weight off his mind, "However, I have gone too far to turn back and there's no further harm in your knowing. My fault was in discussing tribal ritual secrets with the uninitiated. A greater fault was that I discussed these matters, which are men's business, with a woman, Dr. Valda."

He had broken unnumbered years of tribal taboo.

He spoke absolutely seriously. To me the rigmarole about women sounded like fairy-tale stuff, but I didn't appreciate then how strictly the tribal gender barriers were enforced on matters of ritual and secret (meaning gender-segregated) knowledge were enforced.

But Harry listened like a man enthralled. At the end he asked, "Who pointed the bone?"

"That is difficult to discover. There are several koradji among the Wuywurung but nobody is prepared to name one. He may be Ganay, operating from a great distance, two hundred K or more in the far east of the state. If so, I have little hope of finding him."

This was all a bit too much for me. I had to ask him, "Why don't you just ignore the whole thing? He can't really put a curse on you that means anything. Or is it just a matter of being on the outs with your tribal folk, like the kids being twitted by their schoolmates or Miriam being boycotted by her relatives?"

Sammy gave me a puzzled look as if he couldn't see how anybody could get it so wrong. At last he said. "There will be no social consequences. It will simply be seen that I am marked for death and so will shortly die."

Harry said, "You mentioned that the koradji might be Ganay. Would that link him with Bill Gordon?"

Sammy said, as though chewing gravel, "Possibly."

"Have you asked him?"

"I have not." Then, grudgingly, "Our acquaintance is terminated."

"You have quarreled?"

"No. Speak of something else."

Speaking of something else under the circumstances was difficult and in a few minutes he left us.

I said right away, "You'd think he took his bone pointing seriously."

"Most likely he does."

"But he's an educated man!"

Harry said slowly, as if he was sizing up the situation, "So are you, city-educated, sharp as a tack, and believing only in what you can see and feel. But Sammy has two educations sitting side by side. Before he got his New Age knowledge, his first five or six years were saturated in tribal lore, the accepted wisdom and protocol of generations; at puberty he was initiated as a man and had gender secrecy instilled. Those are the early parts of his knowledge of the world. They cling. His tutored brain rejects them but they remain the original basis of his social existence. They are embedded. Later learning denies them but can't smother them. He's been confronted by his grassroots and is unable to deny them."

I asked, "You think he'll die?"

"He might. But he's a nice bloke in his snotty way and worth some small help. What say we visit old Bill Gordon and prod around a little?"

I have to admit it still seemed airy-fairy to me, but if Harry was sniffing at it there could be something in it. So we went to the stables and got a couple of horses and started up the grassy street.

•   •   •

Bill Gordon came to the door and didn't seem surprised by our visit. He was looking his age but very upright and dignified. When Harry asked if we could come in he inclined his head, saying nothing, and led the way to the lounge room. Almost as if he had expected us.

Mrs. Gordon was there, sewing a shirt. She smiled and greeted us and made conventional small talk while we seated ourselves. Then Harry said, "I imagine you will have heard that the Bentinck isolation apparatus has been found," and the old man shot her a fast glance.

She gathered up her sewing, saying she had things to attend to, and left us.

Men's business; no women wanted.

"I have heard," said Bill, "that it was looked for."

"It was found this morning. It seems to be in good condition, so Dr. Bentinck's research can now be continued."

The old man nodded but without showing any great interest. What he said was, "Some people will satisfy their curiosity about matters they will be unable to understand or make use of."

"All knowledge is eventually useful."

The black face crinkled in a disagreeable smile. "Think of nuclear physics: born before its time, used by those clawing for cheap power, never fully understood or properly tamed and now gone with the wind of change. Who could use it today?"

Harry was patient with the stonewalling. "The knowledge remains, ready for resurrection when its time comes, but our need is more immediate."

"*Need,* Mr. Ostrov? I have nothing for you."

"A name."

The black face maintained a polite, questioning silence.

Harry said, "You are spoken of as a kurdaitcha man."

"That word has many meanings, not always understood by those who use it."

"It is said some are interested in morphic resonance, as you are. You have questioned us on the work of Dr. Bentinck, to discover what he knew, how far he had progressed in knowledge."

"And so?"

"I did not know your kurdaitcha grandfather who was murdered by a man named Miraflores because he would not reveal his kurdaitcha secrets, but he surely had secrets to keep. He died because he had some knowledge of morphic resonance and would not reveal it."

"And so?"

"Your people do not write down secret knowledge but pass it on from father to son, mother to daughter. Your grandfather will have confided his secret knowledge to his son, who would have informed you."

"And so?"

"You become the recipient of kurdaitcha lore that only kurdaitcha may share. You become a guardian of knowledge and responsible for the punishment of any who share it with those considered unfit to know. Morphic resonance is not thought a subject fit for women."

Bill was silent.

"In the Area Council a question was asked of Dr. Valda Wishart that indicated that Sam Johns had given her advice about investigating morphic resonance. On the next day a bone was pointed. By whom? By what koradji and at whose instigation?"

Bill made a sweeping, wiping gesture, negating the whole question.

Harry carried on in a reasonable tone when he must have been fuming inside, "If he knows the name of the koradji, Sam can make a proper plea to have the pointing rescinded."

Bill stuck out his head toward Harry as if he would have tried to bite his face. He said in a strangled voice that I can only call a growling hiss, "Sam will die. He has confided a thousand generations of meditation to the grasp of a woman!"

I couldn't help myself; I shouted at the murderous old bugger, "That's a load of crap! Sam has more brains than to fall for it."

Bill switched his attention to me but this time he was grinning.

"Then why are you here? Already he is troubled. He will die, Mr. Kostakis, and there will be no plea. He is a tribesman, a Wuywurung, and he is dying by tribal law."

Harry said, "Come on, Gus," and we got out of there. On the way back to the complex all he said was, "We'll have to keep an eye on Sammy."

I felt he was making a lot out of nothing much, that Sammy ought to be able to look after hisself.

41

It was hard to believe there were so many people in the complex because we hardly ever saw them. We kept away from the laboratory sector, where we weren't wanted anyway, so all we saw of staff was somebody coming out or going in a door or walking down a corridor. We found that they spent a lot of leisure time on the roof, but when we went up there we found a cliquey lot whose conversation was lab talk and who were polite enough but not interested in us; we just weren't part of their daily lives. I had thought they would ask about the past, eager to hear the facts from someone who lived them, but they never did. Thinking it over I realized that nobody in Sammy's family or in his village had quizzed us on our time, not even the schoolteachers, who you'd expect to be curious.

I filed it as a thing to ask Valda about.

I noticed that several of the rooftop crowd were half-breeds, and Harry said, "That's how Sammy knew we went to see Bill Gordon. The bush telegraph never stops working; it makes you think the vidphone was old-fashioned. I'll bet he knew the same day."

That might be so, but it had been in fact a couple of days before Sammy said to us—being very formal and self-conscious—

"It was good of you to intercede for me with Bill Gordon. You could not know it would be of no avail."

I said, "At least we know who the enemy is."

"I have known that from the moment I hinted to him what I intended to do."

Harry was staggered, outraged. "Do you mean you deliberately brought this bone pointing on yourself?"

"I recognized the possibility." He gave that grimace of a smile a person uses to admit the joke is on himself. "I felt myself sufficiently sophisticated to risk it."

"And are you?"

Sammy's answer was careful. "It concerned me more than I had predicted." And it was certain that something concerned him; he had that drawn look of a man losing weight, but I couldn't believe this fairy-tale stuff was really getting to him. He added, "I had not counted on the effect on my family. They will not be ostracized but there will be remarks and allusions in the village, glances and grinning among the schoolchildren. It is better that I stay away from them until the thing is over, not make myself a focus of comment."

Harry asked, "How will you know when it's over, when the curse is lifted?"

Sammy's tone was studied and cool. "It will not be lifted. It will die away. Gossip will cease and life will return to normal." Somehow it sounded more like a hope than a statement, but he wiped the subject off by going on another tack. "Dr. Valda will be here at four o'clock, Harry. She wishes to hear your ideas, if you are ready, about the morphic resonance."

Harry said, "Ready enough."

Valda came to Harry's cell dead on four o'clock. She was like that—everything spot on; I bet she was a terror to her lab staff. Sammy was there to take notes, of course, while I was only being nosy about what went on, but she didn't object.

Sammy had provided an extra chair for her; she sat down and

started in without any preliminaries. "The Bentinck apparatus is in very good condition and as far as we can tell is complete. However, none of us here is a brain specialist because no such branch of study any longer exists. Therefore I have sent for a Last Generation graduate—a man of eighty or so—from New South Wales, to advise on use of the circuitry, particularly the safety aspects. He was an inventor-electrician and is stated to be still fully competent. He has never used Bentinck's machinery, of course, but I trust he can advise what can and cannot safely be done. He will be here tomorrow."

It was all very formal, prepared like a lesson, but Harry had no hesitation about interrupting. He said, "It's only four days since we brought the stuff in and it would take him that long to get here by horse transport even if only from the border. How did you get a message out so fast?"

She was annoyed at being taken off balance in mid-speech, but she answered him, "By radio, Mr. Ostrov."

Harry was taken aback. Me, too. He said, "Your petrol generator couldn't run a station that powerful, not with its other drains."

I thought Valda would say, "Some other time," but she sighed and explained. After all, he might be her guinea pig for the isolation job and had to be humored some. "There are about forty satellites in orbit overhead and still in working condition; they are failing rapidly but we can still use them to contact our laboratories around the world. As well as the laboratories, key villages maintain open receivers on twenty-four-hour watch; they require little power. The satellites orbited late in the last century can be manipulated by ground control to receive a very faint signal from us, augment it, and relay it precisely to the nominated receiver. The satellites won't last forever but we use them while we can."

We could have worked that out for ourselves because all the hardware had been in existence in our day (but there had been hundreds of the things up there then) but we had got too used to the idea of there being no science here at all, except biology.

There was probably lots of useful stuff if we looked for it.

Harry said, "Thank you," as if it hurt him to be so obtuse. Valda did not acknowledge him; she had had no time for him since his performance with Granddad. Her seeing him at all was purely a professional concession.

She continued, "We have a problem with the apparatus: it needs to be tested. As far as we can tell, it is in good condition but it is a century old, and although it has been taken apart and examined and reassembled, we have found no operating instructions. What Gus and Mr. Ostrov have told us makes the application seem straightforward but there may be operating details we need to be aware of." She frowned, hesitated, and began again. "I am making heavy weather of saying that someone will be required to test the assembly. I need not point out the possibility of brain damage."

It may have been coincidence that her eyes roved across Harry on the last sentence, as if maybe she hoped he would put his hand up for test subject and at least win a few brownie points for being useful, but Harry was an old cop who knew better than to volunteer for anything. Nobody said anything and Valda carried on a mite uncertainly, "I can call for a volunteer from the laboratory staff and probably get one. But it seems unfair to ask someone to take a risk on the unknown."

Harry said quite nastily, "It does, doesn't it!"

Valda's lips tightened but she didn't speak.

It was Sammy who said, "I'll do it. If there's a mishap, other shorthand writers are available. My job here is expendable."

Something in the hurry to make his point jerked at my attention. All at once I knew as if he had said it aloud that he wasn't just worried and out of sorts, he was ready to die and didn't care if it happened now or later. My whole attitude to the bone-pointing ritual changed in the space of a thought; it was not mumbo-jumbo to Sammy, it was real.

He kept on talking, not with his usual picking and choosing of his words but letting them tumble out. "I suggested the search for the machine, didn't I? It was my idea. So I ought to be the one to test it. This is a big thing for the future and I want to be part of it."

His babbling kept us all quiet until Valda said, "Thank you, Sam. I'll think about it and let you know."

I could tell she was surprised by the crude vehemence but she let it go with the simple acknowledgement. She turned to Harry and asked him to let us have his ideas about the morphic resonance.

He said, "Let's start at the beginning, the rats and crossword puzzles. This feller, whose name I can't remember, if I ever knew it, tested rats running mazes, with a new batch for every test, and he found that they performed progressively faster, just as if each group picked the brains of the batch before. Then he tried it with human beings, setting them to work crossword puzzles. They each had the same set of puzzles but the groups were kept separate so they couldn't discuss them with one another, and working on different days, and he found that, like the rats, each group solved the puzzles faster than the ones before them. So he developed this idea of morphic resonance, saying that thought didn't disappear but hung around in some fashion, and people working on something that concentrated the mind could tap into it. They wouldn't get the whole thought and so there weren't a lot of easy answers; it was more as though a wisp of an answer was hanging in the air and when they were concentrating it would click into place. A rat would have to decide which way to turn and all the experiences of the rats before him would give him the right answer though he wouldn't know why he made the decision. It just felt right. Same with the crossword fellers—when they came to a hard clue that made them stop and think, they got it a bit faster because their concentration opened the way into the resonance and a tiny bit of the relevant stuff seeped into their brains."

This was basic stuff that we all knew about and I wondered why he was rehashing, until he said, "The concentration was the important thing. That was what Warlock missed out on and we'll come back to it later; it may be the clue to the whole resonance thing."

Valda asked him, "Are you saying that thought persists and can be recaptured even after a few days or weeks?"

"Why not? Warlock gave us the idea that time doesn't exist in the mental regions, so why put a limit on persistence? Without time there is no wastage, no fading. There could be all the thinking since life began, including what rats and insects thought about, all present and waiting to be used. I can't explain the timeless business and I won't try; quantum physics may have answers but I think you'll have to wait a few centuries before any more of those thinkers show up—unless you can catch them in the resonance, and if you can understand what you catch."

This sounded like pretty deep water and I asked him if Warlock said all this.

"No. He was an artist and didn't really have a clue to what was going on down there. Besides, he was confused by his own experience, which was mainly about something else altogether. He saw his preconscious imagery as part of the total experience, not realizing that the resonance world—call it that, got to call it something—was an utterly other thing. You have to remember that I heard Warlock's account in Connor's office in the afternoon and was put in cryo-suspension the same night; when I woke here it was as though I had heard it only a few hours before. I recalled things he had said that puzzled me at the time and I've had a couple of weeks to think them over, and writing it down brought details back to mind. You've read his son's deposition, so you know about his vision of his wife and family—call it a vision for want of a better word—and how he went on from there to something else. It's my idea that the vision was truly in his preconscious mind but what happened next was otherwise. It was a descent— if that is the right word—into the resonance field."

He looked around at the three of us and I don't think he got much encouragement. Sammy was politely attentive but seemed more occupied with his own troubles; Valda was patient but noncommittal, waiting expressionlessly for the point to appear.

Harry said, "Gus was there to hear it and he has pretty good recall. He can check me. The first thing Warlock said that alerted me was when he described his isolation contact with Frankie's mind. He said something like, 'there were other minds around, too, but not so clear.' Then Frankie woke up and contact was lost, but Warlock said, 'I was alone except for the murmur of other minds at a distance.' He was in full isolation, alone with his vision except that there was a background murmur. Check, Gus?"

I'd been listening pretty hard to Warlock because I knew about the rats and crosswords and was expecting some sort of a link. I said, "That's near enough."

"Thank you. Then he talked about falling further into his mind but I think that was only an approximation. He had been fed the idea of exploring the depths of his mind and the feeling of going further down made some locational sense, but in fact he wasn't moving in any direction. I think that in full isolation he had achieved the thing he had been concentrating on and got some sort of an intellectual answer to the question, but that he was now in the resonance area and the mind was free to roam. At first his concentration kept the resonance out but in the end he couldn't ignore it. But it was too big and complicated and overwhelming for him to make sense of it. That's what he tried to describe to us that afternoon. He said, 'Can you grasp the idea of pure thinking without pictures or words or even ideas relating to each other? It was like being wide open and having perceptions pour into me. Everything at once.'

"He said the place, or whatever it was, was full of thought. He tried to impress us with the vastness of the experience, said 'there were minds, so many of them that they could have been all of human thinking since thinking began.' He talked about thoughts so self-centered and stark that they could have been the ideas of animals—remember that—pure greed or defensiveness or the expulsion at birth. And there were ideas so complex that they meant nothing to him. But these were only glimpses; he described them as 'all mixed together in a great combined yell.' At the end he said, 'they weren't people from the past, only their ideas, their thoughts,' and then he said, 'I'm not making sense. I don't think I can. I'm capable.'"

He stopped as if that was all. Valda said at once, "That doesn't take us far. A great tangle of impressions pressing on the mind!"

"Far enough." Harry said. "Remember the rats and the crossword puzzles."

"I don't follow."

"It's the whole point. When Warlock went into isolation he went with an instruction to concentrate on a question whose answer should logically be found in his own mind. And so it was, some extraordinary kinesthetic translation of the real into the surreal—but he was aware of a background murmur and I think it was his emotional commitment that at first kept him out of the resonance ambience. Frankie didn't hear the murmur because his vision of hellfire scared the tripe out of him and nothing else could get through. I say nothing about their sharing each other's minds because I've no ideas about that. What I do say is that in complete isolation the resonance is available."

"As a jumble of thought."

"Rats and crossword puzzles! Warlock made contact with an unknown he wasn't ready for and all he got was an impression of chaos. But the rats and the puzzle-solvers were concentrated on one question whose answer did not lie in their minds, but that other rats and solvers had worked out before them. The answers were already there in the resonance. My guess is that with their brains totally involved in a single question they made contact with some thread of the world mind—if that's what it is—and the answers seeped into their brains. They didn't make real contact, just caught a thread of thought on the wing, so to speak, because of their total concentration."

It began to make sense. We were all quiet, thinking about it. Only the tap and scrape of Sammy's pencil intruded as he took down every word. Then, when he had caught up, he said, "Our kurdaitcha men sought to attain the same state without isolation machinery."

I noticed that he said "our," despite his white skin.

His self-identification seemed to waver uncertainly.

"Perhaps," Harry said, "they succeeded but did not know what they encountered."

"They sought the Dream Time. Some reported visions."

"It is remarkable that they achieved so much without assistance."

Valda asked, "Is that all? You want to go into isolation. Why?"

"Warlock was absorbed in himself and all he experienced was a great jungle without meaning. I want to go to the resonance with questions about things I don't know, as the rats and solvers did, and see if that is the way into the jungle of thought. It might be the way to catch the threads of thought as they untangle, to plug in to the knowledge and experience of others."

Suddenly Valda laughed and said, "Think of it! All the stupidities and lies and errors since life began, preserved forever in morphic resonance!"

It was an unusual jibe from someone who generally looked on the productive side of things, and Harry replied quickly, "I daresay you'll find those if they're what you look for."

She looked him over as if she summed up something unpleasant. "You want to make this test?"

"Very much."

"That is perhaps a stroke of fortune. Every living member of society today is part of a planned whole; none is expendable. And here you are, available for risk."

I had not suspected a streak of cruelty in her, and the mockery was plain; she found him unlikable and saw no need to hide it. Well, we all have a bitchy side to us and it can take only some little thing to find it out.

Harry, being Harry, gave as much back to her. "I take my own risk in order to satisfy my speculations, not to pamper a jerrybuilt civilization whose chances I wouldn't give ten cents for."

His general surliness said clear enough that he didn't like this new world. I'd thought he'd have the sense to settle down and keep quiet about it, but this sounded like war declared and it stung Valda at her sorest point; nobody likes a life's work being attacked. She responded with the ice princess voice kept for insolent guttershit, "You speak with the authority of a moribund society incapable of maintaining itself or of devising a means of its own continuance."

That would have shut me up, but not Harry. He said, "The only good thing I see ahead for your kindergarten is that you and your laboratories full of old men and women will die before you have time to do real damage and the human race will go its own way. It will make its own mistakes, not the mistakes ready-made for it by a bunch of test-tube egos."

She had her mouth open ready to carry on the conflict of spites, which was all it seemed to me, then closed it and nodded as if she understood and made allowance for a fractious brat. Then she just walked out without another word to any of us.

The scrape of Sammy's pencil stopped. Scrupulous Sammy had recorded every nonsense word for posterity. (I have to admit his notes have been useful to my own account. Nice to have the words said dead right.) He sucked at his pencil, which with him was a sign of disturbance and questions to come. When they came he sounded pedantic and pompous after the little slanging match.

He said, "Your extreme rudeness to Dr. Valda aside, what objection have you to our society, Harry?"

Harry answered, "It won't be easy to tell you, because you don't know anything about real people. You've all been brought up to accept what's given you and not think there might be other ways of life."

"To you we are unreal people?"

Which goes to show the danger of free-ranging speech to a literal mind. In our day we were all brought up to accept what we got, but there were always others raised in different ways and so we had a chance to see and compare. And if the result was teenage rebellion and adult bloody murder, at least we had freedom of choice, and even if all the choices were equally shitty at least our mistakes weren't set up at birth. Or were they? It's a hard question.

I think it was hard for Harry, too, because he was slow about answering, still simmering from one attack and now faced with another more placidly launched but just as demanding. Sammy just sat there with his pencil at the ready and waited for him.

Harry swallowed his anger to let hisself think. " 'Unreal' was a colloquialism, a slang word meaning out of touch with the real world."

"We are human, and capable of infinite variety."

"Yes, and that will bring you some surprises. Let me predict: Your children are prepared, trained, dragooned into belief in a system of sexual partnerships designed to perpetuate physical characteristics predetermined by a group of people who will soon be dead. And you, who keep the children in line to hold the belief, will also be dead soon enough. Then, since you are a human race capable as you say of infinite variety, what will the children do when they are at last left to think for themselves? They will ask, Why this way when other ways exist, untried? They will answer by finding out for themselves and the regulated system will crumble and vanish."

"But the norms will have been established."

Sammy was so placid that I suspected this argument was not new to him, but Harry shook his head. "Variations will creep in and be preserved, and men and women from your Forest Genetic will fancy partners from the Coastal Genetic or the people of the grazing plains or the new desert-dwelling group Gus is busy fathering; they will generate cross-bred offspring and soon the whole foredoomed plan will crash."

Sammy said only, "I think not," but didn't elaborate.

"No? Then let's pretend it holds up. What will you get but a whole world of differentiation, genetics with incompatible ideas of behavior dictated by their closed environments, unable to understand each others' ideas, ambitions, moralities, habits; even their languages will drift apart as each develops in its particular way. You will finish up as different races in the one country, distrusting and misunderstanding and eventually hating one another. We called it 'racism' and it was one of the greatest barriers to human peace. You will rediscover war, with Gus's descendants as the race most physically fit to make soldiers."

Sammy sounded less certain as he said, "All over the world the young are being educated in peaceful arts and the rights of others. It is one world. It will persist."

"Will it, Sammy? Communication across the world is already limited to exchange between special location and the satellites are going out of commission slowly but inevitably. Long before the last one goes you will be exchanging messages carried by horsemen while people starve for news of the world. There aren't many machines left and most of those are already useless to you; they were designed to serve billions and not worth preserving for a few scattered tribes. By the time you have the numbers to make industry worthwhile you will have forgotten how to read the books and blueprints stacked in your boarded-up sealed libraries."

Sammy's flying pencil had not missed a word of all this but in the end all he said was, "Harry, all this has been thought of and guarded against."

Harry's laugh was of genuine amusement. "You imagine you can defeat the future by thinking about it? I'd like to be around to see what *Kiev* and *Search* find if ever they come home. They won't recognize a skerrick of it. Squabbling tribes living in huts and rubbing sticks to light fires!"

I wasn't all that sure. If that upset Sammy he didn't let on, only said, "I think your opinion is insecurely founded," and let the subject drop.

42

Valda came to me that night but she wasn't after a roll on the bed; for once I had the feeling she just wanted someone to talk to.

"That damned man," she said, meaning Harry, "has a useful brain clouded by inner rage. What's the trouble with him?"

"Homesickness," I said, because I thought that was at the bottom of it.

Her eyes widened. "Good God! I remember the time as well as he does—dirt, corruption, neglect, wealth trying to pretend poverty didn't exist, industry and knowledge and society all running down into a universal sewer."

"You lived your way through change. He was shanghaied into your new age by the murder of his parents."

"Yes, that was hard." Then she said mulishly, like someone grumbling at an unreasonable obstacle, "But he is an intelligent man; he has had a disorienting shock but he should be able to adapt to the irreversible. Grief lingers but there is no way back. Meanwhile he is all hatred and contempt. His outburst to my grandfather was inexcusable."

"He needed a focus for his rage."

"But the rage must have a limit. You aren't yearning for yesterday."

In spite of good intentions on my part her total lack of understanding got to me. I growled like a chained dog, "You think not? I had a wife and son there."

"Yes, I know, but—" And there she stopped. But what? Wrapped in her ambition, her dreaming about a rebuilt race, insulated by a marriageless life that picked up its pleasures on the run, she hadn't a clue about real emotion, about loss and a familiar past. She could see how things could be made to work without ever seeing the people who had to do the working.

I said, "But nothing. I'd throw your whole pretty picture to hell for a day in my own second-rate dump a hundred years ago."

"You would?" It was a little girl's amazement at the unsuspected. Because I had kept a bland face to events she had told herself I had put yesterday behind me. As any intelligent man ought to, in her view. A century of dedication to making history had taught her nothing; she had had no time to learn and no face-to-face conflict with real life. Or, like the Minders, she had preferred not to look. I expected her now to say something stupid like, Haven't I tried to be nice to you?, but in fact her mind was still toeing the Wishart line. What she said was, "You don't agree with Ostrov's ideas, surely?"

She had roused the past for me and it hurt. Badly. "What I think won't change anything. Talk about something else."

Up against human crankiness—unintellectual response, pure bad temper—she said, "Perhaps I had better leave you; you're in a bad mood."

So I was. I didn't try to stop her from going, but for a cheap jibe I called after her as she made for the door, "I suppose you won't let Harry test the isolation gear now. He's a bad subject, eh?"

She turned to say, "You're not really a stupid man, Gus. Of course he can test the process. We revived him simply as company for you but there is no reason why he should not serve a useful purpose."

That was her cold scientist's voice; intimacy had been rebuffed and her casual relief was being cantankerous.

"Expendable, eh?"

"Indeed, yes."

43

When I saw Harry the next morning I was in mind to do a bit of friendly teasing about his simmering temper and explosions of sheer bad-mannered spite against the Wisharts, but he was so normal and cheerful that I felt he seemed like two men, one on the surface and one snarling and angry below, and the snarler wasn't subsiding with time.

In any case, another thing came up to take our attention. We were taking a turn on the roof where a few of the staff were having a work break when a young woman beckoned to us. The staff never took much notice of us and this woman was one we had never spoken to at all.

We went over and she said, "You work with Sammy Johns, don't you?" Harry said, yes we did, and she went on, "Do you know he's not eating?"

We knew he was looking a little drawn and worried but had put that down to some private problem we shouldn't inquire in to, and Harry asked, "Not at all?"

"He hasn't been into the staff dining room in three days."

Harry said, "He sometimes dines with the Wisharts, doesn't he?"

"Only for some special reason. He isn't eating at all. It's this bone-pointing thing."

"You know about that?"

"Of course. Word gets around."

"And you think he takes it seriously?"

"Yes; he has to."

We knew the curse troubled him, but not to this extent.

A young feller standing and listening nearby put his oar in. "He was brought up by Kooris and initiated into a tribe. He had the tribal stuff dinned into him right up to his late teen years. When a man has had the bone pointed he just gives up and waits to die, or that's what we hear about it."

I said, a bit stupidly because I was upset, "But he's educated; he doesn't believe that bullshit."

The young feller (I don't know his name) said, "Sammy was brought up tribal and he married a tribal wife. His own people expect him to die. Somebody has to talk him out of it."

"Can't you? You've known him longer and better than we have."

"We've tried and he won't listen to us. He just walks away."

Harry asked him, "What makes you think he'll listen to Gus or me?"

"You're with him all the time; you'll know how to get at him. At least you can try."

Harry said slowly, as if he was thinking it out, "I don't think we'd do much good. We've talked to a Koori near here and I understand that the curse has to be lifted by the koradji who imposed it. If he can be found—and the man who knows him isn't likely to tell. But it might be possible to pressure him into telling. Not right away but in a few days."

The young woman protested that in few days Sammy would be in a state of collapse.

Harry assured her, "He'll last longer than you might think. In any case, he can be hospitalized and kept in sedation and fed intravenously until we can persuade old Bill to talk."

"If," I said, "those treatments are still available."

A touch of venom crept into Harry's voice. "You can bet on the Wisharts having some emergency stock. They have to live to celebrate the New Dawn, don't they? Let's ask her bloody ladyship Valda."

That didn't go down well with the New Age folk around us but Harry couldn't care a damn how they thought. He was all at once intent on getting to Valda.

He practically ran down the stairs to the living quarters, with me grabbing at his elbow and trying to tell him that seeing Valda at any time was not easy because of her laboratory schedule. He only said, "We'll see about that," and carried on. Then I tried to explain, between breaths, that seeing her without Sammy being present to record any significant exchange might be hard to arrange, and Sammy's reaction to Harry's ideas could be a very strong resistance.

At the bottom of the stairs he stopped to say, "So we just tell her we don't want him present. God only knows why he has to keep on with his bloody recording; its usefulness must be over by now."

I wasn't sure that his smash-and-grab attitude to seeing Valda would get a result and sure enough our first reception, in the outer office, was ice-cold. The woman clerk or filing girl or whatever she was told us that the doctor could not be interrupted and when Harry threatened to go into the lab and get her hisself she stood in front of the door and insisted that he would only be thrown out if he tried.

His animosity for the Wisharts only really came home to me there; he had reached the stage of resentment where simple enmity became a rage of contempt for them and all their work. Nothing they might be doing mattered in his sight except that it was probably aimed at making things worse for everybody. I hadn't realized how deep-seated his anger was, so far eaten into him that the idea of their affairs being more important than his demand was just something to be swept out of his way. Whatever had got into him—and the murder of his parents had spread now to be the murder of the whole world, or that's how I saw it in a sort of revelation—was likely to end badly. The Wisharts might even see him as needing to be got rid of.

All this flashed into my mind as he raised his hand either to hit the clerk woman or drag her out of his way, and I snatched at his arm to stop him. I said to her, "Listen, miss, Sammy Johns is in trouble and he needs her help."

She didn't move from the door, only said, "We know of Mr. Johns's problems and it is a matter for himself to handle. The doctor does not interfere in civil affairs."

That was a stunner. It seemed the last ones to appreciate what was happening to Sammy were ourselves. Not only that but it sounded like there was a hands-off attitude in the complex. Civil affairs, bejesus!

While Harry dragged at my arm—but he was cooling down as fast as he had burst out—I said, "But there's been a new turn and we reckon she can do something. But we have to tell her about it."

The woman said, "If that is so, she should be told." She spoke to me, ignoring Harry as if he wasn't there.

"You could take a seat over there."

Against the wall, she meant. She opened the lab door and disappeared. We sat down.

Harry said, "I wouldn't have hit her," and I replied, "Yes, you bloody well would." I was thinking that it was more than Sammy who was going to need attention, only I couldn't think what would do any good.

The clerk woman came out after a bit and said, "Dr. Valda will see you during the midday break, in her private sitting room."

I told her, "We don't want Sammy there, though."

"I will inform her."

And that was it.

We had a couple of hours to wait, with nothing to do. Filling in time was our biggest problem in the complex; everybody except us had a job to do. I could have brought my day-to-day account up-to-date but I was too much shook up by Sammy's troubles to bother with it. I had thought of the bone pointing—if I had really thought at all—as something he would at first feel a bit upset about and then shrug off. It would go away; the idea of his actually starving hisself because it was more or less expected of him had seemed plain silly. Now it was real and an insight into what up-bringing and a split cultural heritage could do to you.

Sammy was off somewhere on his own affairs, whatever they were, and I couldn't talk to him but I asked Harry, "What would happen if Sammy said 'up yours' to the bone pointing and took no notice?"

He said straightaway, "They'd find some way to see he died. The koradji wouldn't risk defiance of his power."

Back in the old days I had met a few city Koori with their tribal affiliations growing weaker every year, but I hadn't picked up any idea of tribal life and beliefs. I knew they made some fuss about preserving sacred burial sites and things like that, but that was "country" stuff and didn't concern city living, and they never talked about it anyway. Now it seemed there was a whole mess of menacing and secret stuff we whites—insofar as anybody was full-blooded white or anything else in a mixed society—knew nothing about. My black great-granddaddy had certainly passed none of it on to me but, while it made nonsense in my eyes, in fact it could kill. Simply because you believed in it.

I was trying to say some of this but Harry cut me off, saying he had an idea how Sammy's case could be got around. It would all depend on how Valda saw it, he said and wouldn't say anymore. Which only left me feeling frustrated.

At last the midday break arrived and we made for Valda's sitting room, away down the long passage past the labs.

She let us in, not looking too pleased about the visit but prepared to be patient. "Sitting room" was a misnomer; it was more like an office, all desk and bookshelves and recording machines. There were some straightbacked chairs but nothing to relax on except a sofa in one corner. Valda was very much a straightbacked lady whose relaxations were calculated and private.

She pointed to chairs, sat herself behind the desk, and said, "Well?"

I thought Harry's talk had better be fast and persuasive, but he was aggressive as you like and not at all sucking up to her, "What are you doing about Sammy?"

"Nothing."

"Meaning there is nothing to be done?"

"Nothing that I know of and I am fairly familiar with tribal rituals. The curse can be lifted but not fought against."

"Lifted by the koradji who pointed the bone?"

She softened a little; her face showed a spasm of hurt, immediately controlled. "We don't know who he is; he could be a hundred K or more away, down in the Gippsland forests. Whoever knows won't tell."

"And if Sammy decides to live in spite of the curse?"

"He can't. He can't make a decision against a belief thousands of years old and inculcated in childhood. The one who tried would be at the very least ostracized by all tribes, the curse following by word of mouth wherever he went. Nobody would speak to him. He would be a ghost, literally unrecognized, unseen. He would die of loneliness. What have you in mind?"

"It depends how much time we have. How long will it be before the isolation gear is ready?"

"Is that germane? Perhaps three or four days. The technician should be here tomorrow."

"That should be all right. Sammy hasn't any fat on him but his body will be consuming muscle tissue by then and he has plenty of that." After a pause he asked her, "Do you know why the bone was pointed?"

All at once she became human. Her face collapsed in grief, as if Sammy really mattered to her and her heart had room for humanity; even her hands moved in a little wringing movement. She said bitterly, "Nobody knows. Or nobody will tell. A pointing is not women's business to the tribals but the men have tried to find out and got nowhere."

"Have you asked Sammy?"

"Of course. He only looks and turns away."

"Well, now, Bill Gordon could tell you if he wanted to. He told us. There are kurdaitcha, a few of them, who have been trying to reach the morphic resonance levels, though they call it by other names, for hundreds of years. It is a male pursuit, not open to women. Sammy told a woman how the isolation technique has outstripped the kurdaitcha knowledge and put her in position to take over a male preserve of magical secrecy. It came out at the Area Assembly that he had told you."

I had seen more indication of ordinary emotion in Valda in the last few minutes than ever before. I guessed that in her own way she thought well of Sammy and Harry's last words hit her hard. She shook her head a little, like someone disconsolate.

"We don't realize the power of habit and tradition and the past."

Harry sounded nearly gentle as he saw distress take her. "The Koori lived here alone for sixty thousand years. It needed more than the upstart cultures of Europe to fight beliefs ingrained and deep." He let that sink in before he said, "Still, I think we may do something about it in this special case."

Valda raised her head. "Do what?"

Harry seemed to go off on a tangent. "Do I take it you will let me test the isolation apparatus?" He still couldn't resist a little taunt: "After all, I'm expendable."

Her eyes hardened to everyday Valda. "If you want to try out your ideas, yes. Frankly, I don't see much risk."

"No? I don't fancy brain damage as an outcome. As a reward I want, as soon as my report is made after waking, for you to personally make a trial."

She was puzzled and wary at first, and I think I saw what Harry was getting at before she did. Then she cottoned on and nodded enthusiastically. "Yes. Yes, of course."

I had been quiet all the while, waiting for Harry to show his hand. Now, as much in relief as anything, I said, "Granddaddy won't be pleased."

She looked me over like a crawlie fresh out of the woodwork.

44

The ancient electrician arrived the next morning. His name was Fred something or other I've forgotten; he was bald, skinny, lame in one leg, and short-tempered after several days on horseback, but all things considered in pretty good nick for a man in his eighties.

Harry and I, as the only people to have seen the isolation gear in action, went with him to the storeroom where it had been laid out, and Sammy came along with his pad and pencil to take down the chatter. We explained as well as we could the function of the gear and the old boy took it in without any surprise at the craziness of inventors. He had been one.

"Sounds like a real ratshit setup," was his expert comment, and Sammy noted it for posterity. "Who's going to wear the helmet?"

I said, "Nobody's going to wear it until it's tested. Man, it's been in storage for a hundred years!"

"Then how do I test it? See here, the contact between the doc and the subject is by radio pulse, so how can I tell if the subject's helmet is working if it hasn't got a brain to work on? It has to report back to the doc's register when sensory output is exactly nullified by the input. Can't do that without an output to nullify."

Harry and I stared at each other, being not at all willing. A century packed in grease was no commendation for safety. A man could finish up around the bend and gibbering.

Sammy said, as casually as "Please pass the sugar," "I will test the helmet."

After four days of fasting he looked peaked but not at all worn down; just off-color was all. We had agreed not to talk to him about the bone pointing until we had something hopeful to say, but we knew why he offered: he didn't care. It was an indication of how deeply the whole thing had got to him; risk didn't matter. What amazed me was his calm, the way he carried on so normally with his everyday life, never letting on that he was under strain.

Harry said, "No, you can't do that," and Sammy smiled at him, friendly as you like, as if it was just a matey request.

"Why not, Harry? The grease packing should have protected the internal wiring, which I am sure will be thoroughly checked. There are no moving parts to break down. Besides, I am curious and would appreciate the helmet experience."

"I'll have the helmet apart first, to check connections to the electrodes," said Fred. "Shouldn't be any trouble, except maybe the unexpected." He couldn't care less who tested it as long as somebody did.

That was it. I can't speak for Harry but I know I was relieved to have a volunteer. Harry said, "We'll see. There's something I want to tell you first, so we'll leave Fred to get on with the job."

He led the way back to my cell, which seemed to have become the place for general discussions, and laid straight into Sammy: "You think it doesn't matter whether you live or die."

Sammy was equable, unfazed. "You have heard the canteen gossip, I gather. It does matter. To choose life would be to destroy a thousand generations of tribal lore—if it be possible to so choose, which I do not know. I am not one to throw an entire people into a crisis of unbelief."

"The doom can be lifted."

"If the koradji can be found and persuaded."

"I think Bill Gordon knows his name."

"I will not beg."

That was new—Sammy as the proud loner, facing fate with self-respect intact. In his place I'd have been ready to beg if all else failed; there's a limit to dying for no good reason. Except he thought he had a reason.

Harry persisted, "Perhaps we can find the koradji."

"Still I will not beg."

"But if he is found, others may intercede."

Sammy was silent to that. He was politely attentive to what Harry said, but that was all.

Harry stopped trying to budge him. He said, "There's a thing to know about the test. You heard what I told Dr. Valda, but here's something I didn't tell because it's only an idea in my mind and if you want to make the trial you should know it."

Sammy nodded. "All information will be valuable."

"All right, then. Warlock and Frankie went into isolation with fixed ideas in mind, the questions they had been instructed to concentrate on, and so these were the matters they 'saw' in their mental experience. Frankie was wakened but Warlock remained in isolation, held by his vision, until he became aware of other thoughts. He didn't go to a deeper level; it was there all the time but he was fixed on one idea and his mind didn't listen to anything else until the great mass of thought gradually percolated through to him. Then he just became aware of thought from all time past and present. It confused him because it was an undifferentiated mass he couldn't penetrate. My idea is that if you go into isolation knowing what you want to find, you will locate it, as if your question makes the index to the library and you shut out everything but that. It's only an idea but it's worth trying."

Sammy listened patiently. He considered the idea now with a still face until he was ready, and then said, "And you think I should seek the koradji?"

Harry hadn't expected that so soon but he nodded. "Why not? It could be useful to know who he is."

"I will consider it," said Sammy, conceding nothing, his own man to the last.

With a change of direction, Harry asked, "How do you feel?"

Sammy smiled briefly. "Hungry." After a while he added, "I have—consulted—with some who have fasted."

(Like who? I wondered, feeling pig ignorant of the smidgin of ancestry I had never followed up.) "They told me that the first two days are easy but then the stress begins. It seems to be so. Are you concerned for my readiness to make the test? Don't be; my concentration is excellent."

"Perhaps," Harry said diffidently (and I had never heard him sound diffident before), "you should eat a little today and tomorrow. As a precaution."

Sammy's brief smile flashed and vanished. "Tempter! No!"

He gathered his papers and left us. I supposed he was sick of the subject. I would have been, but I had to ask Harry, "What do you reckon would happen if he shrugged off the bone pointing and just carried on?"

"He would be ostracized by his tribe and even by his own family. And someone would find some way to kill him. The witch doctor can't be defied; the culture leaves only death as an option."

"It seems a hell of a punishment just for talking to a woman. Not even a tribal woman, at that."

"We aren't Koori. We aren't indoctrinated. We can't think their way. And I think he knew what he was doing, what the risk was. I don't know whether he's a fool or a hero or both, doing something scientifically important with the chance of dying for it."

45

We didn't tell Valda about Sammy's testing of the apparatus; she might have raised hell's delight and accused Harry of chickening out. Privately I thought he was glad to be shot of it but he also seemed to have in mind something Sammy would maybe do better than hisself. In a sense, Sammy would know what to look for in the mental depths and would know better what to make of what he found.

Anyway, Fred came to us two days later and said he was ready. He wanted to know if Valda would be with us but we told him her lab routine shouldn't be disturbed until the isolation trip was tested and ready to go, so there were only the four of us in the room.

He wasn't happy about the electrical setup. The lone circuit diagram found with the crated apparatus told him what went where but not what it did, and his dismantling of the helmets had left him little the wiser. He had read the Steven Warlock document, which told him nothing of the technical implications, and he could only hope that what he failed to understand would not kill anyone or mash their brains.

While he talked, Sammy made his meticulous notes of the litany of distrust, blank-faced, showing nothing, doing his job. He looked pretty awful, thin in the face and bright-eyed like a fever patient, but maintained that he was fit for the test and absolutely clear-headed. I wasn't convinced and neither was Harry, but he must have thought it worthwhile to take the chance.

Fred seemed to think of it as a pretty straightforward operation. "The terminals on the helmet should give sensory readings as soon as it is fitted. I don't know what they all are or even which is which, but all the operator in the chair does is flick over the appropriate switch on the control box here and the box sends a radio pulse to its opposite number on the helmet. That operates a computer chip in the terminal, which determines the exact nullifying charge required. The computer tells the box and the box sends another pulse supplying the charge. See—no hands, boss! No human error to bugger the works. We just have to hope the works don't bugger the human. Your man ready?"

A reassuring type, our Fred.

Sammy laid down his pad, said, "Yes," and climbed onto the table. Cool as you like, not a care in the world, all in the day's work. I'd have been shitting myself.

Fred adjusted the helmet on Sammy while he said, "I've stripped this thing right down and can't see anything wrong with it—no corrosion or loose assemblies. I've had the operating chips under a microscope and can't spot any faults. I'd say it's in prime condition; you can see the telltales are registering the sensory discharges already. The thing practically runs itself. All the operator has to do is flick the switches over and check each one to see that its telltale registers exactly zero."

Harry asked, "What if it doesn't?"

Fred scratched his head and said, "Buggered if I know, mate. Open it up and check it over again, I suppose. You want me to operate?"

It was Sammy who said, "Yes; please get on with it."

"Okay, here we go."

He sat hisself in the chair and moved the first of the fingertip controls, with his eyes on the first dial. The needle moved smoothly to the zero spot.

Sammy said, "I can no longer see," but didn't speak again after that, just lay perfectly still without so much as a change of breathing. In his place I'd have been tightened up like a thumbscrew. He had plenty of balls, our Sammy.

Fred flicked over the controls, all eleven of them, and each time the needle showed zero. "That's it. How long do you want to leave him under?"

Harry had his eyes on his watch. "Thirty seconds will be enough. I'll tell you when."

This was not like watching Warlock and Frankie way back when, like two curiosities in a sort of freak show. This was a friend, personal, and I was sweating a bit when Harry said, "Now," after what seemed like forever, and Fred flicked the switches back and the needles all returned to their registering positions. "Seems to work all right," he said, the satisfied tradesman.

Sammy had not moved; he might have been asleep. Harry asked, "Should I shake him? I can't do that guttersnipe whistle of Bentinck's."

I told him, "I can. I was born in the gutter."

I leaned close to Sammy's ear and gave him a real blast from the old streets. It worked like a charm; he opened his eyes, stared at the ceiling for a moment, and then sat up. "Strange," he said, looking around at us. And then, "Unearthly."

He slid off the table and stood leaning against it, frowning while he muttered, "Give me time to collect my thoughts."

When he began to speak I wished we had brought a tape recorder because he had plenty to say, but it went something like this:

"Your idea, Harry, about concentration on a preconceived question seems to have been correct. I felt my senses being nullified one by one and tried to keep my mind free. That is of course impossible, but I let my brain drift idly about whatever came into it and I found myself without warning in a maelstrom. I cannot describe it—literally cannot, because there were no sensory references to cling to, only an immense ocean of thought. And there was no sense of then or now or afterwards, but everything was all at once. I don't mean that it was all present in my mind, because my mind was part of it, but that everything from the beginning of thought was now. I had no solid vision such as Warlock and Devalera had, only a huge confusion until I remembered that I was to seek out the koradji. As soon as the thought came to me the maelstrom receded and I had knowledge of the bone pointing. It did not come in Warlock's or Devalera's visual terms, possibly because what I received was an idea not translatable visually. My mind was flooded by the conception of evil and justice and a conviction of belief, but it was wholly abstract and very powerful. There was a sense of agelessness, of whole populations of believers reinforcing the idea until its potency was unchallengeable.

"But I did not see my koradji, only the conception of generations representing the idea of bone pointing, all of them together reinforcing the power of the idea. There were no single thoughts, only the accumulations of thought expressing themselves as a total of knowledge of the thing conjured up. And there were no names or faces. I thought of people I know and they were at once present to me as mental confusions impossible to penetrate as momentary impressions flitted in and out of their minds and were absorbed into the great mass of thought. But I did not see individuals, only the fleeting contents of their thinking. Remember that Warlock and Devalera saw no individuals, only their own private renditions of them in metaphorical form. It seems that pure thought renders only ideas, not memories.

"I think it is not possible to convey the nature of the experience. It is as though all knowledge is present in your own mind, ready to be called up. That is the best I can do."

There wasn't much we could say to all that. I seemed to me that Sammy hadn't achieved much but Harry was thoughtful as though there were leads to be sorted.

Fred was happy that his cleaning and assembling had produced results but all he said, with a big grin, was, "I reckon I can go home now."

During the afternoon, when I was alone in the cell, Sammy came to see me.

He said, "I told you that in isolation I thought of those I know and received only the confusions of daily impressions. I sometimes saw more, an overriding emotion coloring all thinking. We must have a care for Harry; he dissembles but he is consumed with hate, perhaps murderous hate."

I should have known. He had been too calm, had all too suddenly put off his snarling resentments. I had a sudden prescience of danger biding its time.

I asked, "Who's he got hate for?"

But all Sammy could say was, "I told you I saw no faces. It is ideas and convictions that attract murder, one's own or those of others."

A fat lot that helped.

The next morning was set for the tests by Harry and Valda. Sammy came, too, impassively taking notes and plainly suffering, with all of us feeling obscurely guilty but not prepared to comment; he kept a wall of reserve around him. There was no real reason for my presence but nobody objected; Harry-and-Gus was accepted as a single, faintly alien entity. And there was Fred, looking sour because Valda insisted on his supervision of the trials when all he wanted was to be up and away. I suppose she felt safer with an "expert" in charge "in case of accidents," though any intelligent child could have flicked the switches.

There's not much to tell about the action. Valda hadn't been told of Sammy's preliminary run and she was a touch apprehensive when Harry sat on the table and fitted the helmet. "Sixty seconds," he told Fred, and lay back.

When it was over he came conscious without any help from me, just opened his eyes and sat up. One of those things—some do and some don't.

It was awhile before he said, "It's indescribable; it's everything all at once." And then of course he tried to describe it but couldn't improve much on what Sammy had said. He had gone into isolation with the problem of static time loosely in his mind, hoping for illumination but getting absolutely nowhere. He said, "I picked up all the ideas about time that anybody ever thought of—I could write an encyclopedia about it—but nobody ever thought about it as something that just didn't happen. I should have known that.

There was no sensation of time passing, just the knowledge of everything all at once; it was a matter of thinking of what I wanted to know and it became instantly plain. But no mental pictures or feelings, just bare thoughts like things always known and just called to mind. I thought of each of you in turn and got no hint of personality or appearance, just a jumble of thinking that disappeared into the world mass.''

I didn't quite believe that last. I'd be ready to bet he had looked closely at Sammy and Valda and derived some overall impression of their minds just as Sammy had seen the brutality in his.

"Your turn," he said to Valda and held out the helmet. She didn't hesitate but took it with an air of determination, of somebody not to be outdone in facing the unknown. "Let your mind wander," Harry told her, "until you get there. There isn't any 'there' but I can't think of a better way to express it. I mean only that you don't want to be held up by concentration on personal things, as Warlock was. Relax until the ocean claims you.''

She only nodded to him and climbed onto the table.

"Sixty seconds," he told Fred, "though I don't think the duration means anything.''

The minute passed and like Harry she recovered immediately. I thought that maybe recovery had to do with your state of mind, with how much you wanted to be free of problematic reality. Like Warlock.

Valda was very thoughtful and took her time about speaking, and then she only made the same attempt as Harry and Sammy to describe the impossible to describe.

I asked her, "Did you look for something you wanted to know?''

"Yes, some laboratory research. There was more available than I had imagined, more than I could have assembled in years of fumbling through files of documents. Isolation is the finest tool ever invented.''

She said not much else but left us as though hugely important things were on her mind and all she wanted was to get back to the lab. Fred called after her that he wanted to go home and she called back to him, "Yes, go."

He said, "Well, gents, that's it," and went off whistling.

Sammy also went off, I suppose to write up his interminable notes. Surely no eruption in history was being so well documented as ours.

I looked over the apparatus, thinking that maybe I should take my turn with it but not really all that anxious to try. I don't fancy creepy experiences and I couldn't think of anything urgent I needed to know.

Then Harry said, "Gus, you and I must pay a visit this afternoon. To Bill Gordon. I think we can put the squeeze on him now."

He explained what he had in mind and I cursed myself for missing the obvious.

46

Our visit to Bill Gordon that afternoon was short and quiet but in its way tumultuous. He invited us in almost as though we were expected. There were at least two half-breed aborigines on the Wishart staff and Fred would have talked to whoever would listen; word of the isolation test would have gone up the street overnight.

Mrs. Gordon was not in sight. Men's business! Well, maybe.

Bill had no doubt of the subject of our call; he was polite but not welcoming and he opened the conversation with a definite sighting shot. "I'm told Mr. Johns is showing signs of strain."

Harry shrugged, but I said, "He hasn't eaten for about a week."

Bill nodded. "That is a common reaction, I believe."

I pushed him a bit. "Question is, Bill, whether it is his belief in the bone pointing ritual that drives him or the withdrawal of tribal support."

"I'm sure there will have been no such withdrawal."

"Because he is doing what is expected of a man under the curse?"

He pointed out that it was not a curse but a protocol of tribal justice. "A detected transgressor does not resist."

"What if he did?"

"Then social elimination would proceed. Sixty thousand years of culture is not to be lightly flouted."

I doubted that the ritual went so far back, but that was not the present point. "Still, the penalty seems very harsh, excessively harsh."

He was silent; to him the complaint deserved no answer.

Harry came in at a different angle. "Isolation equipment has been obtained. It has been assembled and was tested yesterday morning."

"So I have been told."

"Bush telegraph, eh? Did it also tell you that Sammy made the first test?"

Apparently his information was not so explicit as that; he showed nothing but he had to think before he spoke, and then he said, "That was an act of defiance. It will earn him nothing." That sounded like a trap slamming down. He added, with a return to good-mannered inquiry, "I trust the test was successful?"

"So much so that I had a run myself this morning." He went on to describe the experience while Bill listened with intense interest. If he was jealous of all his people's attempts over generations being surpassed by a laboratory gimmick, he did not display it; I felt that his thirst for genuine knowledge, even if it was founded on failure and at bottom rooted in sorcery, was as real as any scholar's.

Harry finished up with something he hadn't told us before: "I wanted to see what sort of limits there might be, so I started thinking about unreal things, I thought about the Rainbow Serpent, your people's protector after men were first created, and there it all was, laid out for me, all the thinking of the Koori through generations. I couldn't get any idea of time because it doesn't exist there, but I got a headful of all the forms of the serpent as seen by the different tribes and all its functions and capacities. It was real because a thought is real and is never lost. What I saw did not tell me it was a legend or an irrational belief, only how your people thought of it in their hearts."

I suspected this was a sop to Koori cultural lore, an assurance that the isolation technique would not destroy or destroy the work of centuries. I can't say what Bill thought; he lapsed into a sort of inturned silence.

"And after me," Harry said, "Valda Wishart took the helmet and looked into eternity."

It seemed that took time to penetrate but eventually Bill returned to the present and looked him in the eye with the cold animosity of an animal at the kill.

"Now," Harry went on, "all consideration of men's business and women's business becomes meaningless when women have as easy access to isolation as any. Eternal thought is no longer the longed-for property of a few dedicated kurdaitcha, but is open to all the world. In this matter, men's ritual business no longer exists."

He stood up to go and the old man turned his face to the wall. If he wept we were not to see it.

Three days later, when Sammy was weak and white and shedding flesh, Miriam arrived at the complex and we rushed her to him.

She brought news. The bush telegraph was spreading its web through the tribals, telling that the pointing was lifted. Sammy was a man again.

He could hardly eat by then; he said the hunger pangs were gone, that he only felt tired and wanted to be left with Miriam. She scolded him, once the joy and pity were over, in a tribal tongue that sounded like matriarchy in full tirade, while he simply smiled happily at her and drifted off to sleep. We had to devise a diet, mostly liquid at first, that he could take in gradually, without vomiting the lot over the bed.

Miriam stayed for three days, spoon-feeding him, and he began to put on weight. Curiously—well, I thought it curious—he had nothing to say against Bill Gordon.

47

Valda came in each day to check Sammy's progress and give advice about diet. On the third afternoon, with Miriam only just gone home to her family, she came into Sammy's cell while Harry and I were still there. She gave him a routine inspection together with a lot of small talk about nothing much and was about to leave when Harry stopped her.

"Stopped her" is a friendly way of putting it; what he said and how he said it pulled her up short.

He said, like a copper bailing up some street brat, rough as guts, "Hey, you! I want to talk to you!"

Valda halted in mid-step, turned slowly on her heel and stared at him, not even surprised, just studying the source of insult, and waiting. Sammy became at once still-faced. As for me, I hadn't realized Harry had that sort of coarseness in him.

He grinned at her, and a venomous grin it was, and said, "You got Sammy into this mess with your talk to the Council. He might have died if we hadn't wrong-footed old Bill Gordon and made him take a second thought."

That was too bloody unfair. I interrupted to say it wasn't her fault. "She didn't know about ritual secrets. The Koori keep their ways to theirselves and whites don't know the score. I only know because Sammy told us."

He said, "Shut up and stay shut. Listen, Dr. Wishart, there's a job for you. You got your isolation machine nearly at the cost of a man's life; now you have to pay for it."

Valda leaned herself against the wall, arms folded, expressionless. "Go on."

She had cool nerve. He was in a mood for violence and she knew it. Or maybe she was so used to being boss that she didn't credit danger signals. I couldn't work out what had got into him, but I started to work on a concentration to jump him; he was stronger than me but I had the speed on him and I reckoned I could stop him.

"First of all," Harry said, "you've got to realize the direction your precious New Age is going and then you have to do something about it."

He paused there as if he expected an outburst, but Valda said nothing, continued to watch him like a new bug that should be inspected but not disturbed.

He went on, "The first thing to happen will be the failure of those local generators you depend on for your laboratory power and intercommunication. No spare parts, no more trained technicians, the few that are left growing too old to care—because you aren't training any more, are you? All the bright young folk are being pushed into agriculture and teaching, carpentry and pottery, social theory and local government, and a smattering of a herbal pharmacopoeia to replace organized medicine. With communication lost between world groups and reduced to Pony Express riders even between local groups, how long will it take for them to split into local factions and warring tribes?"

She neither moved nor showed more than a polite interest, while he was intent now on his argument. The moment of possible violence was over. But it might recur, and an uncontrolled Harry driven by deep anger would be a formidable berserker. I could not relax yet.

"And how long do you think your gene diversity program will last once your oh-so-authoritative policing dies with the last of your laboratory policemen, and the careful genealogical tables become debased and misinterpreted and used as instruments of local power? Or when the teenagers become tired of sexual restriction and fuck where the fancy takes them and bring the whole structure tumbling down?''

I suppose that was too much for her; the diversification program was her baby, the real focus of her work. She stiffened and said with a genuine furious stridency, "Two generations will be enough to—" then caught herself and cut her words off, but the pose of patient listening was broken.

"Enough to spread the gene pool, you think? Maybe, but how about your idiot division into physical types, designer-bred to adapt them to topography and climate? The youngsters will soon make hash of that; they'll take the partners they want and to hell with black or white, big or small, slender build or muscled ape. You're wasting your time on people who'll toss all your restrictions into the local cesspit as soon as the pressure is removed. Do you know what the future is? It's a world brought to ruin by your grandfather, your messianic killer of the unborn."

Through all of this his voice had changed. He had begun belligerent and dogmatic, spoiling for a fight, but the tone had changed to a sharp-edged slashing as if each word was meant to cut flesh. This was a Harry I had never seen before, an evil man and a cruel one, bent on the destruction of dreams and visions and dedication. He had begun to sound as if a final pleasure would be to dance on the ruins of humanity. It wasn't as though he had anything against Valda; he needed to tear at nerve ends, and she was the nearest at hand.

The venom was nasty stuff to listen to, not least because it seemed to me he had a good case. It was the savageness that put me off, the showing up of the man beneath the skin. It was hard to credit that his hatred ran so deep.

It was hard to credit, too, that Valda's self-possession let her pass over the direct insult to her grandfather. What she said was, "This is mere diatribe and not original. We have heard it all before in our own discussions. There are competent brains in all the Wishart Laboratories throughout the world; do you imagine they will have missed the obvious? Or taken no steps to ensure against collapse?"

That halted him like a smash in the face. He had to stop and reconsider. He said, with an attempt at arrogance, "Steps you will be no longer here to oversee or enforce! What steps, lady?"

She allowed herself a smile and a mocking silence. In the sudden stillness I became aware for the first time of imperturbable Sammy scratching away at notes, taking all this bitching down for some unimaginable posterity, maybe one so debilitated that they couldn't read his account anyway. Despite Valda's show of confidence, I couldn't see any real future for the New Age.

Harry glared at her; he was actually quivering with rage and his voice cracked slightly when at last he demanded, "Well?"

"Another time," she said casually, "when you are in a more receptive mood."

With all the honors hers, she left us.

Sammy laid down his notepad and lay back on his pillow. "Harry," he said, "you have upset us all. Please go away and recover sanity."

It was the quietest, politest smack in the mouth I ever heard. And Harry calmed down. It was a physical process; I literally watched him change from ranting attacker into the man I knew, as if he had a second personality hidden behind his face. He sat a moment looking down at his hands, then got up and walked out the door without a word.

I said, "He's not really like that."

"As you knew him that may have been so, but that is how he is now. I saw his mind. In full isolation there is no emotional scene, Gus; there is only pure thought. But, as the last almost imperceptible senses fade, there is a passing moment when the minds of those near are open to a rapid glance—if 'glance' is a suitable word. It is mentioned somewhere in your account of the Warlock awakening but without comment. I don't know whether it is an effect of contiguity, dependent on nearness, or might be extended. I can say only that I glimpsed the minds of those present and Harry's was dominated by enmity. Understand that there was no emotional coefficient, only a cold statement, a meaningless core of unassuageable rage. In the final confrontation with the world mind there is no feeling, no sense of personality of any kind, but for that moment—on the way down, so to speak—nearby minds are laid open. Harry's was terrifying."

I had a silly urge to ask what he saw in mine but had enough nous to bite the question back. No man in his senses wants to know the depths; I came near to it with Nguyen's truth drug and what I unearthed then about myself nearly drove me around the bend. Instead, I thought about Harry and how to get at what ailed him.

I tried to tell Sammy how I saw it—how Harry's last sight before waking into a new world was of his parents lying with their necks broke by thugs, and this after remorseful months of patching up his differences with them as he remade his own psyche after a desperate encounter with a truth drug. He woke, with a mind ready for hate, into a New Age that wiped out the past and in his view offered him nothing. He wanted revenge and finding nothing to be revenged on, raged against everything.

Sammy agreed, "Perhaps so, even probably so. But you, Gus, do not display such animus though the actions of Miraflores severed you from wife and child."

I could only say that I am not Harry, that I can be excitable at times but on the whole pretty placid about accepting the world as it comes, that in my heart I cried for the past but faced the fact that there is no going back. I could have said, but didn't, that I saw only bleakness and emptiness for my future in the New Age, an act of living from day to day till the end came in an empty world peopled by a busy but empty race. I was in it but not of it. An observer.

Sammy nodded understanding though in fact he didn't understand. He said only, "We must watch Harry. He will do some-one an injury. Or himself. A general, unfocused hate . . ." He trailed off moodily.

But the hate was thoroughly focused though we didn't realize it then. It only waited on a trigger.

•　　•　　•

I went to Harry and found him lying on his bed, staring at the ceiling. He said before I could speak, "I wanted to tell her something. I started calmly enough." (But you didn't, Harry; you were bitching from the beginning.) "But I lost my way under that superior stare. That bitch rubs me the wrong way and in the finish I didn't say what was really on my mind."

I protested that "bitch" wasn't a fair description, that she was a nice enough woman but resented being under attack.

"Nice enough? That's your cock talking; she keeps it happy."

True enough but it didn't make her a bitch. It wasn't worth an argument so I let it go and asked, "What did you want to tell her?"

"About the world mind, how to make use of it. Not now but in the future when all the generators break down and there's no power for the helmet."

"No power, no isolation. Then what?"

He sat up. "Then a different kind of power. We'll have to see old Bill again. After what he did to Sammy he'll have to help, won't he?"

"Maybe, if you tell me what you're talking about." By now I wanted nothing in the way of new ideas from Harry, not until he'd had time to calm down a bit, but it was best to let him rant.

So he did tell me, and it made sense—of a kind. As he saw it.

48

The next morning we went to Bill Gordon's house. We wanted to take Sammy with us but he was still too shaky to ride; he would have to rely on our version of events.

Bill received us with a kind of stiff courtesy, not quite insulting but less than welcoming, sat us down in his sitting room and waited silently for us to state our business. As before, his wife was not present.

Harry opened bluntly: "We need your advice and perhaps your assistance."

Whatever the old man expected, it was not that. His surprise showed in a suspicious interest.

Harry went on, "Now that the world mind has been penetrated by the isolation technique—" Bill interrupted with one word: "Penetrated?"

"In a fashion. We know what appears to be there, even how to gain a little information from it, but it is too vast a thing for easy comprehension. There is knowledge there, buried and forgotten knowledge; there may also be matters to be avoided, dangers and traps for the investigating mind that we have no way of guessing at."

"The unknown is always dangerous. Tell me what you have done and seen."

Harry gave him a detailed rundown on all the isolation tests since the Warlock business. Bill heard him out in silence, and at the end he said, "Something of this was suspected, but your machine has surpassed our generations of searching. The world mind can be laid open to the world of flesh." He smiled at last, briefly and a touch bitterly. "I confess to jealousy."

"Forget jealousy; this is only a passing thing."

"Passing?"

"It depends on a single machine. There were two but the second one may no longer exist. The machine cannot be duplicated, or I think not. Even if we could locate the metals and their alloys to re-create the helmet there are still nanometric chips to be duplicated and there is neither the skill nor the machinery to do that. The Wishart Labs may be capable but their work is almost purely biological, so I doubt their expertise. In any case, the last of their scientists will be dead in a few decades. The power generators will rust or cease running for lack of oil, and the skills to repair them

or find oil are lacking in an agricultural society. They will be re-
discovered in a century or two as the people find leisure to use
the libraries and reclaim the past, but the way to the world mind
will be rusted and forgotten."

"Then the complex must investigate while it can."

"That will place knowledge in the hands of a few who will
investigate only what suits their immediate plans. Not good
enough."

Bill stayed quiet a long time before he asked, "What is it you
want of me?"

"Information and assistance."

"So ask."

"How many kurdaitcha are there?"

"In all Australia only a handful."

"And how many practice inner contemplation?"

"I do not know all of them. Perhaps two or three. The total
Koori population is very small now and the kurdaitcha are mostly
old. The ancient knowledge is not greatly taught; the young have
little interest."

"But there are some and they are capable of teaching?"

"Yes."

"Can you locate them?"

The old man's eyes mocked him. "Yes, given time; it is a large
country. What do you want with magic?"

"Nothing; I think the kurdaitcha do not deal in magic. I have
one more question: Have those who practice inner contemplation
perceived any hint of the world mind?"

Bill took his time answering, like a man scanning a mind full
of memories. Perhaps that is what he did; the Koori culture is
passed mainly by word of mouth and its stories and stored knowledge go right back—or so they say—to the Dream Time of creation. Swallow that if you like.

He said at last, "There was one who could find far distant
places by dreaming of those who had reached them, dreaming of
mountains and rivers to give guidance from one point to another
until the far place was found. So he found people and places not

known to his tribe. It was an accomplishment superior to that of your rat in a maze but perhaps similar."

"In a state of trance?"

"That is your word; we think in terms of the freed spirit roving and seeing."

"And there have been others?"

"There are many similar stories but few so definite. And remember that the story of the finder was one handed down from elder to young initiate. Exaggerations creep in though efforts are made to preserve the original wording. Even so, there are translations from one language to another and the number of languages in the older days numbered hundreds. So truth suffers but the core of truth remains."

"Now, then, the real question: Could you call in your kurdaitcha contemplatives? We could give each of them experience of the isolation technique and perhaps see similarities to their own deep-trance experiences. Then they could teach others the deep-trance techniques and maybe when there is no longer power for the isolation system they will have learned enough to make their own contact with the world mind."

"A large vision, Mr. Ostrov. To what end?"

"When power and machinery fail and the satellites are no longer available, the planet will be a place of separate countries and peoples. There will be a time of gathering crops and hunting for food until the old discoveries of civilization are found again. It will take a long time, even thousands of years. The libraries will help, but how much more rapidly could man regain his past with contemplative scholars able to tap it directly?"

The old man took so long to respond to this that almost I thought he had gone to sleep on us, but Harry waited with more patience than I would have. And when old Bill did finally speak, it was about something else.

"Gus says nothing. Why is he here?"

•   •   •

Fair enough; I hadn't opened my mouth after saying "G'day" when we came in.

"He records the history of two castaways in time."

So that's what I was for, to record this deathless conversation for the generations, not just a mate tailing along to see fair play or whatever.

"Sammy makes the record."

"Sammy is not present to hear what we say today. He is not yet well."

Bill looked quite expansively satisfied. "I trust he will heed the warning against defiance of ancestral powers. They are very real."

"Indeed so? There is a thing that puzzles me here. I have read of the bone pointing ceremony and of men dying because of it, but never of a truly authenticated case with names and witnesses."

Bill's smile was fixed in place and he waved a dismissive hand. "It is only recently that Koori languages have been written down. Unlike your courts of justice we kept no written records. History was handed on in song and story."

Harry's smile matched the old man's in persistence and fixity. "And the responsible koradji in Sammy's case has not been identified."

Suddenly claws were out and Harry was scratching for blood; the copper was reaching for a nick.

Bill shrugged, which is not a Koori gesture. "A koradji is a tradesman doing what is required of him. Who cares who he is?"

"A nameless man, possibly many miles distant, unknown by the local Koori, doing what a kurdaitcha requires of him—pointing a bone. Who knows if a bone was indeed pointed? The kurdaitcha drops the word of information here and there and within a day such a word from a reputable man spreads through the tribals and reaches the ears of the target, and the target ceases to bother with living. But was a bone ever pointed?"

Bill nodded. "I have no doubt that such a sham could be perpetrated successfully."

Harry dropped his eyes to his hands and said in a small, quiet voice, almost to himself, "If you had let Sammy die I would have come to your house and killed you."

He meant it; it was not the sort of thing he ever said idly and it gave me a cold shiver, but Bill's smile never wavered as he said, "It is pointless to threaten an old man with death, even in retrospect. And, had you killed me, who would have been left to gather your kurdaitcha from the ends of the land?"

It had been, after all, a useless display of menace, like something that had to be spat out because it burned the throat. It was a spike of the hidden hate rising for a second into the light. I had hardly identified it when he picked up the change of topic.

"Then you will find them, Bill?"

The old man's grin vanished; they were at business again. "Yes, Harry. It will take time, perhaps some months. I must first locate them, then there will have to be a detailed message setting out what is required of them. Then I must hope they will come, though I think curiosity will bring them. If even two answer the call, your school of inner contemplatives can begin."

"They will be willing to teach white men, uninitiated men? We will need a lot of students to go out and teach in their turn."

Bill's laugh was genuine. "You speak as though you plan to set up a production line. The method is difficult and the suitable scholars will be few. Should they succeed in tapping the world mind, which is by no means certain, I suggest that at least a century will pass before a single penetration is made."

"I know, I know. It will not be easy. We can build isolation modules to shut out light and sound, heat and cold, provide baths at body temperature to lower tactile reaction. We will think of other aids as we learn more. And they must be willing to teach women."

Bill froze and turned his head away. He muttered, "That strikes at the very heart of tradition. They will not be easily convinced. They will resist, even when they accept that the isolation generator has stripped away all tribal secrecy from the subject. Resistance is inborn through thousands of years. It may be necessary to wait until the first white teacher is trained. I have a free mind but I would find it difficult to instruct a woman."

And that was about it. They talked ways and means for a while and then we went home to the complex.

On the way back Harry was preoccupied. A couple of times he seemed to be muttering to hisself. I felt like I wasn't there or he didn't know I was there; we came out of Bill Gordon's house and he just went somewhere inside hisself.

After a bit it started to worry me and it wasn't the only thing that worried me. I said, "Did you mean that about killing Bill Gordon?"

At first he didn't seem to hear. He came to slowly, surprised that he had someone with him, and said, "What?"

I had to repeat, "Did you mean that about killing Bill Gordon?"

And he said, "Of course I meant it," a bit irritably, as if it was a silly question.

I began to see how serious all his moodiness and bad temper was and I didn't like what I was seeing. "You can't kill people out of hand, Harry. You're a copper, not a judge."

"I was a policeman in an orderly world."

Orderly! Maybe my memory was failing. "This one's a bloody sight more orderly than ours was."

He stopped walking and took my arm. "Gus! This is a despotism of scientists! They created it by an act of mass murder and now they're trying to distort the whole race with their genetic code. When they're done there will be no humanity left, only a set of nursery mannequins fitted to a single set way of life. If I knew how to do it I would slaughter the whole brood in their laboratories and set humanity free!"

This wasn't raving like a man taking leave of his senses; it was the cool pointing out of facts by a man out to convince a blinkered friend. The hard part to take was that I could see how he came to view things that way; it made a sort of logic—but not the sort that should set him muttering to hisself and feeling hisself one out against the world.

I tried to reason with him. "But you said yourself that their plans won't work, that the next couple of generations will see it all fall apart."

He shook his head as if I was a hopeless case. "You heard what your bitch doctor answered to that." The Harry I knew would never have said that even if he thought it, and he said it as though it could never occur that I would object to hearing her spoken of that way. "She said they had thought of that for themselves! She meant that they have ways of preserving their unholy status quo. Little godlets will soon die but they think their botched creation will be preserved."

I supposed she had meant something like that and I had it in mind to ask her about it, but right now I was more concerned with Harry's state of mind. What I needed was a psychiatrist but there was none in the complex or anywhere else that I knew of.

What frightened me most was his attitude of sweet reasonableness as if he had worked it all out and only needed to explain it for others to agree. It was the sort of attitude that covered sleeping violence against the ones who didn't agree.

He hadn't finished. After a while he said, "But it won't be preserved. When the world mind is open to men and women they will see for themselves the way to go with all the wisdom of time to guide them. My kurdaitcha will bring them to their true future."

"My kurdaitcha!" It sounded like another godlet at work. What to think, what to do? With hate and visions boiling together under a tell-nothing surface, what could anybody do except watch and hope it would simmer down to accept what couldn't be changed?

49

There wasn't going to be any watching and hoping. In the end there wasn't time for that; it all blew up so fast and was unstoppable.

By the time we got back to the complex, Harry was working hisself into another lather, only this time it was enthusiasm that had him excited. He was wanting to tell Valda about his afternoon with Bill and the plan to bring in the kurdaitcha, though I can't say he was being pleasant about it.

"Something the scientific bitch didn't think of! Harnessing the past to guide the future when all her precious plans go down the drain!"

I didn't much like him calling Valda a bitch, which she certainly wasn't, but he was on a high and flying with it, and it was best to keep my trap shut for the moment while he piled up a bit of vainglory about how smart he was to latch on to the obvious while her laboratory mind missed out.

He couldn't wait to hunt out Sammy and bring him to my cell and tell him to get to Valda right away because he had news for her that wouldn't wait. Sammy protested that she couldn't come from her work on his summons but he wouldn't take no for an answer and Sammy eventually caved in, to keep him quiet.

It was fairly late in the afternoon and maybe she was finished for the day and tidying up; however it was, she came. And maybe her being free at that moment changed history for a few people.

Actually she wasn't too pleased; I suppose Sammy had told her that Harry was all excited and she thought she had better see what the fuss was about. She came in with a face set for being patient with the insistent infants and asked, "What's your trouble, Harry?"

He went straight at her. "No trouble at all," he told her. "Just the future of humanity."

"You had your say about that yesterday."

"And you didn't like it. But I didn't say all I had in mind and I've taken some action to change things since then."

I couldn't blame her for being wary as she repeated, "Action?"

"I've talked to Bill Gordon. He's going to locate some kurdaitcha who practice inner contemplation and bring them here to experience isolation. Some of them have come pretty close in the past to contacting the world mind and, if they can use the world mind to pick up all their ancestral techniques, with what they find out they'll be on the way to succeeding without the electronics."

Valda was lost, of course. "What are you talking about? I've never heard of such—what did you call them? Contemplatives? Like the old monks?"

"No—like desert people seeking inside themselves for the Dream Time of the creators and guides and protectors. You haven't heard of them because it was the men's business and barred to the knowledge of womenfolk. But the isolation setup has broken that taboo forever." He leaned forward, grinning at her like somebody with a big secret to spill. "That's why I wanted you to try it—to prove that the taboo was broken and the knowledge was open to everybody."

He made me uneasy. His whole tone of voice belonged to a Harry that was foreign to me. It was excited and yet repressed, as if a terrific force was pent up. It wasn't the half-dreamy tone I had heard as we came home from Bill's house but more like an eruption ready to blow, as if his idea about the kurdaitcha had not just taken hold of him but everything else out of his mind.

Valda came and sat on my bed, puzzled and fascinated by the energy of him as he pursued her and stood over her.

He carried on talking and the words began to tumble out of him with spitting and slurring. He was losing control.

He said, "Your isolation machine won't last forever. You know that. The generators will fail for lack of replacement parts. And, besides, who will be able to maintain them after another twenty years? And what about the helmet? Nobody in this pastoral world of yours could rebuild it once it fails. So you need the kurdaitcha. People practiced in shutting out the world, going deep into themselves! People able to set their minds free of the senses! You see?"

But she didn't see. She was confused, petrified by a torrent of words as much like rage as like reason. I held myself ready to interfere if he went over the top, and Sammy seemed coiled tight as a spring.

He yelled at Valda, "Why don't you see? How long do you think your libraries will last once the kids break from your silly genealogy charts? Your whole scheme will fall apart. With no machines, no tradesman, no power, your precious people will have only word of mouth to teach them. When all your books fall into dust because in the dark age nobody can read or write, who will make a society of them?"

He had touched Valda on a raw spot there and she reacted strongly. "There will be no dark age!"

He didn't argue, simply contradicted her. "Oh, there will, there will! Without my kurdaitcha there will be a great gap in every branch of knowledge. With them, all the thinking of the past will be available to men and women! We will set up schools, teach the people to contact the world mind. The world your idiot grandfather destroyed will be rebuilt finer than it ever was!"

This was plain fanatic stuff. He believed what he said, but what had sounded interesting and feasible in Bill Gordon's sitting-room sounded now like ratbag ranting with all the one-eyed conviction of a hellfire-and-damnation preacher. Which, in a way, he was. I had to face a nasty truth, that on the subject of the New Age Harry was as ratty as the Mad Hatter; the tragedy of his transition across a century had unhinged him with hate and grief and his mind was taking it all out on everything around him. And I hadn't a clue to what we could do about it, only some hazy idea that he might have to be put under restraint.

And there was Valda, sitting staring up into his face with stony eyes.

Then, while we were all paralyzed with indecision, a change

came over Harry as if a miracle had picked on this minute to work. The concentration left his face, the tension left his body; he straightened up and stepped back from her and said, in the normal, courteous voice of a man making an apology, "I regret the remark about your grandfather but you will realize that in consideration of vast change there must always be another opinion."

Valda stood and, with absolutely terrific self-control, gave him his answer, "As also on the matter of navel-gazing kurdaitcha, which is visionary garbage. Our school system is not yet fully developed and neither is the genealogical physiology, but be assured there will be no dark age. A short period of stasis, perhaps, but nothing more than that."

Harry took it with a half smile on his face, tolerant, as if her ideas didn't matter. "All on the blackboard or in the laboratory," he said. "All in the system. And Granddaddy Wishart's system has no place for isolation garbage; he doesn't believe in it. The Area Council may think differently! What then? Will the principle of noninterference hold or will Granddaddy start throwing his weight around the council—in spite of your practical experience? Or haven't you told him yet about that?"

From the door, as she opened it, she said, "You are a totally ignorant man who refuses to learn. What on earth does Gus see in you?" Going out, she called to Sammy, "Come with me for a minute, please," and he followed her out.

What on earth did I see in him? Only that a friendship as close as ours was not to be split up when things went wrong and trouble started. But the man I had known and in a way looked up to had become a stranger. Right from the beginning of his days in the New Age he had clutched at his anger and retreated more and more from the man I knew. I could only read it as a red rage against Jesus Miraflores and his thugs, put forever out of his reach and now transferred to Wishart and all his works. As I saw it, what ate at him was a frustration that would never go away.

Yet the habit of companionship dies hard and now, with all

this in my head, I still didn't admit that he was unbalanced clear out of his mind, that some explosion had to happen to satisfy the pressures in him. I thought time would calm him down. That's the way you think when affection and familiarity get in the way; I should have seen that he was clear over the edge.

While I squatted on the bed he wandered over to the window and stood looking out. I tried to think of a useful thing to say and could only come up with, "You came down a bit hard on Valda."

Still looking out, he said, "You don't have to stand up like a knight for your lady; that one can look after herself." There was a little burr of contempt in his tone. I let it go, said nothing.

After a while he spoke, more or less to hisself, "The enemy is the invisible Wishart."

I suppose I was a mite nettled over his reference to Valda when I prodded him with, "Wishart's invisible because you picked hard shit at him. He doesn't want anything to do with us."

"Too bad; I've something to do with him one day."

One day. More of the overflowing spite.

Then Sammy came back and sat at his desk, fiddling with his pencil and looking at nothing with faraway eyes.

Harry said, "A question, Sammy."

Sammy did not turn to face him, merely said, "Yes?"

His attitude toward Harry had always been cautiously professional after the first outburst though he had relaxed while we were at his home; but since the new disagreements with Valda, smelling the way they did like contempt and open enmity, he had kept a formal face and not talked to Harry unless he had to. Now, with his back turned to the man, I could catch the flash of dislike across his face.

Harry had got to the point where he had turned off all the people who had been ready to treat him friendly and he didn't seem to care or even realize it.

Now he asked, "What did Dr. Valda mean when she said that the genealogical physiology of the people was not fully developed yet? Work still to be done? Physical changes yet to be made? Some quiet genes to be activated and set to work?"

Sammy said, "I don't know. Nobody discusses laboratory procedures with me; I haven't the expertise to make it worthwhile."

Harry turned around and stretched as if he needed to loosen up all over. "Then I'll have to ask her, won't I? I suppose she'll have gone back to the lab."

As he strolled out, seeming in no hurry, and closed the door behind him, Sammy manipulated something under his desk and spoke to the empty air: "Mr. Ostrov is making for Laboratory Two."

There were gadgets in the complex I didn't know about, probably a whole lot of them.

He said, "Gus, your friend is displaying disturbing signs of inner trouble. When I spoke with Dr. Valda in the corridor a few moments ago she suggested that we keep a watch on his actions and movements. I regret this, Gus, but it is becoming very noticeable."

There wasn't much I could say; I was the one who had persuaded myself it was a passing flurry of nerves, so I didn't say anything.

I lay back on the bed, all at sea with a problem I had no way of handling, staring at the ceiling while Sammy read over his notes.

It must have been a fair while before the screaming started down toward the labs.

It went on and on, hysterically. Then the crash of doors flung open and running feet and the crazy yelling of men and women in the corridor.

When Sammy and I got out of the cell it was nearly over. Fifty meters down, outside the Number Two Lab, a mob of white-coats, both men and women, surrounded a struggling Harry while more of them poured out of the nearby doors and he hit out at them and bellowed a howling, lunatic rage.

I got most of the story from Valda. The secretary was hopeless; she was terrified out of her mind and had screaming dreams for nights after. It was her screams that roused the lab workers but that was all of her part in the affair.

It seems Harry crashed open the office door without warning as the two women sat at their desks. Valda looked up, startled, and the secretary began to protest but Harry just said to her, "Shut up!," and Valda signed to her to be quiet.

"I am busy, Mr. Ostrov. I will see you later."

He leaned across the desk, hissing at her, "Not later, Doctor! Now, right now! What are you up to?"

She said he had the demented glare of someone suspicious that secret moves progressed against him and determined to unveil them. She had had Sammy's warning but it had not prepared her for a Harry raging and dangerous under the spell of his unresolved hate. To make it worse, she had no idea of what he meant.

He almost screamed into her face, "Physiological changes! What are you going to do to people? What changes? Fiddling with DNA to preserve your idiotic sex charts? Is that it?"

From the side of her eye she saw the inner door to the laboratory open and her grandfather come into the office, attracted by the noise. Harry, intent on holding her gaze, was unaware. He kept on yelling, "Another idea for yoking good folk to your vision of a world tied to genetic perfection?"

Wishart asked, "What is going on here?," in the testy voice of a man disturbed at his work.

Harry straightened and turned to face him, and Valda told me she shivered at the instant change in him from yelling anger to pleased friendliness though there was nothing friendly in what he said. "Ah, the Dr. Supreme himself! The right hand of God! The old mass murderer!"

I'll say for Valda that it took a ton of guts for her to say as if Harry had come in for a quite normal inquiry, "Mr. Ostrov is asking what line our experimental work is following at the moment."

She said the secretary was making little gasping noises of distress but Wishart seemed to grasp the situation enough to ignore the bracket of insults and answer calmly, "That can be simply stated. We proposed to tie a male sexual reaction to the female pheromone so that couples of compatible makeup will be attracted to each other. That's it, Mr. Ostrov, in a nutshell."

There was an empty moment while Harry worked it out. At last he said, "You mean like moths smelling each other out? The way some birds gather a bunch and select the best breeding partner?"

"Broadly, yes. There will be refinements."

Harry said, "I'll bet there will! Refinements to make the hen ruler of the roost while the cocks fawn for her favors!" Then he burst out again in red rage, squalling, "You want to turn men into laboratory animals! Boy toys, without choice!"

Wishart made a pacifying movement with his hands but Valda said Harry moved like a lightning strike (and I knew how fast he could move) and took Wishart by the neck. The doctor was not a big man and Harry shook him in his hands like a leaf and then began to twist his neck, while he made animal sounds in his throat.

Valda jumped on his back, trying to tear his hands away but she might as well have tried to stop a charging bull. The secretary started screaming and couldn't stop, while Harry shook Valda off on to the ground and kicked her in the breast. Then he twisted Wishart's head until the spine snapped and threw the body on top of her.

By then the screaming had done its work and the lab techs were crushing into the office and more were coming from other rooms.

They rushed Harry into the corridor by sheer weight of numbers and gathered around and all over him. That was when Sammy and I raced out to see what was happening. We saw Harry fighting back but the wolves had him and they dragged him down.

He got halfway to his feet, heaving and howling, but a boot took him in the mouth and he went down again on his face.

They were all over him and we were still trying to drag them off while they kicked him to death.

5.

NOW AND FOREVER

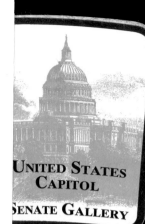

UNITED STATES
CAPITOL

SENATE GALLERY

50

That was three months ago. Sammy's reporting job is finished and he's gone back to his village and I don't see much of Valda. She's developed a lump in the breast where Harry kicked her but she won't say whether it's cancerous or not. She won't even say if she's having treatment. She won't talk about it. She acts like she's had a big shock. I think she still feels dedication to her unfinished work as if she would be guilty to leave a job not done, but she doesn't talk about it anymore. I think the dust-up with Harry made her reconsider the whole New Age setup but she doesn't talk about that either. When she comes to the cell, which is rarely, it is just for small talk; I reckon she has no real interest in me but now and then realizes that the poor bugger from a century back might need a bit of company.

Perhaps after a hundred and thirty years or so, and with no Granddad Wishart on her back now to keep her fueled up, she is just tired of it all and wants a finish.

I don't think about Harry. There's no profit in that, just a big gap.

What I think about most is old Melbourne, the sleazy part of it where I was brought up—the big tenements and the crowds of people and their noise. And the smell of them that I never really noticed until it was taken away.

And Sally and the boy . . .

This New Age is all right, as far as it goes, but it isn't mine and never will be. It's empty. Nobody gives a damn what I do, so I ride out to Sammy's place now and then to have someone to talk to. He's friendly and so is Miriam and so are all the local people but most of all I get on with the kids; they seem to like me and they listen for hours while I tell them about old Melbourne and its crooks and spivs and gangs and squabbling families. Fairy tales, they think, all made up, but they love them. It's a life they'll never have.

The other day something happened. I was riding out to Sammy's place when only a bit of a way beyond the old city limits I came on a swaggie. A real swaggie. I had never seen one but I recognized him from old pictures from before my time.

He had on a shirt and trousers all sweaty and dusty and patched at the elbows and knees, boots with no laces flopped with his stride, and he had on a hat straight out of old prints with corks hanging from the brim to keep flies away. The blanket roll was slung slantwise across his back with cords crossing his chest and he even had a billycan swinging from the bottom of the swag. The only thing out of place was that he was a Koori; the pictures always showed swaggies as white.

He hailed me as we came together and I pulled up the horse. He was on the small side and he spoke English with a rough accent I hadn't heard before.

He said, "I'm from around Alice Springs, mate," (nearly two thousand Ks from where we were, way out in the desert country!) "and I've never been south before. Maybe you can help me. I'm looking for an old bloke called Bill Gordon somewhere in Melbourne."

I reckoned him at about fifty-five and his roundish, cheerful face was absolutely ordinary for a tribesman but I had to ask, "You're a kurdaitcha man?"

His face changed, became wary. He said, "I'm looking for Bill Gordon."

"Get up behind and I'll ride you in to his house. It isn't far." He didn't move, not sure of me, so I said, "He'll be expecting you but I was never sure any of you would come. You're the first."

He decided I was all right and climbed up behind me, saying, "There's a bloke from the west about a week behind me. What do you know about kurdaitcha?"

He pronounced it a bit differently from Bill but there were hundreds of tribes out there with their own languages. "Nothing much," I told him, "but I know he'll be glad to see you."

An hour or so later I dropped him off and whistled for Bill to come out.

"Nice house," said my passenger. "I live in a tent."

As if my mind had come alive after vacant weeks, I dreamed up fantasies as I rode out to Sammy's, imagination fired by the swagman. I had never tried the isolation gear, at least partly because of that little break on the way down into the dark, the point where the minds of those close to the machine became visible for a moment, the point where Sammy had seen the fires blazing in Harry. I didn't want to know what the people around me were really like in their dirty little souls. We all have things in us that have to be suppressed even from our own cheap and hidden sight. I just didn't want to know.

But the swagman stirred something in me, maybe the ever-living little boy who loves legends and myths and high adventures. I had never put real faith in that dreamed-up school for inner contemplation but the sudden arrival of the kurdaitcha man set me thinking: What if it was all true and the world mind could be opened to men and women?

I saw in mind's eye a building somewhere on a hilltop, above the flurry of the world, where the kurdaitcha students lived among all the books saved from the claws of time—white and black and brindle, men and women, old and young—and gazed into their own depths, drawing nearer and nearer to the core of knowledge. The Great University of the World it was, where man learned his own past and got hisself ready for his future.

Some of those students were my and Valda's descendants, the ones with big chests and long, stringy muscles and lean flanks, born to be the world's tireless infantry soldiers and peacekeepers. They were mostly white but some had a touch of the ancestral tarbrush. They were our long-range kids who had given up soldiering to live the internal life.

Down in the valley would be the tough, ox-muscled bruisers dancing attendance on their matriarchal women who held them forever in their pheromonal grip.

The fantasy boggled a little at that one but I comforted myself that it would all somehow sort itself in time.

I went back to the school on the hill where my soldiers of tomorrow stood guard against anyone breaking into the meditations inside.

And inside, where the isolation setup was long-forgotten dust, the contemplatives plunged deeper and deeper into the world mind, finding new marvels, things we had never dreamed of, maybe even the beginning of thought or the Koori Rainbow Serpent at creation's edge . . .

I don't know what put the starships, *Search* and *Kiev* into my head right then, but I thought of them out among the lightyears, settling men on new planets where, it might be, new world minds would form. And in the end the whole galaxy, the whole starscape would end up as a single universe of thought . . .